FOURTH SUNDAY

THE JOURNEY OF A BOOK CLUB

FOURTH
SUNDAY

Dear Reader:

A book club writing a fictionalized tale about a book club? What a fabulous and unique concept! In *Fourth Sunday*, B.W. Read (Because We Read)—six authors from various walks of life—write about seven characters who spend every fourth Sunday of the month discussing books, life, love, and everything in between. Book clubs have become an intricate part of society over the past several decades. They are a way for people to escape reality, relieve stress, and socialize with friends—both old and new.

Without saying, this is an excellent book club selection for existing clubs throughout the nation and the world. So much happens with the seven women in the club—divorce, illness, romantic highs and lows, sexual experimentation, and career challenges—that many will instantly be able to relate to them. Groups and individuals alike will appreciate *Fourth Sunday*.

As always, thanks for the support shown to the Strebor Books family. We appreciate the love. For more information on our titles, please visit www.zanestore.com and you can find me on my personal website: www.eroticanoir.com. You can also join my online social network at www.planetzane.org.

Blessings,

Zane

Publisher
Strebor Books
www.simonsays.com/streborbooks

ZANE PRESENTS

FOURTH SUNDAY

THE JOURNEY OF A BOOK CLUB

B.W. READ

SBI

STREBOR BOOKS

NEW YORK LONDON TORONTO SYDNEY

Strebor Books
P.O. Box 6505
Largo, MD 20792
http://www.streborbooks.com

ISBN 978-1-59309-358-7
ISBN 978-1-4516-0803-8 (ebook)
LCCN 2010940500

First Strebor Books trade paperback edition May 2011

Cover design: www.mariondesigns.com
Cover photograph: © Keith Saunders/Marion Designs

10 9 8 7 6 5 4 3 2 1

Manufactured in the United States of America

For information regarding special discounts for bulk purchases, please contact Simon & Schuster Special Sales at 1-866-506-1949 or business@simonandschuster.com

The Simon & Schuster Speakers Bureau can bring authors to your live event. For more information or to book an event, contact the Simon & Schuster Speakers Bureau at 1-866-248-3049 or visit our website at www.simonspeakers.com.

This book is dedicated to our families,
the members of our book club and
friends who continually supported us through this journey.

In memory of Lisa Hayes Williams

ACKNOWLEDGMENTS

We are forever grateful to Strebor Books and Simon & Schuster, Inc. for giving us an opportunity to fulfill our literary dream.

To Zane and Charmaine Roberts Parker, thank you for accepting our manuscript. Your expertise and coaching have been instrumental in the completion of this project.

We pay homage to the authors of the books we read in our book club. Their stories inspired us to write.

Gail Ross, your literary legal advice was invaluable.

To Arah Jennings, thank you for your creativity and marketing advice, from the "Synergistas."

FRANCESCA COOK

Many thanks to my family and friends for providing unconditional support and encouragement over the years. I would also like to extend a special thank you to my daughter, Kai, for reminding me to be patient and enjoy the journey.

CHYLA EVANS

To Chloe and VJ, who put up with their mother during this process. To Arah, my best friend and the one person who always believed in me and our project.

CLARITA FRAZIER

Thank you, God, for my numerous and continued blessings. Mom and Dad, I know you are guiding me from above and smiling down on me. Keira, as my daughter, you are "my dream come true." You inspire me to be the best person I can be. Tim, as the love of my life, you have taught me how to be free and open. Bill, thanks for the resolute love and support. I couldn't imagine a better brother. To all my "girlfriends," thank you for a lifetime of fabulous bonding moments and memories.

ALLITA IRBY

I am thankful to live in the twenty-first century when literacy is stressed and pushed for boys and girls alike. We must continue to be vigilant to ensure the freedom to learn to read and write exists for all.

Thank you to strong black women everywhere, who have proven that not only can we be beautiful, but intelligent also. This book is an attempt to show that side of us. Not only are we voracious readers, but writers as well.

Without the constant support of my husband, Tim Edwards, I may not have continued with this project to fruition. Your interest and excitement about this book has been unwavering. Like a cheering section, you have been there over the last ten years coaching and cheering me on from the sidelines. You started your literary group (GLC), when our book club was in full swing, attending co-ed book discussions, "meet-the-author" events and book signings along with me. I love you more than you know. Immediate and extended family, you inspire me just by being yourselves. I thank you.

DONNA NEALE

To my coauthors, friends and sisters, I'm so happy that we completed the BOOK. It took some time but what memories, stories and dreams we carry now.

To my parents, thank you for instilling fortitude and commitment.

To my husband, Kevyn, for his unending support of this project and his unconditional love…I think I see Bora Bora. And, to my children, Kevyn II and Alexandra, you are my joy.

YOLANDA YATES

Words alone cannot express the gratitude I owe to Clinton for his assiduous confidence in my abilities and me. Thanks a billion.

PROFILE

GWENDOLYN (GWEN) NICHOLS

AGE: 32

FAVORITE BOOK:
Love in the Time of Cholera, Gabriel Garcia Marquez

FAVORITE DRINK: Kir Royale

FAVORITE CITY: Cape Town, South Africa

FAVORITE VACATION SPOT: Barbados

PET PEEVES:
Complaining—with no suggestions for making things better

MARITAL STATUS: Single

CHILDREN: None

CAREER: Obstetrician/Gynecologist

HOBBIES:
Running, Tennis, Skiing, Soccer, Photography, and Reading

FAVORITE THING TO DO: Outdoor Activities

SPEND MOST TIME DOING: Living out of an overnight bag

PROFILE

NATALIE SEARS

AGE: 31

FAVORITE BOOK:
Genocide Files, Xavier Arnold

FAVORITE DRINK: Fuzzy Navel

FAVORITE CITY: Washington, D.C.

FAVORITE VACATION SPOT: Greece

PET PEEVES: Stupidity

MARITAL STATUS: Single

CHILDREN: None

CAREER:
Chief of Staff, Senate Health and Consumer Affairs Committee

HOBBIES: Modern Dance, Reading, and Tennis

FAVORITE THING TO DO: Relax

SPEND MOST TIME DOING: Working

PROFILE

ADRIANE BUTTLER

AGE: 28

FAVORITE BOOK:
Brothers and Sisters, Bebe Moore Campbell

FAVORITE DRINK: Bahama Mama

FAVORITE CITY: Washington, D.C.

FAVORITE VACATION SPOT: Aruba

PET PEEVES: Stupidity

MARITAL STATUS: Married

CHILDREN: Almost

CAREER: Senior Sales Executive

HOBBIES: Reading, Interior Design, and Sculpting

FAVORITE THING TO DO: Entertain

SPEND MOST TIME DOING: Talking

PROFILE

BRIANNA TAYLOR

AGE: 32

FAVORITE BOOK:
Seasons of Beento Blackbird, Akosua Busia

FAVORITE DRINK: Cosmopolitan

FAVORITE CITY: Washington, D.C.

FAVORITE VACATION SPOT: St. Croix, Virgin Islands

PET PEEVES: Pretentiousness

MARITAL STATUS: Single

CHILDREN: None

CAREER: Anesthesiologist

HOBBIES:
In-Line Skating, Aerobics, Piano, Tennis, and Shopping

FAVORITE THING TO DO: Eating and Wine Tasting

SPEND MOST TIME DOING:
Working at the hospital (passing gas!)

PROFILE

ALLANA SMITH

AGE: Forty-something

FAVORITE BOOK:
In Search of Satisfaction, J. California Cooper

FAVORITE DRINK: Kir Royale

FAVORITE CITY: Washington, D.C.

FAVORITE VACATION SPOT: Hawaii

PET PEEVES: Noise

MARITAL STATUS: Married

CHILDREN: Two Stepchildren

CAREER: Business Consultant

HOBBIES: Reading, Dancing, and Gardening

FAVORITE THING TO DO: Reading and Vacationing

SPEND MOST TIME DOING: Consultant work

CAMILLE CASTILLE

AGE: 39

FAVORITE BOOK:
Topping from Below, Laura Reese

FAVORITE DRINK: 1989 Silver Oak Cabernet

FAVORITE CITY: Washington, D.C.

FAVORITE VACATION SPOT: Cancun, Mexico

PET PEEVES: Traffic

MARITAL STATUS: Twice divorced

CHILDREN: Two (Jade, 10, and Tyler, 7)

CAREER: Entrepreneur/Banker

HOBBIES: Tennis, Reading, Working Out, and Eating Out

FAVORITE THING TO DO: Fall in Love

SPEND MOST TIME DOING: Being a taxi for my kids!

PROFILE

DESTINY DAVIS

AGE: 37

FAVORITE BOOK:
My Soul to Keep, Tananarive Due

FAVORITE DRINK: Margarita (frozen) with salt

FAVORITE CITY: Washington, D.C.

FAVORITE VACATION SPOT: Paris

PET PEEVES: Pets

MARITAL STATUS: Single

CHILDREN: None

CAREER: International Finance Consultant

HOBBIES:
Furniture Shopping, Interior Decorating, Reading, and Dancing

FAVORITE THING TO DO: Shopping

SPEND MOST TIME DOING: Working

FOURTH SUNDAY

The spring-like day in March of 1997 had all of us in a glorious mood. The temperature hovered around seventy-four degrees and the sun gave off a golden glow through the wooden plantation shutters. The tulips were in early bloom and the birds were chirping away. The weather conditions prompted us to chitchat about upcoming vacation plans and reminisce about past excursions. We even discussed the possibility of renting a beach house for a couple of days in the summer. While socializing, bonding, networking, and laughing, the time slipped away. We were preparing to discuss the book when Old Man Winter returned with an attitude. But the weather wasn't the only thing that changed. One of us was transformed from carefree to uncertain. And just like that the group's relaxed demeanor came to an abrupt end.

The blast from the ambulance siren and the flickering of the red and blue lights declared an emergency. Piled in the Range Rover, we succeeded in keeping up with the tattered ambulance that was traveling faster than the thirty-five-miles-per-hour speed limit. The traffic was unusually heavy for a Sunday in Washington, D.C. At one point, some fool, showing no respect for the ambulance and certainly not us, swerved in between our car and the ambulance, causing us to lose our escort. Not to be deterred, we made good use of the horn and ran a red light to reclaim our position. The ambulance was transporting a very important person in our lives and we had no intention of losing sight of it. We had never experienced such a road trip, nor had life's experiences prepared us for what we were about to face.

University Hospital was like a scene from the television show *ER*. Although under complete control, everything seemed so chaotic and everybody was moving one hundred miles per minute. That is, everyone except us.

"Paging Dr. Brown. Paging Dr. Brown. STAT to Labor and Delivery."

The hospital's fine reputation, the clean, almost sterile, atmosphere, and the accommodating admission clerk who favored Claire Huxtable from *The Cosby Show*, should have put us at ease. It didn't. We were all on pins and needles. Who would have thought that we'd be huddled together, comforting each other in a hospital, when two years ago we barely knew one another. A book club had united us in sisterhood—Adriane, Allana, Brianna, Camille, Destiny, Gwen, and Natalie. We started out loosely connected by a desire to discuss literature. Slowly, this common thread evolved into a tightly woven fabric of emotional support, intellectual stimulation, professional guidance, and most important, friendship and love. As we settled into the less than comfortable vinyl furniture outside Labor and Delivery, we couldn't help but begin to reflect on our lives and the changes all of us had endured over the last two years.

GWENDOLYN
(GWEN)

GWEN

As usual I'm late for book club. I still have two more errands to run, plus get gas, before I make my way to Destiny's. I promised myself that I would try to be on time for the meetings this year. It would be a first. I was late for every meeting last year. Although I was in good company with Brianna and Camille, I was ready to graduate from the "late group."

The errands took more time to complete than I expected, so I was really late for the book club meeting. As I drove down Destiny's tree-lined street; I saw a flashing red light moving toward me with a white Range Rover on its tail. As the duo neared, I could see that Camille was behind the wheel of the Rover. In rapid sequence, I beeped my horn, flashed my high beams, and rolled down my window. This got Camille's attention and within a moment, our cars were side to side in the middle of the street.

"What's going on? What's wrong?"

As if they were in a choir, all the women in the car answered in unison, "It's Adriane. Her water broke."

"Why is she in the ambulance?" I asked.

Camille responded, "Something's not right. Adriane is having contractions and she almost passed out on us."

Instead of continuing the conversation, I turned my car around and joined the caravan to the hospital. Just as I fell into place behind Camille and the ambulance, my beeper went off. The screen read, "Adriane Buttler, thirty-five weeks, in labor, going to the hospital."

Driving along, I called to mind how it all started...

I was sitting in the call room on a Wednesday evening in December of 1994. I'm certain that it was a Wednesday because I had become hooked on the trite TV drama *Beverly Hills, 90210*. My residency would be over in six months and I had started my countdown. It dawned on me then that many of my peers already had an eight-year jump on me in terms of having a real life. Eight years had passed since college graduation. A lot of my friends were married with kids and starting their second or third jobs. I spent the first half of the eight years in medical school and then the last four years in residency. When teased about looking like a sixteen-year-old, I would always say that all these years of education and training had spared me the toils of life as a twenty-something—no late-night partying, no rushing to get to Happy Hour, and no stress of trying to keep up with the Joneses. I put in a lot of grueling hours over the last eight years, but something told me that it was nothing like the dog-'em-out, wear-'em-down stress of everyday life that I was about to experience when I left residency in six months. Those feelings, however, didn't overshadow my desire to finally have a "normal" life.

I started thinking about all the things that I wanted to start doing again. I wanted to take piano lessons. I wanted to take tennis lessons. I wanted to do some more volunteer work at the children's center. I wanted to sleep in on more than one weekend of the month, and I didn't want to read another textbook for a long time. I laughed to myself. I couldn't remember the last time I read a novel. It must have been at least six months before when I went to Jamaica with my friend Brianna Taylor. For me, the perfect vacation was sitting in the shallow water in a chaise longue reading a great book. The water could be the Atlantic Ocean, the Pacific Ocean, the Caribbean Sea, or the Gulf of Mexico. As long as the temperature was above ninety degrees, I was happy. Another thing I would add to my list of things to do after residency was to start a book club. I had read an article in *Essence* magazine touting book clubs as the latest fad. I thought it would be great to read a book, and then discuss ideas and thoughts about the characters, plot, and theme with friends.

Once I had an idea in my head, I would usually forge ahead until the idea became a reality. Sometimes it takes me a while to put a plan into action, but I strongly believe in the motto "Better late than never." It was two months later before I started making plans for the book club. I happened to be at the hospital, which was no surprise since the hospital had become my surrogate home for the last three-and-a-half years. On a piece of official University Hospital stationery, I jotted down a few names of people who I thought would be interested in participating in a book club. Then I pulled out my daily planner, which also served as an address book, and started calling people from my list of potential book club members. The first name on the list was Natalie Sears.

Natalie and I have known each other since high school although we did not become friends until I came back from medical school. From the outside looking in, Natalie always struck me as the "academician." However, over the last few years, as I got to know her better, I also got to know her fun and adventurous side. I can remember one Black Caucus weekend when Natalie dragged a group of us to the Chicago Connection party. Initially, we all had the same response to her invitation, "Sorry, but I'm broke."

Quickly Natalie said, "Don't worry about it. I'll take care of everything." We all got dressed up in our best after-five outfits and headed over to the Washington Hilton Hotel, where the party was being held. The mood was light and festive. We each saw at least ten people we knew in the lobby of the hotel and shared a silent thought—Why go into the party when there are enough people to party with in the lobby? Nevertheless, we proceeded to the entrance of the party and soon realized that Natalie had not taken care of everything. She'd led us to believe she had enough tickets for all of us, when in fact she did not have any tickets. I wasn't worried because my mother always told me to have money with me whenever I went out, so I'd stuck fifty dollars in my purse before leaving my apartment. I could see some of the other women getting a little warm as small beads of sweat formed on their foreheads. Natalie must have noticed this too, 'cause she connected herself to a group of older gentlemen and walked with them into the party. We followed her lead and ended up in the party alongside her. I laughed as I recalled that evening. Natalie's stunt was not about trying to get over by not paying because she didn't have the money, but about having the guts to live on the edge, to live outside the box. We ended up having a great time at the party after spending the first hour trying to ditch the older gentlemen.

I picked up the phone and called Natalie. I shared my ideas about the book club with her and she thought it was a good idea and told me to count her in. The next person on the list was Adriane Buttler.

I have known Adriane for about fifteen years. In fact, it was Adriane who introduced me to Natalie. She and Natalie were close friends, although nothing alike. Where Natalie was usually reserved, Adriane was outgoing and outspoken. When Adriane had an opinion about something, good or bad, she let a person know. She was quick to give someone a compliment and she always brought out the good in others. Adriane was also very creative. Even though she worked in corporate America from nine to five, her real passion was making arts and crafts. Adriane was one of the first people I knew to make her own window treatments, which looked exactly like those showcased in the homes of the rich and famous. She painted her walls with faux finishes and designed and built a rock garden with a waterfall in her backyard. One of her other many talents was working a scarf. I always teased Adriane that she should write a book entitled *100 Ways to Wear a Scarf*. It seemed that she had a different scarf for each day of the week during each season. Moreover, she had ten different ways to tie the scarf around her neck, not to mention all the other different places that she would tie a scarf—around her waist like a belt or around her shoulders like a shawl. I called Adriane and shared my ideas about the book club with her and she too was excited. She kept me on the phone for almost thirty minutes, giving me titles of books we should read. Adriane is well connected in the Washington metropolitan area, so by the end of our conversation, she had also given me a list of ten other women who she thought might be interested in joining our club.

My next phone call was to Brianna. As the phone was ringing, a smile came to my face as I remembered the first time I met Brianna. We became friends the summer before medical school. We both participated in a program our school set up to help minority students get acclimated to the first year of medical school. The twenty students participating in the program stayed in the dormitory together. On the first day of the program, we all met in the lobby of the dorm. I'll never forget that scene. The first person I saw was a guy who looked like he was twelve years old. He was playing with his calculator as he mumbled a physics equation. Then I saw a woman with straight, red hair and pale skin with freckles, who was explaining to one of the other students that she was one-twelfth American Indian, a fact that she did not mention again during the entire four years of medical school. And the next person I saw was Brianna. She was dressed in a linen skirt suit with matching three-inch sandals and an accompanying backpack. Mind you, it was about eighty degrees at 7:30 a.m., and everyone else was dressed in sundresses or shorts.

On our twenty-minute bus trip from the dorm to the medical school campus, all Brianna talked about was finding an apartment for the fall semester. I wanted to tell her to please shut up because we all had to find a place to live. Instead, I only asked myself what I was doing spending my last free summer with a bunch of misfits. Luckily, not all first impressions are lasting. Some of these "misfits" became my support system during the four grueling years of medical school. In fact, the three of us—Brianna, the guy who looked like he was twelve years old, and I—became roommates.

After medical school we all went our separate ways. Brianna went to Boston to do her residency in anesthesiology followed by a fellowship specializing in the management of chronic pain. However, she was returning to D.C. in the next couple of months after years of being away. I thought the camaraderie of a book club would be great for her because she recently called off her engagement to the love of her life and she needed to get reacquainted with friends.

There was always some drama surrounding Brianna and her love interests. During our last year of medical school, Brianna started dating Jackson, who everyone thought was such a straight arrow. In fact, he was described to me as someone who would never hurt a fly. Well, one night as I was getting dressed to meet Brianna and Jackson for dinner, I received a call from the owner of a local car dealership. It seemed that Jackson, who everyone thought was so straight, had stolen a car off a dealership lot. While "Action Jackson" was fleeing the crime scene he'd dropped a matchbook with our phone number on it. After this incident, all of Brianna's male callers had to be inspected by us before she could go out. It was the house rule! Now that Brianna was moving to D.C., that rule would need to be reinstated since her luck with men had not changed.

Finally, Brianna answered the phone. I invited her to join the book club, and just as I anticipated, she thought the book club would be a great diversion. She also helped me add some other names to the list of potential members.

One name she thought of that I had not was Camille Castille. Sounds like a movie star, huh? Well, when one meets Camille, they know immediately that she is part of the jet set crowd. After attending medical school in California for four years, Brianna and I had become pros at spotting the jet set. In fact, Camille was from California but we didn't meet her out there. We met her in the lobby of my apartment building one weekend when Brianna was visiting from Boston. Camille was dating and would soon marry a friend and neighbor, Eric Nobles. I went out with Camille and Eric many times. Despite her Hollywood glamour image, Camille was really down to earth. She had two kids from a previous marriage to a professional athlete, owned businesses out in L.A., and had traveled around the globe. I thought that Camille could definitely add a different dimension to the book club. I made a mental note to extend an invitation to Camille the next time she was in town. Brianna and I said our good-byes. I hung up the phone, only to pick it up again to make one more phone call.

My last phone call that evening was to Allana Smith. I met Allana in Cancun, Mexico, at the Jazz Festival earlier in the year. We met at breakfast one morning, and started hanging out with each other for the remainder of the vacation. Allana is a little older than I am, but her age did not hinder her enthusiasm for partying from sundown to sun up, downing Tequila shots, and exploring the ruins of Chichen Itza on mopeds. We continued our friendship when we returned to D.C., although recently, I had not seen her much. On the third ring, Allana answered the phone, dragging out that last syllable as in a church hymn: "Hel-looo."

"Hi, Allana, it's me, Gwen. You sound very perky for it to be so late." It was 10:30 p.m. I had been a little hesitant to call at this hour because if Allana was not at a social event, she would start dozing off at 10:00 p.m. "Sorry to call you so late, but I'm thinking about starting a book club. Do you think you'd be interested in joining?"

"Oh, that sounds like a great thing to be a part of. I'd love to join. Any concrete plans for the first meeting date or the first book to be reviewed?" she asked in a business-like tone.

Allana is the constant organizer. It figures that she would be the only one to ask about specific details. "No," I responded. "The details have yet to be worked out. I just wanted to see how much interest I could generate. I'm really excited. So far, four women including myself have said that they would be interested in participating in a book club. You'd make five."

"Okay, count me in. I also have a friend, Destiny, who I think might be interested in joining. She reads all the time. I'm sure you'll like her."

Allana and I said our good-byes. I promised to get all the details to her as soon as I knew them myself, and she promised to bring her friend Destiny to the first meeting. Luckily, the rest of the evening was slow at the hospital. By the time the sun came up on Thursday, I had sparked enough interest to start the book club and also gotten seven hours of uninterrupted sleep. The next night

I called a friend who I knew was already in a book club and picked her brain about the format of her club. The following weekend I met a woman at a dinner party who was talking about a book that her book club just finished reading. I expressed interest about how her book club meetings were run and she was more than happy to share ideas with me. For the next two months, whenever I ran into an old friend or met a new acquaintance, I would mention the book club and invite them to the first meeting in May. Camille moved to D.C. in April and accepted my invitation to join the club. After considering a number of choices, we decided the first book would be Bebe Moore Campbell's *Brothers and Sisters*. I looked down my list of names and smiled. Mission accomplished. Natalie Sears, Adriane Buttler, Brianna Taylor, Camille Castille, Allana Smith, and maybe Allana's friend Destiny Davis, and I, Gwendolyn Nichols, would be the inaugural members of The Book Club.

3

GWEN

The first book club meeting was off to a great start. Since I was unexpectedly on call, Natalie agreed to host the first meeting at her home. So far my pager had been quiet. I hoped it would stay that way. Looking around the room, I felt proud that after only five months from the time of conception, the book club was actually happening. Almost everyone I invited showed up and everyone was talking animatedly.

"Bebe Moore Campbell really hit the mark with *Brothers and Sisters*. I can totally relate to Thelma. Corporate America is a bitch! My new senior executive, sales position is not much different than the occupational service representative position I had right out of undergrad. The way I see it, I busted my ass for two years to get an MBA and created $30,000 in additional debt for nothing but the same old shit! Granted, I make more money and I have a little more authority, but other than that, there really isn't much difference," Adriane complained.

"Yeah, Adriane, but you have to admit your job isn't all bad. You get to make your own schedule and pretend to work from home." Natalie laughed. "What I wouldn't give to have some down time during the work day!"

"That's true, Natalie. I guess there is a plus side," Adriane replied. "I can arrange my schedule as I please for the most part, but when I do go to the office it is always a trip. Remember Humphrey, the guy in the book who had it out for Thelma? Well, I work with a zillion of those crazy people every day. Of course there are only a couple of us in management positions. I don't know how *Black Enterprise* magazine keeps rating my company as one of the top twenty best companies for African Americans to work. When my company fills out the questionnaire they must list all the mail clerks, receptionists, and custodial engineers to fill their quota. I need to write Earl Graves and tell him they're lying! The most tripped-out thing is a lot of those clerks and receptionists have college degrees while those other idiots barely finished high school. They are everywhere and they all act the same. I went to a meeting the other day and it was downright scary—all shiny bald heads and gray hair. I wanted to run." Adriane laughed.

"Well, corporate America may be full of crazy people, but believe me when I tell you that crazy people are everywhere! Have you read the paper lately and caught any stories about the crazy *elected* officials who run our country?" Natalie quipped. "At least potential applicants at your firm have to meet some sort of minimum educational and experience criteria. Sometimes I think all elected officials have to do is show up on the Hill. It is amazing how little so many of them know about so much. You thought Dan Quayle not knowing how to spell 'potato' was bad. The stupidity that graces the Senate and House halls every day is astounding. The stories I could tell. For example, at a hearing last year, the distinguished ranking member of my committee, and I use the word 'distinguished' loosely, got up to leave the hearing halfway through. Well, even though he has been on the committee for seven years, somehow he mistook the door to a storage closet for the exit. I guess he was embarrassed, either that or very stupid. So instead of coming right out and finding the appropriate exit, he stayed in the storage closet for the next forty-five minutes. The hearing is still going on, mind you. Sometimes I shudder when I think people like him are elected to represent us and make the laws that govern the land. But enough about the crazy people Adriane and I work with. Let's get back to the book. Allana, do you think it is realistic to have true friendship with a white woman like Mallory and Thelma did in the book?"

"I think you can develop meaningful relationships with people of different ethnic backgrounds," Allana replied.

Beep, beep, beep. "Gwen, is that your beeper or mine?" Brianna asked.

"It's mine," I replied. "I'm on call. I'll call the hospital from the kitchen." I apologized for the interruption and excused myself. I've been doing this doctoring thing for four years now and you'd think I would be used to my beeper going off, but I wasn't. Somewhat irritated, I answered my page. "Hi, this is Dr. Nichols. Did someone page me?" I couldn't wait for my residency to end, only one more month to go.

While waiting for the person who put me on hold to return, I heard Adriane say, "Shit, I would have gotten that brother, Humphrey, straight!" I then heard the ladies roar with laughter.

"Oh, Gwen, thanks for calling back," the voice on the other end of the phone replied. "It's Ken. We just got a maternal transport. The patient is a thirty-year-old G1 P0 at thirty weeks' gestation with a complete placenta previa. Reportedly, she bled about two hundred cc's earlier this morning. When she initially arrived in Labor and Delivery, she was contracting every ten minutes or so. Her contractions have stopped now after IV hydration and her bleeding has decreased."

Ken Mays was the third-year resident covering Labor and Delivery. I liked Ken, but I couldn't help thinking that every time Ken called me it was for some type of obstetric or gynecological catastrophe. Typically, a residency program is structured so that there is always a senior and junior resident working together. The junior resident has to discuss all patients that he/she evaluates with the senior resident. Since the time Ken was a first year resident, it seems like we have always been on a team together with me being his senior resident. We have managed a lot of challenging patients together like the patient in labor with undiagnosed twins, the patient who had cardiac arrest in the Emergency Room and required an emergency cesarean section down there or the patient with an underlying psychiatric disorder who wouldn't acknowledge her pregnancy even when she was in active labor with a full-term fetus. That had been fun trying to convince her to push the baby (that she wasn't acknowledging) out! Somehow along the way in my residency, I had gotten a "black cloud," which in medicine means that you are the doctor that gets the tough cases or tough patients. So, I have gotten accustomed to "craziness" at work.

"Ken, check her hematocrit and coagulation factors. Make sure her type and screen are kept active at all times. How does the fetal monitor strip look?" Ken reassured me that the fetal heart rate was stable. I then asked Ken to notify the attending physician on call that day about the new patient's admission and told him that I would be on my way to the hospital.

While hanging up the telephone, I took a minute to gaze out of the window and noticed two squirrels chasing each other. At that moment I thought, wouldn't it be great to be a squirrel? No troubles, no responsibilities. Just running around all day long and having a good time. I really have no complaints about my life—great family and friends, a fine and loving boyfriend, great health, and a bright future in medicine. Only when I had to be stuck in the hospital on such a gorgeous day would I start contemplating the life of a squirrel. Right now I have no time for squirrels. The patient that Ken called me about is a first-time mom who's bleeding because her placenta is right over her cervix, which is the exit for the baby from the womb. The bleeding could mean that she might lose the baby. I had to say good-bye to the ladies and get going.

By the time I arrived at the hospital, the patient that Ken called me about had stopped bleeding for now and was being closely monitored. However, I had more than enough work to do to keep me busy for hours. Labor and Delivery was packed with patients— ten women waiting to be mothers. One woman was going to need a cesarean delivery. She had been eight centimeters dilated for the last four hours. I discussed the need for the cesarean delivery with the patient and her husband. After all of their questions were answered, the patient was wheeled back to the operating room. The patient already had an epidural in place so the surgery started right away. Ken performed the surgery. My role as chief resident was to act as first assistant and teacher to help Ken perfect his surgical skills. Just as we were finishing up, a nurse waltzed into the operating room and announced that two women out in Labor and Delivery weren't doing well.

"The lady in room one is having difficulty breathing, and we can't get a fetal heart rate in room two," she said.

Another responsibility that came with the role of chief resident besides teaching was triaging cases. I knew that the woman in room one was HIV positive and had bronchitis. The patient had a complete pulmonary evaluation late last night and did not have pneumonia. This patient was well known to the OB team. She often used coughing or the onset of pain to get attention. She knew that as soon as she mentioned that she was HIV positive, every-one would jump. Knowing this, I sent Ken to room one. The fact that the nurse was having a difficult time finding the fetal heart rate in room two troubled me more. The patient in that room was a healthy thirty-three-year-old who was having her fifth child. All of her previous deliveries had been vaginal without any complications. The patient was full term, so why were the nurses having a hard time finding the heart rate? Because of the size of a full-term baby, even the most inexperienced nurse should be able to locate the fetal heart rate. This nurse was one of the most experienced nurses working that day.

When I walked into room two, the patient was complaining of shortness of breath. She also seemed agitated. The nurse had the fetal heart monitor in her hand. She was fumbling with it trying desperately to find a steady heart rate. Something didn't seem right. Instinctively, I told the patient that I needed to do a vaginal exam to insert a fetal scalp electrode. This instrument is placed on the fetal scalp and gives an accurate reading of the fetal heart rate. Just as I was doing her vaginal exam, Ken walked in and said room one was stable. He then asked, "What's happening here?" With my hand still in my patient's vagina, I calmly ordered Ken to quickly bring the ultrasound machine into the room. What I was feeling was very disturbing—there was no presenting part. This means that the head was no longer in the pelvic area. The only other time I had seen something like this was when a patient had ruptured her uterus and the fetus had been extruded into the abdominal area. Ken quickly reappeared with the sonogram machine. I ran the transducer over the patient's abdomen and what I saw confirmed my suspicions. I could not make out a distinct uterine wall. All I could see was the fetus with a sluggish heartbeat surrounded by placental tissue floating in the abdominal cavity.

"We're going back for a C-section," I announced. "Please call anesthesia." Ken and I helped roll the patient to the operating room. At the same time, I explained to the patient that it was necessary to perform a cesarean section to save her baby and that she would most likely need a hysterectomy.

Although the patient barely had a blood pressure and was groggy by this time, she nodded her head, signaling that she understood the necessity of surgery. I did not share with the patient or with Ken the likelihood that by the time we performed the operation the baby may already be dead. The anesthesiologist could not be found. Even though I had never done this before (but had read about it in my obstetric textbooks), time was of the essence in this case, so I proceeded to make the incision after infiltration of a local anesthetic instead of the patient being under general anesthesia. Upon entering the abdominal cavity, Ken and I saw only blood. Then I saw the fetus and placenta. At that moment, I felt an immense tug on my heart. I had never lost a baby in labor and there was no way this baby could have survived this uterine rupture. I quickly delivered the fetus from the abdominal cavity and clamped the umbilical cord. Miraculously, I could feel a heart rate. The baby started crying and moving. Then, the baby did something that made me positive that he was all right—he peed all over me! At that moment, I smiled, passed the baby to the pediatrician, and then turned my attention to the mother's uterus, which was beyond repair. By this time, the anesthesiologist had arrived and stabilized the patient, which allowed us to remove the uterus. Two hours later, Ken and I left the operating room. Both mother and baby were stable and our shift was over. And I'm sure the book club meeting was over too.

4

GWEN

Delivering babies conjures up images of my past for some reason. The circumstances of the delivery dictate the memory. Today, I saw myself as a little girl. I have always liked being outdoors. How could I help it? My birth order was the second out of three, and I was sandwiched between two brothers. They had me climbing trees, playing basketball, football, baseball, or any other game with a ball. We also rode bikes, go-carts, and any other kids' vehicles. There were very few things that I was afraid of. My brothers erased the emotion of fear from my repertoire after they placed a garter snake in my bed. I guess as a child I would have been described as a tomboy. I didn't mind this description at all. In fact, later in life, I attributed my competitive edge to my tomboyishness. In high school and college, I excelled in athletics, specifically track and field and soccer. The state records I set in various events in track and field are still standing today.

Luckily, my parents, Johnny and Vera Nichols, tried to make sure that I was a lady too. I took ballet and tap, played the piano and violin, and took English riding lessons. Against my wishes, when I was a junior in high school, I made my debut in a debutante ball. I did not see the benefit of such a social event, but it was a simple thing to do to make my parents happy. I had a good relationship with my parents and brothers. Unlike some of my friends, I actually enjoyed spending time with my family.

My brothers and I each had our different challenges as we were growing up. One challenge that we faced together as a family was when my father's company went bankrupt. My father owned a real estate development company. During the mid-seventies, the real estate business hit rock bottom. Subsequently, my parents liquidated most of their assets, including our cars and the summer home, to stay afloat. Up until this point in my life, I had always looked at my father as the rock of our family's existence. I guess it was because he had his own business and always seemed to be in charge. My mother always seemed quiet in comparison to my father. She worked too, but erroneously I viewed her job as only a hobby. I saw a different side of my mother during this time. She was the one who carried the family through this financial disaster. My mother had been purchasing investments separate from my father, and the proceeds from these investments paid the mortgage, college tuition for my oldest brother, and other major household expenses. In addition, my mom made sure that my father still felt like a productive part of our family and society even though he was out of work for about a year. I learned three things from my mother. The first was that probably one of the most important times to show your man how much you love him is when he's down and out. I also learned that a man's ego is very fragile and it is devastating when one of the main things that define him, like his job, is disrupted. The third lesson that I learned was that a woman doesn't have to announce her successes. My new-found admiration for my mother did not diminish my respect for my father. I never mistook silence for passivity again. I also decided then that I would rather be a behind-the-scenes girl than someone always in the limelight.

My parents stressed the importance of academic proficiency, and as I had done in other areas of my life, I excelled academically too. I was the valedictorian of my high school class, graduating with a 4.0 grade-point average. I went on to matriculate at Harvard University where I graduated cum laude. When it was time to go to medical school I shocked everyone. All of my professors assumed that I would stay on at Harvard, but I packed my bags and headed for California. The decision to leave New England was an easy one. What I struggled with was whether I should go to New York to be close to my boyfriend of four years whom everyone thought I would marry, but I knew I would not; or to spread my wings and head for the West Coast. Anyone who knew me knew where I was going before I announced it. I didn't do the expected. I did what I thought would make me happy.

California ended up being all that I had imagined and more. If asked to describe medical school, I would say that it was labor intensive—in class eight hours a day and then studying another six hours every, I mean every, night. But I did not find the material hard to grasp. I guess a Harvard education was good for something. Medical school was not the only thing that had my attention while in California. Years before while still in college, I had worked on a research project at one of the hospitals in Los Angeles, during the summer of the 1984 Olympics. It was then that I met Sloan.

Sloan was five years older than I was and already in medical school. I was completely in awe of him. He was six foot, three inches tall with golden brown skin and biceps, triceps, and quadriceps to die for. His voice was always even keeled, his tone always calm, and his touch always strong. So it was not long before I had a huge crush on him. However, two problems existed. He had a live-in girlfriend whose name was also Gwen, and he had a female classmate from medical school, Wendy. Wendy was working on the research project as well, and I believed that she also had a crush on him. Nevertheless, I enjoyed working side by side with Sloan in the lab, eating lunch with him and slipping out in the middle of the day to go swimming with him when things were slow. Of course Wendy was always around, and I knew that every night he went home to his Gwen.

From the time that I had made the decision to go to medical school on the West Coast, I could not stop wondering if I would run into Sloan again. Whenever I went out to parties, I would scan the room for his face. When I went to the beach, I would pray that I would spot his physique. When I walked through the hospital, I would strain to hear his voice. Sometimes when I slept, I would dream of his touch. Finally, in between my second and third years of medical school, after taking the first part of the National Board Examination, I saw Sloan.

The examination had been a two-day experience from hell, so naturally I was oh so happy when it was over. I rushed home to change into my bathing suit as my roommates and I had decided to meet at the beach at 5:00 p.m. I caught a quick glimpse of myself in the mirror as I changed. I looked whipped. I had studied nonstop for the last three weeks and then spent the last two days mentally stressed. All of this showed on my face—no California glow, instead I had bags under both eyes and a nonexistent hairstyle. At least the headache I had since the third hour of the first day of the exam was starting to subside. I threw on my favorite baseball hat and headed for the beach. I was responsible for bringing drinks to the post-Boards beach party, so I made a pit stop at Krueger's. I was almost out of the store when I remembered that I had forgotten to pick up a bag of ice. As I approached the freezer, I tried to decide whether I should get a large or small bag. I opened the door of the freezer and picked up a large bag. It was heavier than I expected. As I turned, slightly off balance due to the weight of the ice, I saw Sloan, or at least I thought it was him. He was standing across from me picking through bags of frozen vegetables. Just as I started to move, he looked up. Our eyes met for a split second. My mind began to race. Should I put my head down and walk away? That would be rude. Should I smile and then walk away? That would be acceptable. Or should I suck it up, smile, and say, "Excuse me, is your name Sloan Taylor?" I guess the same thoughts were going through his mind but his synapses were firing a little quicker than mine because after a brief—let's say about a nanosecond—delay, this gorgeous man said to me, "Excuse me, Gwen...Gwen Nichols?"

I don't know what I said but I think it was something like, "Yes, Sloan, it's been ages." We hugged each other in the frozen food section and caught up on each other's lives as we waited in the checkout line. Sloan worked as a trauma surgeon at City Hospital. We exchanged phone numbers and promised to get together. Somehow I got to the beach and for the next two weeks, all my roommates heard was Sloan Taylor this or Sloan Taylor that. I was on cloud nine. I wore a smile all the time. I even slept smiling. I felt like that little girl back in 1984, totally in awe of this gorgeous man.

I got a reality check once school started again. In the third year of medical school, you finally get out of the classroom and work on the wards in the hospital. Hours are long but you're so excited to be in the hospital that you don't notice your fatigue for the first month. I never heard from Sloan after our meeting in the grocery store. I assumed he either had a wife or a girlfriend. I resigned myself to accepting that he was unavailable.

Finally, one night when transporting a patient to Radiology, I ran into Sloan again. To my surprise, he seemed genuinely excited to see me, and proceeded to apologize for not getting in contact with me. He explained that he had been preparing a lecture that he recently gave at a trauma conference in Miami. I said that I understood and we made plans to go in-line skating the following Saturday. I was rapturous the rest of the week. Neither my roommates nor I could wait for Saturday to come.

Saturday could not have been a more perfect day. The sun was bright and not a cloud was in sight. I got a good night's rest on Friday, so my skin had that pampered glow. My mind was relaxed and carefree. I felt great. I had not been that sexually charged in a long, long time. Sloan picked me up in his Porsche Carrera, which got me even more excited. It wasn't a bourgeois thing—I just love Porsches for their sleekness and speed. We in-line skated, swam, sunbathed, and talked, like old times. I felt chemistry between us. I prayed that I wasn't re-creating the feelings that I had developed for Sloan when we worked together back during my college years. What I felt was wonderful. It was not just sexual attraction; it was something more. I remember feeling an overwhelming sense of happiness and tranquility, as if I had just been reunited with my best friend in the whole wide world. Don't get me wrong; there were definitely pheromones brewing between us. There was no pressure to act on these feelings. We ended our afternoon by making plans for dinner, deciding to have a barbecue at Sloan's house on the beach. When Sloan picked me up that evening, I had that casual but sexy look. I blow-dried my hair so that it hung to my shoulders. My skin was sun kissed as if I had just worked out. I had on a khaki miniskirt with a black T-shirt and black thong sandals. I'd treated myself to a pedicure earlier in the week so my toenails were painted Tahitian Coral. A sterling silver ring and bracelet completed the ensemble. Dinner was great. Again, we laughed and joked like old friends. The chemistry was in the air but we restrained ourselves. We ended the night with two pecks on the cheek and promises to see each other again. We kept our promise. For the next four weeks, we saw each other whenever one of us was not on call.

For Labor Day weekend, we decided to go to a bed and breakfast in Carmel. My girlfriends teased me that if I came home without getting any, I should start thinking that either Sloan was gay or he just wanted to be my friend. I knew the attraction between us was getting stronger. I thought we were both ready for an intimate relationship, but I didn't share these thoughts with my roommates. I packed a few simple but sexy items along with my diaphragm and condoms. We got to Carmel about 9:00 p.m. The temperature had dropped into the seventies with a slight breeze. The bed and breakfast was a cluster of individual cottages, each with a fireplace and a porch. After we unpacked the car, we went for a walk along the beach. The moon was a tiny sliver but there was enough light to see our shadows. We looked good together. Without warning Sloan picked me up and ran into the water. I was startled at first by the icy temperature of the water but once I felt Sloan's body on mine, I felt warm and relaxed. When I felt his full luscious lips on my body, I knew I was in heaven. We swam for what seemed like an eternity with our bodies skin to skin, relaxed on the beach, and then made love to the rhythm of the waves with the moon winking down on us. That was the beginning of a wonderful relationship.

My fourth year of medical school flew by. Once it was over, I was ready to move back to the East Coast. I missed my family and friends. I missed the four seasons. I missed Utz potato chips. And I missed plain old folks. I was very tired of the generally superficial, shallow people of Southern California. This may be a bit of an overstatement because I did meet a lot of substantial people and left behind some great friends when I moved back east. But to me, the overall feel in Los Angeles was too plastic. I cannot tell you the number of times I was mistaken for an actress or a model as if they were the only two professions in Los Angeles. The only thing that could have kept me in Los Angeles would have been Sloan. I was ready to settle down and get married. I had communicated these desires to Sloan in numerous heart-to-heart conversations. But he made it crystal clear to me that he was not ready. So, I packed my bags and moved to Washington, D.C., to start my residency in obstetrics and gynecology at University Hospital.

Sloan and I kept in sporadic contact for the first year after I moved back east. We would call to extend birthday or Christmas wishes. Then, for no special reason, we stopped calling each other; I guess we stopped missing each other. The last time I heard from Sloan was in 1995. He sent me one of those cute friendship cards. His note in the card said he had been offered an unbelievable position at a hospital in the Washington, D.C. metropolitan area. I dismissed the note because I was totally consumed by my residency and my life in D.C. I had completed my residency by this time and was enjoying an active social life. It was summertime. All the hot restaurants had their patios open and business was hopping. After a long day at work, there was no better way to unwind than to sit outside with friends sipping margaritas or white wine spritzers. My Happy Hour partner, Bob, had been bugging me about meeting his friend. Bob never said his friend's name, but kept telling me how he thought that the two of us had so much in common and that we would make the perfect couple. Finally, our blind date was set up. I was going to introduce my friend Natalie to Bob and he was going to introduce me to his friend. You can imagine how shocked I was when I realized that Sloan was my blind date. We had a wonderful reunion that night. We talked until the wee hours of the morning about our lives, the breakup, and the relationships in the interim. We realized how much we missed our friendship and companionship. For me, that day marked the start of a different type of relationship—I resolved in my heart and mind that what I wanted most was to enjoy Sloan's company. I no longer wanted our relationship to be strained by the weight of marriage ultimatums. We didn't just pick up where we had left off back in California; instead our relationship grew from the base we had already established. For now, I was happy enjoying life after residency.

Once again, Sloan and I were spending all of our free time together—going to movies, going out to dinner, playing tennis, running, and even spending a week in Bermuda. When we got back from Bermuda, I had a letter waiting for me from one of Sloan's previous girlfriends. I thought the envelope looked odd. My name and address were written in two different-colored inks, as if someone wrote my name first and then my address later. It's funny, the content of the letter was definitely meant to shock. But to Sloan's credit, I already knew everything. The night of our reunion, he'd told me a story about one of his ex-girlfriends. Apparently, near the end of their relationship, she found out she was pregnant. This supposedly happened while she was on the pill. They decided together that termination was the best option since Sloan was not promising her a future. In fact, Sloan said he went with her when she had the procedure. However, the woman, who seemed to be crazier than a bedbug, did not take her separation from Sloan well. She continued to call Sloan for months, threatening to have their non-existent baby. Interestingly enough, the calls always seemed to coincide with the onset of a new relationship. Sloan believed she made these calls to scare away any potential new girlfriends. I thought that he was being a typical man by not taking responsibility for protecting himself from an unwanted pregnancy or a sexually transmitted disease, and trying to rationalize, weakly, his irresponsible behavior.

I showed Sloan the letter and told him that he needed to resolve this situation and that I never wanted to be involved with any nonsense like this again. I wasn't mad, but I felt violated. I didn't know this woman, yet she knew my name and address. If he did not resolve this situation, I was prepared to leave him. Appropriately, he called the woman, in my presence, and told her that she was totally out of line to send me such a letter and that if she ever did anything like this again, he would take legal action. I don't know what legal action he could have taken, but in his deep, professional baritone, it sounded official. He assured her that if this was a stunt to make me leave him so she could have him, it was a futile effort. Moreover, to this woman's horror, Sloan shared with her that I already knew everything in the letter.

I thought Sloan's threat scared Girlfriend. But I was wrong! One night when I was over at Sloan's house working on a presentation for grand rounds, I heard a sound coming from the backyard. As I got up to take a look outside, I heard Chris Rock's voice in my head talking about how black people couldn't be in horror films because when we hear a weird sound, we don't go toward the sound to check it out, we run the other way. Well, I didn't heed Chris's advice. I turned the back porch light on and what did I see sitting on the steps, but a woman. I paused for a second; deciding whether or not I was in danger. After I determined that I was not, I opened the door.

"May I help you?" I asked.

"Can you help me? Yeah, you can help me," this woman said as she turned around and pointed to her abdomen. "You can help me get through this pregnancy."

Oh shit, I said to myself. I couldn't believe this crazy babe was at the house. It had been a couple of months since I had received that letter from her. Sloan said he went with her to terminate the pregnancy. Was he lying to me? If he was, by this time she would be close to her delivery date. But the woman didn't look like she was pregnant at all! She didn't know who she was messing with; being an obstetrician, I surely knew she wasn't still pregnant. She was starting to get even more agitated now as she rose to her feet and moved toward me like she was going to enter the house. I was now rethinking my danger clearance.

"Where's Sloan?" she asked. "I should be living here with Sloan, getting ready for our baby. He loves me; he told me that I was the only woman for him."

I had been standing by the door but had not closed it completely. At this point, I closed the door with a deliberate bang, signaling to this woman that she was not getting into this house. I then forced her to sit back down by positioning my body in front of her, blocking her forward path. If we had been playing chess, I would have said, "Check."

I was trying to figure out whether she was high on something or crazy. Or if she had some type of psychiatric illness—manic depression, paranoid schizophrenia, or delusional disorder. Her speech was not slurred, her clothes were not disheveled, not one of her hairs was out of place, no alcohol breath, and her movements weren't really jerky. I decided that she wasn't high.

I remained standing. "I'm sorry; I didn't get your name."

"I'm Sloan's wife, Linda. We're having our first baby soon," she continued as she patted her abdomen.

"Really," I said. "How far along are you?"

"I'm not telling you anything about my pregnancy," she screamed.

Now I was really thinking, *oh shit*. I wasn't in the mood for this. I wanted to finish my presentation and go to bed. I had to be up at 6:00 in the morning. Plus, now Girlfriend was getting loud.

"Linda, you know you really need to keep your voice down. It's late and you shouldn't be over here. In fact, you weren't invited, so technically you're trespassing."

"Trespassing? Please. I told Sloan to tell you about me a long time ago. He's such a wimp sometimes; he said he didn't want to hurt you. He wants you out of his house now. He says that you're messy, can't cook, and can't satisfy his needs like I can. If you know what I mean," she says as she winked.

Why am I out here with this woman? I asked myself.

"You know Linda, Sloan did tell me about you. He told me that you terminated your pregnancy a long time ago; he said that he went with you when you had the procedure." Now her eyes were getting big like she'd just seen a ghost.

"You know what else, Linda?" I stated with authority. "I'm an obstetrician/gynecologist. I'm trained to be able to tell when a woman is going to have a baby soon. You are certainly not having a baby anytime soon. You're probably not even pregnant, and if you are pregnant, it's not Sloan's baby." Checkmate.

Her wide-eyed gaze turned downward, and then the tears fell. I found myself stooping down, patting Linda on the shoulder, and encouraging her to go home. I told her that she was going to be okay, but she had to come to terms with the fact that she was no longer in a relationship with Sloan. She kept saying, "I'm not okay, I won't be okay," as she staggered off the porch. At that moment, I thought maybe this woman was so distraught about having an abortion that she was just calling out for help. I took the pen that I had behind my ear—bad habit—and quickly jotted down the number to a support line for women's health issues on a piece of paper I spotted on the porch. I put the paper in Linda's hand just before she turned to walk away. Her pitiful whimper made me feel sorry for her. After that night we never heard from her again.

Unfortunately, it would be another woman who would next invade our relationship. It had been nine months of bliss. No drama, no big talks about the future. Just lots of fun and hot sex. Then, I got the dreaded phone call.

"Hey, Gwen, give me a call. We need to talk." I don't think I'll ever forget that message. On the surface, I thought our relationship was going well. But deep down inside, I knew something was not quite right. Sloan was acting distant. Not in a mean way, but in a way that was different from his normal behavior. I thought that maybe Sloan was acting as he was because he was so independent and afraid of losing his freedom. I returned Sloan's call and we made plans to meet. When I got to his house, I asked Sloan what he wanted to talk about.

"Well, Gwen, we always said we could be honest with each other and that we would always be able to talk about our feelings," he said. I realized then that this was not going to be a good conversation. Anytime someone says, "You always said we could be honest," you know they're about to tell you that things aren't working out. You're about to be dumped. I stayed calm. I knew Sloan and I had a special bond and I believed in this bond. I also knew that there was more to this story and I was ready to hear it.

"Yeah, Sloan. We always said that we would be able to talk. Tell me what's on your mind." After some hesitancy, Sloan proceeded to completely burst my bubble. He shared with me that he thought he still had unresolved feelings for Gwen, the woman he was dating when I first met him as a medical student. I knew that they had gotten back together and broken up many times over the years but it never occurred to me that he had residual feelings for her. I tried to understand whether Sloan wanted to have a relationship with this woman or if he was feeling nostalgic. After I thought about it for a while I realized that, of course, he wanted a relationship with this woman; otherwise, his feelings wouldn't be affecting our relationship.

Call me arrogant or call me crazy—I wouldn't accept this to be our fate. But, before I could stop myself, I heard these words coming out of my mouth.

"Fine, Sloan. If you think you have unresolved feelings for this woman, then I think you should go to her and tell her. I think we need to put our relationship on hold." That's when his tears fell, and if there's one thing that really tugs at my heart, it is seeing a man cry. To me, a man represents strength and impermeability, so if a man cries, he must be really hurt. At that moment my rational, objective side kicked into gear. Always the physician, healer, and provider, why was I even considering his feelings at this time. "Why are you crying?" I asked, bewildered. "You tell me that you have been harboring feelings for some woman that you dated years ago. I should be the one crying."

"Gwen, that's not why I told you. I don't want us to break up."

I almost choked. "What did you think was going to happen if you told me that you had unresolved feelings for some other woman?"

I heard myself continuing in a very calm, almost eerie tone, "Sloan, I do believe in our relationship. Hey, I thought that we were meant to be together forever. If you don't believe in it, then that's fine. I want to be in a relationship where my mate is with me one hundred percent."

I think I was so flabbergasted both by what Sloan had told me and how he was responding that I did not feel the knife in my heart until I left his house.

As I drove home, I felt like I was in a fugue state. This wasn't really happening to me. Yet, it *was* happening to me, and I felt terribly lonely.

Over the next few weeks, my stupidity reached new heights as I continued to call Sloan again and again to see if he told the other Gwen about his feelings. I guess I was being a pest. But I felt that Sloan was going back to the past because he was afraid to face the future. He was afraid of commitment.

"Sloan, if you think that you have all these feelings for this woman, then you should be running back to her. Our relationship was a good one. We had a stronger relationship than some of our married friends. So, you should be ecstatic with this woman," I said sarcastically.

"Gwen, if you're going to harass me every time you call, then maybe it's best that we don't talk to each other."

This is how our conversations went for at least two or three months. Finally, after months of getting my hopes up that Sloan would realize that he had made a mistake, I realized that I needed to move on with my life. I lost weight. I was evil to my family and probably some friends too. I went out with different guys, but I wasn't interested in any of them. I told myself that I had to stop comparing every man to Sloan. Otherwise, I'd never find another companion. Of course, as soon as I had gotten used to being by myself and enjoying it, Sloan started calling me, beeping me, and even writing me. I didn't return any phone calls or letters. I was determined to move on and not look back. One morning while I was stretching before a run, the phone rang. I thought it was Camille calling about getting together for lunch.

"Hello."

"Hi, Gwen, it's me, Sloan."

I was quiet for a minute because I really was caught off guard. "Hi, Sloan. Is everything all right?"

"Yes, everything is fine. Why do you ask?"

"Well, you paged me three times yesterday. You made it pretty clear that you didn't want me to be a part of your life and that you didn't want to be a part of mine. Yes, I'm the one who pulled the trigger on our relationship and actually said the words, 'I'm done.' But, you had already broken up with me emotionally. So, I figured something must be wrong if you were calling me and wanted to talk." I had practiced that line so many times. I was thrilled that I finally had the opportunity to use it.

"Gwen, you know that's not what I want."

"The way you've talked to me and acted toward me in the past months, that's exactly what I thought you wanted. It's okay. I'm not a bad person and you're not a bad person. I still care for you. Maybe in time we can be friends."

There was silence on his end of the phone. I guess Sloan couldn't believe that I had told him to leave me alone. "Gwen, you know I still love you. It's just that I'm afraid."

I didn't even let him finish his sentence. "Afraid of what?" I really wasn't in the mood to hear this crap. I had been telling Sloan that he was afraid of commitment, the future, the unknown, or whatever you wanted to call it since we broke up the first time.

"I'm afraid that I won't be a good husband or a good provider," he said. I couldn't believe Sloan was saying he was afraid of not being a good husband. That was the one thing that I was sure of. From the first time that I met Sloan, he had been the epitome of strength to me. He was intelligent, articulate, and compassionate. I couldn't believe he doubted himself and the stability he brought to the relationship. I thought back to how my mother supported my father when he doubted himself after his first business failed. But then I stopped myself in mid-thought. Sloan was the one who had initiated the breakup. I was starting to enjoy my life again. I was not sure if I wanted to be in a relationship with Sloan for a third time. I didn't know whether I could trust him with my feelings again. I wanted to know whether he was coming back to me because the other women wouldn't take him back or because he really wanted to be with me. I questioned whether I was the default girl.

He told me that after speaking to her, he realized the feelings he thought he had for the other Gwen were nothing. Over the past few months, he really wanted to be alone so that he could reflect on what it was he really wanted. The other Gwen was merely an excuse for him to avoid the reality of his commitment phobia to me, the Gwen who really captured his heart. He also made it clear that he had not slept with any other women. I didn't care one way or another. While we were apart I took a long hard look at our two relationships and realized that Sloan was not good for me emotionally. Plus I had finally met a nice guy whom I really enjoyed spending time with, and there was no pressure. This guy had recently gone through a bitter divorce and was willing to be monogamous but wasn't ready for anything more. Our weekends were filled with dinners, movies, picnics, black-tie affairs, ski trips, and, I loved making love with him. I knew I'd eventually want something more substantial, whether from this relationship or from another, but right now I was fine. One day I looked up and I was happy without Sloan. I acknowledged to myself that I missed him, but I felt strongly that I would never go back to Sloan if he couldn't commit. Besides his commitment issues, Sloan had involved me in a lot of mess—getting a letter and a visit from Linda, the crazy girlfriend; and his on-again, off-again relationships with Gwen and whomever else. I didn't want to be bothered with any more foolishness. I was getting too old for childish games.

He was persistent though. Over the next nine months, Sloan

kept calling me and asking me to spend time with him. He had the nerve to get angry if I had other plans. It was amazing. Now that he was ready to commit, he expected me to have the same feelings that I'd had for him before. He was surely mistaken. It was truly the turning of the tables. Our phone conversations would always get to the point of Sloan badgering me about why we weren't together and what it was that I saw in my new friend. On many occasions, I found myself saying to Sloan that if he was going to harass me during our phone calls, then maybe it was better that we didn't speak right now. I was very forthcoming about my new relationship and my lack of desire to have a relationship with him at this time. He didn't get it that I had moved on. More important, he didn't realize how much he had hurt me.

At some point, my new relationship fizzled out. There was no catastrophic event—no cheating or lying or ex-wives showing up. We both just realized that our time together had been wonderful but it was only meant to be for a finite period. Maybe we each were put in the other's life to help each other get over bad relationships. It reminded me of a poem on friendship that says that people come into our lives for a reason, a season, or for a lifetime. I would say that we were meant for each other for a reason or season, but not a lifetime.

About a month later, I ran into Sloan at the Smithsonian, at a lecture on the state of Black America. Cornel West, Henry Louis Gates, and Kweisi Mfume were on the panel. Sloan was looking good. We spoke to each other at the end of the lecture and shared some "nicey-nice" chit-chat. As I stood there, face to face with him, I realized that I was no longer angry or hurt. I was in a neutral zone. Sloan called me every day for two weeks after that chance meeting at the Smithsonian. By the third week we started spending some time together—meeting for a drink, catching a movie, or checking out an exhibit at one of the museums. We had an unspoken limit of spending three hours at a time with each other. Gradually, as I let myself feel the love that I felt for Sloan before, we started spending more time together. I was actually surprised that my feelings were still there for Sloan. He finally apologized for hurting me like he did and for the first time, he took responsibility for us being in the situation that we were in—not dating, not married and nursing many battle scars. Over the next few months, I slowly shed the covers that kept my feelings for Sloan in check. I no longer felt like the schoolgirl with a massive crush on the most popular boy in the school. I now felt like an equal partner. I finally realized the wealth and strength that I brought to our relationship, and I believed that Sloan could finally be committed to me and us. We fell in love again. My heart paused and a delightful shock tingled my spine the moment that we both realized that we wanted to spend the rest of our lives together. It was amazing. For the second time in my life, I felt an overwhelming sense of happiness and tranquility.

5

GWEN

The Christmas holidays were over and things were settling with work and Sloan. I now had some time to spend with friends. Everyone, including me, was excited about the upcoming birth of Adriane's child. Adriane's circle of friends was so wide that multiple baby showers were given for her. Not to be outdone, the book club decided to give her a shower two weeks before Valentine's Day. If it had been up to Adriane she would have had the shower at her house. But we wanted to give her a special treat that didn't require any work on her part. We arranged an elaborate affair at The Black Sax, one of Allana's husband's restaurants. Two of Adriane's many favorite colors are black and gold, so the invitations were done up in those colors, as were the balloons, ribbons and linens. The floral centerpieces for each table consisted of white hydrangeas in gold and black square vases. Allana kept saying that baby shower colors are supposed to be blue or pink. "Why are we using black and gold?" she kept asking. She finally got over it. We kept the invitee list small, mostly book club members and a few people whom Adriane added to the list. Brianna invited one of her friends. The chef prepared a special menu of spinach with pine nuts, grilled shrimp and chicken, and roasted red potatoes in a creamy butter sauce. He also made a German chocolate cake designed to look like a baby cradle. When Adriane arrived and looked into our loving eyes she cried.

"I can't believe you guys did all of this for me. Look at the food. Look at the cake. Are all those gifts for me?"

"Yes, Adriane, all of this is for you," I responded. "Maybe you should sit down."

"Yes, maybe I should. I feel a little overwhelmed," Adriane said, wiping the tears from her eyes.

As soon as Adriane sat down the ladies came over to hug her. Destiny, who was always doing something, started fixing Adriane's plate to get the baby shower in gear. Once Adriane's plate was fixed the ladies dug in. While enjoying the food and each other's company, we discussed motherhood and raising children. After dinner and kudos to the chef, Adriane opened her cards and gifts. She read each card aloud, and then cried. She opened each gift, and cried again. And then she made a thank-you speech and we all cried. Before she could start in on the story of her life, we teased her that we only had the restaurant for a couple of hours. Adriane's response was "Y'all ain't right." That day we waited on Adriane hand and foot. She enjoyed the special attention we gave her. When Destiny served her some cake, she commented on how she could get used to being served.

Most of the guests had departed. Allana and Destiny were packing up the leftover cake and baby shower gifts while the rest of us were sitting at the table drinking champagne, when Brianna said, "Girl, I'm so excited for you and Sloan."

"I'm so excited too. I don't think I've ever been happier. You know, when Sloan and I got back together this time, I wasn't sure whether I would ever be able to really love and trust him again."

"Gwen, you know I love you to death and I want you to be happy," Camille chimed in. "Are you sure about Sloan this time? He is a good guy, but do you think he is over his fear of commitment? Have you asked yourself whether you're marrying Sloan because you're ready to get married now and Sloan is available? I'm sorry to say this, Gwen, but how in the hell can you go back to him? Did you forget all the pain that he has put you through? Are you sure that he is sincere this time?"

"I hear you, Camille. You're asking some really poignant questions that have crossed my mind. I have put a lot of thought into this. I don't think I've ever stopped loving Sloan. You're right, I'm so ready to get married now, and I can't wait to have a couple of kids. Yes, I did have some anger toward him for all the back and forth he put me through, but I'm not angry anymore. I've never loved anyone like I love Sloan. I like who he is as a person. Yeah, he had some major commitment issues, but what man do we know who didn't grapple with issues of commitment, especially concerning tying the knot? A lot of women go through this with their mates. Unfortunately I'm one of them."

Adriane put her two cents in. "You know, Tim pulled some craziness on me right after we got engaged. I was working on a deal with the Mexican government that required me to spend weeks at a time in Mexico. Well, when I returned one weekend after being gone for about ten days, Tim started talking about how maybe we didn't have such a strong bond with each other and we shouldn't be getting married because while I was away he didn't feel like he was going to die without me. Now, what kind of crap was that?! I almost called the wedding off myself on the principle that I was marrying an idiot, because in my mind, only a fool would have said what he did."

After we all laughed and agreed that yes, most of the men we knew had some struggle with commitment at some point, I continued. "I acknowledge that Sloan had more issues than most with commitment, but I never doubted that once he got that monkey off his back, he'd be a great husband and father. He's got a heart of gold. He's kind and genuine. I always believed that he wanted to make me happy; he simply didn't know what to do with all of his feelings. It scared the shit out of him.

"When we were apart I missed our friendship and now that we're back on track, I feel complete. I'm not saying that I need a man to be complete, but I'll be honest with you, I feel happier and I feel like everything else in my life is smoother with Sloan around."

"Okay, okay, okay, you still haven't said why you think Sloan is sincere this time," Camille said.

"Well, you know how he used to close down or try to run away when he felt himself becoming vulnerable as we were getting closer emotionally; well, he's no longer doing that. He's inviting me to share his life; he's calling to ask my opinion on what he should do with some real estate deal. Now, you know the old Sloan would have no problem talking to me about the deal, but he wouldn't be calling me to ask for my opinion after every conversation with his attorney. He genuinely acts like he wants me in his life. I really think he's ready to be committed to me. Maybe I should be worried that he's finally ready to settle down and I happen to be around. But, I'm not."

A little light-headed from drinking too much champagne, Brianna spoke up out of nowhere. "Gwen, there is no doubt in my mind that Sloan loves you. I don't know how many times I told you that you two belong together. Anyone who sees you two together can see how much you both love each other. People always say that it's the woman who glows when she's in love, but I swear; Sloan is the one glowing right now."

"It's funny you say that because strangers stop us on the street to tell us that we look really happy and in love. In all the other relationships that I've had, I never felt this feeling that I have with Sloan. I was trying to explain it to Natalie the other night. I feel like there is something literally soothing my heart and soul. I wouldn't describe it as hot passion or admiration or attraction or even comfort. It's some moving force that keeps me bonded to him. I know this sounds weird but I can't find the words to explain it. You guys know that he can really get on my nerves and he can make me so angry sometimes, but at the end of the day, I still feel the bond."

"That would be *love*," Adriane said. "I know the loss you're at trying to explain your feelings. I feel that for Tim. Gwen, that's what keeps couples together. You know, life is not always kind. Circumstances, work pressures, people, and I'm not just talking about other women or men, but family, will try to come between you and Sloan. You've got to have that unexplainable bond to get you through those times."

Just then a woman whom we did not know appeared at the table. Brianna immediately jumped up.

"Sarah, I'm glad you could make it. Everybody, this is Sarah. I met her at a Washington Bullets game. Sarah, this is Gwen, Camille, Adriane, Natalie, Allana, and Destiny."

"Good evening, all. I've heard so much about all of you. Congratulations, Adriane. Sorry I'm late for the shower. From the looks of things, it looks like it was wonderful. Here is a little something for the new one. I hope you like it," Sarah said with a smile.

Reaching for the gift, Adriane said, "Thank you. I'm sure we will love it."

"Have a seat, Sarah. Would you like a glass of champagne?" Brianna asked.

"That would be nice, I've been running all day," she responded.

"Would you like me to see if I can still get you something to eat?" Brianna eagerly volunteered.

Touching Brianna's arm, Sarah said, "No, no, champagne is fine."

While Brianna poured Sarah a glass of champagne, Allana said to Sarah, "I understand you are a big fan of basketball."

"Yes, I try to make most of the games here and away."

Destiny chimed in, "Patrick and I went to a couple of games last year. Who is your favorite player?"

"I really don't have a favorite player. I just like the sport," Sarah answered.

"Gwen, didn't you and Sloan go to a couple NBA games too?" Destiny asked. There was no response. "Gwen, did you hear me?" Destiny inquired.

"I'm sorry, what was that?" I asked, dazed.

"Girl, did you have one too many over there? I asked you if you and Sloan had attended NBA games."

"No. I mean, yes. Yes, we did attend a few games. I was remembering something that happened a while ago. Sorry," I said, a little flustered. *Sarah? No, it couldn't be,* I think to myself.

Immediately after residency, I'd joined an established practice of three Black female physicians. I was very excited because I would be joining with a friend, Angela. Angela and I met in medical school and quickly became friends. Then, the unheard of happened. We both ended up at University Hospital for our residency. A computer program assigns the residency positions, so the chances that two friends from the same medical school would be assigned to the same hospital are slim. In any event, I thought I was stepping into an ideal practice situation. There was no doubt in my mind the physicians practiced sound medicine, but there was something about their personalities that made me uncomfortable.

One of the doctors never smiled and didn't seem too thrilled to have Angela and me joining her practice. I had heard rumors that she was having an affair with a doctor at University Hospital.

The other doctor was a shopaholic and was said to have embezzled money from the practice. Being a fair person, I ignored the uncomfortable feelings and the rumors since I did not know them to be true.

Initially, I really enjoyed working in the practice. Then, little things started to bother me. First, two of the partners smoked. Before starting my office hours in the morning, I would have to wipe away cigarette ash from the desk and spray the office with Lysol. By the end of the day, my hair and clothes would smell like I had been smoking. Furthermore, as a physician promoting health maintenance and prevention, I found it hypocritical to have an office that smelled like a chimney stack. The second thing about the practice that began to wear on me was that the nursing staff would sit at the front desk and eat. This was not my idea of professionalism. Again, being a fair person, I never said anything about these things except to my mother. I shared with my mom that I thought both of these habits were not only unprofessional but also disrespectful to patients. I wish these were the only things that dissatisfied me. No luck! Tax time came around and I was levied with a large tax payment. I started rehearsing what explanation I was going to give the IRS for not being able to pay my bill since I hadn't been paid in two months. Luckily, after many conversations with the partners, I got my back paychecks on April 14 and never had to have that conversation with the IRS. But my patience was wearing thin. I was working twelve-hour days and spending at least two nights a week in the hospital and yet I continued not to get paid. The toll of the work schedule showed on my face. Everyone kept telling me "you look tired" or asking, "Are you okay?" Moreover, I was becoming a grouch. Actually, some people may have better described me as a "bitch." Finally, after missing five more paychecks, which meant no pay for an additional two and a half months, I reached the end of my rope. The only things keeping me at the practice were my patients and my friend Angela.

"Angela, I don't know about you, but I can't continue to work without getting paid," I said one day over lunch. Mind you, it was a free lunch at the hospital since both of us were broke.

"Oh, Gwen, don't be so hasty. Why don't we set up a meeting with the senior partners and see if we can come to some type of arrangement to get paid?"

Angela convinced me to hang in there for an additional month. We had a meeting with the partners, who promised to pay us all of our back pay within the month.

One evening, I was in the office late dictating some letters to referring physicians. All the nursing staff had left about an hour earlier. I heard the back door of the office open and I assumed it was the cleaning team. There was no reason for me to be alarmed as I had been in the office late before and knew that the cleaning woman entered from the back door. I continued dictating. About a half hour later, I realized that I hadn't heard the vacuum cleaner start up yet. I thought this was a little odd since the cleaning woman had been there a while. I poked my head out of the office and noticed an almond scent coming from one of the partners' offices. At that moment, it hit me that someone was burning a candle. I approached the partner's office and what I saw stopped me in my tracks. Through the slightly cracked door I saw one of the partners, and she was naked. I'm thinking, it's true, she's having an affair. I backed away from the door, struggling to hear the other voice. I thought I would recognize the voice of the particular doctor with whom she was rumored to be having an affair. His voice was very deep but with a soulful Southern drawl. Then I heard the other voice coming from inside the office, but it wasn't that deep and there was no Southern drawl.

The woman said teasingly, "I'm going to need a little more cash this week. Because of you, I was late meeting a client, which cost me a commission. We get so little time together. Whenever I'm with you I want my tongue buried in the sweetness of your pussy for as long as it takes to make you quiver."

I heard my partner say, "I'm short on money too. We've got to pay our new associates this month. I've given you a lot of money over the last couple of months. A trip to Paris and then to Italy for some wine conference and your season tickets to the Washington Bullets, among other things. This adds up, you know, Sarah."

I thought to myself, *Sarah? Who is Sarah?*

Sarah shot back, a little put out, "How do you think your husband would react if he found out his precious little wife is licking my clit and bumping my pussy every chance she gets? Better still, what would the medical community say about a medical staff president carrying on an illicit lesbian affair?"

I quickly covered my mouth. So she is having an affair. And with a woman. I'll be damned. This was too much. I was tiptoeing back to my office when Sarah's voice got louder as she demanded money. Once in my office, I thought, *shit, no paycheck again this month.*

Since I had already agreed to stay, I kept my word. I also didn't say anything to anyone about what I had seen and heard. To no one's surprise, the end of the month came and went without mention of a paycheck. On many occasions, the partners hinted that Angela and I could get by without our paychecks since we were single and without any financial responsibilities. We had to remind them that we had rent, school loan payments, car payments, and other expenses. I couldn't believe it but Angela was willing to continue to work despite not getting paid. But as time went on, even Angela finally understood that the partners had no allegiance to us. We notified our attorney and within two weeks, we had in our possession a lump sum equaling twelve paychecks. Then we resigned.

I shook myself back to reality and focused my full attention back on the group before me. We continued chatting for nearly another hour, which gave me an opportunity to learn more about Sarah.

NATALIE

6

NATALIE

When we arrived at the hospital, we were told that Adriane had been taken directly to Labor and Delivery. We jumped into the elevator and headed for the third floor. When the doors opened at the Labor and Delivery floor, a roomy and festive-looking waiting room appeared. Gwen suggested we sit in the waiting area while she checked on Adriane. Before Gwen disappeared behind a door marked "Hospital Staff Only," she assured us she would come back soon to give us an update on Adriane's condition. Camille told us that having had two children herself, she thought it was a good sign that Adriane was brought to Labor and Delivery. "If it was something more serious she probably would be down in the Emergency Room or in another wing. The fact that she is on the Labor and Delivery floor probably means she just went into premature labor. Having a baby is no joke but once Adriane gets an epidural she won't have any problem pushing that baby out," Camille continued.

I felt a lot better now that we were in the hospital and Gwen was here. I figured even if there was some problem with the pregnancy, we were at the best place for it and I had confidence in the medical staff. Now all we needed was a report from Gwen to confirm everything was okay. I guess the powers that be heard my plea because a few minutes later Brianna came out and told us Adriane was indeed in labor and so far everything looked fine.

Brianna was truly a welcome sight, having missed today's book club meeting because she was on call. She told us that Adriane was three centimeters dilated and that everything seemed fine. At this statement there was a collective sigh of relief. Brianna indicated that she had to run, but told me to come with her because Adriane had asked to see me. I followed Brianna through the staff-only door and down a hallway that looked a lot like a hall in someone's home. There was a southwestern feel to the wallpaper and on one side tasteful pictures of landscapes were displayed. On the other wall there was a big collage of baby pictures. I assumed moms and dads whose babies were delivered at the hospital had donated the pictures. I snuck a peek into the first room on my right and I caught a glimpse of a woman lying on her side with one leg being stretched practically over her head. Her husband, I assumed, appeared to be stroking her hair. She was moaning. I knew that I wanted a family in the not too distant future, although a husband would be a nice prerequisite, and at the moment I had no prospects. However, seeing delivery up close and personal was enough to make me give adoption some more thought. I hurried on after Brianna, who was at least ten paces ahead of me. Brianna pointed out Adriane's room and I followed her inside. Adriane's room looked like a den. There was a reclining chair, a TV, a dresser, and several pictures hung on the wall. There also was a waist-high machine with some probes connected to Adriane. I figured that it must be the maternal/fetal monitor. Adriane also had a pulse oxymeter on her finger. She seemed calm and in good spirits. Gwen was in the room with her.

"Hey, girl! Are you ready for motherhood?" I asked Adriane.

"Well, I'm pretty frightened about the actual delivery, but I figure I'll get through it!" she exclaimed. "The epidural Brianna gave me hurt like hell, but it seems to be working. Most of the crazy pain is gone now, but I still have this pain in my middle. I guess it will go away when I have the baby."

I asked Adriane if she had been able to get in touch with Tim.

"I had to fight with the EMS techs in the ambulance about making a phone call, but you know I made that call!" she said. "While the techs were trying to get my vital signs I was fumbling in my purse for my phone. I'm glad I called when I did because if I had waited he would have been in the air. He was on the way to the airport when I called him. When I told him I was in labor, he could barely get out a sentence he was so excited. He told me he would call me from the plane as soon as he could. He should be here in about three hours. He told me to hold on until he got here. I also called my mom. She should be here soon."

"Don't first-time moms take a while to deliver?" I asked Gwen.

"It depends on the mom, but usually a woman's first labor can take about twenty-four hours from the very first contractions to delivery. And sometimes the epidural slows things down a little. So, there's a good chance he'll make it here. But the reason we called you back is because if he doesn't—"

"You're my replacement coach!" Adriane cut in.

I didn't quite know what that would entail but it made me a little queasy. I was excited to see the new baby, but I wanted it to be after it was all cleaned up and in the nursery. I wasn't too sure about seeing the actual birth part. I smiled, hopeful that my trepidation did not show on my face. I figured I needed to rise to the occasion...

I guess I failed because Adriane said brightly, "I saw that! Don't worry, it will be easy. You'll just help me with my breathing and stuff."

I smiled for real this time and laughed. "You know me much too well, Ms. Buttler," I replied.

"Oh yeah, I forgot. Since you're sitting in for Tim, I get to yell and scream at you and even hit you if the pain gets too unbearable. I hope you brought some padding to protect yourself!" All four of us laughed at that one.

"Don't worry," Gwen said, "we have a room filled with stuff for first-time fathers. Padding, earplugs, barf bags; you name it, we've got it!"

"Really?" I asked, thinking I might actually need some stuff from that room. Gwen and Brianna looked at each other and burst out laughing.

"Oh, Natalie," Gwen quipped, "you really are just like a first-time dad!" Gwen fiddled with one of the machines and then told us that she would be back soon. Brianna received a page and followed Gwen out.

"Adriane, I can't believe you're having a baby! It seems like only yesterday we moved into our first apartment."

Adriane and I were roommates for two years. The summer I graduated from law school and Adriane finished college we both were living at home going crazy, so we decided to get an apartment. We only lived about ten minutes away from our families, but it made all the difference in the world. Adriane was a total extrovert and was happiest when entertaining friends. Consequently, we always had a house full of people. I was totally cool with that except Adriane was a total slob. Her room looked like a tornado hit it at all times and the kitchen was always a mess. I'm not the neatest person, but I take after my mom in the kitchen department. I cannot go to bed with a dirty kitchen. That meant I spent quite a few evenings cleaning up her disgusting mess. Finally, we had to have a little talk; a talk that soon turned into a shouting match. We ended up compromising. Adriane became a little better about cleaning her dishes and I learned to leave her shit in the sink, crust and all, until she got around to it. I smiled at the distant memory of that fight.

"Hey, what are you smiling about ?" Adriane asked.

"I was just thinking about our fight about the dishes. You know, now that you're going to have a baby, you'll have to clean out the sink every now and then and even eat vegetables, or at least feed them to your kid."

"Yeah, I don't know how I'm going to handle the vegetable thing, but I figure I'll have lots of time to do dishes in the middle of the night when I can't get the baby to sleep! Speaking of sleep, you look pretty tired, Natalie. I know things have been going crazy at your office the last couple of days. You never told me what happened this morning with Thorton's interview."

"Oh, Adriane, after the baby is here I'll give you all the gruesome details. Right now I don't even want to think about it! I'd rather think about your impendent bundle of joy."

"It's so weird sitting in this bed waiting for the baby to come. Soon I'll have this little person to take care of. Someone who will be totally dependent on me. I hope I am a good mother."

"You will be. Even though you're younger than I am, and Gwen and Brianna for that matter, you've always been the mom figure."

"Yeah, I know, I'm the maternal one. Gwen's the free spirit and you're the rational, calm one, always in control."

"Hey, you forgot Brianna," I said.

"Yeah, I know; how would I describe Brianna? Professionally she has it together, but she seems a little lost lately, ever since her engagement fell apart. She's always experimenting with something new and traveling here and there. I wish she could find herself and be happy. Sometimes I really worry about her," Adriane said.

"She seems to be happier now and more settled than usual," I replied. "And as I said before—always the mom. Brianna is fine and you're just a worrywart!" Just then Adriane's mom appeared in the room with a big smile on her face. We hugged and then she gave Adriane a big kiss. I decided to give them some time to themselves, so I told Adriane I would be back soon and headed in the direction of the waiting room. As I walked down the hall I thought about how Adriane had described me—rational, calm, and in control. She was right. I like to be in control, not of other people so much, but in control of my own life. My head rules and only on occasion does my heart take over, usually taking me in the wrong direction. I guess sometimes that is what makes life worth experiencing.

7

NATALIE

I was a good kid who followed the rules and respected authority—except for my rebellious period when I lived in Paris
during my freshman and sophomore years of high school
and hung out with all my little white friends. Friends who were
allowed to curse their parents. Well, I never went that far, but let
me tell you I did lose my mind a little bit. I tried to run away but
my mom locked me in the house (yes, in the house not out of it!).
This was after I had been grounded for life after having a party
while my parents were away.

Now that I think about it, how did I turn into that out-of-control
teenager? I only vaguely remember parts of that infamous party;
we were all so drunk and it was so long ago. Most of the kids I hung
out with from my high school, The American School of Paris,
were there. In France, at that time, sixteen was the legal drinking
age for beer and wine. Alcohol was sold at almost all stores, even
their equivalent of a 7-Eleven. Sixteen appeared to be just a number, however; I don't recall ever having a problem buying alcohol.
I even remember buying a bottle of champagne at the corner store
a block away from my school one lunch period, and drinking it
with a friend in my English class. We then went to class drunk
and laughed all the way through the discussion of *Macbeth*.

The party was held on the Fourth of July, the American Independence Day celebration. Obviously this was not a holiday in

France, where they celebrate their Independence Day, called Bastille Day, on July 14th. I remember Michael Jackson's *Off the Wall* album playing on the stereo and how I thought I was so cute in my yellow checkered top that I had purchased at one of the chic Paris boutiques. That didn't last long though. At one point during the party I remember walking back to my bedroom and catching my shirt on the handle to my bedroom door. I jerked away to free my shirt, tearing all of my buttons off in one motion. As I continued to prance around with my shirt wide open, one of my girlfriends caught me before I could expose myself further and got me into a new blouse. I cringed at the memory. What could I have been thinking? Clearly not much. While I was dealing with the loss of my little checkered shirt, some of my class-mates started hanging out of the large bay windows at the front of our apartment, attempting to sing "America the Beautiful" while throwing firecrackers on the cars and people below. Another young man from my school, in all his drunken wisdom, urinated on the mirrors that lined my apartment building's first-floor lobby. I recall begging the concierge in my rambling French to please not call the police and please not tell my parents. The concierge must have taken pity on me because she cleaned the glass and never told my parents.

It seems so odd that, at fourteen and fifteen, drinking was a major factor in my social life. I hardly touched liquor in college and law school, when folks tend to experiment, and now I can barely drink a glass of wine or anything else. When I do drink it has to be a sweet cocktail like Fuzzy Navels or Kahlua and creme; stuff where you can barely taste the liquor.

My experience in Paris was bittersweet. It was an amazing ad-venture in that I had an opportunity to travel, learn a new language, and experience a different culture with a luscious history. I also learned about racism first hand.

Before moving to Paris my family lived in a place called New Columbus. I was six when we moved there from New York. New Columbus was a brand-new city housed between Baltimore, Maryland, and Washington, D.C. The founder envisioned a place where affordable housing, good schools, and recreational centers were all available and accessible to the residents. The biggest draw to the early inhabitants of New Columbus was the fact that it was also built on the spirit of integration. In the early seventies America was just beginning its experiment with racial mixing. I grew up with loads of white friends. In fact, I had mostly white friends until we moved to Paris. I spent the night at their houses and dined with their families. I knew little about racism and rejection due to skin color. I can still remember my mom admonishing me that I should hold on to my black friends because black friends were important and would probably outlast the friendships I had with my white friends. "Natalie," she would say, "white friends are fine and good, but you are not white; remember that." I could not understand her concern. In my view, friends were friends and my friendships would last forever! Well, everyone must learn sometime, and for me the lesson came a little later than for most. Moving to Paris opened my eyes. Interestingly enough, it was not the French who treated me differently because of my race, but the white American schoolchildren, who turned out to be a little different than the New Columbus friends I was used to.

I remember one friend, Liza Wuzinski, a teammate on the freshman basketball team, invited me over to her house for dinner one evening. Her family was from Ohio, but her father's military job had brought them to Paris. After dinner as we poured over her mom's *People* magazines trying to catch up on all the gossip from the States, Liza told me that in Ohio she did not have any black friends, mostly because her parents didn't like my kind. But as she told me proudly, "They like you. You're different. You're not like them, you're more like us." I remember looking at her in a puzzled way. "I am them," I replied, "and I'll never be like you." Well, after that incident our friendship was never the same.

The most hurtful incident happened during my sophomore year. By now, I had settled into Paris life and found my clique of friends. There were a group of us, boys and girls, who hung out together at school and on weekends. A senior named Donald Keyburger whom I knew fairly well (the school was so small you couldn't help but know everyone) had a crush on one of my girl-friends, Gabrielle. Gabrielle was Brazilian. Her father worked in the Paris branch of a Brazilian bank. Since I was friends with both of them I became their go-between. You know how kids are at that age. There was lots of note passing and talking among her friends and his about who liked whom. Finally, the two of them got together and proceeded to make out in the locker room every chance they got. A couple of months later Donald and his friends threw a big party. Everyone was invited—except me. I couldn't understand it. I was the one who had hooked him up with Gabrielle. I was a closer friend to him than a lot of my friends, or so I thought, and all of them were invited. How could he humil-iate me this way? I was much too proud to crash the party or ask Donald about my perhaps "misplaced" invitation. Gabrielle and my other friends wondered about my non-invite, but seemingly not too much. Several offered to call as soon as they got home from the party to fill me in on all the details. It was as if everyone understood that this was the way it should be. The Saturday night of the party I cried and cried. My mom and dad hurt for me and tried their best to console me, but to no avail.

Life's funny; a couple of years ago I was cleaning out some boxes and came across my old yearbooks from Paris. The turnover at the American school was tremendous each year. Most families stationed in Europe with the government or private business had short tours—two to three years—therefore it was a ritual to get as many people as possible to sign your yearbook, since many would not return the following year. As I looked through my two yearbooks, I saw that Donald had written the nicest notes in both of them, telling me what a nice girl I was and thanking me for hooking him up with Gabrielle. In fact, his notations were some of the nicest I received. Go figure, I guess I hid my hurt well. If he only knew the teenage angst he caused me!

When I returned to New Columbus after my two-year stint in Paris, I learned a thing or two about racism stateside. I was so excited to move back and pick up where I had left off. My white friends quickly embraced me while some of my black friends became leery of me. I was different now. I had lived abroad, I spoke another language, and I was in advanced placement classes. I also had a bunch of white friends. Together these characteristics made me suspect in their eyes. This all changed, however, the summer of my junior year.

That spring, my mom and I were constantly at each other's throats. I believed I was grown, as most sixteen-year-olds do, and we clashed constantly. She told me in no uncertain terms, "Both of us cannot stay home together this summer. Get a job or go to summer school." The idea of earning my own money was an exciting prospect, so off I went job hunting with Carla, one of my closest friends since third grade. She was petite, blond, and blue eyed. We lived on the same street and basically grew up together. She even came to Paris to visit me the summer of my freshman year. That spring we made getting a job our raison d'être. We went everywhere filling out applications. The fact that we had the exact same qualifications—none—did not deter us. We applied at Friendly's, Clyde's, the Fish Net, and every other restaurant in our local mall. We were hell-bent on getting a job in a restaurant. I can't recall why now, especially since we were not old enough for waitress jobs.

I vividly remember my interview at the Fish Net. Carla and I inquired about the openings listed in the local newspaper. We were provided applications and were told that the manager would be with us in a moment. The manager interviewed me first and told me he was very sorry but that no hostess positions were available. Carla interviewed immediately after me. I'll never forget waiting for her in the lobby of the restaurant, trying to figure out where we should go next, when she came out of the interview smiling with excitement as she announced to me that she had been hired as a hostess. My mouth flew open in disbelief, though I tried to hide my disappointment and be happy for her. When I told her what the manager had told me she didn't seem to believe me. "Things like that just don't happen. Maybe he likes me better." At sixteen I was too timid to prove my point by questioning the restaurant manager about his decision, but I believed it was due to only one reason—race. Later I found out that Carla received offers at two other places that turned me down. After that our friendship was over. In retrospect, it wasn't really her fault. But I couldn't hang out with her anymore. I blamed the "system" on her.

Without a job I was forced to go to summer school. I only needed one credit to graduate from high school, so I signed up for advanced English. I was pretty perturbed at my mother for forcing me into summer school, but it would turn out to be a blessing in disguise.

I am a little sorry to say it, but of course every black person in New Columbus was in summer school. Consequently, I had a ball. I met so many new people. And the folks who had shunned me after I moved back from Paris now embraced me. It was like

I was now "down" or something. Whatever the reason, I did not care. I was having too much fun. Classes were only half day, and I had the whole afternoon to goof off with my new friends. The friendships I made that summer lasted throughout the school year and beyond.

My senior year was spent juggling my relationships with my black and white friends. I hung out with my white friends at school, though I regularly ate lunch at the "black table" and socialized exclusively with my black friends on the weekend. There was very little intermingling. And that's how it has been ever since. I still have a few white friends from New Columbus and maintain a few friendships from college and law school. These friendships have their place and are important, but they are very different from the friendships I share with my black friends, like the women in my book club, who are more like sisters. My white friends and I send holiday cards and we do dinner every now and then and keep abreast of the professional goings-on. That's about it. And I'm not ashamed to say I like it that way. We are different. They can never fully understand what it is like to be a minority. And you know what, they don't have to. My white friends in New Columbus, those who grew up in and experimented with integration, have moved on too. They know the deal. We all do. I bet they don't have one close black friend now. As for the New Columbus concept, I think all of us who grew up in the early years—those whose families moved to New Columbus because they embraced integration—are better off. We have a better understanding of one another and will pass that understanding on to our own children and that's important. But as far as changing the world, my life in the Senate has shown me that those in power like to keep it. In my view it will be a long time, if ever, before America heals its ugliest scar—racism.

I guess if those three experiences are the sum total of the racial incidents I recall as a youth, I'm pretty lucky. By the time I moved on to college, law school, and the working world, I was better prepared for reality. The incidents my friends and I experience now as adults are too numerous to tell. All black professionals know the drill. It's called life.

8

NATALIE

I peek into the waiting room and see Camille, Destiny, and Allana. Camille and Allana appear to be asleep and Destiny seems deep in thought. Since Allana and Camille are asleep I decide to dash to the bathroom before updating them on Adriane. As I hurry to the stall I glimpse my reflection in the mirror. Adriane was right; I look like a tired hag. The past several months have been so chaotic. Last year, I was promoted to chief of staff of the Health and Consumer Affairs Committee in the Senate. I am one of the few African Americans to serve in such a capacity. It was a difficult transition for me. Many of the committee staff secretly grumbled about my promotion, particularly Mark Levin, the senator's press secretary and my nemesis. He had lobbied hard for the job and could not believe he lost out to a black woman.

Jack Thorton, my boss, is the chairman of the Health and Consumer Affairs Committee. Last fall he was reelected for the fourth time, assuring his tenure for another six years. His recent Senate race was very close and the black vote was instrumental in his victory. I campaigned tirelessly for his reelection and it was my effort and that of the team of volunteers I organized to get out the black vote that put him over the top.

After Thorton's reelection, his chief of staff, Ed Marky, took a job with a blue-chip law firm to cash in on his ties to the powerful chairman. Ed nurtured me and lobbied for me to succeed him.

When I was first chosen, Mark Levin and others touted my promotion as an affirmative action appointment, a choice, in their
words, that Jack Thorton made solely to appease his African-
American supporters. I tried to prepare myself for the inevitable
negative reaction by some when I was offered the job. Luckily, in
time much of the grumbling ceased.

I have worked hard to build relationships with other Senate
staff, both Democrat and Republican, and take the time to know
the issues inside and out. I have to. Any mistake I make will be
totally blown out of proportion. Although many of my colleagues
may believe otherwise, there's a lot of mediocrity in this place,
but as a black female I do not have that option.

As I continue to ponder my reflection in the mirror, I think
about how badly I need a vacation. Last summer we read *How
Stella Got Her Groove Back* by Terry McMillan, in which the main
character takes an impromptu trip to Jamaica to relax and
rejuvenate. That Winston sure sounded fine. I wish I had some
time to gallivant on a tropical island with a handsome young
black man who took pleasure in catering to all of my needs. And
boy, did I have some unfulfilled needs! I must make a mental
note to plan such a trip whenever I can get a couple of consecutive
days off! Unfortunately, time off is a scarce commodity in my
line of work. I realized I hadn't done anything exciting or
adventurous in a long time. I used to hang out regularly when I
first finished law school and first started working on the Hill.
There was always a party or reception to go to. That life gets old
quickly though, and it seems that my party days are now behind
me. A "Stella" vacation might be just what I need to rejuvenate!

Hmmm, Jamaica, I thought. I haven't been on a relaxing vacation
in years. My last trip to Jamaica was a disaster. I had just finished
law school and my boyfriend at the time had a summer job there.

Unfortunately, the relaxing, romantic vacation turned into the trip from hell. My boyfriend's job was based in Kingston, and he had little free time to spend with me. Kingston, while a thriving city by Caribbean standards, was hardly the beachfront mecca I had anticipated. Far from it, actually. I wondered if I could list the vacation-from-hell atrocities with a straight face. I had the pleasure of experiencing another hand in my pants as I was pickpocketed at the corner market. It turned out the seemingly well-to-do widow who rented a room to my boyfriend was hard up for cash because she was accused of ordering the hit that killed her husband the previous spring, and all their assets were frozen until the case went to trial. I crashed my boyfriend's moped into a beat-up car that was already covered with about a thousand scratches, but was nonetheless surrounded by every Jamaican within a two-mile radius, all of whom claimed to own the car and demanded money for repairs.

To top off the trip, I missed my flight home. But after employing my "ugly American" act, I was able to scream my way onto an intra-island flight that would take me from Kingston to Montego Bay where I could get a flight home. Unfortunately, the intra-island flight I screamed so hard to get on was a four-seater propeller plane that the pilot had to wind up by hand. To make matters worse, the other three passengers, one of whom had to sit on two boxes of bananas due to my presence, were in the Jamaican military and were dressed in riot gear replete with machetes and grenades. I was so happy to be on my way home that I didn't think about the fact that I was on a plane with strange men with weapons and that no one knew where I was until I was in the air and it was too late for me to do anything about it. I ended up crying the whole twenty-five-minute flight to Montego Bay.

Well, maybe a trip to Jamaica is not an ideal getaway. That's okay. Instead of going to Jamaica, I'll have a "Stella" vacation in the Cayman Islands. But right now Adriane needed my attention and Camille, Destiny, and Allana needed an update.

Destiny was drinking a Pepsi when I entered the waiting room and Allana and Camille were engrossed in whatever was appearing on the television.

"Hey, girls, I have good news. The epidural kicked in and Adriane's quite comfortable. Other than some queasiness, she's her old self—talking away. Tim is on a plane on his way home. I've been anointed Adriane's birthing coach until he gets here!"

"I figured everything was probably okay," Camille said. "Thanks for bringing us the update."

"I'm going to call Rod and fill him in," Allana said. "He was concerned when I called him earlier to tell him that Adriane was in the hospital."

"Is Gwen still with Adriane?" Destiny asked.

"I'm not sure. She examined Adriane and everything looked okay, but she left a little while ago to check on some tests. She said she would be back soon. Did she stop by the waiting room?"

"No, we haven't seen her since she went back to check on Adriane," Destiny replied.

"Oh, Natalie, I've been meaning to ask you about your boss," Camille said. "I wanted to ask you at book club, but as usual I was late and then Adriane got sick. How's your bill coming? I know you have been working overtime the last couple of months. Plus, I caught a glimpse of *Meet the Press* this morning. The piece about your bill was good but then Jennison started slamming Thorton about some Africa statement. I had to take my son to basketball practice so I missed most of it. What happened?"

The last six months have been a mess. This morning was the worst, but surprisingly enough I was pretty calm and detached. I plopped down on the sofa suddenly realizing how tired I was and embarked on my story.

"It all started when we introduced Thorton's Consumer Bill of Rights legislation last fall. The legislation is really worthwhile but it has gotten caught up in all sorts of political games. Now finally it has the chance to move and Thorton gets involved in some stupid racist bullshit. That man and his mouth are really getting on my nerves."

The legislation, which sought to ensure that beneficiaries of managed care plans were not denied appropriate care under increasingly restrictive plans, had garnered wide support from consumer groups. Managed care providers, however, were less than enthused because limiting or managing services was how they were able to contain costs and experience vast profits. I recognize and acknowledge the positive effect of managed care in bringing down rising health care costs nationally, but in some cases I believed their policies had gone too far. We held hearings on the legislation the previous September. Mark and I were responsible for finalizing the hearing details and securing the witnesses.

While the legislation had several supporters on the committee, Senator Charles Rednecky from Kansas was a staunch opponent. Senator Rednecky had a dominant personality and was often able to persuade members who were "on the fence" to lean toward his way of thinking. Also, the managed care lobby was well financed and had provided quite a bit of campaign funds to Rednecky and his cronies on the committee in the last election, and they were lobbying hard to squash or water down the bill.

Mark and I fought constantly about the hearing logistics and panel composition. "We need no more than three panels of witnesses and to the extent possible we should divide the witnesses as follows: Health and Human Service's Secretary, consumers and

academics, state regulators and national insurance represent-
atives," I told him.

"I think we should forget the balance and go for victims," Mark
replied. "The more victims the better. CSPAN and CNN can
get it all on tape and the networks can show footage on the six
and eleven p.m. news broadcasts. We could also set it up so that
Rednecky is filmed leaving the hearing with victims taunting and
chasing him down the hall. Finally, we can close the story by having
Thorton make a statement on his bill while the victims cheer. I
talked to Joe Slipperd who said he can help set it up." When Mark
finished he had a big grin on his face like he had come up with
the solution for world peace. "So what do you think, Nat?"

"Well," I responded in a measured tone, "the purpose of our
bill is to protect the interests of the consumer, and human interest
stories will be key to making an effective argument. But come on,
Mark, the last thing we need is a circus. Don't you remember last
month's melee when the disabled protested in front of Senator
Dorcas' office and blocked the halls with their wheelchairs? And
come to think of it, didn't Joe have something to do with that
major disaster?"

Picketing Senator "Dorkass," as we called him, was actually okay
in my book, since he was forever linking shit he shouldn't together
in the same sentence, for example: black women, welfare, and too
many babies; or young black men, violence, and genetics. Plus,
he was as far right as you could get. He had recently introduced
legislation to change Medicare and Social Security Income eligibility
requirements to make them so restrictive that most disabled individuals would no longer qualify, hence the demonstration.

Unfortunately, the demonstration got out of hand. While trying
to get to his office past the throng of disabled people, Senator
Dorkass and his staff knocked one poor woman with multiple

sclerosis off of her motorized scooter, and the woman broke her wrist. To make matters worse, there was a bomb scare when about two hundred or so protesters were finishing their lunch in the cafeteria and heading back upstairs to members' offices to make visits. Well, after Oklahoma City, folks here in the Capitol are pretty cagey about bombs, and do you know that more than a few of the disabled protesters hopped out of their wheelchairs and ran on two good legs to the exits? Apparently, in order to have a more convincing throng of protesters some overzealous staff bulked up the throng with healthy, able-bodied volunteers.

"Earth to Mark. Are these details refreshing your memory?"

"Yeah, that was a mess, Natalie, but this would be different— we will have real victims," Mark said. "And the MS victim breaking her arm would have been a real coup for our side if the story hadn't been overshadowed by the fake victims."

"No way, Mark," I said, exasperated. "We are on the right side of this issue. The initial press on the bill has been very favorable, and our polling numbers are high. There is no need to take chances on a demonstration that could get out of hand. Call Joe and squash the victim protest and in the future, let's keep your good ideas just ideas until you check them out with me. Oh and Mark, quit calling these people 'victims.'"

The hearing went well and generated a lot of favorable press coverage. Rednecky had successfully held up the legislation in committee for several months. Now it appeared that a deal was finally imminent. We worked diligently with Rednecky's staff throughout the fall and into the winter recess, which began in late November and ended in January, to finally hammer out a deal on the managed care bill. Senator Thorton was scheduled to appear on *Meet the Press* with Tim Russert to unveil the agreement. Only a few loose strings remained to be worked out before Rednecky and his cronies would sign on the dotted line. Unfortunately, Mark ignored this fact and leaked the "unfinalized" deal to the press. Mark owed a favor to a reporter for the *Daily Times*, an influential paper in Memphis, so he gave this reporter an exclusive scoop. So the *Daily Times* prints a cover story the day before we agreed to announce the deal. Senator Rednecky's staff was furious. I spent all Friday afternoon and evening renegotiating with them. We didn't finish until late in the evening and both Senator Rednecky and Thorton had left for the weekend.

Early Saturday morning I go into the office and before I can turn on my computer, my phone starts ringing. I answer it quickly so that it does not roll over to my voicemail. It's Kim Lewis of Rednecky's staff. "Hi, Natalie, I'm glad I caught you," she says.

"Me too, I literally just walked into the office," I respond.

"Well, to get straight to the point, the senator was unable to take a look at the changes. As I mentioned yesterday, he is spending the weekend in Florida with his wife and asked that staff limit any work faxed out to him. He simply is not available to make the decision this weekend. I have arranged a meeting with him when he returns Monday afternoon. We should be able to iron out any last-minute details then. I think it would be wise to postpone the mark-up scheduled for Tuesday until at least next week. I'll have a better sense of his issues, if there are any remaining. "

"Oh shit," I mutter under my breath. She has totally fucked us. We need to mark-up soon if we want to get this bill moving. The mark-up refers to committee consideration of a bill. During the mark-up the committee can amend the bill under consideration or even offer an alternative. If the committee approves the measure it can then go to the full Senate for consideration. I bet her scrawny ass didn't even call Rednecky, but I say simply, "No problem, we want a deal and Senator Thorton will not move forward without one. It's too bad that we were not able to work something out, since both senators agreed earlier this week that they wanted the details worked out by Friday. But if your boss is unable to take a look at the proposed language we'll postpone mark-up. We don't want any surprises."

"Gee, I'm so sorry," Kim says in her most genteel Southern drawl. "I tried, I really did. I guess the *Daily Times* article was a little premature..." she droned on, twisting the dagger in my back. "Oh, and by the way I saw a teaser for *Meet the Press* tomorrow. I look forward to hearing what Thorton has to say about the 'done deal.' I guess Thorton and Russert will have lots to talk about..."

Not anymore, you asshole, I think, but say instead, "Thorton always has lots to talk about with Tim Russert. Let's touch base on Monday."

We hang up. I have a headache, a big headache, literally and figuratively. "Fuck, fuck, fuck , fuck, shit , shit , shit. Okay, Natalie, enough of that, let's get a plan of action. Problem one: no deal, thus no announcement on *Meet the Press*. Problem two: no mark-up. I start a list of the actions we need to undertake to fix these problems. Number 1: Kill Mark. Number 2: Get Charlie Meyer, the labor union counsel, on the phone so he can work up some talking points on the Ford Motor Company strike and Thorton's role in the negotiations. That will have to suffice as the big issue for the show tomorrow. Number 3: Kill Mark. Number 4: Alert all committee staff that the mark-up is off. Number 5: Kill Mark. Number 6: Call Thorton.

"Damn, I hate calling Thorton on a weekend, and I really hate calling him with bad news. I can't kill Mark yet, I need him to grovel on the phone with Thorton, and then I'll kill him. He's such an idiot sometimes, why does he still have a job?" *Why ask stupid questions?* I ask myself. Mark is a good ole boy, the son of one of Thorton's sister's best friends, who also happens to own a huge chicken farm. Knowing that Mark's relatives raise chickens for commercial use has nearly led me to eliminate them from my diet. Mark's family gives lots of money to Thorton's Senate campaigns. I wonder if this is why Thorton thinks Mark walks on water. Whatever the reason, it is clear that as long as Thorton is Senator Thorton, Mark will have a job. It makes me sick, but that's politics sometimes. Often it's not what you know but who you know. Right now I don't care how much money Mark's family gives, his ass is coming in to work and making this call to Thorton with me.

I walked straight into Mark's office and had a seat. I fumbled around the many newspapers strewn across his desk until I found the committee staff phone list and proceeded to dial his home number. Before I could get to digit number seven, however, the man of the hour appeared in person. "Hey, Nat," Mark said sheepishly. "I just heard the deal was off."

"Yeah, Kim just called with the good news. The *Daily Times* article really got us on this one. Leaking the deal to the press before the deal was done was a bad move, Mark, a very bad move."

"It's like I told you yesterday, Nat. I told the reporter to hold off until Sunday, after the announcement on *Meet the Press*. The reporter broke our agreement."

"And like I said yesterday, reporters make news for a living. After Thorton announces the deal on TV the story is no longer an ex-clusive. You of all people know this; therefore you should have kept your big mouth shut until Saturday and let the reporter announce the deal in the Sunday morning edition concurrent with Thorton's announcement on TV. Now everything is a complete mess."

"I told you, Nat, I thought I had it under control."

"Tell it to the boss, Mark; I'm sick of this shit." We dial the senator's home number. I had alerted him earlier that we should have word of Rednecky's stance and that I would be calling.

His housekeeper, Ruth, answered the phone. "Senatah Thawton's residence, may ah hep you?" she asked.

"Hi, Ruth, it's Natalie and Mark from the senator's Washington office. He should be expecting our call."

"Well, hiya, Natalay, it is nice to tawk to you. Jus one moment, please." I like Ruth; she is like a sweet grandmother. Unfortunately, she was more likely to be my grandmother than Thorton's. She's black, as are all of Thorton's many house staff. And for some reason it bothered me to go to events or strategy sessions at his home and be waited on hand and foot by numerous black servants. It was reminiscent of a time before my birth, a time my parents worked hard to ensure I would not have to experience. I didn't like the fact that Thorton, my boss, felt comfortable in and essentially advocated such a lifestyle. His staff always seemed so proud and happy to see me. It was like they put me on a pedestal or something. In my view, we were one and the same. And I'm sure Thorton saw it the same way. We all served him, just in different ways.

"Well, hello there, Natalie, how's the deal coming? Did Rednecky sign off?"

"I just got off the phone with his staff. Apparently, he did not have time to review the changes and will not make a decision until Monday afternoon," I replied.

"Well, goddamit!" he said, his voice booming. "This thing was supposed to be wrapped up by Friday. What the hell is he doing, anyway?"

"He is spending the weekend in Florida with his family. To be frank, sir, I think he and his staff were ticked off by the *Daily Times* article and they would like to take some time before giving the go-ahead on this deal. I know for a fact that the managed care groups started calling as soon as they heard about the article on Friday."

"Can someone explain to me how that article got in the paper? I recall only giving my okay to an article to run concurrent with the announcement on Sunday, not before. Why was that article published yesterday if the deal wasn't done?"

"Well, sir," Mark mumbled. "I thought I had an understanding with the reporter and—"

Before Mark could finish, the senator exploded. "Mark, you just fucked up, that's what you did. You fucked up. I do not pay you to fuck up. Your job is to cover my ass and to ensure that it looks pretty and smells good at all times! I do not pay you to make stupid decisions that I did not approve! Natalie, what the hell am I supposed to talk about tomorrow, my house in the country?"

"I thought you might focus on the impending Ford strike and your role in the negotiations. I called in Charlie Meyer to work up some talking points on the issue."

"That'll do for about four of the twenty minutes I'm allotted," he replied sarcastically. "It looks like I'm on my own. Make sure you get the talking points to Ed in the state office. He's going to accompany me to the TV studio in the morning. Oh, and Natalie, put some time on my schedule on Monday to discuss that damn article." *Click.*

It took a few weeks longer than I expected, but finally everything is in place on the bill and I'm excited that the committee will mark-up its first piece of major legislation under my leadership. Last week, Rednecky and Thorton ironed out their differences and the managed care legislation is ready to go. We have broad support within the Senate, and the administration has signaled its support for the bill.

"It sounds like the legislation is on the right track," Camille remarked.

"Yes, the legislation is in good shape but, as you can see from the show today, Thorton is a mess!" I replied. "Right now though, I refuse to think about his troubles. I'm focusing positive energy on Adriane, Tim and the soon-to-be-here baby," I continued. "I need to go back and check on my birthing duties. I'll come back out soon with another update."

I walked toward the Labor and Delivery Hospital Staff Only doors and smiled as I thought about Adriane. She was going to be an amazing mom. I have a large circle of good friends, but Adriane is one of my closest. She is the one I confide in most regularly. I can tell anything to Adriane because of all my friends she is the most nonjudgmental. She can see the flaws in someone, accept them, and still be their friend. To Adriane friendship is sacred. Nothing you can tell her would shock her or make her judge you as bad or wrong. She has very strong opinions, both good and bad, and she doesn't hesitate to express them. She is the epitome of honesty. We would talk several times a day about nothing and everything, though that has been sorely lacking lately. She's also the one whose shoulder I seek when my heart is broken yet again.

Adriane and Tim's house is a second home to me. Unlike mine, their refrigerator regularly has food inside. I often drop by for sustenance after working late or on the weekends. Adriane and Tim respect each other and allow each other space to pursue their own interests while maintaining a fierce devotion to their family. Tim loves Adriane with all his heart and I truly believe his number one goal in life is to make her happy. He knew from their first date that he wanted her for his wife. In some ways Allana and Rod's relationship reminded me of Adriane and Tim's. They too seemed to have developed a deep connection and respect for each other that would stand the test of time. When I think about these couples I often wonder why I was unable to inspire the same level of devotion in my many boyfriends.

Sometimes I envied Adriane's relationship. Of course I knew, both intuitively and from the perch of a best friend, that her marriage wasn't perfect. All relationships had ups and downs. Unfortunately no matter how high the highs, my relationships always ended with the lows. None could weather the cyclical motion of good and bad over time. I was single at the moment, well, it's actually been quite a bit longer than a moment—my choice after a particularly difficult and emotionally draining relationship. Chris and I dated for two years, which was a pretty long relationship for me, but we were very different. He was smart, funny, ambitious, and cared for me deeply. He was also white.

We met in law school. He was tall with curly brown hair, which he wore a bit on the long side, and had an infectious smile. He was athletic but not a jock. We were the best of friends. We sat together in class and crammed for exams together. We frequently spent hours talking about everything, politics (my favorite topic), art and architecture (his favorite topics), campus intrigue, and who we were dating. It wasn't a romantic thing though. We rarely socialized together. He did the white boy, beer keg thing and I went to parties and get-togethers with my black friends on the weekends. After graduation I came to D.C. to work on the Hill and he joined a prestigious law firm in the area. We agreed to keep in touch but basically went our separate ways until a couple of years after moving back to the area, when I ran into him at a bookstore. We agreed to have lunch and then fell into the same pattern of hanging out and talking for hours, except something had changed. One night we made plans to catch a foreign film in Northern Virginia. Afterward he suggested we take a walk along the harbor in Georgetown. It was a beautiful evening so I consented, though I was a little apprehensive about running into people I knew. Up to this point our outings were usually during the day and never had the feel of a real date, just good friends spending time together. We walked down to the far end of the pier and sat down on one of the benches to watch the boats go by. Chris was leaning back with his legs outstretched in front of him. I sat sideways on the bench, facing him with my legs tucked underneath me. I don't remember how long we sat there talking, but when I looked at my watch I realized it was nearly midnight. I suggested to Chris that we should get going and in response he turned sideways so he was facing me directly. He looked at me for a long moment and then he surprised me by stroking my hair and pulling me toward him. He kissed me tentatively at first and then more passionately. His touch was soft but certain. To my surprise, I didn't resist. And when he slowly pulled away and stood up, offering me his hand, I took it. I didn't know where this would lead but I decided to follow. If you had asked me if I would date outside my race, the answer would have been an emphatic no. And yet, here I was dating a white boy, or man, I guess I should say. He wasn't even European, just regular old American white. This wasn't a summer fling or vacation affair. It was the real deal and I truly loved him. Unfortunately, we didn't live happily ever after in interracial Never Never Land. At first, I thought I could handle it. But I couldn't. I was never totally able to be open about the relationship with my family or friends. Adriane is the only one who really knew the extent of things. The relationship ended because I could not handle my business. I was never comfortable in public nor could I ever let down my guard completely when I was with Chris. There are parts of me that I didn't think he could ever understand. How could he? How does someone who has never experienced racism and always had the benefit of white privilege know how it feels to be part of a society that had to force others to value them? Although I truly believe I want to raise my children in a colorblind society, I failed to achieve that standard in my own life. I could never see past what he was. He didn't believe race mattered. But it did and does, and always will; at least that's how I felt. Ultimately, it was easiest to walk away. That was three years ago. Since the relationship ended I've dated sporadically but nothing really serious.

Well, there was Derek. I remember the Saturday morning of our breakup clearly.

It started innocently enough.

"Natalie, sweetheart, are you awake?" I crack one eye and slowly focus in on Derek's face. I smile up at him. He appears wide awake, chipper almost. He kisses me gently and says, "You know that exhibit you wanted to see next weekend? I think we should check it out today. Next week isn't good for me."

"Sounds good," I mumble, still not fully awake. I close my eyes and cuddle closer to him. "What's next week?" I murmur.

"Jill's coming for the weekend," he says softly but firmly.

"What?" I try to scream, but instead it comes out as a hiss. All drowsiness evaporates as I open my eyes fully and focus on Derek's mouth forming the words "I think I'm going to marry her."

What?" I say again. This time I'm able to add volume, transforming the hiss into a screech. Cuddling clearly over, I disentangle myself from Derek and the sheet strangling my right leg, and step off the bed directly onto Derek's size thirteen shoes, promptly turning my ankle. I didn't see his shoe because the camisole I had worn last night was lying on top of it. Last night we went to a jazz club and afterward went to play pool. Halfway through the game we were spending more time kissing each other than cueing up. By the time we got home we couldn't take our hands off each other or get our clothes off fast enough. I was surprised my camisole had even made it to the bedroom.

"Shit," I yell, as I stumble to my knees, ankle throbbing. Afraid to immediately put weight on it, I crawl to the bathroom, which is situated directly across from the bed. As I put the seat down on the commode—What is it with men?—I say, "Did you just have an epiphany? Why am I learning about this in the morning?" I flush and wash my hands and limp back into the bedroom.

Derek, who has not moved, continues to lounge on the bed. "I love you, Natalie. I knew we were meant to be together from the moment I saw you."

"Then why are you marrying her?" I ask, my voice quivering a little.

"I love you both. It's just timing. I met her first. We've been together for four years. We have a history. You've been toying with me this whole time. I've been a convenient diversion. I know you're not interested in anything serious. You're married to your job."

I look at Derek like he's crazy. What the hell is he talking about? I wonder. Just because I have a demanding job doesn't mean I don't want to get married…one day. I suck my breath in and roll my eyes like the black woman I am, and reach for my camisole. I retrieve my panties from under the bed and glance around the room for my skirt. Nowhere to be found. I stumble out into the hall, my ankle still throbbing, and see my skirt scrunched up at the bottom of the stairs. I pull my skirt halfway over my hips and then wonder why I'm getting dressed. Derek's the one who should be getting dressed. This is my house. I stomp back up the stairs, put my hands on my hips, and stare at Derek. He is standing stark naked in the middle of the room. If it were twelve hours ago, hell, if it were twenty minutes ago, the sight of his body would have driven me crazy. His broad shoulders, narrow waist, and deep chocolate complexion drove me wild. Derek took sex to another dimension. I would definitely miss that. Damn. I shake my head to remind myself that all of that is now in the past.

"Should I go?" he asks.

"I think so," I say with much attitude.

"We still have the week."

"I don't think so," I say with even more attitude. I walk into the bathroom and turn on the shower. "Lock the door on your way out."

Later, I hear the phone ringing, and grope for it. I realize it is not next to my bed, because I am in the guest room. I jump out of bed and am immediately sorry as my leg buckles under my weight. I forgot that I twisted my ankle earlier today. I hop the rest of the way to my bedroom and pick up the phone right before the answering machine kicks in. "Hello," I grumble.

"Hey, Natalie, it's Adriane. Did I catch you at a bad time? You sound out of breath."

"Hey, girl; no, I'm fine. I was in the guest room so I had to run to catch the phone." After my shower, I was too pissed to sleep in the sheets Derek and I had made love in the night before, and too lazy to do laundry so I decided to go back to bed in the guest room. I didn't tell all of this to Adriane.

"How are the two lovebirds?" Adriane giggled.

"He's going to marry her," I responded.

"Marry who?" she asked.

"His girlfriend," I said indignantly.

Silence.

"Well, don't you have anything to say?" I asked Adriane.

"I'm sorry, Natalie." More silence, then, "but honey, what were you expecting out of this relationship? It's only been six weeks, for God's sake!"

"I know, but six weeks of being with someone every day and night can be more serious and meaningful than dating someone for a year and seeing them once a week. I fell in love with him," I whined. "I could have married him."

"Natalie, you knew that he had a girlfriend when you started this thing. What did you think was going to happen? Besides, you barely saw him; you've been working non-stop."

"He told her about me; he told her about us. I figured it meant something. He said he loved me."

"I know it hurts, Natalie, but this too shall pass."

"Adriane, I knew from the first time I talked to him we were destined to be together."

"I know, honey, you told me. You've had a rough patch. Your breakup with Chris was tough and Derek was the first guy you've shown interest in since then. I know you say Chris is a distant memory but I think you took that breakup harder than you will admit. Do you even think you really loved Derek or were you with him to prove you were over Chris?"

"Funny, Derek said he thought he was only a diversion for me but it's not true. He made a calculation—he took the known—his stupid girlfriend of four years—over the unknown. The bird in the hand rather than one he believed to be in flight. I probably would have done the same thing. Figures I'd meet a man who isn't afraid to commit. He just isn't committed to me."

"Stop whining, Natalie. If you ask me you were mostly interested in the sex. That's all I ever heard about, anyway. You never talked about Derek in terms of a future. Remember the February sexy book club, when we had the women come with all the sex toys? We all laughed at Camille when she picked out not one but two dildos! But all she had to say was, 'Men come and go, but these babies will take good care of me in the interim and with less hassle and disruption to my kids.' She seemed quite happy with her little purchases, so I suggest you get one and keep on walking!"

"Thanks for your support, Happily Married Lady Expecting a Baby." I pouted.

"You know I am always here for you. Stop moping and come over and hang out with me and Tim. I'm cooking and I know you don't have anything in that wasted fridge of yours. I'll see you in thirty minutes," Adriane said with finality and hung up.

I laugh about the Derek episode. He was fun but never the one—if "the one" even exists. But I stop laughing when I think about the state of my life. Even with all of my friends I hate to admit that I am lonely. My current existence, I'm not so sure it should be called a "life," consists of work, work, and more work. While my job is challenging, invigorating, and exciting at times, I am beginning to realize it is not enough. My time belongs to the senator and I never have time to do anything for myself. My longing for a stable, loving relationship and the American dream of a home and family becomes more intense with each passing year. I cannot distinguish whether this longing is due to society's expectation of what a woman should have—a marriage and children—or if it is my own deep-seated desire. Whatever it is, I am deeply frightened of becoming one of the statistics I so often read about—a professional, accomplished, and single, black woman.

As the hospital Staff Only door slowly shuts I turn and wave to my three friends and just catch Destiny saying, "Adriane's baby will be the newest edition to our book club. I can't wait to meet him or her." I think about my book club friendships, which have grown into so much more than the sharing of books. Statistic or not, I have a lot to be thankful for and good friends who are there for me through the good and bad are at the top of my list.

The past twenty-four hours had really drained me and I took the opportunity to cut my stay short because I wasn't ready to admit how angry and empty I felt about what had happened. I sigh audibly as I think about yesterday, and to think it started out so promising. "I finally thought I had a free day. I remembered thinking in the morning—my bill is on track and the prep for *Meet the Press* is complete. I figured I was safe, but then around 2:00 p.m. my beeper goes off. One of the not so glamorous parts of my job is always being reachable just in case Thorton needs me. Getting an unexpected page on a Saturday afternoon is rare, however, and I wonder worriedly what it could be about. I checked the number, it was local but I didn't recognize it. As I fumble in my purse for my phone to return the page, I try to recall Thorton's schedule. He was in the state and had a breakfast meeting with a business coalition and later he was supposed to attend a charity golf tournament to raise money for the state university.

"When I dial the number, Mark answers. My heart sinks. A call from Mark on a Saturday always means trouble. The senator is finally scheduled to discuss the managed care legislation on *Meet the Press* tomorrow and I wonder worriedly if Rednecky had reneged on the deal again.

"Hey, Nat, how are you doing?"

"I'm okay. What's up?"

"I got a call from Sherman Keter; he said there might be a flap about a statement the senator made this afternoon."

Sherman Keter headed up our state office. He was scheduled to attend the breakfast and charity event with the senator today. He was a pretty unflappable guy. If he called to say the senator had made a gaffe it was probably true. While Thorton was a good legislator he had a tendency to speak his mind without always thinking about the consequences first. This would not be the first time his mouth got him into trouble.

"Well, what did he say?"

"I'm not exactly sure; Keter is faxing a transcript to the office, something about the genocide in Rwanda. I scheduled a conference call with Keter and Jim Kindle to discuss the statement and his response at 3:30 p.m." Jim Kindle handled press in our state office.

"Rwanda? Why was the senator talking about Rwanda?"

"I don't know all the details yet, Nat. Sherm can fill us in at 3:30 p.m."

"Do you think the statement will be picked up nationally, or is it likely to stay local?"

"It's too early to tell. When I get to the office, I'll check the AP wire and call some of my press friends in the state to see if the story is deemed newsworthy enough to go national. I suspect that even if the story is local today, tomorrow it will be national since Thorton is bound to get questions on *Meet the Press*." I knew Mark was right. There was no way we could get out of this one. Finally, we were getting somewhere on important legislation and now it would be overshadowed by Thorton's inopportune and stupid comments about Rwanda. *What in the world did Thorton say now?* I thought to myself. If Sherm told Mark to call me on a Saturday, I knew it had to be bad. I could feel a black cloud en-gulfing me. "Fuck, that man infuriates me sometimes!" I mumbled to myself.

"Mark, I'll stop by the office for the 3:30 p.m. call and we can go from there."

"Okay, Nat. I'll see you then." Mark actually seemed relieved that I was coming in. Probably because the senator's statement had something to do with Africa and Mark was clueless as to how to handle issues that involved race. I'm sure his response to the problem will be to promptly dump the whole mess in my lap.

As I settled in at my desk that afternoon, Mark yelled out from the conference room that he had Sherman and Jim on the phone. I walked across the hall and sat down.

"Well, guys, what's the story?" Mark asked.

Sherman began, "At the business breakfast today a local reporter asked Thorton about the U.N. tribunal for Rwanda. Thorton replied that the genocide in Rwanda was a terrible situation that should never be repeated and that the tribunal was necessary to bring the individuals responsible to justice. That was the gist of his statement to the press."

"Okay, so what's the big deal all about?" I asked.

"Well, unfortunately, during the charity golf tournament, Thorton remarked to Mark Cass, a big campaign contributor and president of a big waste management company in the state, that Africa was a mess, and the leadership since the time of colonization was nothing but a bunch of barbaric crazy dictators, as evidenced by the recent genocide in Rwanda. Apparently, he must have been over-heard, because at the charity golf tournament a reporter for the *African Herald* asked him if he had indeed made such a statement." The *African Herald* was the oldest black newspaper in the state.

I could think of at least three or four things wrong with his statement, including the presumption that European colonization of Africa was a good thing; the connection of barbarism with all African people; and a generalization of the genocide in Rwanda to all of Africa. Most of all I was struck by the arrogance of his statement and the inherent sense of superiority.

The genocide of the Tsutsis in Rwanda at the hands of their neighbors and previous friends, the Hutus, was atrocious. Whole families were literally hacked to death with machetes by their countrymen. Tsutsi women were raped repeatedly. It was a hor-rible situation and the United States, the U.N., and Europe did nothing to prevent or stop the killings. In my mind the crimes were truly depraved, and the people who committed them were hardened criminals who deserved the maximum punishment. But

I believed we were all to blame for allowing such crimes to occur in the first place. "Ethnic cleansing" seemed to be endemic all over the world at the moment, and white Europeans were no strangers to this type of activity. In my view if Thorton was going to make such a statement he could have at least been more inclusive in his condemnation!

Thorton's statement was sickening and I believed the story would have legs, at least in the black community. And in my view he owed his election to the black community, and thus should be at least appreciative of, if not accountable, to them. His statement showed he took blacks in his state, and the nation, for granted, and that he clearly misread his mandate. I knew that the task of getting him out of this mess would require quite a bit of intervention from me. I wasn't happy about it and wondered silently if at some point my job and moral compass would become too conflicted for me to continue. At the moment, however, I had work to do. I had to help Mark and Jim craft a thoughtful and apologetic response, and somehow force Thorton to agree to issue it and make a similar statement on the news tomorrow morning. I sighed and got to work.

I finally arrived home after a long night. I ended up staying at work until nearly 9:30 p.m. Thorton was unapologetic and would not agree to sign off on the statement of apology Mark, Jim, and I had crafted. Although the statement was simple and straightforward, Thorton would not agree to release it. I had long since learned that when Thorton was in one of his belligerent moods, it was impossible to change his mind. He had clearly decided that any response to his statements would be much ado about nothing and was not willing to admit he had misspoken.

"Now, Natalie, why are you so upset with me? You and I both know that the situation in Rwanda was out of control. When I heard about the tribunal's findings, I expressed outrage."

I wasn't sure if his statements expressed outrage or contempt, but I kept my thoughts to myself. I ignored Thorton's comment and continued. "The apology we have prepared is short and sweet. It expresses your regret for making the statements and apologizes for any offense the statements may have caused. In addition, the apology notes that the atrocities in Rwanda were terrible, as are those occurring in Eastern Europe, and must not be repeated nor tolerated in the future."

"Natalie, I hear you, but this is not that big of a deal. By making a statement I am making it into a bigger issue than it is or it deserves. Trust me on this. It will all blow over," Thorton responded.

"Senator, tomorrow you are scheduled to discuss the Consumer Bill of Rights legislation on *Meet the Press*. I think this issue is going to come up. We must be prepared. We have worked so hard on the managed care legislation and I don't want this to overshadow all of our hard work."

"Senator, I agree, we should at least reach an agreement on how to respond tomorrow should a question about the statement arise," Mark chimed in. *It's about time he piped up*, I thought to myself.

Unfortunately Mark's words made no difference. Thorton responded in his most patronizing tone, "I have been a senator longer than the two of you have been adults. I do not believe a statement is necessary. The American people are not interested in this issue and I doubt it will be a topic of discussion tomorrow. If the subject does come up, I will handle it. Mark-up is Tuesday and that is what you should be focusing on."

Well, I was one American who *did* care about his statement, and I suspected I was not alone. Somehow I had to move past the polite correctness that characterized our conversation and get on to the nitty-gritty.

"Senator," I began again softly, "you made the statements and only you can retract them. However, I must tell you that I disagree with your approach to this situation, and I do not agree that the statements are no big deal. I think your statements will be perceived as insensitive to some and offensive to many." When I finished, I noticed Mark was looking at me with horror. Thorton was not used to being challenged, and was known to rant and rave when irked. Most staffers, and I was no exception, kept their opinions to themselves and only gingerly raised direct issues with their bosses' conduct. I paused as I waited for Thorton to respond. When he did, his response surprised me.

"Were you offended, Natalie?" Thorton did not usually care what his staff, or anyone else for that matter, thought.

"Yes."

"I see." There was another long pause and that was it. He said he would talk to us on Monday. No resumption of the discussion. No apology to me. No word of remorse or even understanding. Nothing.

As I crawled into bed I was left wondering about my inability to articulate my true feelings on the issue. I should have told Thorton exactly how I felt in clear language, but I didn't. What made me feel worse was I knew that even if I had been able to tell him how I really felt, he probably wouldn't have gotten it. He, a man of privilege his whole life, could never understand why I would feel contempt for his dismissive tone and noblesse oblige manner. I felt like a wimp. I was too tired and depressed to call Adriane or even Gwen or Allana. Plus, I figured I was probably the only one of my girlfriends in bed at 10:00 p.m., alone, on a Saturday night. Everyone else had a life. Instead, I was grappling with how to cover my boss' ass for a statement that belittles me and anyone who looks like me. I picked up the phone to make a call but think better of it and hang up after two rings.

I woke up around 9:00 a.m. this morning and puttered around

the house until ten. I turned on the TV just in time to catch a teaser for *Meet the Press*. There were two pictures on the screen—one of Thorton and another of Rednecky. The announcer beckoned the viewers to tune in to hear about pending managed care legislation with key members of the Health and Human Services Committee. As the commercials began I put down my orange juice and riffled through the Sunday edition of the *Washington Post*.

When the program began, I got quite a shock. Joseph Jennison was subbing for Tim Russert. I had mixed emotions about this wrinkle. Jennison was an up-and-coming black reporter on the network. He regularly covered Congress and had a bi-monthly column in *Newsweek*. He was smart, articulate, and known for asking probing questions that sometimes caught his guests off guard. I had met him briefly a couple of months before at a Hill reception and dinner for a departing member of Congress. The reason I had mixed emotions was because while I wanted Joe to do a good job, thus enhancing his opportunities for more visibility on the network, I knew Thorton was in for a hard time regarding his Rwanda statements. As I sat watching Joe discuss the various topics the show would cover over the next hour, I couldn't help noticing how good-looking he was. His skin was a deep brown, the color of polished ebony. He had gleaming white teeth and a beautiful smile. His expressive eyes were framed by long, jet-black lashes. And those lips, wow! How did I miss those delectable pieces of eye candy? I was really lunching when I met him. I recalled thinking he was attractive and seemed very nice, but our conversation was brief because his wedding ring was gleaming and I was running home to pack for an early trip the next day. I only stopped by the reception to pay my respects to the retiring senator and his staff, and to get a few munchies, of course. On my way out I ran into a colleague who made the introduction.

The program began innocently enough. The round table panel of journalists led by Jennison discussed a number of issues in the news the previous week. The conversation was lively and at times gently combative. The Treasury Secretary talked about the Federal Reserve's recent decision to lower interest rates and the banking scandal that threatened to collapse the Brazilian economy. As they droned on about finance issues, I waited anxiously for the discussion with Thorton and Rednecky to begin. Finally, after yet another commercial break, Joe launched into the managed care issue. "Over the last decade, there has been a dramatic increase in the number of employed individuals enrolled in managed care plans and a significant decrease in the number enrolled in unmanaged, fee-for-service plans. The shift has been driven by an employer focus on controlling health care costs. To keep costs down, however, managed care plans have increasingly employed management techniques that seek to restrict patient access to expensive services and specialists." The picture then turned away from Joe and continued with a series of graphs that showed the increase over time of American families enrolled in managed care plans. This was followed by vignettes of individuals and families who had been denied certain services or procedures by their managed care plan and how they had been adversely affected. After Joe finished the last vignette, he turned to Senator Rednecky, who was in the Washington studio, and Senator Thorton, who was doing the interview from an NBC affiliate in his home state. "Today, we have Senator Thorton, chair of the Senate Health and Consumer Affairs Committee, and Senator Rednecky, also of the Health and Consumer Affairs Committee, to talk about their bill, the Consumer Bill of Rights."

The interview itself went very smoothly. I was pleasantly surprised; so far no mention of Rwanda. Joe had been very polite to the senator and provided him ample opportunity to discuss the merits of the legislation. When the interview was over Joe thanked Rednecky, who smiled and nodded his thanks to Joe. Then Joe turned to Thorton and said, "Thank you for participating on *Meet the Press* this morning. Before you go I wanted to take a few moments to talk about the situation in Rwanda." Then, looking directly at the camera, Joe said, "It appears that in addition to being one of the premier authorities on health care in the Senate, Chairman Thorton also has a keen interest in foreign affairs, particularly African policy." His sarcasm was not subtle. Thorton appeared unfazed, except I noticed he began rubbing his neck, a sign I had come to recognize as a nervous gesture he used when he needed a quick response but was at a momentary loss for words. Joe continued, "Specifically, sir, could you tell me and our audience if you said the following statement yesterday?" Joe then proceeded to read a statement that was nearly identical to the statement Sherman Keter had described to Mark and me the evening before.

Thorton ignored the statement and responded, "Yesterday, during a breakfast with business leaders in my home state, I was asked about the tribunal findings. My response was that the genocide was a terrible situation and that the tribunal's work should be supported and the perpetrators of the violence should be brought to justice." Thorton's response was true, but the problem was Joe didn't ask him about the statement he made to the press. Joe was asking him about the statement he made later in the day.

Joe then pressed, "Sir, do you deny making the statement I read earlier, in which all African leaders were described as barbaric crazy dictators? My sources indicated that this statement was allegedly made later in the day at a charity golf tournament."

I had to give it to Joe; he certainly had the facts right. I wondered how Thorton was going to get out of this one. Thorton's mouth had gotten him into a number of tense situations over the years, but somehow he was always able to talk his way out of the mess or with time the situation resolved itself.

"Well, I don't exactly recall saying those exact words—" Thorton began in response to Joe's question.

"Perhaps this will jog your memory," Joe said and proceeded to play a tape of Thorton saying exactly the words that Joe had read. After the tape finished, Joe asked the senator if the voice on the tape was indeed his voice and if his memory was a little clearer now.

Thorton's neck rubbing was becoming more fervent and his forehead was starting to glisten with sweat. I thought he was going to have a heart attack. The worst thing was I found myself rooting for Joe to nail Thorton, even though I knew it would require long hours on my part to help clean up the mess he made.

Thorton coughed a little and then said, "I seem to recall that uh, um, that, ah, perhaps I may have said the statement in jest to a colleague. Obviously, I, um, do not believe African leaders are barbaric or crazy as a whole. I was referring to those leaders who encourage their followers to commit acts such as those that are coming to light in Rwanda." That is the real issue here. Thorton certainly was trying his best to wiggle out of this one.

"I see," Joe said. "In your statement you actually linked the downfall of colonization to the lack of current leadership in Africa. Would you care to discuss the colonization of Africa and the merits of that practice and how you believe the independence of African nations has been detrimental?"

Thorton was now visibly shaken. His face went blank. He did manage to get out a weak response about focusing on the relevant issues of the here and now—like bringing the perpetrators of the violence in Rwanda to justice and preventing any reoccurrence. I kind of felt sorry for him; floundering was not in his vocabulary, nor was being bested by a black man, I'm sure. He was definitely twisting at the moment. But shit, that's what he gets for mouthing off. He should have known better.

"Finally," Joe said, "one last question, Senator. How would you compare the events in Rwanda to the ethnic cleansing atrocities happening now in Eastern Europe? Would you also label the perpetrators there as barbaric, crazy dictators, and do you lament the collapse of the Soviet Union as you do the loss of colonization?"

The camera turned to Thorton and his face was no longer blank. His mouth looked grim and his eyes were filled with thinly disguised anger. "Let's set the record straight, Joe," he said coldly. "The statements that you read today were made by me as an aside to a friend. I should not have made them and I apologize for any offense that may have been taken. I believe strongly that events such as those that occurred in Rwanda and the current ethnic cleansing activities in Europe are wrong, and that those who commit such acts must be punished. Regarding the statements, I discussed them with my staff yesterday and a full statement of my apology will be made available immediately following this program."

The camera turned to Joe, who was now smiling broadly. "Well, it looks like we are out of time. Thank you for being a guest today on our show, and I hope you will appear with us again soon. That's it for our show today. Please tune in next week when our guests will..."

The show was over, and it was a disaster. At least Thorton would now release the statement of apology. Maybe he'd also learned a lesson. I guessed that the story would now be quite a news item, given the drama of Thorton's denial and then the playing of the tape. I imagined Thorton at this moment. I knew Sherman Keter was in for an earful. Thorton is probably ranting and raving about how he was blindsided. I certainly wasn't going to accept any responsibility for his fiasco! We tried to prepare him yesterday and he wouldn't listen.

The phone rang and I picked it up. "Hello, Mark." I knew as soon as the show was over Sherman would call Mark about releasing the statement.

"Hey, Nat," he responded. "Did you see the show?"

"I sure did."

"Jennison was really hard on Thorton, and Thorton is ballistic."

"Actually, to tell you the truth, Mark, I thought Jennison went easy on him. It could have been much worse. Thorton, of all people, should know that actions or statements have consequences. Have you spoken to Sherm?"

"When Sherm and Thorton left the studio, there was a crowd of reporters outside. Thorton decided to give an impromptu press conference. It is going on now. Sherm has a copy of the statement we drafted last night and he and Jim will make sure it is distributed in the state. I'm in the car on the way to the office to distribute it on the wire. I know my phone is ringing off the hook. I'm not looking forward to fielding calls this afternoon. What time will you be in the office? I expect the senator will want to talk about damage control."

"I won't, Mark. This is a press issue—you handle it. You can page me if something urgent comes up."

"But, but..." Mark stammered, clearly stunned at my response. So was I, actually. As chief of staff I was expected to be involved in all major decision-making and certainly be on hand to help devise a response when there was a crisis. But I figured the senator should stew a little about this gaffe. If the senator wanted to fire me over this, so be it. I figured that would be unlikely, given that he needed me a little more than I needed him right now. Plus, I had no intention of having him try to trot me out to defend him. As far as I was concerned he was on his own. Another reason I didn't feel like going in to work was because for once I had something fun planned to do—book club at Destiny's house.

BRIANNA

9

BRIANNA

I can't believe that I have to pull a twenty-four-hour call
today. Luckily it's been busy so time is going by fast. I wish
I could have attended the book club meeting at Destiny's
instead of being here at the hospital. *Jack & Jill* will make for an
interesting discussion since there was always something going on
with the plot and because it was set in Washington, D.C. Most
of the places James Patterson talked about in the novel I knew
firsthand. I was so engulfed in the story I could not put the novel
down. I wanted to know the ending, but I didn't dare skip all the
chapters in between and go directly to the last chapter. I wanted
to read every mystifying word. The book kept me up three nights
ago when I was on call. Instead of getting sleep in the call room,
I stayed up all night reading and found myself exhausted from
sleep deprivation the next day. It's one thing to be up all night
taking care of patients because you have to. It's a completely different story when you stay up all night because you don't have
common sense.

Just then, my pager went off. I did not recognize the number.
I found the closest phone and dialed the number on the pager
screen.

"Hello, this is Dr. Taylor," I answered.

"Girl, get up here now! I need my epidural!" exclaimed Adriane.

"Adriane, is that you?" I asked.

"Yes, this is me," she yelled.

Moving the phone from my ear, I said, "Where are you?"

"In your hospital, about to have a baby."

"Alright, I'm on my way," I said. I went directly to Labor and Delivery on the third floor. Adriane does not handle pain very well. If I allowed her to suffer one minute more than she had to, I was definitely going to be cursed out.

"I wasn't expecting to see you in Labor and Delivery this soon."

"Me either. I went into labor at the book club meeting," Adriane answered.

"You must have scared the hell out of the ladies," I said, laughing, while making room for myself and the epidural cart in between the bed, the baby warmer, rocking chair, side table, and the tray table. Bumping into furniture and operating room tables was definitely a job hazard of anesthesiology. Once I maneuvered behind Adriane, I asked her, "Are you going to listen to me while I put in your epidural?"

"Yes, Doctor, but if you don't put it in now, I can't be responsible for my actions," Adriane said with a smile that lasted no longer than two seconds.

"Okay, I want you to round your back like the letter 'C' and try your best to relax your muscles," I explained. "That's perfect. I found a great space here in your lower back area. You're going to feel a pinch and some burning now that I'm injecting the local anesthetic to numb the skin in this one small spot." I immediately noticed her back muscles tightening when I numbed the skin. I knew that she would not move her body position despite the burning of the anesthetic as it was going underneath her skin. "Girl, that was the worst part. Now that the skin is numb, you should feel the pressure of the needle but not the pain." I said all of this while I was advancing the needle. When I finally felt the difference between the muscle layers and the epidural space, I told Adriane, "I'm almost done. I am going to put the epidural catheter through the needle and then remove the needle so only the epidural catheter remains in."

Adriane asked, "How large is the catheter?"

I replied, "It looks like a long strand of angel hair pasta. Don't worry. You won't even know it's there." Once I secured the epidural in place with huge wads of paper tape, I directed Adriane to lay flat on her back with her hip tilted off to the side.

"Hey, why do you have me in this weird, uncomfortable position? How am I supposed to breathe with my stomach on my chest?" she said with her face scrunched up.

I told her, "If you want your entire belly to be pain-free, then you better stay on your back and wait ten minutes so the happy juice can numb the nerve roots. Call me crazy, but I don't want the baby squashing your aorta, which happens to be your shared blood supply right now. Chile, just do as you're told."

My beloved friend came back to being herself and started smiling again. She calmly said, "Relief is on the way." I sat with her until the meds completely kicked in, which took about fifteen minutes.

"What's up with this Southwestern décor? We ain't in Texas," quipped Adriane. "I think that the hospital should have Destiny redo the entire floor. Don't you have any influence around here?" she asked me.

I replied, "Yes, but I don't have any say in whom they hire to decorate."

"Well, I think you should have some hand in that. Girl, I'm tired as hell and I'm still not feeling well. I think I may try to take a nap," said Adriane.

"What's wrong?" I asked.

"Well, the pain is gone now—thank you, but I still feel weak. The nausea won't stop."

"Hmmm, well, why don't you try to take that nap? You will need all your strength for pushing," I told her. "By the way, where is your husband?"

"In the air. He's on his way," replied Adriane.

On that note, I said, "You better get some sleep now. Believe me, you will need it."

"You're right, can you get Natalie for me? I need a pep talk before the real work begins. Make sure you tell the girls what's going on. And tell them I'll see them later," Adriane said softly. I closed her door and walked toward the waiting room.

The troops were all there. I told Destiny, Allana, Camille, and Natalie that Adriane was fine. Then I told them what she said about Destiny picking up the hospital account and becoming the interior designer. We all laughed because in the middle of everything, Adriane was still thinking about how we could get involved in something and get paid. "I'm going to go back and check on her before she gets into a deep REM sleep. Natalie, Adriane requested your presence, so come with me. See you all in a few." We left the group and walked down the hall.

We stopped by the name board on Labor and Delivery and I noticed there were no new patients yet. I had to remember to mention to Gwen my concern over Adriane's complaint of persistent nausea. As we approached Adriane's room, I could see Gwen's silhouette. I knew she would be in shortly after I'd put the epidural in. No sooner had we arrived in the room than Natalie asked Adriane, "Are you ready for motherhood?" Things got really interesting after Natalie found out that she might have to be the replacement coach. I really couldn't tell if the look on

Natalie's face was one of true shock or dread. Either way, we would have to work on increasing her level of excitement about participating. After Adriane finished fielding Natalie's interrogation as to the whereabouts of her husband, Tim, I made sure she was comfy cozy.

"Adriane, are you feeling the pain of your contractions?"

She replied gleefully, "How 'bout I feel nothing."

I told her, "If it's alright with Gwen for you to feel nothing, then it's all good to me." I looked up at Gwen and told her, "Don't give me attitude if Adriane doesn't know when to push."

Gwen responded, "Adriane, you know usually I like it when my patients can at least feel the pressure of their contractions. It allows you to push more effectively. But for you, Miss Thang, I will make an exception."

My pager went off at that moment. I told Gwen, Adriane, and Natalie, "I have to go. My boss is looking for me. I'll catch up with you all later." I waved good-bye and left the room. I told Gwen that I would catch up with her after I spoke with my chairman. Walking to his office, I wondered what he wanted to see me about now. Smiling, I thought how familiar those words sounded. I recall always wondering what my parents wanted to see me about when they called my name out loud. Those childhood years seem like they were just yesterday!

My mother took my brother, Brandon, and me to the Philippines when I was seven and my brother was four. Even though it was over twenty years ago, I still vividly remember the experience. It is hard to forget being in a foreign environment for three months, especially during the rainy season. After seeing the way my mother grew up, I knew that there was nothing I could not accomplish if I only tried.

Even though my mother and father were from two different

continents, they had similar values. My father is nineteen years my mother's senior. He married at the prime age of forty-five. Prior to matrimony my father was a swinging bachelor. When I emerged from the birth canal, I became the apple of his eye, his pride and joy, his heart. My father made it his life's goal for me to succeed and to let no one block my path. In doing so, he often made harsh and unreasonable demands but they were supposedly all based in "love." Love, however, can be a dangerous thing.

Somewhere around the age of seven, I told my parents that I wanted to be a doctor. I truly do not remember ever wanting to be anything else. From that time on, my father decided to start my journey down the medical path. He decided that he would bond with me by having weekly one-on-one talks. These talks lasted for hours. I truly believe this is when I formed the ability to literally sit for hours on end without moving. From the age of seven to sixteen, my father and I had this same weekly talk as well as other lengthy lectures. He would talk about his life experiences, his family, and his unfulfilled goals. He was hoping that I could learn from his mistakes instead of creating and suffering from my own. As I sat there hour after hour, it struck me that my father was a very smart and articulate man. I never understood why he became a hospital administrator instead of a politician. No matter how he started the conversation, three to five hours later, he would come full circle. I myself would forget how the conversation started. I wonder if I learned my communication skills from my father. I have often been accused of running points into the ground.

I worked hard to make my parents proud of me, though my teen years were dramatic for them and me. Since I skipped first and sixth grades, I was two years younger than my classmates although physically I did not stand out. I did everything I could to blend in with my peers. In junior high school, I was elected to the student government, joined the cheerleading squad, participated on the yearbook committee, and joined the Spanish club. I participated in all these activities to meet as many people as possible and to avoid having to go home and listen to my dad lecture me. One would have thought that I was a bad kid as much as my father found it necessary to address me.

When my friends started dating, pure fear struck my father's heart because he thought that I wanted to date as well. I truly think he had a psychotic break in my tenth-grade year. It was if his whole purpose in life was to make sure my legs did not spread apart. He felt that every male individual in my life was going to get me pregnant. I was not allowed to visit girlfriends and all visitations at my house were supervised either by my mother or father. My only saving graces were having a very loving and sensitive mother who tried to make allowances for me whenever she could, and also being blessed with a great set of friends who accepted my situation at home. To this day, I hold dear two friends from high school—Bernard and Terri. Bernard and I have actually been friends since elementary school and he can talk about me like nobody's business. He knows me better than I know myself sometimes. Terri was my hanging buddy. If I couldn't go out, she wouldn't go out. There is definitely comfort in numbers. I never completely felt left out because I had Terri. If we couldn't do something together, then we would talk on the phone for hours. I think the only reason I did not rebel during this period in my life was because I had friends in school. Evidence of this came in my senior year when I was elected to the senior valentine court. I remember feeling so honored that my classmates voted me onto the court.

Somehow I managed to graduate from high school at the age

of fifteen without running away from home, abusing drugs or alcohol, or becoming pregnant. I considered all these possibilities at one point or another just to escape but my friends kept encouraging me to be patient with my parents and to continue to be understanding. My friends were always by my side, supporting me. I came to realize early on that friendships were essential to my well-being and balance.

10

BRIANNA

After high school, I left my friends and family behind to fulfill academic, professional and personal aspirations. But things didn't work out the way I had envisioned. At twenty-nine I was, gladly, done with school and was supposed to be preparing for a blissful married life with a man who lived in Charleston, South Carolina. But my life turned 180 degrees on tax day of 1995 when he decided he made the wrong decision about marriage and kicked me out of his apartment at 4:00 a.m., or so he tried.

Two weeks prior to this incident, we took a weekend road trip to Charleston to view the neighborhoods, hospitals, and to seek employment. We found out three weeks prior to the trip that he would be stationed there. He had a four-year army commitment that he had to fulfill immediately after his graduation from residency. I, on the other hand, had two months left before completion of my pain management fellowship. That left me with the arduous task of writing about fifty letters to the hospitals in the surrounding area, which included Beaufort, South Carolina, as well as Savannah, Georgia. I was lucky enough to interview with a dynamic solo female practitioner who wanted to form a partnership with another female anesthesiologist. Apparently, the "good-ole boy" network was alive and kicking in conservative Charleston. There was one anesthesia group in the city that had a hold on the contracts with all the hospitals. In this group of twenty anesthesiologists, there was one female. This situation spoke for itself. I had never heard of such a monopoly in the Northeast, at least not where one group had a lock on all the business in town. So when the female anesthesiologist proposed that we join forces and hit the hospitals on the outskirts of town, I was enticed. After talking for about an hour, she offered me the job right there on the spot. I could not believe how lucky I was. Having the chance to be a pioneer and set up chronic pain clinics was a golden opportunity, especially for someone coming straight out of a fellowship.

Charleston was definitely a place I could live even though I am very much a city girl. The sunny, warm climate on the water would be a welcome change of pace from the torturous cold winters I had experienced in Boston. My girlfriend from Howard University lived there with her husband and two children. She had been there for about five years and was very involved socially. I knew that she would help me adjust to the new environment.

During the drive back to Washington, D.C., my fiancé and I discussed how things had worked out so perfectly. He was about to finish his residency in orthopedics and I was about to finish my fellowship in pain management. In planning our future together, I decided to prolong my training in Boston, even though I hated that city, just to take advantage of the opportunity to train at one of the Harvard University hospitals. Completion of the pain fellowship would allow me to follow him wherever he was assigned, even if it was in Timbuktu. I figured that I could not go wrong with the additional training I obtained. When we got back to D.C., I wrote a letter accepting the job offer in Charleston. I was truly grateful for the many blessings bestowed upon me. In two months, I was about to start a new life with the man I loved with my entire being, move to a new city filled with the love and warmth of my friends and in-laws to be, and embark on what I hoped to be a prosperous career. Then, in a day, it all came crashing down around me.

You know, I've always been told, "If you look for trouble, you'll find it." Truer words could not have been stated. But a woman has to follow her instinct. For two to three months prior to that infamous tax day, my fiancé had been acting strange. More specifically, his behavior pattern changed. Since he and I were both in medicine, I knew what an acceptable turnaround time was for answering a page. What used to be a return call minutes after he was paged turned into hours, sometimes even twenty-four. Being four hundred miles away in another city, you know my antennae had to go up. Our conversations became shorter in duration and often he would sit on the phone in dead silence. This was quite a change from me often falling asleep on him because he was so long-winded.

I flew in late on the night of tax day. I was so tired that I went straight to the shower and jumped in the bed. Once in bed, I knew something was wrong because I had to initiate intimacy. I couldn't remember the last time that I had to initiate anything with him. I definitely could not sleep then. This was a jumbo-sized red flag. I was not going to wait for the tractor-trailer to run over me. I did just what any intuitive woman would do—went looking for answers. Since I was unable to sleep, I went into the kitchen to get some milk and found leftover dishes of foods I never knew he liked. After seeing someone for two years, you tend to learn their likes and dislikes, especially when it comes to food. There were leftovers of what appeared to be a home-cooked exotic meal. In the cabinets, I found spices that were not there a month before. Since I pretty much stocked his kitchen, I knew exactly what was in his cabinets. Unless I missed something, I was unaware of his participation in gourmet cooking classes. I stood there reading the labels on the McCormick bottles: turmeric, marjoram, and coriander. This was a man who loved his meat and potatoes seasoned with nothing but salt and pepper.

My mind started to race. I wanted to question him then and there but realized it was 3:30 a.m. Instead, I decided to sit down in his second room, which he deemed his entertainment room. As I was listening to his snoring in the other room and trying to calm myself down, I looked at the floor and noticed a thin piece of metal sticking out from underneath the 4 x 6 cobalt blue and yellow area rug. I pulled it out and upon further inspection it turned out to be a hairpin. I began wondering if he was doing more entertaining than I'd thought. I started walking around in circles, trying to stop my mind from racing for a few seconds so I could decide what to do next. During the fifteenth walk around the room, something on the corner of his desk caught my eye. I felt myself being summoned by several piles of paper on top of the desk. I rummaged through the papers and found a credit card bill. There on his Visa bill was a list of restaurants that I had never been to. These restaurants, in fact, were ones that I was going to ask him to take me to. Unfortunately, I had not been there with him. The bills weren't cheap either. I thought we were supposed to be saving money. That was the reason given to me as to why he was not coming to Boston as often to visit me. He had not come up to visit me in two months. This was another drastic change. He used to come up two to three times a month. Not once every couple of months. I was starting to see a picture I did not like.

This issue could wait no longer, so I stormed into the bedroom, turned on the light, and immediately started questioning him. He just looked at me dazed, then started calling me all kinds of bitches and told me to get the hell out of his apartment. I refused to leave his apartment at four in the morning even though he threatened to call the police. I dared him to call them. I couldn't wait to put on public record that I was charged with refusing to vacate my fiancé's apartment merely because I was questioning him.

I didn't leave the apartment until mid-morning. And I didn't move to Charleston after completing my responsibilities in Boston. Instead I moved back home to Washington, D.C., put my things in storage, and moved in with my parents since I was jobless. Within a month, I signed a contract for a new job, bought a new car, and moved into my own apartment. A few months later I got a call from my ex-fiancé. He admitted he was having a relationship with one of his colleagues. The relationship started around February as I'd suspected. I was so relieved to know that I was not crazy and that my suspicions were right. To me, there is nothing worse than having a gut instinct about something and not being able to prove it.

I reconnected with Gwen without delay. We were both getting over rough relationships and were not particularly interested in dealing with the male species. So we just hung out.

Oftentimes we went to Rock Creek Park to in-line skate. During the weekends, parts of the park would be closed off to traffic allowing bikers, walkers, and skaters access to one of the most beautiful areas in D.C. Even though in-line skating was work, I found it very relaxing to exercise along the stream under the lush foliage. I never understood, however, how Gwen was able to fit skating into her already busy schedule. But she did. She is a natural athlete and exercises constantly because she enjoys it. Part of me exercises due to pure joy, another part of me exercises only so I can eat. I want to be able to go to any restaurant and eat any cuisine without having to worry myself to death about weight gain. For me, having to calculate the caloric fat and carbohydrate content of every morsel going past my lips just kills a meal. Hell, I gave up on men; I couldn't give up on food too!

11

BRIANNA

Eventually the highlight of my life became the fourth Sunday. Reading the books for book club meeting was fine, but I loved the dining portion of the fellowship. The ladies traditionally went all out preparing delectable foods for the meeting. Sometimes the food incorporated in the novel was prepared by the host of the book club meeting. And sometimes we dined out at restaurants. In either case, as long as we were eating, it was fine by me. One month we read *Coffee Will Make You Black* by April Sinclair. The meeting was held at Montego Bay Cafe. I got to Adams-Morgan at four o'clock but it took me fifteen minutes to park. Montego Bay Cafe was right in the middle of Eighteenth Street, where it is almost impossible to find a parking space. I could already taste the jerk chicken, peas and rice, stewed cabbage, and fried plantains going past my lips. I was surprised to see how packed the restaurant was. Destiny, Gwen, Natalie, Allana, Adriane, and Camille were all sitting in the back waiting for me.

"Hey, guys! What's up?"

"You're late as usual," said Camille.

"You've got that right if I'm coming in after you." We both laughed because we knew there was a perpetual contest between the two of us as to who would arrive last. I won this time. I thought I'd done well by arriving at 4:15 p.m. since the parking was so bad. "Whom do I owe money to?" I said as I stared at a glass of rum punch waiting for me.

"Just sit down and enjoy yourself," said Destiny. I hugged everybody at the table, then squeezed in to take my place. It was just like my friends to look out for me, but then again we always looked out for each other.

Natalie began the discussion of the book by saying, "This was a great coming-of-age story until the end. I personally didn't get it. Why did Stevie have to be gay, and if she had to be gay why did she have to fall in love with a white woman?"

"Oh, Natalie!" Allana exclaimed. "I don't think she was gay. Stevie was just learning what sexuality is all about. She was a confused young girl."

"I don't think so," Natalie replied. "All of the telltale signs were there. She was practically having sexual fantasies about that nurse."

"Yeah, but remember what the nurse said; maybe her feelings weren't sexual at all," Camille chimed in.

Adriane countered, "Hmmm, that's possible, but I'm not convinced. I really think the author was setting the stage for a lesbian in the making. I bet her next book confirms it. It says here on the back flap that April Sinclair is working on a sequel. Mark my words, I bet you Stevie is gay or has a lesbian encounter in Sinclair's next book."

"Well, what's wrong with that?" I asked. "Experimenting with one's sexuality is not a crime. There are a lot of confused people out there and it's better to figure out who and what you are than to be always wondering and trying to fit in."

"Don't get me wrong, Brianna; I have nothing against anyone's sexual orientation. Who a person decides to sleep with is his or her own personal choice. But over the past eighteen months we have read the three E. Lynn Harris books and now this. It seems like everyone is gay. I'm starting to get paranoid," Natalie said.

"Girl, I know how you feel. Did you read the article in last month's *Essence* about the group of women in D.C. who had formed a support group because their husbands were gay? It was a trip because the women in the group still loved their husbands and refused to leave them, even though essentially their marriages were a lie!" Adriane exclaimed.

"I don't get it," Gwen said. "Why sleep with a man you know is gay? First, you could possibly expose yourself to HIV and AIDS, and second, your man admittedly wants another man. What an ego crusher; why put yourself through that?"

"Well, at least the women in the *Essence* article know what's up and can take steps to protect themselves," Allana chimed in.

I addressed the group and said, "It's hard for me to tell if you all liked the book or not. Right now, we need to rate the book so we can eat."

After soliciting a vote from everyone at the table, the final book rating was 2.5. The rating system was developed at the second book club meeting. The score of 1 denotes an excellent book, 2 is good, 3 is fair, and 4 is poor. The waiter arrived with our food right after the noting of the rating. We settled down and ate our dinner. After dinner we discussed the book a little more, then bade one another farewell. Adriane and I remained and I had another cocktail while we delved into work dramas. The conversation started out pretty general, and then Adriane said she had some shit she was dealing with at work. I asked her if it had anything to do with that big account she'd brought in.

"You guessed it. The Tolbert account was going to be the vehicle I would use to drive me straight to the top. Instead, this may be what halts my vertical movement in the firm."

"What?" I replied, setting my drink down on the table.

"For the past four weeks, I have been out of town working closely with the senior vice president on the Tolbert account.

One night, we were working late in his hotel room as usual. We were reviewing a slide presentation he was giving the next morning. While I was sitting in a chair at the desk, I suddenly felt his lips kissing the back of my neck and his hands starting to grope for my breasts. I immediately stood up, knocking the chair over and spilling all the slides out of the carousel. I told him, 'I have to leave!' I ran out of the room like a bat out of hell. I bolted down the hall, took the stairwell to the floor below, and somehow managed to find my card key despite my hands trembling and my mind reeling. Once in my room, I locked my door, took the phone off the hook, and sat on my bed in darkness. I kept going over in my mind all the times before when we were together and how I could have missed any hints or innuendoes."

"Did you call Tim?"

"Girl, are you kidding? He would have hopped on a plane and pulverized that man. Not that he would not have deserved that and more. At that moment, I had to figure out how I was going to handle the situation. I called you and Natalie but neither of you returned my call."

"Adriane, I am so sorry. You should have said 'urgent' or something on your message. You know how I get sometimes with running around. I get home late at night, then I just fall out. If you had paged me, I would have known that it was very important. What are you going to do?"

"The easiest thing would be to just let it go. I could press forward as if nothing ever happened and hope that he will take the escape route I provide him. I could also try to talk to him and salvage the situation by saying that I would be happy to put this behind us. Otherwise, I would be putting everything at risk by bringing it out in the open. I may be viewed as a troublemaker and then where will I be?"

"Come on. I would hope that by now you have developed equity within the company and they value your integrity and professionalism. It would be in the firm's best interest to create an environment in which diversity in terms of race, gender, and age prevails."

"Bre, our chosen professions are a little different. In corporate America, I work in an environment where fewer than five percent of partners in privately held firms are female. There are about the same numbers for female vice presidents. It is a man's world. Who do you think is expendable?"

"Okay, you've got me. Medicine is not quite that bad. Our numbers are a bit better when it comes to the number of females in the profession. It still remains pretty bleak when it comes to the number of women who are academic chairman of hospital departments. On an up note, presently at least one-third of all entering medical students are female."

I continued, "You should go to the human resources department for counseling. At least speak to a representative and review the policy regarding sexual harassment."

"That's a good suggestion but what I think I'm going to do is speak to a colleague, John Turner, at the firm. John has been not only a mentor but also a good friend. He has looked out for me in so many situations. I think he feels there is a special bond because we're both African American."

"Adriane, that's fine but make me a promise. At least go and see my brother Brandon. His law firm, Taylor, Frazier, and Browning, has prosecuted several major companies in cases of alleged sexual harassment."

"Alright, I promise I'll go see him this week or next week at the latest." Adriane finally smiled. Then she excused herself and walked quickly to the bathroom. When she returned, she stated that the stress of this situation was really getting to her. She had been feeling nauseous for the past week. I told her it was time to leave since it was going on nine o'clock. We walked to my car and then I drove her to her car. I told her that I would check on her later.

Driving home, I continued to think about Adriane's situation. I hoped her decision to speak to her associate and mentor was a good one. This episode further supported my hypothesis that some men ain't shit. That's probably why some men have intellectually challenged me, few have physically dominated me, and rarely has a man spiritually and emotionally fulfilled me.

12

BRIANNA

Last fall, Destiny's cousin Travis sent her tickets to a Washington Bullets game. Destiny and I had planned to have dinner first, then go to the game. However, a deadline at work changed at the last minute and Destiny paged me to say she would not be able to attend. I called Gwen, Allana, Adriane, Natalie, and Camille. No one in the crew could go. I couldn't even get a co-worker to accompany me. I really wanted to go because I had never been to an NBA game and my call schedule was fairly light that week.

I was finding that the difficult part in having a group of friends who were also professional was not being able to count on them for last-minute activities. Everybody was busy doing something. I have to give at least two days' notice if I expect anyone to be available. That is the one nice thing about being in a relationship. If you and your significant other are in the same city, you usually have someone to attend functions and events with. I was starting to miss this convenience. I thought that it was actually good for me to attend the basketball game by myself. It was time to be more independent and to become comfortable going places alone.

The only thing that I was a bit hesitant about was going into downtown D.C. to the sports arena at night by myself. As in any major city, crime exists. Luckily, D.C.'s crime rate has decreased. The renewed commerce interest in the downtown area has sprouted many other entertainment venues. Now there is more foot traffic as visitors come to hang out. As I drove into town, I realized how beautiful our nation's capital truly is. The art district that sits right besides the sports arena is home to a number of art galleries. None of which are owned by African Americans. How this happened in "Chocolate City" is beyond me. I suppose it is all about the Benjamins.

To my amazement, I found a parking space fifty yards from the entrance. I knew then that I was meant to be there. When I got inside, I was initially disappointed because it appeared that only forty percent of the seats were filled.

I made my way to my assigned seat that was located in center court, about ten rows back from the front. Two seats away from me, I noticed an attractive woman who appeared Hispanic. She looked up at me and immediately greeted me. "Hi, my name is Sarah. I thought that I was going to have the whole row to myself tonight."

"Hi, I'm Brianna. It's nice to meet you. I would be happy to move back a row if you need space."

"No, no. I'm happy I have someone to talk to." *Great, just what I wanted. Someone to talk my ear off when I truly came to watch the game.* "Brianna, do you come to many games?"

"No, actually this is my first one. How about you?"

"I attend all of the home games." Well, this woman was obviously a fan. I was hoping that she would not be a fanatic and start cursing and screaming. I was not up for all that.

Luckily, the players soon came out. I took that opportunity to ask super-fan Sarah about the individual players and the coach. As I thought, she knew the statistics and background information on all the starting players. I was actually glad she could give me insight because she made the game more enjoyable. It was very pleasant talking to her. During halftime, she offered to get refreshments for me but I declined. I just wanted to sit and observe the crowd. I could people-watch all day. You can learn a lot from people's facial expressions and gestures. From my brief interaction with Sarah, I could tell that she had a great deal of enthusiasm and energy. She talked with her hands and she also had large hazel eyes that were very expressive. She returned just before the second half. The opposing team was extremely talented. They won by twenty points. Unfortunately, the game was not very exciting because the Washington Bullets were behind by at least ten points the entire time. Sarah advised me to come to another game. I told her I would. "If you come back," Sarah said, "make sure that you sit next to me again. Since I have season tickets, you'll know where I'll be."

The traffic was not that bad. Since I'd parked on the street, there were no long parking lot lines to contend with. I decided to drive through Adams-Morgan on the way home. As I passed by Montego Bay Cafe, I remembered the talk that I had with Adriane about her senior vice president. I was so concerned about her. Since the news of her pregnancy spread through the office, things between them seemed to have settled down. She never went to my brother Brandon for legal advice, nor to human resources for counseling, nor did she tell her husband. With a baby on the way, they would need more money, and she couldn't risk putting her job in jeopardy. For now, she was hoping that what occurred was a one-time event that would not happen again. If she were not pregnant, however, I don't think her decision would be the same because Adriane usually does not take too much shit from anyone. I too would have to agree with her decision to put things on hold while she prepares for the newest member of her family. I just hope that her anxiety over that shit don't stress her out.

By the time I got home, it was eleven p.m. I was exhausted. I was glad I went to the game though. It was cool having my own personal super fan nearby. I was also looking forward to attending another game. I checked my voice mail and listened to Destiny reminding me of the next book club meeting. As soon as I put the phone down from checking messages, it rang.

"Brianna, hey, it's Allana."

I replied, "What's up? What's going on?"

"Rodney and I just got back from that jazz club Bailey's."

"Did you have a good time?"

"Girl, I met the nicest guy. Did you see this past week's Sunday supplement to the *Washington Post*?"

"You mean the article about the piano player?"

"Oh Brianna, you should see him slam those keys. He is really fabulous."

"Why didn't you and Rodney call me before going over? I could have met you over there."

"To tell you the truth, I forgot he was going to be there. Since we were in the Silver Spring area, we decided on the spur of the moment to stop by Bailey's for drinks. You should go see him; he's playing again tomorrow night."

"I wish I could but I'm on call tomorrow for twenty-four hours."

Allana asked, "Can't you switch with someone?"

"Since it's 11:18 p.m., it may be a little late for me to attempt schedule maneuvering. I'm sure he'll play somewhere else."

Immediately Alana jumped in and said, "He's single."

Of course I had to ask. "How do you know?"

"I asked him directly. I also told him that I had a very good friend that I wanted him to meet. I got his business card."

"Well, hold on to that business card. I'll get it from you later. I have to be at work at seven a.m. so I need to get some sleep. I'll see you at the book club meeting. Tell Rodney I said hello."

"Okay, Brianna, have a good day tomorrow. 'Bye."

I hung up the phone. All I could do was shake my head because Ms. Allana was always trying to fix somebody up, especially me. I suppose that's what it's like being a newlywed. You want all your girlfriends paired up and as happy as you are. As I drifted off to sleep, I knew that my night would be filled with hoop dreams and music.

13

BRIANNA

Destiny and I decided that we would take a trip somewhere. After mulling over brochures and special deals,
we narrowed down our choices to Paris or Hong Kong.
Paris was her first choice since it's one of her favorite cities in the
world. Hong Kong was my choice. Every true shopper knows
that Hong Kong is paradise. In between shopping, we could also
eat to our hearts' content. One of my favorite restaurants is
Maxim's, which overlooks the bay next to Kowloon. There, the
waiters and waitresses in short coats whiz by your table with their
steel-wheeled carts crammed with what seem like at least two
hundred types of dim sum. Whether it's dim sum, tapas, or appetizers, the small portions make me feel like I'm not eating much.

I was to meet Destiny downtown at the travel agency, but she
called me at the last minute to cancel. She had to meet with
Camille and go over some financial issues. Since I was already
downtown, I decided to get a bite to eat in Chinatown. Every
once in a while, I have to eat at an authentic Chinese restaurant.
That's the Asian side of me jumping out. I can only go three days
at most without rice before I start to crave it.

I love to personally select a crispy duck from the window and
watch as they carve it in front of the table. After eating half the
duck, I looked my watch and realized that since it was only 7:30
p.m., I could probably catch the 8 p.m. Washington Bullets game

at the Verizon Center, which was three blocks away. Luckily, my car was parked one block away from the Verizon Center, which made it even more convenient.

When I got to the window to purchase my ticket, I realized that I might see Sarah again. I asked the ticket agent for seat B111 in Row CC, which is the same seat I had before. Lo and behold, it was available. I thought that was a sign. Now the time was 7:55 p.m.

As soon as I approached my seat, I saw Sarah. She looked surprised to see me and said, "You came back. I'm glad. This should be a much better game than the last one you saw." I sat next to her and had the entire game narrated. By the time the game ended, my mind was stuffed with information about the players, undergraduate schools attended, and statistics about the league. I was ready to play "Jeopardy" and select the category Men's Basketball for $300. We exchanged phone numbers and then Sarah asked me, "Do you want to grab a drink or something?" I told her that I'd eaten before the game, but I could go for a glass of wine. She told me that she collects wines and had tons of bottles at her place. I decided to test her and see if she had Camille's favorite wine.

"Do you have a 1989 Silver Oak cabernet sauvignon?"

Her eyes lit up and she said, "Yes, I love that wine. It's one of my favorites although I have many. Why don't we walk to my place and I can show you my wine collection."

"How far is the walk?"

"I have a condo in the Lansdowne Building. That's about five blocks away."

"Okay, let's go." I had never seen the inside of the Lansdowne building but read in the *Washington Post* that the building went through massive renovations and the condos were all split-level and started at $500,000. While walking to her condo, I found out that her dad was a wine sommelier for Lespinasse in New York City. Sarah had no choice but to learn about wines. I had a feeling that I was also going to learn more trivia and information pertaining to wines.

As I entered her condo, the high ceilings immediately impressed me. The spiral staircase, office loft, and beautifully shirred draperies made of a pewter-colored raw silk trimmed in violet were amazing. The furnishing was immaculate. In her kitchen stood what appeared to be a chrome Sub-Zero refrigerator but was in fact her wine cellar. It held approximately three hundred bottles. She pulled out the 1989 Silver Oak cabernet, opened it, and put it in a decanter. Next she pulled out two crystal bordeaux goblets that had the Riedel label on the base.

Sarah also had an upper loft, where six floor-to-ceiling bookcases filled with books spanned the walls. All shelves were packed. At some point, I knew that we would also talk about literature.

While the cabernet was breathing, Sarah pulled out her prized possession. She had a 1966 Lafite Rothschild. I figured it obviously had to be a good year since that was the year I was born. She said that her dad decided to save it for her when she was five years old. She had wines from all over the world including Australia, South Africa, Chile, Spain, Italy, and of course, France. Most of the collection was from Italy and France but there was also quite a bit from California.

When we finally started drinking the wine, it was perfect in temperature and texture. Sarah told me that she traveled extensively with her father when he went on business trips. I thought, *What a great job, that required you to visit vineyards and purchase wines for clients. With the vineyard visits, you'd know there's going to be some good eating. I could never do this. I'd be big as a house.* I was still glad I picked anesthesiology.

While Sarah was describing her visits to the different vineyards in various countries, I dozed off. I don't know what happened. I guess I just felt so extremely comfortable. This person was someone I practically just met and there I was asleep. When I awakened, I became startled because I forgot where I was. When I remembered, I realized that Sarah had put a blanket on me and was sitting at the other end of the couch with my feet in her lap. I looked at my watch, which read 12:30 a.m. I had no intention of being out that late. I immediately got up and told Sarah I had to go. I thanked her for her hospitality, apologized for falling asleep on her, and made sure that she understood it was no reflection on her as a host.

As I walked to my car, I could not believe that I fell asleep in a strange person's place so easily. I knew that I was still a little tired from being on call two nights ago but this was weird. Why did I feel so comfortable? As I approached my car, I pulled out my car keys and saw the little piece of paper on which Sarah had scribbled her name and number. I wasn't sure about learning any more about men's basketball, but I definitely wanted to learn more about wines and what type of books she reads and collects.

14

BRIANNA

After months and months of begging Camille, Destiny, Natalie, Gwen, and Allana to accompany me to a wine tasting, I gave up and decided to go on my own. I was a little more perturbed at Camille because she encouraged me to join the Wine Tasting Association but was never available to attend events. Adriane was not subjected to my pleas since she was baking a bun in the oven. I paid good money for my membership and was determined to get the most out of my dues before the end of the calendar year. The main event for December was the Italian wine tasting at the embassy on Sixteenth Street in D.C.

The Wine Tasting Association organized wonderful events at the embassy of the country whose wines were being presented. It provided an opportunity to get a glimpse of the décor inside these palatial buildings. After receiving the quarterly pamphlet, I realized that I missed the tastings at the French, Australian, and Portuguese embassies. The Italian wine tasting seemed spectacular. The chefs from the top two Italian restaurants in the city would be serving hors d'oeuvres. Also present would be ten importers offering a variety of wines to taste. Each importer had between eight and twelve wines apiece for sampling. This was simply too good to pass up. This was the perfect way to learn about the grapes of Italy. Somehow, I still had to catch up on France. I really wish I had gone to the French tasting just so I could understand the regions and which grapes were grown where. At least Italy was similar to California labeling in that the grape grown determines the type of wine. For now, I just had to slow down and learn one country at a time.

Luckily, I got off from work around 3:00 p.m. That gave me enough time to go home, return a few phone calls, get dressed, and get downtown by 6:00 p.m. The Italian embassy has a circular driveway with a black ornate wrought-iron gate covering the entrance. I passed by the building all my life not realizing that it was an embassy. Immediately upon entering the building, you get swallowed by the grand marble foyer lined with Corinthian columns. The foyer opened into a high-ceilinged ballroom. Before entering the ballroom, a member of the Wine Tasting Association was there to greet me and give me a name badge, a wineglass, and a piece of paper with a list of numbers from one to ten in one column and the names of wines in a second column. I was then instructed to go to each of the ten tables and taste the wine with the numbered brown paper bag over it. After tasting the wine, you had to pick the name of the wine you'd tasted from the second column. I never would have thought that a wine tasting would involve tasting wine from a brown paper bag. You would think that brown paper bags were saved for hard liquor like Jack Daniel's.

I decided that it was best if I filled my stomach with food so that the wine would have something to cling to. Better that it cling to food first rather than brain cells. The food section was packed, of course. The chefs were making fresh appetizers and giving pointers on cooking as well. I had no interest in cooking, only consumption. I grabbed some crackers since that was what everyone else was doing. I learned a long time ago, when in Rome, do as the Romans do. After nibbling on prosciutto, cannelloni, rotini in truffle sauce, and crostinis, I navigated my way back to the ballroom.

I started at table one and decided that I would methodically make my way through the wines listed in the second column. The Italian wines were totally different than the California wine varietals. Thank goodness that Chilean, Australian, German, and South African wines were similar to those in the good old USA. I felt as if I knew a smidgen when dealing with those countries. The second column on my paper might as well be in a foreign language: barolo, barbaresco, chianti, brunello di montalcino, dolcetto, orvieto, lambrusco, vernaccia di san gimignano, and moscato d'asti. I quickly found out that I loved the prosecco and moscato d'asti. There is something to those little bubbles. I like anything sweet, especially dessert wines. I definitely had to lay off those two.

By the time I got to table ten, my palate was having a hard time differentiating any subtle nuances. I definitely was not swishing and spitting the wine as we were instructed. I enjoyed tasting the wine as it went down my throat. Despite eating the crackers to supposedly clear the palate, my taste buds were buzzing.

I looked up at the crowd and estimated that there were about 150 people in attendance. Guests remained split between the food section and the wine tables. In the middle of the floor in front of wine table number five, I caught a glimpse of a brown-haired woman who looked like Sarah but as soon as I saw her, I lost her again. I couldn't believe it was really her—I had not seen her since that time I dozed off on her in her apartment back in August. I thought about calling her a few times. In fact I actually picked up the phone but never dialed her number. She left a few messages but I decided not to return the calls because I had a mysterious feeling whenever I was in her presence or thought about her. I started to walk over to that area where I last saw her and then thought to myself, *Why would she be at this tasting? She knows more about wines than half the people here.* I turned around and headed toward the main desk in the foyer so I could find the answers to the numbered brown-bagged wines.

As soon as I took a couple of steps, I heard my name. "Brianna?"

I turned around again. "Sarah? Hey, I thought I saw you but I figured that you wouldn't come to something like this."

"I come to these tastings often because I know a lot of these importers. Believe it or not, they actually invite me to get my opinion on new products. What brings you here?" Sarah asked.

I replied, "I considered myself pretty educated on wines, but after I met you I realized I had a lot to learn. My girlfriend encouraged me to join the Wine Tasting Association. She thought it would be a fun thing for us to do in addition to me gaining some knowledge."

Sarah asked, "Are you finished tasting all the wines you were interested in?"

"Frankly, I didn't know enough about Italian wines to even know what to be interested in. Prior to coming today, I'd heard of chiantis and barolos. But now I have a better idea about which are whites and which are reds and the lighter-tasting wines versus the big, bold flavors."

Sarah just smiled at me. "Well, I'm glad you came. It sounds as if you can order wines in a restaurant, at least."

I agreed. "Most definitely. I want to check my 'assignment sheet' before I leave."

"I'll wait for you out front."

Somehow I muscled my way through the crowd to the table with the answers. I was totally shocked—seven out of ten right. That's the equivalent to a C. The format turned out to be effective for me since I'm so goal oriented. The challenge made me focus more on learning. I wished Camille, Natalie, Allana, and Destiny were here. We could have turned this into a party.

When I walked outside, Sarah was waiting for me in her SUV. She rolled down the window and said, "Why don't we get something to eat while your alcohol level is dropping?"

I realized she'd made a good suggestion. My little Italian delicacies were long gone. It was only 9 p.m. Plus, I was not in the best driving condition. I replied, "Okay," and climbed in.

Sarah made a U-turn on Sixteenth Street and then made a left onto Columbia Road. "Should we eat in Adams-Morgan?" she asked.

"Yeah, I think we should change countries and do Brazilian."

"Have you ever been to The Grill from Ipanema, Brianna?"

I couldn't believe it; we were on the same wavelength. "It's only my favorite restaurant in Adams-Morgan. Those green mussels in the broth are to die for."

Sarah said, "Alright, that's where we're going."

We found a place to park across the street from the restaurant right on Columbia Road. So far the parking gods were smiling on us. The restaurant was not that crowded so we were able to get a booth in the front corner. I drank water immediately. The mussels were on our table in five minutes. After sopping five pieces of bread in the broth, eating the mussels, and downing two glasses of water, I started feeling normal again. During the meal, I found out that Sarah was a fundraiser. She appeared to know her way around the political circles of D.C. I was surprised that she did not know Natalie. I was also surprised how kind and thoughtful Sarah was toward me. She sat right next to me in the booth and continually dipped my bread in the broth. As soon as I had one piece in my mouth, she had the next one ready. She also kept pouring water in my glass from the carafe the restaurant placed on the table as we were seated. While she was talking, I noticed how fluid her body language was. She appeared so confident and radiant about everything she discussed. When she laughed, she would toss her head back, tilt it to the side, and shrug her shoulders. Her whole body laughed. She just seemed to be so open.

"Hey, Brianna, I think we should get going. You have to be at work at seven, right?"

"Unfortunately, yes, I do. You're right, I've gotta go." We left the restaurant after she paid the bill.

While riding back to the embassy, I decided to check my messages. To my surprise, there were messages from some of the girls. Natalie said, *"Bre, I should have gone with you to the tasting. Even though I don't like wines, I sure could use a drink now. Focusing on legislation during recess is driving me crazy."* Camille begged for forgiveness. *"Bre, I'm really sorry I couldn't go with you tonight. Next year, I will definitely make it a point for us to go to a least one function quarterly. Call me and tell me how it was."* Destiny said, *"Next year, girl, I'm there eating cheese and crackers with you. Give me a call tomorrow."*

Then I heard Sarah's voice. *"Brianna, here we are."*

Before I could say anything, she leaned over and kissed me on the lips. I didn't move. I wasn't sure what to do. I did notice at that moment she smelled of jasmine, gardenia, mandarin, and lime. Her lips were full and very soft. All I could do was say, "Thanks." I opened the door, got out, and waved good-bye. I was grateful the valet had left my car out front. As soon as I started my engine, Sarah drove off. I blasted the music and drove home. I couldn't stop thinking about that kiss. I had never been kissed by a woman. I didn't understand why I thought it was a natural end to the evening.

15

Interrupting the reminiscing of the last two years of my life, I got off the elevator on the ground floor and walked toward my chairman's office. I had no idea why he wanted to talk to me. I knew that it could not be about signing my medical record charts because I completed that two days ago. I knocked on the door and then entered.

"Dr. Taylor, how are you this morning?" asked Dr. Paney, the chairman of anesthesiology.

"I am doing well. Spring is my absolute favorite time of year. I missed this the most while I was in Boston. It would remain cold until May and sometimes June, and then all of a sudden it was sixty-five degrees, up from thirty-five."

Dr. Paney replied, "I am very happy you moved back to the area. I hope you stay on staff here. So far, you have received compliments from both the nurses and surgeons."

I said, "At this time, I have no intention of leaving. As long as there is an opportunity to expand the chronic pain service, I'm all yours."

He smiled, then said, "It has come to my attention that the patient that you took care of three days ago remembered a portion of his heart bypass surgery. Do you have any idea how this happened?"

"Yes, I do. The patient was experiencing a heart attack and lost consciousness. His blood pressure was very low. There was no time to wait so I immediately put the breathing tube in his lungs to get oxygen into him. The cardiothoracic surgeon was there at the time watching the procedure so that he would know if surgery was going to be necessary. After I made sure the patient was getting oxygen, we immediately took him to the operating room for emergency heart bypass surgery. I started him on medication to maintain his blood pressure. Since his blood pressure was so low, it was dangerous to give him any drugs that would put him to sleep because his blood pressure could drop to nothing. It was truly touch and go there for a while before the skin cut was even made. Once his chest was open, the surgeon quickly put him on the bypass machine. Only at that point was I able to give any medicine to prevent memory. What is his status now?" I asked.

The chairman replied, "The patient is still in the intensive care unit but is going to be moved to the step-down unit today. The breathing tube was removed yesterday but he remains on high-dose adrenaline to keep his heart working well."

"I will go up and talk to him about his condition and the events leading up to his surgery. I hope that he was not frightened by what he heard," I said.

"Brianna, it sounds like you did the best you could to provide comfort without jeopardizing his life. Those situations are truly stressful and critical. There is no doubt that the populations of surgical patients that have the highest percentage of recall are the cardiac bypass patients. This is the time, however, where communication between physicians and patients becomes key. I want you to make sure you speak with him and answer any questions he may have regarding the events leading to surgery as well as the anesthetic care he received. If his family is there, make sure they are present as well."

"Dr. Paney, I completely agree with you. I really think that we, as physicians, forget to empathize with the patients and their families. We become accustomed to reacting quickly in emergency situations and forget that for the patient and his or her family, it is a unique experience. If we do not explain what took place, people tend to assume that something was done incorrectly."

Dr. Paney replied, "We must never forget to be vigilant and to be aware of what our drugs can and cannot do. As anesthesiologists, we do more out-patient surgery, giving shorter-acting drugs so that patients are not too sleepy at the end of the day. For in-patient surgery, we have to switch gears and give longer-acting medication, realizing that each person breaks down drugs in their system differently. You cannot use a cookie-cutter approach."

After thanking my chairman for bringing this case to my attention, I walked out of his office toward the elevator. While waiting for the elevator, I thought about how truly frightening it could be to actually remember your surgery and what the operating staff was saying. Personally, it would totally wig me out. Every time I read an article referring to awareness under anesthesia, it heightens my sensitivity for vigilance. The "happy juice" drugs (as I like to call them) are truly fabulous. Patients move themselves over onto the operating room table and have absolutely no memory of doing that or of what was said.

I immediately went to the cardiac care unit to visit my patient. This would be a first introduction since he was unconscious when I'd arrived to take care of him. Upon my entering the unit, we immediately made eye contact. His bed was directly in the center of the action. He looked up at me as if he recognized me. It amazed me how well he looked. I introduced myself to him and explained how sick he was prior to and during surgery. He stated that he remembered hearing the order for the paddles so that I could shock his heart. In fact, he said that my voice was familiar to him. He expressed his gratitude for the care I gave him but stated that he was worried that he might wake up while under general anesthesia if he were to have surgery again. I explained, "The incidence of awareness under general anesthesia is 0.1–0.2 percent. Your case was a very special situation due to the circumstance of your extremely low blood pressure. The team worked very hard to keep you alive. In the future, should you require surgery, hopefully the conditions will be different and it won't be life threatening. Usually sedation medication is given before you are put off to sleep which immediately makes you forget everything. Generally, patients wake up in the recovery room not realizing that their surgery has been completed."

The patient asked, "Dr. Taylor, will there be any bad side effects from the experience of my surgery?"

"Outside of the complications from the corrective surgery for your heart, there may be recurrent dreams from the memory. Did you feel anxious or have any fear associated with your memory?"

"No. Actually it was weird. The whole thing just didn't seem real. I guess things happened so quickly, I didn't have time to feel scared. Somehow I knew that I would be alright."

"Well, that's the most important aspect of awareness under anesthesia. The outcome of the event is based on how you viewed it. Since it didn't scare you, hopefully you will not have nightmares. Sometimes, we refer patients to psychologists if there appears to be negative implications." With that being said, the patient appeared satisfied with the explanation and did not have any more questions. I told him to please feel free to call me at any time if he had questions or needed to talk. He again thanked me for being there and taking care of him.

I walked over to the nursing station, hoping that his chart would be in the rack. Upon viewing an empty chart rack, I started the chart search. The one constant that exists in all intensive care units is the fact that the chart rack is always empty. Its sole purpose appears to be decorative. The problem is that the chart is going to be with one consulting team or another. If a consultant does not have it, then the unit secretary is transcribing orders off the chart, which was written by a consultant. This time, it took me less than a minute to find it. After overcoming the challenge of finding a seat with desk space to write, I reflected on my conversation with my patient. I was pleased that he understood what happened and why. I looked back toward his room and observed him simply staring out the window. While I was writing a note in his chart about what we had discussed, my beeper went off. I looked down at the screen on the beeper and saw the extension for Labor and Delivery. Instead of phoning, I decided to walk over there. I wanted to check on Adriane to see how she was doing and catch up with Gwen. Maybe I could steal a few minutes to hang out with Destiny, Camille, Natalie, and Allana.

ALLANA

16

ALLANA

I watched Natalie disappear behind the Hospital Staff Only doors and hoped she, Brianna, or Gwen would come back soon with a report on Adriane's condition. I began daydreaming about having my own "bundle of joy" with my soul mate, Rodney. Both of us are in our mid-forties. What am I thinking? This is ridiculous! I have never had a child of my own, and at our ages, it would be incredible and unwise. After two children by a previous marriage and a vasectomy, Rodney had volunteered to have the procedure to reverse the vasectomy if I wanted him to. But the risks could be great. The doctors think we could get pregnant without any problems. They said people our ages have babies every day. But everybody is different. Each pregnancy is unique; the cost and the heartache some couples go through. I wept inside thinking about the potential pain and anguish. Here I am in the waiting room with Camille and Destiny, thinking about myself when I should be concentrating on Adriane. Up till now, Camille was the only one in the group with children. She has two beautiful and well-mannered children at that. But Camille has said many times, "Not another child is coming out of this body, honey!" There were no questions regarding more children in Camille's mind. Destiny had mentioned to me several times that she had decided not to have children of her own. I knew Gwen wanted children but I wasn't sure how the other ladies felt about motherhood.

Yep, motherhood is probably out of the question for me. Especially since my aches and pains are starting to nag at me of late. I have the feeling that something is wrong inside my abdomen. The irregular bleeding between periods dampened some of the joy of what should be the happiest time of my life. After all, I am starting a journey with Rodney, one that I hope will allow us to grow old together and continue our friendship and love. Rodney and I promised to take care of each other for the rest of our lives. To live up to my end of the deal, I need to find out what is depressing me so. I think I need a complete physical.

I've never been concerned with my inner physical well-being. I guess youth fools you into thinking about your outer appearance only; especially since I grew up in the male-chauvinistic fifties, sixties, and seventies. To keep up with the trends, my style went from sexy and glamorous—James Bond girls and Hugh Hefner bunny types—to not wearing a bra in the seventies, to a natural style in the eighties, and now an ethnic chic mix in the nineties. The ethnic chic style suits me better now because it's comfortable and it allows me to show my age gracefully.

17

ALLANA

I'm an army brat. I'll admit it, if I am pressed. It depends on to whom I'm speaking. Some civilians have perceptions that people who grew up in the military are spoiled or bourgeois. What they don't understand is that in the 1940s and fifties, the military offered many opportunities for people of color. So my father, who was from a rural area near Montgomery, Alabama, made the military his career so he could find more opportunities for his family. Before he married my mother, he traveled to Korea, Europe, and the South Pacific and had seen the world, and was thus a "worley" even before I came to be. "Worley" is a term that means "world traveler," like a "homey" is a "home boy." Being a worley, one looks at life a little differently than most. You see more than one side to people, places, and things. You have to in order to survive. In order for me to survive, I project an extroverted image although I am more introverted.

My parents met and were married in my mother's home state of Georgia. She was nineteen and my father was twenty-nine. A year later, I was born in Frankfurt, West Germany. My sister was born six months after my first birthday. We babies spoke German before we spoke English, thanks to a German nursemaid who helped take care of us. She also cooked and cleaned our four-bedroom apartment, which was located off base. I remember the carved cherrywood furniture and ornate tapestries in earth tones that adorned the walls. The decor had a hunting lodge feel, with trophies of preserved fish and birds and racks of antlers over doorways. Mr. and Mrs. Smith, my parents, looked like the movie stars Errol Flynn and Greta Garbo. He wore a pencil-thin mustache and she wore her hair in a shoulder-length pageboy parted in the center. Both of my grandmothers were coffee colored and both grandfathers were cream colored. That made us café au lait. Mrs. Smith was the only girl and the youngest of seven and Mr. Smith was the oldest of three children. They loved to entertain. I remembered jazz (33-1/3 RPM) recordings on the turntable, laughter and tinkling ice cubes in crystal glasses, silver ice buckets and martini shakers. Even though they liked to have fun, they were conservative in their thinking and child rearing. Especially Mrs. Smith. She held the apron strings very, very tight.

My sister and I were rambunctious kids. You name it, we did it. Little Sister and I imitated characters from *Gunsmoke*, *Wagon Train* and *The Cisco Kid*. I was Cisco and she was Poncho. We had cowgirl outfits and cap guns. We played Jacks and Ball, Hopscotch, jump rope, Tetherball, Kick ball, Red Rover, Red Light-Green Light, Swing the Statue, and Mother May I. We rode horses, swam, skated, and skied. All of this had a military base, integrated influence. We were Brownies and Girl Scouts well into high school. That was my parents' way of controlling us and keeping us out of trouble. TV was a huge pastime in small town USA. The sixties' TV shows we watched were *American Bandstand*, *Hullabaloo*, and *Shindig*. Sis and I looked like brown Annettes and Gidgets. We didn't quite identify with Diahann Carroll's weekly show about a nurse, Julia, raising her son, Corey. After all, she was "old" to us teenagers.

My first year of public school was as a freshman in junior high school in Oklahoma. It was a culture shock to be in the minority—a military dependent in a sea of civilian kids who were predominantly white. Undertones of racism were felt there. The Beatles invasion brought that British influence of hair and clothes. It was Carneby Street, miniskirts, fake hair and eyelashes, sheath dresses, and white Courreges boots! Yves Saint Laurent and Rive Gauche were plastered everywhere. We moved back to Germany from 1965 to 1968, where we lived in Stuttgart and Munich. We saw fashion up close and personal. I just knew I wanted to be a fashion designer. Some of my favorite groups, other than the Beatles, were the Stones, the Dave Clark Five, and the Kinks. But things changed when I was watching German television one day—*Beat Club from Bremen*—and saw Jimi Hendrix. Here was a musician with wild, straight and kinky hair and tight-tight pants, talking to me with his guitar. He had big hands, big lips, and was plucking the strings with his tongue. I thought he was so sexy! After that I started collecting Hendrix and the Experience paraphernalia from teen magazines, newspapers, and albums. My locker door was plastered inside with pictures of Hendrix and his band. I had the best collage. Classmates would stop by to ooh and aah over my idol. When he and his group came to Munich to perform, I was forbidden to go; never mind my plea that "everybody else in school is going." I cried myself to sleep and didn't speak to my father for two weeks.

While in Germany, we missed a lot of what was going on stateside in the way of black awareness, afros, and Black Power. I heard "soul" music but didn't see "our" images until much later when new kids transferred into school from the States. They brought with them cultural news of Martha Reeves and the Vandellas, Smokey Robinson and the Miracles, the Temptations, and little 45 records. With the new kids came dances with names like the Mashed Potatoes, the Camel Walk, the Stroll, and Mickey's Monkey. We returned to the U.S. of A, again during the summer of '68, following the Martin Luther King assassination.

18

ALLANA

I remember the day I learned Adriane was pregnant. It was another book club Sunday and Rodney and I didn't make it to church. Bill, a friend from Virginia, had stayed over that weekend. I heard Rodney and Bill in the family room. The aroma of waffles and bacon was in the air. I should have been down there with them, but instead I was updating the book club roster.

"Hi, guys," I said sheepishly as I walked into the room. "Sorry I didn't come down earlier."

"Where are you going? To work?" asked Bill, laughing as he looked at my tote bag of books and binders.

"No, smartie!" I shot back. "I'm on my way to book club at Camille's. Sorry I'm rushing out." I grabbed a waffle in a paper towel. "Destiny's here and I'm driving."

"Okay, honey," said Rodney. He gave me a good-bye peck on the cheek. "See you later."

On the way to Camille's, Destiny and I chatted away. "I missed the last meeting at Camille's. You said her place in Potomac is really posh, right?" I asked Destiny.

"Yeah. It's sorta contemporary. And she has it beautifully decorated," replied Destiny.

"Oh, yeah," I say.

"Well, I wonder how the meeting will go today. I think the group needs some structure. I mean, we're all over the place. Some of us get here late. And some of us don't stay on the subject. I don't have all day to gossip. And I wish we would stick to the meeting dates and the book selections. You know what I mean?"

"Aah, yeah," Destiny said. "I think I'll propose some new guidelines."

It was a beautiful, sunny day, great for that Beltway drive. Destiny and I were the first to arrive. We knocked on the solid wood door and we heard, "Come in, it's open."

"Come on up, you guys!" called Camille, in her lyrical way. "Hi. I'm just finishing up a few things. I'm trying a recipe I saw in a magazine. It's got walnuts, butter, and cinnamon in it. It's very rich!"

"Oooh, sounds good. I think that's a little too rich for me. I'm watching my intake these days. I've put on a few pounds since our wedding," I said.

Before long, other club members started to arrive. I heard, "Hey, girl!" I turned around.

"It's Adriane!" I exclaimed. "You're pregnant! I haven't seen you in months! Congratulations!" We hugged.

"Congratulations to you on your marriage! I had something for you. But I couldn't tell you where it is now!" She laughed. "We have changed things around at the house in an effort to get the room ready for the baby. I've been working like crazy!"

"Don't mention it!" I said. "I'm so glad to see you! You look great!"

"Thanks," she said, distracted. "What smells so good?"

"I'm trying this coffee cake recipe. You want some?" offered Camille.

"Yeah, give me some," Adriane said.

"You know you're not supposed to have that," added Gwen, who overheard everything.

"I can have a little piece!" was the retort from Adriane.

"Okay. But just a little piece," Gwen conceded.

Camille waved her hands. "Hey, everyone let's get started."

I said, "We have a lot to cover this meeting. We need to get organized. How about rules, mission statement?"

"Oh, no. This sounds like another book club I know of," Adriane said. "They have rules. You get demerits if you're late. I couldn't stand that shit! And there's a waiting list to get in!" We all finally settled down. I facilitated the administrative part of the meeting and Destiny took notes. And of course Camille led us in the discussion of the book.

When I returned home, the guys were watching the Sunday lineup of ball games. When they saw me, they looked up, expecting to hear all the gossip. "How did it go?" asked Rodney.

"Fine. We have our first male member," I informed them. They looked surprised and anxious.

"Who?" Boyfriends, mates, and spouses have tried without success to gain access to the book club for the last two years. Regular meetings don't start until all males have left the premises. We're not prejudiced. It's just that the club members voted to keep the club exclusively female to facilitate bonding and to maintain serious literary discussions.

"One of the members is pregnant, with a boy!" I informed them.

"Oh. I thought you all had some 'hard heads' there!" Rodney grinned.

"We did. Just the soon-to-be little one. Ha! Got ya!" I laughed.

This year we did decide to have a coed book club meeting. Natalie proposed a cookout this summer. Camille suggested we could invite our significant others. Adriane recommended the book *The Genocide Files* by local author N. Xavier Arnold. She knows him. She said he is self-published and thought we should "help the brother out."

My husband joked, "Well, you better tell the guys six months in advance, so we men will have enough time to read the book!"

I smiled. "Yes, dear."

Rodney and I met on a Friday in 1995. Back then it was not unusual for me to go to Happy Hour every Friday. This particular Friday, something told me to go to a new restaurant in the Maryland suburbs. Brianna called me at the office. "What's up?"

"Not much. I heard about a new restaurant in Lake Tree. Let's check it out. Okay?"

We decided to meet at the restaurant. It was a balmy evening. The restaurant was in an affluent area. When we arrived, we noticed the parking lot was filled with Benzes, BMWs, and other foreign cars. I think I saw a Fiat and a Jag. I thought this was an indication that the patrons of the restaurant were of means. As we walked through the doorway, we were greeted by a wave of mellow jazz coming from the overhead sound system. Brianna and I exchanged looks and smiles. *This should be interesting.*

"This is exactly what I need at the end of a hectic week."

"Me too," she said.

A young woman asked us how many. We said two for dinner and she guided us to a banquette seat along the wall covered with purple, black, and gold fabric in ethnic patterns. The tables were dressed with cloth napkins in crystal goblets and stainless steel place settings. The hostess handed us menus.

"Your waiter will be right with you." We settled in and relaxed.

The first person I noticed moving around in the dining room was a man who had the physique of a football player. He had on dark slacks and a white dress shirt, no tie, with the sleeves rolled up. And he was carrying a pitcher of ice water. As he moved from table to table filling glasses, he engaged each patron in conversation. A lot of the tables were filled with smiling women watching his every move. He looked like Franco Harris, the former Pittsburgh Steeler running back, without the beard.

Rodney approached our table and introduced himself as one of the owners. The first words out of his mouth were "I've coined a new term. It's 'Nashee.' I use it to describe people who complain for the heck of it; you can't please them. It means 'nigger shit.'"

Brianna and I looked at each other and laughed. "Yeah, we know what you mean."

"I've been all over the world and there are no people like my people. I love my people. I'm new to the area. I love seeing all colors, shapes, and sizes of folks in the D.C. area. It's a change from New England. My parents retired on the Cape. Retired military."

"Which service?" I asked.

"Air Force," he said.

I said, "I was an Army dependent." We discovered we were in the same city in West Germany when his brother and my sister were born.

"We must have played in the same sandbox; there weren't many of 'us' over there," he said. He went on to tell us about his travels all over the world while growing up. I thought to myself, *I like this man, his voice, and his look. I would never tire of this.* After a while, he was summoned to another part of the restaurant, and Brianna and I went on to enjoy our meals of corn-encrusted catfish, salads, and glasses of wine.

As we prepared to leave, he came over to say good-night. He looked me in the eyes as he handed me his business card and said, "I want a number." I took his card, saw a number written on it, so I responded in kind—I took one of my business cards and wrote a number on the back and handed it to him. I guess that was all a part of that mating ritual. I see you. You see me. We like what we see. What next? I couldn't wait to get home to see if the ritual worked. Did he call?

When I got home, I called my office voice mail just in case. I heard Rodney's deep melodious voice. "I did ask for a number, not your work number. That's what I get for not checking the number on the back of your card against the number on the front. Now I guess I will have to wait for you to call me, since I don't have another number for you." I just smiled to myself.

Our next conversation was over the phone. I found out he was a jock in high school, which earned him a college scholarship. He played wide receiver and special teams. Instead of playing professional ball, Rodney went to graduate school and received an MBA. After school he pursued a career in real estate. Now he was a real estate developer for commercial business complexes and malls. He also co-owned several restaurants. Rodney's parents were from the South, like mine, and he was first-born like me. He likes dancing, so do I. We both like traveling and meeting people. Rodney said he was looking for a special person, so was I.

After hanging up with Rodney, I lay in bed thinking about the hunk I'd dated three months earlier. Although I thought of him less and less, I still would fantasize about the sexual escapades we had. We used to talk dirty to each other over the phone. In between our soft moans we would describe what we were or were not wearing. Sometimes I would grab the pillow and use my hands to find that special spot and satisfy my need. I loved it because the gratification was instant and I didn't have to be bothered with a nincompoop in my bed. Rodney, on the other hand, stimulated my mind and I prayed he would be able to stimulate my libido as well. But I wanted to take things slow. I really liked Rodney and I didn't want to ruin things by jumping in the sack too soon. I wanted us to be friends first, then lovers, if it was meant to be.

I called Natalie the next day to tell her about Rodney. I knew she would be able to relate to his experiences because they were similar to ours.

"Girl, we have so much in common. Our parents grew up in the South, Alabama and Georgia. Both of our fathers were in the military and moved their families all over the country. Natalie, I think I found my prince, after all of the frogs I've kissed."

"Yeah, I've kissed quite a few myself," Natalie replied.

Natalie and I continued to talk for hours about the frogs we'd dated. Even though there was an age difference between Natalie and me, her frogs looked, jumped, and sounded just like my frogs.

"Well, I can't wait for you to meet Rodney. Maybe he has a friend. Would you be interested in a 'mature' man?"

"Allana, don't you mean 'old'? I'll keep looking for someone in my generation. I'm not ready for worms just yet. But I would love to meet your prince."

"You shouldn't knock worms until you've tried them," I said, laughing.

19

ALLANA

Rodney and I became inseparable. Twelve months after meeting, we bought a house together. We found the perfect house about a mile from my townhouse. Our new single-family home sits in a small community of thirty homes carved out of a national park. Woods surround the development on three sides; there are three cul-de-sacs and no main street to speak of. It reminded me of the setting of the book *Linden Hills*.

I led the book club discussion of that book because I was the host for that meeting. The author, Gloria Naylor, included so many interesting topics that I didn't know where to start. Of course we discussed the main character, Luther, and his many accomplishments and faults. Then we talked about how the female characters stayed in bad marriages or relationships regardless of the abuse they suffered just because their men were "successful." The club had a field day with this topic because our members are in stark contrast to the women in Linden Hills. The ladies in the book club don't look for a man as a symbol of success because they are successful in their own right. They look for a man to be a partner for them, to add value to the relationship, to bring spiritual nourishment to the soul, to bring male wisdom, and to lead his family.

"But I don't want no ugly man!" one of the ladies yelled out.

"An ugly man! What is an ugly man? You can be pretty on the

outside and nasty ugly on the inside. Believe me, I know from experience. I've dated plenty of ugly men," Camille said.

"You know how it is, most people want pretty offspring, so they like to marry people with nice textured hair, an acceptable complexion, and a high IQ," Brianna chimed in.

"Just like Luther did," I said.

"What nationality are you?" one of the book club members asked me.

Stunned, I said, "Who me?"

"Yes, you. I've never been able to detect your accent and I've always wondered what your ethnic background is," was her reply.

"I'm American black, white, and Native American," I responded.

The club member would not back off. With all eyes on the two of us, she asked, "Which side is white?"

Looking a little put out, because I don't like to discuss my personal business, I said, "My father's side. He never discussed it. But my mother told us that my father's parents were mixed. I don't know if they were married or not. A lot of things happened in the backwoods of Alabama in the 1800s. We used to visit Alabama every year in the summer. We would drive up to a big white house, but we never got out of the car and went inside. A white woman would come out to the car to see my father and his family. She would always comment on how my sister and I looked— beautiful girls, light skin, straight hair, and keen features. When we left her, we would go down the road to the end of the property and visit with a friend of Dad's. There we would run and play in the pear and apple orchards with his children while the grown folks visited."

Camille broke the tension by commenting that she has relatives in Alabama, too. You never know what's going on behind the wood shed. We found out that before coming to America, some of my ancestors were in the slave trade in Sierra Leone. I was thankful for Camille's interruption. And I was glad when the meeting was over. It was the first time a book club meeting mentally and physically drained me.

In *Linden Hills*, the wealthy lived at the bottom of the hill and the renters lived at the top. In our neighborhood, Forest Hills, the whites live at the bottom of the hill, non-whites in the middle, and blacks at the top. Rodney and I jokingly call it the United Nations because the homeowners are from Cameroon, Ivory Coast, Guyana, India, the Philippines, Florida, New York, Oklahoma, Colorado, and Maryland.

Setting up house with Rodney was an experience. We had two households to move, not to mention a storage unit full of stuff. How were we so lucky to move the day of the first snowfall of December 1996? I kept Destiny abreast of everything, selecting options for the house, settlement, and moving. I asked for her assistance in selecting window treatment. I wanted honeycomb shades for the family room and kitchen. She gave me names of places to check. We would compare notes and prices by phone. The evening Rodney and I were ready to hang the shades, we called Destiny and Patrick to assist with the project because Patrick had a drill. They showed us women how simple it was (yeah, right) and then the guys went to work. Destiny helped me unpack. I didn't know where to start in the kitchen. Where should I put the pots and pans and dishes and glasses? I looked to Destiny's organization skills and took her suggestions and input. I was having an anxiety attack and couldn't think clearly enough to decide where to store foil or bowls.

Destiny gave me a look like "You don't sound like yourself." I wasn't myself. It was tough adjusting. I was no longer independent. The partnership aspects of being in a relationship, making decisions together, and considering another's feelings were weighing on me. Rodney and I were engaged but not married yet and these thoughts kept running through my mind. Eventually I got into a routine.

During the first year in the house, we went through three cleaning services. First we had a white woman who was very good. She fired us because we forgot to leave a check for her on the second cleaning. She explained by voice mail message that she could no longer clean for us because she had a bad experience with people who forgot to leave a check—she'd cleaned their whole house for them and she never got paid. The second cleaners were a two-woman team, one black and one white, who came out for an interview. They accepted our offer and began work right away. After one cleaning, we were not impressed enough to call them back. The third group was a national franchise, Sunny Maids. Our neighbors used them, a team of three Africans. We thought, Good—keep the money in the black community. But when I saw one of the women pick up a dirty scatter rug from the kitchen and drop it on the cream-colored carpet, I knew this arrangement would be a training ordeal. As it turned out, the metal fixtures around the sinks and faucets were not wiped, the kitchen floor had to be redone several times, and they told us they did not scrub shower stalls. I noticed when they moved things, they did not replace them in the same order. There also appeared to be a language barrier. When I complained to Destiny and inquired about her maid service, she said, "What maid service? Child, pleeeez, I am the maid!" I couldn't figure out how she maintained her career and her house. Where I came from in the Midwest, you either did one or the other—became a housewife or a career woman.

Six months after playing house, we decided to make the living arrangement legal. The intimate wedding ceremony was beautiful and the honeymoon in Barbados was one ecstasy-filled moment after another. Even though we had already set up house and had many an opportunity to explore every inch of each other, I brought a few toys to Barbados that allowed us to take sex to another level. I showed Rodney some new things and he did the same for me. The honeymoon ended quickly though, because the first two months back home, we fought every weekday morning.

One Tuesday, Rodney and I were getting ready for work and I was running late as usual. Rod almost yelled, "Are you ready to go?" I could tell he was exasperated with me by the tone of his voice.

"If you have to leave, leave! I'll take the Metro from the College Park station!"

I continued getting ready and then called his name. "Rodney!" I went downstairs. No Rodney. I noticed his lunch sandwich, banana, and cake were gone from the kitchen counter. I opened the garage door. The truck was not in the driveway.

"I'll be damned! That Negro left!" No good-bye. No kiss. He left me in the shower and didn't set the house alarm! I flew to the phone and paged him. The phone started ringing as I listened, my heart pounding.

"Hello."

"Have you lost your mind?" I practically yelled.

"No," he said. I thought I detected a smile in his voice.

"You left me and didn't say good-bye or give me a kiss. And you didn't set the alarm!"

"You turned away from me when I was talking to you. You acted strange," he replied.

"I was getting ready for work and preparing the house for the cleaning people. I was moving things out of the way. Even when things get picked up the night before, there are still the last-minute items we use to get ready for work that I put away before I leave the house. After I'm dressed, the last thing I do is put the bath rugs in the laundry room!" I tried to explain.

"Yeah, well, I just needed to go. I told you I can't expect people in my office to be on time if I keep coming in late!" Rodney said.

"I'm not talking about that! I know that! I don't understand why no kiss, no alarm! I'll talk to you later!" I was frustrated at this point.

"Yeah, we'll talk later!"

"'Bye!" I exclaimed.

"'Bye!" We hung up, mad. I threw on my white Keds sneakers and put the pedal to the metal to the subway parking lot. I hopped out of the car and stepped into freshly mowed grass! Ugh! Now my white sneakers were green. That man! We'd had our first major miscommunication.

I arrived at work in a better mood, having had time to relax and read a few pages of *The Poisonwood Bible* by Barbara Kingsolver on the train. As I checked my voice mail messages, my ears perked up when I heard Rodney's voice.

"Hi, this is Rodney. I'm sorry about this morning. If you could step outside yourself and look at how you act this time of every month. You become a very, very difficult person to deal with. I may be copping out, but I'm trying my best to be cool. But it's hard when you are jumping up and down, hollering and acting like a crazy person. I never know if I'm coming or going. So I just stay out of your way as much as possible. Maybe it's a coward's way of dealing with the situation. But what am I to do? I don't know how to help you. To tell you the truth, you are driving me crazy. Don't misunderstand me. I love you, baby, we just need to work some things out. 'Bye."

20

A few months later, I found myself sleeping in often. One morning I opened one eye and peeked at the digital clock on the night table—10:05 a.m. Ummmmm, the bed felt good. Why was I so tired? Could it be because we were out the night before at a film premiere at DAR Constitution Hall, went to Chinatown afterward for Mongolian barbecue, and didn't get home 'til 3:00 a.m.?

I felt sad because my girlfriends were out of town. Brianna was in Germany for a medical conference so I couldn't call her. Gwen was in the Dominican Republic, Destiny was in North Carolina visiting her cousin, Camille had gone to a resort in Virginia for a romantic weekend, and Natalie had to work all weekend. I remembered when I was single and traveling to Hawaii, Cancun, and Martha's Vineyard on holiday. I love being with Rodney but those were some fun times. I don't know why I'm getting depressed so often these days. I have good friends, a wonderful husband, a great family and extended family. I'm beginning to think that my depression is hormone related. Lately, the mood swings have started to pop up more and more often. I've noticed more "power surges," or hot flashes. I prefer the nineties' term "power surge" because the word "power" has a positive spin to it. The flashes are uncontrollable. I'm grouchy and irritable. Rodney has noticed it and continues to comment on it. It's time to do something about this. What's happening to me? I don't like myself sometimes. I don't care to be around people much anymore. I decided to get to the bottom of this so I made an OB/GYN appointment. Most of my close friends are in their mid to late thirties, and I don't feel comfortable discussing these issues with them, not even Gwen or Brianna, who are doctors. I was concerned about menopause, mood swings, my sex drive, hot flashes, and spotting between cycles. Americans have such an obsession with youth. Even though I was a late bloomer I noticed that my hourglass figure is now pear shaped. However, I still have a youthful spirit. I heard all the horror stories of fibroids, bleeding, and hysterectomies. *Maybe I need hormone therapy*, I told myself.

When I called to make an appointment, the receptionist pointed out that my last PAP test was less than a year ago.

"Well, I have some concerns," I heard myself say to the male voice on the other end of the phone.

"If you're in pain, we can see you right away."

"Oh, no, just some things I've noticed. I think I need to be examined." How could I tell him about hot flashes, mood swings, a change in menstrual flow and duration of my periods, body aches, depression and being just plain miserable all the time?

"Okay," he said in an understanding tone. "Would you like a male or female doctor?"

"Female, please."

"Okay, I've scheduled you for January twenty-first with Dr. Lois Johnson."

"Thank you," I said gratefully and hung up. During the week that followed, I wrote down questions and concerns to discuss with the gynecologist.

I recall being in my thirties and having several older girlfriends.

One in particular was always talking and complaining about physical ailments, night sweats, and hot flashes. I didn't know what to say or do in response. But I remember it strained our relationship because she was always, I mean *always*, talking about some bodily function or other and frankly, it turned me off. Not to mention her sudden bouts of irritability, during which she would sometimes blow up at people. I grew distant from her, didn't call her as much or do things with her. I felt guilty but her negativity was too much for me at the time. I was out of my supportive role, divorced after fifteen years of a bad marriage. I was living on my own for the first time in my life and enjoying it. I was working on Allana and doing exactly what Allana wanted. This meant dating different types of men, going to Happy Hours, traveling, or just hanging out. I had left most of my married friends behind and formed friendships with women from work or grad school. This went on for four or five years before I even thought of settling down again.

January 21, 1997 came soon enough. Armed with questions, I kept my GYN appointment. How could I describe Dr. Johnson? She looked like Secretary of State, Madeleine Albright, in a lab coat. Her coat was open so I could see her tailored, knee-length tan dress. With it, she wore stockings and chocolate brown pumps and pearls à la June Cleaver. I thought, uh oh, a Republican in her mid to late fifties. Did I mention the blonde bob courtesy of L'Oreal? Yes, I prejudged her. We had an interesting visit.

"What brings you here today?" she asked.

I recounted my fears about hot flashes, length of periods, and mood swings. "One thing I know about menopause is that periods stop coming. Am I entering menopause? All of this is confusing to me." She invited me to ask all my questions. When I finished, she proceeded to give me all the answers and a tape to view.

Later, while watching the video at home, I learned that at some point the ovaries stop producing estrogen. The main symptoms of estrogen loss are night sweats, irritability, hot flashes, brittle bones, and vaginal dryness. The doctor had told me that during menopause, women are exposed to an increased incidence of osteoporosis. Osteoporosis is a porous, thin bone condition caused by loss of estrogen, which serves as a stimulant for bone growth. For this reason, all reproductive age women should be taking 1000 mg of calcium a day. During menopause, however, it should be increased to 1500 mg a day. It is recommended that one stay on estrogen replacement therapy (ERT) for five to ten years once started. I watched the Premarin video and it also mentioned taking progestin with the estrogen. As a result of taking progestin, there may be a light monthly discharge of the endometrial lining. I had mixed feelings about all this information. I knew I wanted the mood swings and night sweats to stop. I recalled seeing people in costume and carrying pictures of horses, protesting the use of Premarin outside of a National Institutes of Health building, drawing attention to the use and treatment of pregnant mares to collect their urine to make this drug. A couple of the people were on bullhorns shouting, "Stop the inhumane treatment to mares! Cruelty to animals!" I could not get the picture out of my mind of mares impregnated again and again and kept in little stalls to harvest horse urine for their estrogen.

The doctor and I decided to measure my estrogen, FSH, and LH hormone levels via a blood test before making a decision to implement hormonal replacement. Low levels would indicate that I was in menopause and would benefit from replacement therapy. Sometimes women experience symptoms of menopause but their hormone levels are normal. This is called perimenopause. Even in that setting, some women respond to hormonal therapy. After three days, Dr. Johnson called me back and told me that my hormone levels were normal but on the low side. She reminded me of our conversation about whether or not I should have replacement therapy.

After thinking about it for a couple of weeks, I called Dr. Johnson for a prescription. She called me back.

"So you have made the decision to go ahead?" she asked. I told her yes, and that I wanted the option where I still had a period every month at the same time.

She quipped, "A lot of women pick that option, so we will know when we can wear our tennis whites." She told me she would write a prescription and I should take the pills as prescribed—the little brown estrogen pill every day and the little white progesterone pill for days 14 through 28 only each month. I went to the pharmacy that day thinking, *Well, this is another rite of passage.* I discussed it with some friends my age and I discovered some were already on hormone replacement therapy (HRT) faithfully. Some were considering it because they were experiencing the same symptoms I was; I just didn't know it. I realized how little we really talked.

A month passed and I called for a follow-up appointment. Dr. Johnson was no longer with my health plan so I made an appointment with another female doctor, Dr. Patel. Between the time I made the appointment and actually saw her, I started spotting between periods. I shared this information with Dr. Patel and she assured me that this is often normal when women start hormonal replacement therapy. She explained that spotting is an indication that the tissue lining may be overgrowing, a condition called endometrial hyperplasia. Bleeding could also be a sign of endometrial cancer. Since my hormonal tests were normal, I understood that my chance of having cancer was small, however we decided to go ahead with additional tests. The first thing she wanted to do was stop the hormones and do an endometrial biopsy.

The East Indian gynecologist was in her thirties and proficient. She had a hint of an accent, brown skin, and shoulder-length, straight black hair. I felt comfortable in her presence. She lied to me though. She said I would feel a little sting and some cramping from the long tube she would insert through the cervix and into my uterus. When she performed the biopsy, it was a *big* pinch and a pulling sensation! My *"Ouch!"* was followed by her "I'm sorry. It's all over. You can rest here, take your time and come out when you're ready." When I got dressed and went down the hall to her office, she had the lab slips ready for my blood test and pelvic sonogram. She said she would call me with the results.

Gwen had been quite busy lately delivering babies. I didn't want to impose but I called her to talk about my experience. "Will you answer some questions for me?" I asked.

"Sure, no problem. What's up?" I recounted my long story about Rodney, my libido, the mood swings, and how I thought HRT would be the answer to my problems. She listened quietly.

"How old are you?" she asked.

"Forty-five," I said.

She mused, "Well, everybody is different. Some women don't do well on hormones. There are things you could do like diet, eat soy products, and take herbs like black cohosh, dong quai root, or ginseng. Vitamins E, B6, and B12 are good, too. That will keep you from killing Rodney and keep him from killing you." I had to smile at her humor. She was just the person I needed to talk to at that moment. She explained to me that if I was still having periods (which I was) and my hormone levels were normal (which they were) that I was not in menopause yet.

"Yeah, well, I've read about perimenopause and that's no fun." I pouted.

"What are your symptoms?"

"Mood swings, irritability, indifference to loved ones, hot flashes." I also told her about the scheduled blood test and sonogram. She said the results would give me more information about what was going on and suggested that I also get my thyroid and testosterone levels checked. She further explained that sometimes in the perimenopausal period, the drop in testosterone causes some of the symptoms that I had been having. I thanked her for talking to me. She was easier to talk to than I'd expected.

"No problem. You can call me to talk anytime. Be good to my buddy, Rodney," Gwen said.

"Thanks. I'll be in touch."

"No problem."

In the next month, I had two transvaginal sonograms. The first one showed three uterine fibroids and a 4-cm, tubular-shaped mass in my ovary. The second sonogram showed a 7-cm complex mass in my ovary. I learned that a complex mass was a cyst that had both fluid and solid materials within it. I asked Dr. Patel exactly where the fibroids were. She said, "There was one six cm on top of the uterus, one three cm on the back, and one four cm on the right top. We could remove the cysts laparoscopically. The time frame is not urgent. Your biopsy was normal and the sample tissue was benign. We can continue the hormones if you choose, if they're helping you with your symptoms and if you are not bothered by the bleeding."

I responded, "I'm not sure about the procedure you mentioned, Doctor."

"Laparoscopy?" she asked.

"Yes," I replied.

"Laparoscopy is a procedure where two or three tiny incisions are made in your abdomen. Through one of these incisions, air is pumped into the abdomen to allow the space between your skin layer and organ layer to expand, and through the other incision, a telescope-like instrument is inserted that allows one to see inside the abdomen. Through the third incision, instruments can be inserted to remove objects that should not be within the abdomen such as fibroids or cysts. The operation takes between one to two hours, with two hours in recovery," said Dr. Patel.

"You might be out of work for two weeks. I should add that your ovary produces a bag of clear fluid every month. That is a simple cyst called the corpus luteum that would support a pregnancy if you were to conceive. If there is no pregnancy then you get your period and the cyst goes away on its own. Sometimes, though, the cyst can grow or stay around for a couple of months. When the bag is filled with fluids and has solids in it, it is considered complex. Any solid mass has to be examined for the possibility of being cancerous. There are, however, cysts and masses that are benign such as endometriomas, hemorrhagic cysts, and dermoid cysts. It's best that we take a look. Why don't you just think about it?"

"Why not just stop my periods altogether and be done with it?"

"Because you're not menopausal yet. It seems that your periods are normal. Are your symptoms bothering you? Is that why you want to stop your periods altogether?" She continued, "It is not necessary to begin hormone therapy to make them regular or to make them cease altogether. There is another option of low-dose birth control pills to regulate your cycles. I would like to check you again next month with another sono to look at the simple cysts. I expect them to be gone or to be smaller in a month."

"In the meantime, what can I do about night sweats?" I asked.

"There is clonidine, which helps the hot flashes. You take one pill at bedtime and you have to decide whether you want to continue the hormones." She also said, "To be on the safe side, we could also give you a PPD test for TB or tuberculosis. You would come back to have the skin test read in forty-eight to seventy-two hours. Sweats can be a symptom of TB. We want to rule it out."

I was on overload. I did decide not to get the TB test done. I then asked about checking my testosterone level like Gwen had suggested. Dr. Patel thought that was a good idea, too.

On my way out of the clinic, I saw a poster for "Managing Menopause (For Men and Women)" and "Effective Problem Solving for Couples." I thought, *I'll discuss that with Rodney when I get home. Maybe that's just what we need.*

When I got home, I called Gwen to discuss the doctor's visit.

"What do you think?" I asked Gwen.

"If it were a complex cyst, I would recommend it be taken out," Gwen offered. "That could represent a possible malignancy. If it is a simple cyst, it can be watched. Simple cysts go and come all the time. If it were complex, a laparoscopic procedure would be done for removal of the cyst. That would be an outpatient procedure. A laparotomy is an open incision made for removal of the ovary, uterus, or both."

"Oh, I see."

Gwen added, "If women have horrible periods with a lot of pain or bleeding, a low-dose pill is offered. If a woman is menopausal, hormone replacement therapy is offered. The breakthrough bleeding goes away in the first year on hormones. The advantage of hormone therapy is that it helps relieve the symptoms of menopause. Estrogen protects bone density and helps fight osteoporosis. It may also aid in the reduction of heart disease. There is new data that shows estrogen may also protect against the development of Alzheimer's disease. But later associations are not as well studied as the benefits of estrogen to stop hot flashes."

"That's interesting, but I don't like the idea of being on a medication for the rest of my life. I read that even after periods cease naturally, some method of birth control should be used for a year," I said, then sighed.

"The time will fly by," Gwen said. "Remember what I told you about diet and exercise. It helps."

"I'm going to join a health club."

"Good," Gwen commented.

"Hey, are you going to be able to make the book club meeting at Destiny's house?" I asked weakly.

"I plan to."

"Good, I'll see you on Sunday."

My exhausting daydream led to a cat nap.

CAMILLE

21

CAMILLE

Sitting in the hospital, awaiting news on Adriane, brought forth bittersweet memories of hospitals for me. My first year as a teenager was a life-altering experience that is forever etched in my mind and also on my body.

My father grew up in Almeter, Louisiana, during World War II. His father, the medical director of a prominent and revered colored hospital, decided the public school his kids was supposed to attend was inadequate, so he sent my dad and his siblings to prep schools in Massachusetts.

It became a family tradition and now, it was my older sister, Rachel, and my cousin Tanya's turn to go to Richfield Academy in Richfield, Massachusetts. Dad gassed up the motor home and Aunt Joanie, Tanya's mother; my younger brother, Drew; Billy, who worked in my father's garage as a mechanic; Rachel; Tanya; and I set out on the long road trip. My cousin Richard, a lanky twenty-year-old who always wore a broad smile and a floppy, light-brown 'fro, decided at the last minute to go along for the ride since he didn't have anything to do before returning to Emory University for his junior year. After dropping Rachel and Tanya off at school, we turned around and headed back to Chicago. Driving all night, we reached Indiana, southbound, around 6:00 a.m. The sun was just peeking over the horizon and a fine mist from the dew began settling in the atmosphere. Everyone was asleep except for Billy and my father, who were co-pilot and pilot. Aunt Joanie was on the front couch and directly across from her was Drew, scrunched up on one side of the club table and chairs. Richard and I were asleep on the bunk beds at the back of the coach. Suddenly, there was a loud sound of crunching metal and screeching tires on the pavement. The driver of a tractor-trailer heading northbound, who fell asleep at the wheel, swerved into us and smashed into the back end of our motor home. Cabinets flew open; dishes fell out; the stove, which was in the kitchenette located in the middle of the coach, came dislodged; my aunt Joanie was tossed off the couch and onto the floor; and Drew fell off the chair and on top of Aunt Joanie, fracturing her rib. Richard and I were the only ones in the back of the coach, where the brunt of the impact was felt. The front engine of the truck ripped off the back end of the motor home. I had been on the top bunk and was thrown into the mangled engine of the tractor-trailer head first. It seemed like everything was going in slow motion and all I could hear were screams. I smelled gas, saw bright head-lights…and then nothing.

I was knocked unconscious so I don't remember much about what happened at the scene. But I was told it was chaotic. My father was running around frantically trying to find me, in his bare feet amid the broken glass and the smell of burning oil and rubber. He was yelling my name incessantly. "Camille! Answer me!" Aunt Joanie and Drew were struggling to get out through the side door of the coach. Billy was searching through the metal debris for Richard and me when he saw my feet sticking out of the tractor-trailer's engine. He lifted the remnants of our stove that had been pushed into the engine of the tractor-trailer, and pulled me out.

The first thing I remember is waking up in the hospital in

Elkhart, Indiana; dazed, scared, trying to figure out where I was. There was a dull pain in my legs and a throbbing in my head from a concussion. I felt tightness from a thick gauze wrap that went from my wrist to my shoulder. I was experiencing dizziness from the morphine drip and nausea from the smell of Betadine and alcohol. I was hooked up to a maze of beeping monitors with IV tubes in my left arm. My mother, who had not been with us, was at my side. She had been driven from Chicago to the hospital at record-breaking speed by Don, my father's friend, as soon as he was notified about the accident. I remember that she was amazingly calm, probably because of her nursing background, while repeatedly telling me in soothing tones, "Everything is okay, honey. You are doing fine. I am right here with you."

"Where is Dad?" I asked over and over.

She replied, "The doctors are examining him; he strained his neck and has to have a neck brace, but he would not let them touch him until we got you stabilized. He's got a little bump on his head, and cuts on his old rusty feet, but he's just fine."

"What about Drew, Aunt Joanie, Billy, Richard, Rachel, and Tanya?" I asked.

"Don't you remember, baby, you all dropped Rachel and Tanya off at school. They weren't in the motor home. Drew fell on top of Aunt Joanie and broke her rib but she's okay. And Drew is out in the hall waiting to see you. Billy's okay, too. So you stop worrying about everybody and just rest," she demanded softly.

"What did you say happened to Richard?" I asked with my eyes half closed. My mother did not respond.

I had fallen asleep again from all the medication, but when I woke up, the doctor was checking my chart and talking with my mom in hushed tones. The doctor, a gentle-looking, white-haired man, told me that I had suffered third-degree burns on my arm, right side, and back when I was thrown against the hot engine of the tractor-trailer. Drew came into the room and kidded me, "It's about time you woke up; you've been sleeping for days." When I saw my dad for the first time, he looked like a huge marshmallow with his white hospital gown and his white neck brace. He is tall at six-foot-four, with wavy, dark-brown hair and piercing green eyes. He consumes any room with his presence. When he saw me he said, "Hello, Sunshine, how's my girl doing?" No matter how bad I was feeling, a warm sensation came over me when I heard his voice. My eyes welled up and I became flush. I asked, "When am I going home?"

My dad said, "We are going home very soon, baby. You have to go to a hospital in Chicago so we can take care of you."

It was not until a helicopter was transporting me to Cook County Hospital in Chicago along with my uncle John, an internist, that I finally learned what happened to my cousin Richard.

He had been killed instantly when the tractor-trailer ran over him after he was thrown from the motor home. No one had wanted to tell me Richard's fate until I was out of danger of going into shock. I often think about why I survived the accident and Richard didn't, and why winning a silly kid's contest to see who could finish an ice cream cone first is ultimately what saved my life. The last conversation we had was when we'd stopped at a gas station on the way back. We had gotten chocolate-dipped ice cream cones and we were joking around as usual. We argued about who was going to get the top bunk and who was going to get the bottom. We ended it by racing to see who could finish their ice cream cone first, and I won, which meant I got the top. I have repeated this conversation to Richard's mother and sister several times, because they wanted to know what frame of mind he was in before he passed. They were happy to know he was laughing.

I spent the next month in the Cook County Hospital children's ward, which was five minutes from my house. I received excellent treatment from the doctors and nurses, but anyone who has been treated for burns will tell you it is the most painful recovery you can experience. With third-degree burns, you don't feel anything at first because all of the nerves are dead. I had a debridement operation, which simply cleaned the burn sites and left me with raw exposed flesh. The worst part of the treatment was the daily whirlpools where one set of bandages were soaked off and another set of bandages were put on. The drip of water on my raw flesh was excruciating. At first, I thought the nurse was trying to kill me! I was screaming with pain. After the first week, my mom and I had to literally walk every nurse through the quickest way to get me in and out of the tub in order to minimize the pain. Some were more willing to listen than others. There was one elderly Jamaican lady who said, "You do not tell me; I tell you what you will do." We definitely did not get along with her. My family doted over me because they thought they'd nearly lost me. "It's a miracle that you are alive," is all everyone kept saying. That miracle changed my life.

For as long as I could remember I had been in the shadow of my sister, Rachel. She was tall, slim, very athletic, a cheerleader, and Miss Popularity. I was plump and awkward and although I had friends, I was not nearly as popular as Rachel. I thought everything she did was so cool. She always had a boyfriend and was part of the "in crowd." I remember thinking how unfair it was that Rachel could eat anything—ice cream, candy, and cookies— and not gain weight. I, on the other hand, gained weight just by looking at food, which I over ate to ease my loneliness. I remember many a day sitting in the window watching my sister and her friends while I ate peanut butter and applesauce sandwiches with a big glass of whole milk. I was teased a lot by all of my siblings about my weight, but Rachel really knew how to make me feel bad. She would make me do things for her, slave for her, and if I didn't, she would not let me hang with her and her friends. This all changed after the accident. Since Rachel was away at school, this was the first time that I felt people recognized me for myself. I was visited regularly by my brother, James, and my cousin Winston, who constantly made me laugh despite the pain I was in from my burns. My father visited me every night and brought me so much food, like Fannie Mae fudge, cookies, and fruit, that the doctors would make extra rounds to my room to sample some of my goodies. I don't know if my father felt guilty because he was the one driving or whether he just was sad to see me hurt, but he stayed with me every night until I fell asleep. We developed an enviable father-daughter bond, one that I treasure and thank God for every day.

At the end of my stay in the hospital, my mother brought me my old clothes to wear home and I was amazed that they were all too big. I had lost thirty-five pounds without even knowing it and I was thrilled! There was a silver lining to suffering the pain of skin grafts and debridement operations; I went back to high school as a quasi celebrity. Everyone had heard about the accident and wanted to know how I was doing. It was wonderful to see people that I didn't think knew my name come up to speak to me. This was a confidence-building period for me.

At prep school the next year, my relationship with Rachel and Tanya changed, because I felt like their equal. I had an insatiable appetite for sports like swimming and tennis, but little interest in the opposite sex, so I found myself home alone during my junior and senior prom.

College was a different story. I let my hair grow halfway down my back instead of the afro style I wore in high school. And I really tried to keep in shape despite the late-night study binges on pizza and ice cream. My roommate, Tina, was a Snickers junkie and we always had plenty of munchies around. Tina was from New Orleans and was the type of person everyone wanted to hang around. She was smart, funny, loads of fun, and most important, she had the ability to make insecure people feel good about themselves. In fact, one night I got one of her "followers" to type a paper for me by promising her that she could hang out at our apartment! At five foot nine I towered over Tina's five-foot-two frame. And her 34DD bust, after a breast reduction surgery, made my boobs look like mosquito bites. But those measurements didn't stop us from wearing each other's clothes and looking good in them to boot. After growing up with a complex about my appearance, I finally believed, with Tina's help, that everyone has the potential to be beautiful; it's just a matter of the right packaging. And, apparently, I now had the right packaging because I was in one relationship after another.

Wilcott University in Tennessee was a culture shock to me because I had always attended small schools where the majority of students were white, and I'd never heard of fraternities and sororities. At Wilcott, considered the Harvard of the South, fraternities and sororities ruled the campus. In addition, two other black colleges were within the same city boundaries, so it was one big party all the time. I almost flunked out after my first year and did not get serious until my parents threatened to transfer me. I was heavily involved with a Meharry Medical College student so I was spending all of my time off campus. His name was Larry, and he was my first long-term relationship. He was caramel colored, medium height, and had blue eyes with light-brown curly hair. He was a brilliant student who read medical books like novels and came from a family of doctors in Sugarwood, Maryland.

We had a lot in common and he was so smitten with me that I

think I ended up taking him for granted. He would do almost anything I wanted and he definitely could envision us getting married. Despite Larry's unwavering devotion and love for me, I didn't take his proposals seriously. I was crazy about him, but at twenty years old, I wasn't thinking about settling down and being called Mrs., besides the fact that he also smoked a lot of weed. I broke up with him right before his graduation; I did not want to have drama with his family when they all came for the ceremonies. The last time I heard about Larry, he was recovering from a serious drug addiction that nearly destroyed him, his practice, and his family. Larry was a perfect example of my flawed thinking that someone who has the right exterior credentials and is attracted to me should automatically be the object of my desire, without really understanding who they are as a person. Women are conditioned to believe that when a man chooses them, they should be inclined to reciprocate. Instead, women should find out who they are and choose a man that fits their personality.

Growing up, I tried to please my family by making good grades, and playing well in sports. Then it became an issue of what kind of men I dated. They all had to fit this certain package—well educated, great career aspirations, and probably most important, the right appearance. I was superficial enough to not let myself consider any man who was too short, too fat, or too bald, even if they had terrific personalities. I would bend over backward to attract the "cute" guys who were so popular with most women, even if they acted like jerks. I will never forget one of my college classmates, an Italian stud named Kyle who was fine and knew it. He was the starting forward on the varsity basketball team and an honors student. He was tall with thick black hair and an air of confidence that could not be mistaken. I had never dated outside of my race before, but something about him intrigued me. After exchanging glances at various times on campus, he stopped me one day in the cafeteria. He said he had been admiring me for some time but was hesitant to come up and speak because we were, after all, still in the bastion of white conservatism in this elite Southern university. He was from a large Italian family in New York and had dealt with black women before. He seemed very nice, so when he asked me to cook dinner for him one evening, I was receptive.

We decided that Friday evening would be good. I prepared my famous lasagna and a green salad, and after a long perfumed bath, I dressed in my sexiest black leotard and jeans and welcomed him into my recently cleaned, half rummage sale, half Sears–decorated apartment. He was wearing a white polo shirt with jeans that fit him like a glove and had actually bought a bouquet of flowers. He wore the fragrance Quiet Water, which smelled great on him. I was so nervous that after just my first sip of wine, I had to excuse myself to go to the bathroom because my bladder would not hold anything! With dinner there was small talk and jazz playing in the background. I was just starting to relax a little when Kyle said, "Wow, I am really feeling that workout I had at camp today. I could use a massage, would you mind?"

I said sheepishly, "Okay, I can rub your back. Come sit on the couch."

"Wouldn't the bed be more comfortable?" asked Kyle innocently.

I wanted to be mature about the situation and after going to pee once more, I led him into the bedroom and he immediately removed his shirt and plopped on the bed face first. I began to massage his shoulders and neck, then his back. By the time I got to his lower back, he started to loosen his pants to pull them down and I didn't know how to react, so I giggled and said, "You don't need to pull them down. I'm not going any further."

Kyle pulled me down on top of him and started to kiss me. I could tell that he was used to doing this and I thought about telling him to stop, but instead I asked if he wanted anything more to drink and pulled away in an effort to get up. He pulled me toward him again. "I've always been attracted to you and I think you feel the same way about me."

I just giggled some more and tried to think of some clever answer. "I like you, too; that's why I invited you over."

Kyle started to kiss my neck and simultaneously move his hands into the front of my leotard and slip it down on my shoulders. I was not in the habit of going anywhere near this stage on a first date and did not intend to go any further, but I think that due to the combination of too much wine and wanting to seem cool and mature, I was not as in control as I needed to be. I couldn't believe that he was being so forceful, pressing his manhood against me and rubbing my breasts. I was almost fighting with myself. In my head I knew that this was not right, but the hardness of his muscles also felt good and my body was responding. He eventually had his way. I didn't really enjoy the act and felt guilty as soon as it was over. And of course, Kyle immediately jumped up and threw on his clothes while making some excuse about needing to be at practice early in the morning.

A couple of weeks later I missed my period. I began feeling very tired and queasy after eating. I couldn't believe I could be this unlucky. I had thought about having Kyle wear a condom but everything happened so fast. I told Tina what happened and she told me that she had thought she was pregnant by her boyfriend Tyrone once a few months back, and she had been tested and found out she was not. I could only hope this would be my outcome too. Tina went with me to the campus clinic so I could get tested. As soon as I found out that I was pregnant, I knew that

I wanted to terminate the pregnancy. I was twenty years old with my whole life ahead of me, and I certainly was not in love with Kyle so in my mind, there was no question about whether it was the right thing to do. I did not even want Kyle to find out about it, which is why I asked Tina to go with me to the clinic.

The family planning clinic at Wilcott was a pleasant, clean place with very competent counselors, doctors, and nurses. First, I was examined. Then I had to speak with a counselor to make sure that I knew all of the options available to me. The counselor wanted to make sure that I was not being unduly pressured to go through with this procedure. I assured her that was not the case. Once the session was over, I had to sign a bunch of releases and was led to a room where I had to undress and put on a hospital gown. Then I was put in an ambulatory bed and rolled into the surgical operating room. I was transferred to an operating table and directed to put my feet in the stirrups. The doctor and two nurses came into the room and began explaining the whole procedure. I was given a local anesthetic, which allowed me to feel everything the doctor was doing but without pain. I could feel her inserting a rod into my uterus, then I could hear this suction sound. The whole procedure took less than twenty minutes and I was then rolled out to a recovery room where they monitored me while I ate cookies and drank orange juice. I felt cramping and waves of nausea but nothing unbearable. I stayed there for a couple of hours and then, still cramping, I was allowed to leave. Tina was with me in the recovery room and she drove me home. This would be a significant event in Tina's life because she was never able to have children, even after spending thousands of dollars on fertility drugs.

The abortion was my second life-altering experience. I made a promise to myself that I would never again do anything so stupid. It was then, in my junior year of college, that I decided I better get serious about life and my future. I became much more cautious about the men I dated and I did not entertain male guests alone for a very long time. Most of the guys I hung out with after the incident were friends only. Ironically, the bad experience actually helped me to have more successful relationships because they usually began with a foundation of friendship. I immersed myself in my classes and became more involved in school activities like business lectures, theatrical productions, and political debates. My grades improved and I ended up graduating with honors in economics.

Thinking about Adriane back there in Labor and Delivery attempting to bring a new life into the world brought to mind my third life-altering experience. Motherhood. There was a definite contrast in my delivery experiences. With the first child, my first husband, Everett, was there every minute of the fifteen hours, trying to tend to my needs. However, my second pregnancy was especially vivid because I remember calmly discussing, with Everett, our pending separation on the way to the hospital. We had tried several times to resurrect a roller-coaster marriage and this had been one more failed attempt to make it work. I remember going through a very long and lonely twelve hours of labor, during which I walked the hospitals halls alone to deal with the pain while my soon-to-be ex sacked out on the waiting room couch. The most excitement came when the expected six-pound baby girl turned out to be a nine-pound baby boy. I guess this was an affirmation of Everett's masculinity because he immediately began calling everyone in his family to announce his accomplishment. There were large red roses and balloons everywhere once word got out about the birth of our son. Interesting how the birth of a boy commands so much attention, especially from Everett and his "boys."

Of course, our relationship did not start out that way. I met Everett Vance during Christmas vacation in my senior year in college. A group of my friends, home from school, had an annual party the night after Christmas to have a chance to see everyone during the holidays. An old high school buddy, Pam, called to say that she wanted me to meet a friend of hers and asked if she could bring him to the party. I said fine, although I was a little curious since her call came out of the blue. That night, I was having a great time at the party dancing and seeing old friends when Pam came in with Everett, a rookie football player who had just moved to Chicago from Arkansas where he had been a college star. I had no idea about football and had less than a clue about this muscle-bound man with a silk piano scarf draped over a tight sweater, winter white pants, and driving gloves! To top it off, he had enough gold chains to give Mr. T a run for his money. I thought, *this must be a joke; how could anyone think that I would be interested in someone like him?* We talked for a while and to my surprise, he seemed pretty down to earth. He said he had asked Pam to introduce him to me because both my brother and my sister had gone to school near his hometown of Little Rock, Arkansas, and he had heard a lot about me from mutual friends. Plus, when he saw my picture, he thought I was *hot!*

Everett asked me if I would go for a quick spin with him, and although I didn't want to leave the party, I consented because I was a little intrigued. We stepped outside the restaurant and he had his sparkling new, white Mercedes sedan double-parked right at the entrance. I thought, *this guy is full of himself,* but he was funny and we ended up talking while we rode along Lake Shore Drive looking at the Christmas lights.

I said, "How does a country boy end up looking like a player in the big city?"

"I am proud to say I am a country boy. I was raised to honor patience and go after the best life has to offer, which includes women. If you think I am a player, you are wrong. I have seen a lot of places and met a lot of people because of my athletic career, but the one thing that I know for sure is I am not interested in playing emotional games. I am having a great time enjoying the fruits of my hard labor but I would love to find my soul mate eventually."

I thought to myself, *Hmmm, we'll see.* Everett returned me to the party and said he had to go home but wanted to call me, so I said okay. I'm usually very busy with family events when I'm at home and over the next few days, I missed several calls from Everett. When he finally did catch me, he wanted to invite me over for dinner. I was leaving in two days but we made plans for the following night. He picked me up and took me to his apartment in a North Side high-rise. He wanted to prepare dinner, which I thought was a little unusual. As I stepped into his apartment, I could tell immediately that he was proud of his dwelling. It was quite the bachelor pad, complete with breathtaking views, fabulous stereo system, and mood lighting with all kinds of objets d'art and paintings. I wondered how someone just out of college could afford all of this, but I learned that he had been recruited as one the first black running backs for the Chicago Bobcats, with a hefty signing bonus.

Everett's culinary talents impressed me. He prepared beautifully seasoned, herb-baked chicken, fresh corn, and broccoli. He even had one of his mother's famous sweet potato pies imported from Arkansas for dessert. Everett dressed much more conservatively this evening and actually looked very handsome in his black wool slacks and black turtleneck with black alligator loafers. As we talked about school, home, and family, I began to see a much more complex person than my first impression had provided. Everett drove me home and asked if he could call me at school, then he kissed me good-night and I thought I had never kissed anyone with lips that soft and full.

Everett and I spoke once or twice while I was at school, then we lost contact. I was so busy trying to finish school, but I did think about him and thought that I would like to see him again. After graduation I came back to Chicago and went to work for my father. As a graduation present/business trip from my father, my sister, Rachel, and I went to Europe and Africa. My father was doing business with some oil exporters in Lagos, Nigeria, and we were glorified couriers, carrying important papers for him. It was a fascinating trip and I loved all of the countries we visited, including Cameroon, where our great-aunt was the U.S. ambassador for President Jimmy Carter. Rachel and I helped her plan receptions and we visited the local Peace Corps camps. We stayed at the ambassador's residence, which looked like a hotel, complete with pool and tennis courts.

Upon our return to Chicago, I continued working with my father and prepared to take the GMAT for business school. One day I saw Everett's name in the newspaper and wondered how he was doing, although I had started dating someone else. Then, in November, I heard on the news that Everett was in the hospital with a serious football injury. I knew how it felt to be in a hospital, and I remembered how great it was to have friends visit. So I decided to go see Everett. When I got there, some people were already waiting in the lounge to see him and I felt a little silly thinking that I could just mosey on in without interfering or without an invitation. One of the ladies waiting was Everett's "play cousin" Jackie, a cute, short, light-skinned woman with short curly hair. She asked who I was and when she heard my name, she immediately perked up and said, "Everett talked about meeting you. I live in Hyde Park and I know your family." We talked about the people we knew in common and she seemed very nice. She said she would let Everett know I was there. A few minutes later, she came out to tell me that Everett wanted to see me so I went in.

Everett was sitting up in the bed with two nurses tending to the several IV's and monitors that were hooked up to him. A friend of his whom I also knew was sitting in a chair on the other side of the room. The room was filled with flowers, balloons, and cards. There was even a six-foot-long poster with well-wishes from the team hanging on the wall. Everett broke into a big smile as soon as he saw me and I could sense something was different about him. We talked for a while and he explained how even though he had a very serious staph infection and he was going to have to practically learn how to walk again, he had taken this as a sign from God that he was living life too fast and he needed to slow down. This became a kind of bonding experience for us because we had both been through a life-threatening event and wanted to make the most out of our lives as a result.

Everett recovered faster than expected due to his determination and he was back in the starting position for the Bobcats by the end of the season. We started seeing each other throughout his recovery and by January 1980 we'd begun to date exclusively. We were married in June 1982 and divorced in 1991. Marriage to a high-profile athlete is not all parties, shopping, and TV cameras following you everywhere. Everett was a low-key, quiet guy with very expensive tastes. He was known for being the best-dressed teammate down to his Gucci underwear. He also drove the fanciest cars but never wanted to go anywhere! He became more and more involved with the born-again Christian movement after we were married. We attended at least two to three church services per week and he read the Bible every morning from five to seven a.m. His interpretation of the Word meant that he was increasingly restricted in his desired lifestyle. For example, we had beautiful Chinese rugs in our condo but, all of a sudden, the dragons in the design were demonic so we had to get rid of them. He only wanted to see G-rated movies and socialize with other like-minded Christians. Everett grew up in this religion and his mother is particularly devoted so it came naturally to him. But this was not natural for me even though my parents, Drew Sr. and Kathy, raised all five of their children to attend church, it was mostly on holidays. I believe I made an honest attempt to rationalize his beliefs and support Everett's religious persuasion, but I did not understand the restrictions and I was not about to disassociate myself from my family and friends if they did not have the same religious preference. The deal breaker was when Everett informed me one day that he heard a sermon that convinced him to reject oral sex! One of the best aspects of our relationship was our sexual compatibility—he knew what I liked and vice-versa. The elimination of oral sex was not up for debate!

Everett and I had a tumultuous marriage. Part of it was due to the ups and downs of his football career and everything that comes with being a professional athlete, including racism among the players, coaching staff, and the owners; ostracism by some team members if you were having a bad season; all types of drugs; the physical strain on the body; daily competition among peers; and the inability to trust anyone. Everett wasn't a superstar but he had a burning passion to play in and win a Super Bowl; to the point where I believe he tried to bargain with God. He thought if he was a diligent Christian who read the Bible every day and went to church relentlessly, that God would grant his prayer of going to the top of his game. It was not enough that he succeeded to a level of playing pro ball that only one percent of athletes achieve.

When it looked like he was not going be a starter in Chicago, Everett's agent negotiated a deal to move him to Denver, Colorado, to play for a new football organization called the United States Football League (USFL). I will never forget my shock when he announced the deal to move him to Colorado had been signed and he was going to be the highest-paid player ever to move from the NFL to the USFL. It was a multi-million-dollar contract that made sports pages headlines for weeks. When news like that goes public, people assume that millions of dollars just gets deposited into your checking account—similar to lottery winners—and they start lining up for loans. Everett received a salary divided up in payments over a four-year period; and the contract was supposedly guaranteed by an insurance policy paid by the league. We flew into Denver and Everett immediately had to go to camp, which left me responsible for finding a house, moving everything from Chicago, and setting up a new life in a place where neither of us had family or friends.

Arriving in town on the tail of news stories like ours, we found that everyone wanted to be our friend and we had no shortage of people wanting to help us get situated. One of the first people we met was a jovial real estate agent by the name of Willy Barris, a former pro football player who was built like a chocolate fireplug, short and stout with a wide, white grin. It was fun looking at the beautiful homes in Cherry Creek, an upscale neighborhood near Denver University. Everett loved contemporary designs so when we found a new development that was uniquely constructed as a stucco modular design with an open floor plan, including large picture windows and fifteen-foot ceilings, he was ready to move in. There were mini-bars with sinks and refrigerators on every one of the three levels, with a floating bridge between the kitchen and the breakfast room. A travertine marble fireplace separated the master bedroom from the huge master bath. It seemed as though things would work well in Denver and Everett was excited about the team.

Unfortunately, after a great first season, the new league started to have financial problems due to slow TV advertising revenues and some of the smaller-market teams were in trouble. By the end of the second season, the ratings had dropped significantly and the league was forced to dissolve. It was also at this time that I found out I was pregnant with our first child, Jade. Everett had always lived up to his Gemini dual personality but the stress of playing for the troubled team made him more moody and distant. To make matters worse, we found out that Everett's attorney did not follow up with the league to make sure that the premiums were paid on the insurance policy that guaranteed his contract. It lapsed, causing the policy to be cancelled. We went from weekly salary payments of $30,000 to zero in a day! This is when I learned it is easier to accumulate assets than to liquidate to recoup money. We had a house full of expensive furniture, paintings, clothes, and jewels, with a Benz and a Jaguar in the garage, but no cash flow to keep up the lifestyle. Everett had to go back to Chicago to see about trying out for the NFL team again and filing a lawsuit against the USFL for defaulting on his contract. Meanwhile, I was in Denver, pregnant and trying to make the best of a bad situation. I needed reinforcement so I asked my best friend, Michelle, to come and stay with me. We had been friends since high school and we were in each other's weddings, which were within a year of each other. We stayed in touch despite the fact that she lived in Laguna Beach, California. Michelle's visit

really helped me to make it through a rough time. She is an awe-
some cook, her famous fried chicken and biscuits were great
comfort food, and she even went to Lamaze classes with me.

The separation from Everett was taking its toll on our relationship. When we did speak by phone, the conversation was strained.
He kept saying, "You have no idea what I'm going through. You
don't understand." I admit it was hard to be in his shoes but he
made life tough for me because of his inability to communicate.
Then, after a very long year, Everett was finally picked up by the
Los Angeles Waves, and that gave him a fresh start. He wanted
his family back so he tried to woo me. Jade and I moved back to
Chicago and I resumed working for an investment banking firm.
He wrote letters, sent flowers and gifts, and begged me to give
him another chance. I was torn because I was ready to move on
with my life without him, but I also wanted my daughter to have
a father. My sense of family devotion won out and we moved out
to Los Angeles in 1988.

Things were great for another year. And I was happy when I
learned that I was once again pregnant. We lived in a cute townhouse in the beach cities outside Los Angeles, which encouraged
a laid-back lifestyle. We were within walking distance of the
beach and spent a lot of time biking and jogging on the sand.
Everett was still moody but seemed to be trying to communicate
more. We were involved with team Bible studies and it was a
good way to socialize since Everett was still very religious and
did not go to clubs or parties that served alcohol. Our relationship became tense again when problems arose with the current
team. Everett had been the starter until there was a change in
coaches; the new coach decided he wanted to go with another
running back that he had recruited so he arbitrarily made Everett
the backup. The mood swings became greater, and that was

when I found out that he was seeking comfort from another woman, a model named Beverly who worked in Los Angeles. She and Everett had met at a team promotion event. The groupies in Los Angeles were notorious for their aggressiveness and they made it a point to show up at the games and afterward, to greet the guys when they came out of the locker room. I called it the "show after the show" because the women were usually dressed in little short skirts, low-cut tops with fake boobs, weaves, and a ton of makeup. It was easy to tell the wives from the groupies. The players loved the attention from both. I remember Everett asking me one time, during a heated discussion, "Why don't you love me? Everyone else does."

I replied, "Because they don't live with you!"

I believe it to be a prevailing pattern with high-powered men; they want to believe that they can be good husbands and fathers, but they get caught up in the public message that they deserve more. The constant temptation of women throwing themselves at them only reinforces their belief. I never thought women would be an issue with Everett, not because of his loyalty to me, but because of his devotion to God. When I found out that he had violated my trust, I was amazed at the hypocrisy of his actions. We separated again and this time, despite his many attempts to earn forgiveness, I'd had enough.

Even before my divorce, I searched for a way to combine spending time with my children and having a business. That's when I learned how expensive child care was in my area of Southern California. I decided to start my own child care business. I attended UCLA and earned my child care credentials, then began with a small preschool in my neighborhood. I was fortunate to meet some wonderful women who became teachers at the school. Timing is everything; a year after I started the school, I learned that a major aerospace company in the area was interviewing potential directors for their own corporate-sponsored school. I met with a panel of parents and management from the company and must have impressed them because they chose me to head up the first corporate-sponsored child care center in El Segundo, minutes from my quaint beach bungalow in Redondo Beach.

My friend Michelle and I became closer than ever. She helped design and develop the child care center, including accompanying me to a little town in Italy to research the best child care facilities in the world. We incorporated a lot of their ideas and philosophies. The center was so successful that we kept a waiting list. Everett came to visit after I opened the center and he was impressed with how much I had accomplished in a relatively short time. I think it was bittersweet for him because it reinforced the fact that I did not need him to succeed.

As for my social life after Everett, my friends and I did things that were "mommy oriented." But then, once a month, usually on someone's birthday, we would get *fine* and go out to a fancy restaurant or a nightclub and go buck wild, pretending that we had no kids, no husbands, and no boyfriends. One time we went to a very trendy restaurant in Beverly Hills, with red suede cushioned seats in round booths placed close enough for you to see a famous movie star or producer eating lobster tails with drawn butter or angel hair pasta with huge prawns right next to you. We were seated just across from a group of well-dressed, middle-aged blonde women with dark tans, dripping with tasteful jewelry, seemingly waiting for their dates to arrive. They initiated a conversation with my girlfriend, Vicki, who is married to Ramon White, the now-retired pro baseball player and is stunningly beautiful and extremely sociable. The women offered to buy Vicki and our whole table drinks in honor of my birthday.

We thought it was a nice gesture and accepted. The women said they were waiting for the sons of the president of Mexico to arrive. They indicated that they had flown in for the weekend and were out on the town. I thought it was peculiar the way they kept complimenting us on how striking we all were and asking what we did for a living. After offering to pay for our dessert, which we chose from a scrumptious array served on a silver platter, they gave us their cards and asked that we stay in touch with them. The women then turned to welcome their dates, who had just arrived. It was not until we were heading upstairs to the club that we looked at the card and realized they ran an escort service and were trying to recruit us as call girls. This, in addition to the tall, well-built stud muffin who came to our booth to inform me that the maitre d' had sent him over to be my special birthday gift for the evening, made for an interesting night out for our posse.

I was crazy busy with the center and my kids, who both attended the center, so I didn't have time to think about dating, but out of the blue, a great guy came into my life. I met Jake at a UCLA benefit concert where my good friend, Bill Ferry, the R & B singer, was performing along with other artists to benefit a charity. I was running late as usual and had to wait in the lobby until after the first song concluded. To my surprise, a young man came up behind me and whispered, "May I ask a favor of you?"

I turned around to see a tall, caramel-colored young man in his late twenties with the black silky hair and a well-proportioned body. I thought to myself, *I'm waiting in a very nice concert hall at a very swank event, so why not?* I looked into his piercing eyes and said, "It depends upon the favor."

Jake went on to say, "I know you don't know me and this will sound strange, but my friend is the conductor for tonight's performance and he gave me two tickets for myself and a friend, however, she was unable to attend at the last minute and I know he will feel badly that I didn't use both tickets. So...would you mind if I introduce you as my date? It will only take a few minutes of your time."

I just looked at him with my mouth open wide and thought, *This guy has got to be either crazy, or very creative with pickup lines.* I laughed and said, "You are original, I'll give you that!" There was something about the way he looked at me with his light-brown eyes and his extremely long lashes that matched the rest of that silky hair. I found myself saying, "I'll think about it and let you know at intermission." The doors opened and we went to our seats. My friend Linda, Bill's wife, was waiting for me. The concert was wonderful but my thoughts kept wandering back to that strange but intriguing conversation. At intermission I told Linda about my encounter, and of course, she had to meet him to check him out. We went out to the lobby and sure enough, Jake was waiting. I introduced him to Linda and she immediately started questioning him about his background. It turned out that he was a graduate of Northwestern University School of Drama, had toured with Second City performers, and had just returned from Thailand where he had a co-starred in a movie. I informed him that I was also a graduate of Northwestern (business school). We laughed about how we both preferred California sunshine to Chi-town hawk and I even let Jake introduce me as his date to the conductor, who did not suspect a thing.

After a great show, everyone gathered in a reception room in the back of the auditorium, beautifully decorated with a flower garden patio. Champagne and hors d'oeuvres were plentiful. I was with Linda when we greeted Bill, who was already changed into casual clothes and was signing autographs. Then I noticed Jake walking toward me with a big smile. At the same time, Bill saw

Jake and said loudly, "Jake Mallet, long time no see. How are you?"

Jake went over to Bill and warmly shook hands. "Hey man, great show as always, and I see you keep great company as well."

Bill looked at him and then at me. "Oh, so you've met Camille. I know you appreciate quality when you see it."

Jake said, "I certainly do!" Then he turned to me. "I would like to buy you that drink, if you will allow me." I laughed as he led me out to the patio, which was filled with fragrant flowers. We slipped into a conversation about relationships and remained talking for over an hour. I was amazed at how easily I opened up to him. I guess it was because of the way he seemed to intuitively feel things that I was feeling, like his guess that I had been in a long relationship and had been hurt. He also had gone through his share of busted romances, especially out in LaLa Land with all of the superficial actress types he ran into and swore not to ever date again. I knew that it was getting late and I had to go so Jake just politely kissed me on the cheek and asked if he could call me. The encounter grew into a two-year romance that I refer to as my transitional period. With Jake's constant encouragement and support, I grew from having no self-esteem and feeling totally inadequate about my ability to have a successful relationship, to a confident, fun-loving, self-fulfilled woman. I moved to a new place, ran two businesses, and had a ball doing the most spontaneous, crazy things with Jake at my side, like the time we took off on a weekend trip to San Diego and went parasailing, dined by the ocean, and made love by candlelight on the balcony of our hotel suite.

Jake helped me get over Everett by being everything Everett wasn't. He communicated well and was always ready to go out to jazz and comedy clubs, and of course, all variety of movies. Jake was five years younger than I but very mature and knowledgeable on many subjects. He was well traveled because of all the movie locations and he loved to cook and experiment with food, wine, and ways to surprise me. The only reason that Jake and I broke up was that he was offered a series that took him to Canada for three years. We tried to make it work for a few months of long-distance dating, but I had learned early on what long separations could do to relationships. We agreed it was better to be friends, but I still think of him as the one that got away.

One year later, I went through one of the most stressful and exciting periods of my life. It started with a whirlwind, multi-city relationship that resulted in a wonderfully romantic proposal on a midnight boat ride along the Seine River in Paris and then my marriage to Eric Nobles. The backstory begins with my visit to a psychic. I used to visit a well-known psychic when I lived in Los Angeles. I was scheduled to take a business trip to D.C. and she told me that I would meet two men at the same time and in the same room. Prophetically, I arrived at the conference and on the second day, I was in the hotel lobby, a grand, luxurious room with several cozy conversation areas, speaking to some friends. One of them introduced me to Mark Hines, an aerospace engineer, also from California. We had an instant attraction and went out to dinner the next evening. On the other side of the room was Eric Nobles, a political appointee who lived in D.C. but was on his way to Russia for a business trip. He came over to meet me at the suggestion of my brother, who went to school with him. There was also an attraction with Eric but it was more intense because I was intrigued that my brother, who never introduced me to anyone, would all of a sudden arrange this meeting. I later found out that Eric had seen me at a reception and asked my brother to set it up. Since Eric was leaving the next day, we spent most of the day together, talking over a delicious lunch of Spanish tapas and walking down Connecticut Avenue on a beautiful, warm fall day.

Although I had a great dinner date the next night with Mark, I was still thinking about Eric. So ultimately I selected Eric to be my significant other. The fact that he could travel so much worked well for our relationship. He would send for me to meet him in different cities and then he would come to Los Angeles for meetings. The rendezvous were wonderfully romantic and I believed that I had finally met someone whom I could depend on.

After the engagement, the drama came with moving my two kids from Los Angeles to D.C., selling my business to an angel-turned-asshole ex-partner, selling my house, as well as planning a three-city coordinated wedding. It was a pleasure telling Everett about my pending marriage since he was arrogant enough to believe that the kids and I would always be at his beck and call and ten minutes away whenever he felt like visiting. The shock on his face when I told him first about the wedding was clear, but when I told him we were moving across the country, he became visibly ill.

Eric introduced me to tons of people in D.C., which was great because, despite the fact that I have a huge family clan here, I needed my own network of friends. Gwen Nichols actually lived in the same building as Eric when we were dating. Gwen and Eric were good friends and several times when I was visiting him, we would get together with Gwen and her boyfriend, Sloan. Once I moved to D.C., Gwen became my OB/GYN. She asked me if I was interested in meeting some of her friends. She suggested that I come to this book club she was starting and I agreed to come.

The women I met at the book club were a great group of professional black women. All of the women were grounded and funny as hell. This circle was a good fit. I felt at home here because the women reminded me of the friends I left behind in Los Angeles. One big difference was my friends in Los Angeles had kids and the ladies here did not. Once I got settled in D.C., I started hanging out with all of the ladies in the book club, but I still was a mom, and I had a lot of responsibilities, especially since my kids were transitioning to a whole new world as well. Gwen, Natalie, and I joined a tennis league and played in matches every Saturday. I ran with Gwen often because she was training for the Marine Corps marathon. I took long weekend trips with the ladies whenever I could arrange for a babysitter, and Brianna and I took hand dancing lessons, because I found out that hand dancing is the dance of choice in D.C. and I was still doing the hustle, Los Angeles's dance of choice.

People are considered fortunate if they have two or three close friends as they go through life, the kind that you know that you can depend upon under any circumstances. The rest of the people you meet fall under the category of associates or acquaintances. I count myself as extremely fortunate because I seem to find true friends in most of the cities I live in. And Gwen, Adriane, Natalie, Allana, Brianna, and Destiny would prove to be no exception. From the start of our friendship they accepted me for who I was. Just like a family does.

22

CAMILLE

It was 7:30 p.m. and I would need to leave the hospital soon to pick up the kids from my friend Jennifer's house. She has two kids the same ages as Jade and Tyler (seven and ten years old) so we swap babysitting. Being the only mom in our book club made my time management skills essential and perhaps more in demand than the others fully understood. I told Jennifer I would return around six, but called to explain the situation once I arrived at the hospital. She said, "The kids are fine. They are playing Monopoly with Jason and Marsha. Take your time," was her response. Time—seems like there is never enough time in a day!

Even when it was my turn to host the book club meeting I was running late. As usual, I had a million things to do all at once. Jade had a basketball game for which she told me if she was late one more time the coach would not play her, and I was supposed to drop Tyler off at a playmate's house. I had yet to fix the refreshments. Plus it was the first book club meeting of the year, and I was supposed to type up a schedule so that we could list the books we selected to read and the hostesses for the next twelve months. The only thing I had managed to do was finish the book, which I didn't do until 4:30 a.m.

The book was called *Erotique Noire/Black Erotica*, edited by Miriam Decosta-Willis, Reginald Martin, and Roseann P. Bell.

It was a steamy collection of works, the writing was so beautiful, yet the images and emotions it conjured up were titillating. The sexual aspect of a relationship becomes so minor in comparison to the concept of trust, respect, and friendship. I realized this notion all of a sudden one morning when I was lying in bed wondering how much longer I could live in an unfulfilling situation. My marriage to Eric had become a nightmare. He turned out to be so different from the image that he had represented to me and my kids when we were dating. He decided after one year and three months that he preferred being by himself and that the responsibilities of having not only a wife but also two kids was too much for him to handle. Eric thought that kids should be "seen but not heard" and expected them to behave perfectly. In addition, he wanted to continue the spontaneous getaway trips that we'd taken before marriage. I don't understand men who think they have given up everything just because they gave up their bachelorhood. Eric was forty years old when we met and he confessed that he had never met anyone to whom he could relate to on so many different levels. He claimed to love independent women, however, after the wedding he turned into this possessive, controlling person who did not want me to be around men personally or professionally. It was almost like a Dr. Jekyll and Mr. Hyde situation.

From that point on, my whole focus was on getting out of the mess I was in. The separation and divorce were not complicated. I just wanted to be free. I did not want anything from him. Jade and Tyler were happy to see me acting normal again. We moved into our own house and I set up my life as a single parent once more. I was glad the kids were adjusting because I certainly had to bring them kicking and screaming from the comfort of their home in California. They loved the California lifestyle and Jade especially was in awe of her dad. She was just beginning to understand the perks of having a quasi-celebrity for a father, like when her friends wanted autographs and always wanted to come to our house to play. I put them both in therapy just to help with any potential separation anxiety from Everett and Eric.

After the divorce from Eric, I continued working as a vice-president in the private bank of a major financial institution. Because of my position, I was obligated to attend social functions like dinners and sporting events and theater, and I met several successful business people, some of whom became good friends. I thought another man would be the last thing I would have in my life, but the opposite was true.

His name was Marshall Wren. Marshall was a furniture retailer and designer. Besides being a millionaire by his fortieth birthday, Marshall was also an avid sailor and had invested in his own racing sailboat that he and his crew race in various competitions around the area. Marshall is tall, about six-foot-two, and very striking with jet-black hair, chocolate coloring, and hazel eyes. He walked with an air of confidence that makes most people at least notice, if not admire, him. A native of Trinidad, Marshall spoke in a deep bass voice with a subtle British accent that cut right through me the first time I heard it on the telephone. Just as Jake provided the spark I needed after the breakup of my first marriage, Marshall helped to make me feel whole after my second divorce. Eric, my second husband, who seemed too good to be true, was just that—a dud.

My faith in romance was renewed when I flew to Chicago the weekend after our January book club meeting, with the kids, for my brother Drew's, birthday. The same weekend, Drew was going to surprise his longtime girlfriend Sabrina. Drew had recently accepted a fabulous job offer, which would relocate him to

California from Chicago. Although he had been close to popping the question to Sabrina for some time, I guess he decided this was the right weekend. He called me a couple of weeks prior to tell me about his surprise and needed my help. He instructed me to wire funds for him to New York to a jeweler friend. His plan was to be carried out during a wonderful dinner in the exclusive Carlton Club restaurant in Chicago. My other brother, James, who was known as a ladies' man but was really a sweetheart, organized a small dinner party where Sabrina and I joined Drew and another friend of James, whose name is Gail, under the auspices of celebrating Gail's birthday. For dessert, the waiters brought out Gail's birthday cake while we sang "Happy Birthday." As Gail was opening her birthday cards, she suddenly looked puzzled at one of them. She said to Sabrina, "I think this one is for you." As Sabrina opened the card and started reading it, her face went from confusion to delight as she read aloud, "Will you marry me?" At the same time, Drew stood up, went over to Sabrina, knelt down in front of her and presented her with a black box. She opened it and screamed! It was a four-carat, princess-cut diamond in a platinum setting to set off the brilliance. I knew it would be stunning but I was amazed. Then we were off to a two-story suite Drew had reserved at the Suisse Hotel, one of my favorites in Chicago. It had a panoramic view of the lakefront and there were huge bouquets of roses and buckets of champagne for the celebration. Drew and I even planned for my parents to join us on their way back from an affair they attended that evening. They were as surprised as Sabrina about the announcement, but they were thrilled because they loved Sabrina, and we spent the wee hours of the night toasting and laughing.

Back in D.C., I was looking forward to seeing Marshall and I was happy when he called to arrange a dinner meeting. Marshall was referred to me by a mutual lawyer friend and was interested in having a business line of credit established with the bank. Since I was selected as the bank's point person for clients who were affluent minority professionals, it was a natural fit for us to meet. He was wearing a beautifully tailored blue suit and a yellow power tie with a white five-point handkerchief like politicians and newscasters wear. We made plans to meet at Morton's for dinner, and it was such a beautiful summer evening that we sat out on the patio and ordered wine with delicious appetizers. We had that spark of chemistry that sends an underlying air of excitement to even the most mundane of conversational subjects. The conversation flowed very well and we found ourselves going off on tangents like personal interests, sports, restaurants, and hobbies. When Marshall mentioned his passion for sailing, I thought, *now there is something you don't hear every day, and wouldn't that be something nice to do.* We spent hours talking and when I finally had to leave to get home to the kids, Marshall walked me to my car and, like the perfect gentleman he is, kissed my hand and asked if we might see each other again soon. I invited Marshall to join me for lunch in the bank's elegantly appointed dining room on the ninth floor with gorgeous views of Washington landmarks. There we continued our discussion about banking and everything else. I found myself laughing out loud at some of the stories Marshall shared about his boating experiences and the places he had journeyed to. After a delicious lunch of lobster bisque and Dover sole with a fresh grape sauce, Marshall asked me if I would care to go for a sail sometime. I found myself ignoring my standing rule to not date clients and said, "Perhaps I can allow some time in my schedule," trying to contain the eagerness I felt to jump at this invitation.

"Oh, by the way, Marshall, I have a friend who has developed a beautiful line of furniture and furniture designs. Do you think you would be interested in meeting her?"

"I'm always interested in new ideas and new things to invest in. Why don't you arrange for me to meet with her," Marshall said.

I called Destiny at work and shared with her the interest Marshall had expressed. She responded like I told her she had just won the lottery. She was so excited. She wanted to immediately go home and work on her designs. Destiny had really done her homework and had even filed for an intellectual properties patent application to protect her interests. She had been following the furniture design market and was in tune with the trend toward refinishing wood pieces with an antiquing treatment that went perfectly with the new "Shabby Chic" designs.

Soon after our conversation, Destiny and I met with Marshall at his office in Georgetown. Destiny brought a couple of her pieces and her design portfolio. Marshall looked at everything for several minutes without a word. He touched the furniture, inspected the details, and looked at every page in the portfolio. Finally he looked at us and said, "I have seen several applications to treat furniture and I have seen many furniture designs, but my educated opinion is that you have a million-dollar baby in your midst!" He went on to say that he would be willing to set up an exhibit to showcase pieces of the furniture in his showroom. He also said that he would invest the money to have the sketches drawn for the exhibit. Marshall hit his intercom button and asked Val to come into his office. "Destiny and Camille, this is Val. She is my partner in crime," Marshall said. "She will manage this project."

While Destiny and I exchanged pleasantries with Val, Marshall walked over to his office kitchen and took out a bottle of Tattinger champagne that he said he kept on hand for special clients. He felt that this was an occasion worth celebrating and wanted to toast to our success. Destiny and I looked at each other in disbelief. She had dreamed about this happening but had dared not assume that it would catch on and make such an impact, especially with someone like Marshall who knew so much about the business. I became numb with exhilaration; I could not take it all in so I started laughing. After Val and Destiny set up a meeting to discuss Destiny's business plan, Destiny left, gibbering about all of the things she had to get together and smiling from ear to ear. I turned to Marshall to thank him for the wonderful meeting. Marshall took my extended hand to shake it and held on while he said, "Would you be able to find time in your schedule this weekend for a trip to Annapolis?"

I smiled. "I think so."

We planned to meet on Saturday morning at 10:00 a.m. at the pier on the Potomac where Marshall's boat was docked. Marshall told me he was going to invite our mutual lawyer friend Ken and his fiancée, Paula. It was a warm Labor Day weekend and I knew that this would be a perfect place to watch the fireworks as well as get away from the crowds. Marshall was pulling up the cushion fenders on the boat when I walked up. He was wearing a black T-shirt with a design from one of the new trendy restaurants on the waterfront along with red swim trunks and gym shoes. I couldn't help but notice how toned his legs and arms were, and his tan that made his whole body look bronzed. Ken and Paula arrived and I quickly learned that I was the only novice in the bunch.

Ken and Marshall had grown up together and had been life-guards on the beaches of Trinidad. Ken was also an excellent cook and was the self-appointed ship chef. Paula had been coming out for sails since she met Ken three years ago and loved it almost as much as the guys. We all helped out with the preparations to set sail and Ken brought enough groceries to feed an army. He and Paula are vegetarians but Ken could create fabulous meals where you would not even miss the meat. Marshall had a favorite wine stocked on the boat, and as soon as we set sail he pulled the cork and we sipped wine while listening to Michael Franks and Jon Lucien on the CD player, and watching the pier get farther away. We had a lively conversation about a mixture of topics, from world events to relationships in the black professional world to the best jokes ever heard.

The breeze was just right for the sails to carry us at a brisk pace, and with a few instructions from our captain I was able to take the helm and steer the boat for a while. It was such a gorgeous night and the Labor Day fireworks going off in various places all along the harbor made it seem almost magical. I thought to myself, *It's no wonder how the seductive reputation of men and their boats came about.* I felt so far removed from reality that I thought I was free to do anything I wanted, and Marshall was just the person I wanted to do it with. He was strong yet gentle, sensitive yet funny, and the way that we were able to communicate with such ease made me realize what a struggle it had been to relate to many of the men that I had been out with since the breakup of my second marriage. As we continued to talk we made subtle moves toward each other; first sitting across from each other, then side by side, then touching each other with light taps and then brushing against each other. It was like a dance and Ken and Paula couldn't help but notice the chemistry heating up between us. They continued to talk with us but then excused themselves to go up to the stern side of the boat to watch the fireworks, leaving us alone.

It was then that Marshall turned around, looked at me, and said, "Do you mind if I do something I have been wanting to do since the first moment I saw you?" I smiled, and he leaned over to kiss me, just lightly with several small pecks first, but when he saw that I was responding, he became more passionate, letting his tongue gently touch my lips, then my tongue, until we were in a full embrace. He felt so wonderful when he wrapped his arms around me that I think I audibly swooned in satisfaction. We continued to talk but now there were kisses and hugs in between every sentence. His voice became a whisper as he went on to tell me how attracted he had been to me from the beginning, and how he couldn't help but think about what he would like to do with me if he had the opportunity. He was definitely smooth and I began to think that he could only be this good if he had plenty of practice.

So I inquired, "How many other women have you brought out on this boat recently? I would hate to believe that I'm just the flavor of the month."

Marshall laughed. "I know it seems like I'm coming on very fast but I promise you it is just because I think you are not only gorgeous but you are very smart. I love your wit, and I can't keep my hands off of you! Yes, I admit that there have been other women out on this boat but I'm usually just into being friends and having a good time as an entertaining host. I have not reacted to anyone in a very long time the way I am reacting to you."

"Maybe I want to believe you because I know the same is true for me. After everything I had been through in the past with my failed relationships, I feel as though there is no point in playing games and not being honest about the way I feel." We kissed in a wild embrace and sat holding each other saying sweet nothings until Marshall had to prepare to dock the boat in Annapolis. Ken helped him to dock and then went to work in the kitchen preparing dinner. I was amazed when forty-five minutes later he emerged with a scrumptious salad topped with artichoke hearts, avocado, and a delicious Caesar dressing, followed by tortellini pasta smothered in a rich classico tomato sauce with broccoli and fresh shaved romano cheese. For dessert we had fresh blueberries soaked in Grand Marnier covered with whipped cream. Maybe it was the mood and the wine but we were all a little giddy. Ken shot a little whipped cream at Marshall which led to Marshall retaliating with his own flick of cream right in Ken's face. When I laughed Ken decided to come back with a shot of cream to my cheek. What ensued was a chase around the boat and Ken and Marshall being pushed overboard into the chilled harbor water. Paula and I were laughing so hard that we were doubled over on the deck. The guys climbed back onboard to dry off with our waiting towels.

Marshall and I went downstairs to the master bedroom so that he could take a shower. He took off his shirt and shorts and replaced them with a dry pair of black shorts that made him look so handsome, I was getting a little excited. I think that he picked up on my vibe because he came over to where I was sitting on the bed and leaned over to kiss me while gently guiding me to lie back on the bed. I allowed myself to be guided and invited him to lie with me while we explored each other, kissing, licking, and touching in all of the most erotic places. Marshall suddenly stopped and said, "I hope you know what you are doing to me. I am so excited that I am about to explode, however, I don't want you to think that I will not control myself. I will not let anything happen that we both don't want to happen."

I thought, this is a great form of reverse psychology that men use to let women know that it will be their decision to go further so that women feel safe. Although my body was telling me that I could easily enjoy every minute of an intimate sexual act, I felt that things were moving a little too fast and that it would be premature to go further. Instead we enjoyed holding each other until we fell asleep.

I was up first thing in the morning with a surprisingly clear head for the amount of liquor that I had consumed the night before. I went up top to the deck while Marshall lay in a deep sleep. It was such a beautiful morning that I decided to go exploring the surrounding area of Annapolis. I found the showers that were for the boaters and quickly bathed and brushed my teeth, which felt like sawdust since I had missed my normal routine of brushing right before bed. I walked around and browsed at some of the antique shops and restaurants in this quaint little neighborhood and by the time I returned, Ken and Paula were up and Ken was already preparing a breakfast of bagels and scrambled eggs with tomatoes, onions and jalapeno cheese. Marshall was just stirring from his bed and I went in to say good morning. He saw me, rubbing his eyes to get adjusted to the light, and said, "Hello, beautiful, I missed you, where have you been?" I told him of my activities and he was glad that I had enjoyed the town. He smiled at me. "I want to kiss you but I don't dare until I get rid of this dragon breath." Then he hopped up and went to find the showers.

We had Ken's delicious breakfast and pulled out of the harbor to return home. The whole trip back was filled with listening to oldies but goodies on the CD and laughing and talking while we baked in the morning sun. Marshall came over to sit with me on the deck and handed me a box. I looked inside and saw a little gold sailboat charm. I was so surprised, I said, "When did you get this?"

"I picked it up when I went past a little shop on the way to the showers." I gave him a big hug and a kiss. "I just wanted you to have something to remember this trip," Marshall replied. I melted.

As we returned to the dock on the Potomac, I felt a little melancholy to see this special time together ending. I hated the fact that I had to come back to the reality of my hectic life with all of my responsibilities.

I called Destiny to tell her about my wonderful weekend. I had to tell someone so that I could relive it out loud. She was thrilled to hear about our union and said that she had sensed an attraction between us. For the next few months Marshall and I enjoyed many wonderful days and weekends together when our schedules permitted; going to movies, fabulous restaurants, bank functions that I conveniently invited him to as my "client," and cozy evenings at his home. These evenings were like my spa treatment—where else could I go and have a bubbly Jacuzzi with champagne and flowers followed by a heavenly massage and a gourmet dinner prepared by a fabulous man?

Thinking about my wonderful weekends with Marshall made my mind drift back to the January book club meeting at my house. I'd finally completed my tasks with moments to spare when the ladies had arrived. The *Black Erotica* book club meeting was full of exciting discussion and a natural digression into some of our own past sexual experiences. One of the enjoyable aspects of our group discussions is that we feel so comfortable with each other that even more intimate details are not held back. The short stories that *Black Erotica* offered were very relevant to our own experiences. The touching stories of young love, the excitement of first encounters, and the intrigue of alternative sexual lifestyles got our conversation flowing. I commented on my experiences with Everett and Gwen shared the story of one of her many romantic evenings with Sloan. Destiny, who is usually quiet when it comes to personal matters, even told us what products to buy for a soothing bubble bath with your mate. Brianna mentioned an occasion she'd shared with her ex-fiancé; while the experience was a tender one, it only heightened the pain she felt when that relationship ended. Love can be this fantastic ride, full of excitement and thrills. However, it can turn into a nightmare that is hard to recuperate from. Prior to hearing about her unfortunate experience, Brianna had impressed me as someone who would plan the perfect Martha Stewart wedding after a storybook romance and probably be pregnant within one year of marriage. Though Brianna has a wild side too.

Some of her explicit escapades surfaced when we discussed *Topping from Below* by Laura Reese. The author was unknown to me and the rest of the book club members. This sadomastic murder mystery made our book club list due to a referral and I'm glad it did. Ms. Reese spiced up my life and kept me turning the pages and indulging in some masturbation until the wee hours of the morning. Although the book contained some kinky stuff, it was really about the lives of two sisters, one of whom was mysteriously killed. It struck me as odd that one sister would have such low self-esteem and the other sister thought the world of herself. But then I thought of my relationships with various women in my life, and how we all seem to suffer from a disease I call "anorexia of the mind." This is the condition of seeing yourself totally differently from the real world perception.

After the book club meeting was over, Destiny stayed for a while to help me to clean up. I poured us glasses of wine and we began talking about Destiny's Designs. I went over the budget that she had given me and I figured out how much in initial financing she would need. I knew that Marshall was going to guarantee the loan, but to have it be in the name of Destiny's Designs would give Destiny a financial track record. Things were going great with Marshall and Destiny was crazy busy.

Marshall had been a perfect gentleman the whole time I had

spent with him. He is the kind of guy who lives in strict adherence to his principles because they are the most important things in life to him, or so he says. Consideration of others is among those principles. He is careful never to impose on anyone and his caring manner is obvious in everything he does, like calling to leave me a voice mail every morning so I would have a pleasant thought to start my day, or sending flowers for no special reason. Sometimes I think he should have been alive in the Middle Ages when things were done simply and elegantly, like scented, monogrammed notes written with ink-filled pens in long, fluid, poetic lines. I often found love notes hidden in my purse or left in my car to remind me of his feelings for me. Besides being a successful businessman, Marshall is athletic, a nature lover, and tremendously spiritual. He keeps a picture of his grandmother, along with those of his children, in a place of prominence in the house because he believes that they all communicate spiritually. Marshall is truly one of a kind! Did I mention he could cook too? For my fortieth birthday—you know, the one where you start to question your level of desirability and youth—Marshall invited me to spend a very special long weekend in his country home. I met him at his house, a five-acre estate in Antioch County, Maryland, where we had a mouth-watering dinner of rack of lamb with sautéed spinach and champagne. Then he led me upstairs where I was met with a vision of flowers, balloons, and a stack of presents wrapped with beautiful ribbons. I was speechless. The gifts included a butter-soft Coach bag, wonderful perfumes, and lovely silk pajamas from Victoria's Secret. And this was only the beginning of a magical birthday celebration.

Marshall expressed his desire to have a dinner party for ten or twelve of our friends, as a kind of "coming-out" party for the two of us. We decided on the Saturday before Thanksgiving. I invited

Gwen and Sloan, Allana and Rodney, and Destiny and her friend. Marshall invited two couples. We planned a beautiful affair, complete with petite printed menus, appetizers, and a main course of lamb roast in wine sauce, bass stuffed with shrimp and crab, mushroom risotto, and a dessert selection of pumpkin cheesecake and caramel flan. Everyone got along great and Allana commented that it seemed as though Marshall and I had been married for years. After dinner it was brandy and cigars and an impromptu *Soul Train* line when Marshall cranked up the seventies Motown hits on the stereo. When the inevitable slow dance came on, Marshall whispered to me, "Come on, I want to hold you close and not let go. You were a wonderful hostess tonight."

I responded, "I think we make a great team."

DESTINY

23

DESTINY

I felt like a fish out of water sitting in the waiting room of the hospital. My past experiences had not primed me for the rhythmic beeping sounds, disinfectant smells, and the ticking of the large, round black-and-white clock. Since I was born, my family and I never required the services of an emergency room or hospital. There were no broken bones, no stitches, and no serious illnesses. And I have no recollection of visiting anyone in the hospital as a child or as an adult. I guess my lack of exposure to the world of medicine is why I'm so squeamish when it comes to hospitals, doctors, and blood. The closest I get to the medical profession is my annual checkup with my primary care physician, my dental visit twice a year, and my annual gynecological exam. I believe I inherited my medical phobias from my mom. She despised hypochondriacs. So she didn't believe in running to the doctor for any- and everything. That is, until she was diagnosed with hypertension. Now she's visiting some doctor or alternative medicine specialist every other month.

I peeped at Allana and Camille from the corner of my eye and observed the two of them napping. Even though they looked uncomfortable with their heads and necks slumped over the arm of the sofa their presence projected peace. I liked what I saw—friends, willing to go the distance. I couldn't help thinking I had Allana to credit for my position between her and Camille on the lightly stuffed sofa in the family's waiting room of the maternity ward. I finished my Pepsi and put the empty can on the end of the coffee table, rested the back of my head on the wall, closed my eyes, and joined my friends in a nap.

24

DESTINY

A couple of years ago, Allana called me to talk about a
book club she was joining. She didn't ask me to join. She
casually spoke about how nice it would be to network
with some positive sisters and enhance the mind with diverse literature. I remember the conversation well. Allana, in her worldly
accent, said, "Destiny, my girlfriend Gwen is starting a book club.
Membership entails reading one book a month and meeting every
fourth Sunday to discuss it. I know how much you enjoy reading
so I told her you might be interested. Doesn't the book club
sound like a great idea?" she asked.

"Yes, Allana, it does. I heard some women at work talking about
their book club just the other day. I was going to inquire about
it but I got busy. I would love to join a book club, especially a
book club that you are in, if you are asking." I laughed.

"Good, I'll call Gwen and tell her you are a yes," Allana replied,
delighted.

"Call me with the details," I said before ending the call. It wasn't
like my Franklin Planner was overflowing with things to do,
places to go, or people to see. Besides, I thought it would be nice
to meet some new people and discuss books we read. Allana was
right. I like to read. Always have. I'm a surface reader though. I
read the words and I take the author's journey, but I don't really
personalize the contents. I have worked at not taking things per-

sonally. That is my learned persona, which has truly been a safe-guard, a shield, and my saving grace over the last thirty-seven years.

Thirty-seven years on this planet Earth and life ain't been half-bad. Matter of fact, life's been pretty damn good. Not perfect, mind you. I don't display the beauty of Halle Berry, nor do I strut the body of Angela Bassett. Quite the contrary. My mane is not long enough, not short enough, the wrong texture, not curly enough, not straight enough, always talked about, too thick, too nappy, too short, too long, too damaged, too brittle, definitely not the preferred head of hair. But, if I may say so, I am always dressed for the part. It's my hair that's always auditioning.

My facial features are not unique or chiseled like an African sculpture. And since I don't have any Chinese or Native American in my family tree, I don't have slanted eyes or high cheeks. My eyes are not blue, green, or gray and I don't have dimples. How-ever, I have a beautiful set of pearly whites that complement my brown complexion.

Some of my body parts are under reconstruction, the other ones I can live with. That slightly flabby area that is called the stomach or waistline is being gruelingly exercised into the shape of a not-so-flat pancake. And my gluteus maximus is being challenged to soar from no man's land to paradise. On a scale from one to ten, (with one being the lowest), some people might rate my appear-ance as a 4.5. Because compared to the video queens, the rich and famous, and the Hollywood wannabes, I'm your average-looking Jane, not Kanesha. However, I would rate myself a 5.5. And I am sure I could step up a notch on the scale if I had my hair and nails done once a week, routine facials, pedicures, massages, ate nutri-tionally, and acquired the services of a professional weight trainer three times a week. All of which sounds so luxurious and self-rewarding. But I am sort of cheap when it comes to stuff like that.

I honestly don't want to spend hundreds of dollars a week on improving a look that's not half bad.

As careers would go, I consider myself semi-successful. My six-digit salary from an international consulting firm would not qualify me for a write-up in *Fortune* magazine, but it allows me to live comfortably. The Ph.D. that I received from Duke is really paying off. "You get all the education you can get, baby girl, 'cause can't nobody take it away from you" is what my mama used to say. I thank my mama every day for those words of wisdom. I also thank the good Lord too, for allowing me the opportunity to work so that the bank can't take anything away from me. Especially the 4,000-square-foot, three-level villa that I purchased five years ago in a picturesque area in Mitchellville, Maryland, and the 1994 white-on-white, Mercedes-Benz 500SL that I purchased last year. The Dreamer—that's what I call her because she's my dream car. I use my black SAAB to kick around town in. Never have materialistic things called out my name as did the Dreamer and my home. Well, that's not totally true. There were those Chanel suits that I had to have, and of course that chocolate-brown, cashmere Valentino coat that I bought from Neiman Marcus. But the villa and the Mercedes are different. It's like they were made for me.

I bought the Dreamer from a woman who was a delegate for the World Bank. She had accepted a new position and was being sent on a one-way trip to South America. This meant she was anxious to get rid of many of her worldly possessions, and I was looking forward to relieving her of one of them. Arranging a meeting with her to look at the car was challenging because she was trying to wrap up her personal and professional affairs. But we eventually stopped playing phone tag and she provided me with a time and an address. Her house in Washington, D.C., was as she had described it; a cream-colored Tudor-style house with colonial blue shutters and a well-manicured lawn right off Foxhall Road. Every house in this high-rent district had a real estate value of well over a million dollars and hers was no exception. When I arrived, she had the car brought over by a man who worked at the garage where it was stored. Her description of the car was not exaggerated; it was in pristine condition. The mileage was low and the engine was sound according to my mechanic, who gave it a seal of approval before I gave her the check. We didn't really haggle over the price because I had done my homework. Matter of fact, I think I got a pretty good deal because I told her I wanted to think about it for a couple of days, which caused her to lower the price because she wanted me to make a decision right on the spot. So I did. The Dreamer only had 7,000 miles on it when I brought it home. And now it has 9,500. She is as sweet as vanilla ice cream and as gentle as a man who has just reached an orgasm. She also attaches herself to a curve, at 80 mph, like a baby clings to its mother's breast at feeding time. My dream is now a reality for thirty-six payments of $1,650.66. She looks real fine backed into the garage of the villa.

It was the fourth Sunday in May. I lounged in the sitting room of my bedroom, watching *Made in America* with Whoopi Goldberg and Ted Danson on HBO while trying to decide between two outfits that I pulled from my cedar walk-in closet. Should I wear the ankle-length, black knit dress with black mules or the wheat-colored, two-piece linen pantsuit with brown mules? It was my first book club meeting and I wanted to make an impression as well as be impressed. I did not want to appear overdressed. So I picked the linen pantsuit and brown mules. I accessorized the outfit with two-carat diamond stud earrings, a three-carat diamond tennis bracelet, and my new eighteen-carat-gold Omega watch.

Natalie was the host that month, and Allana picked me up an hour early so we arrived at Natalie's house before the scheduled

1:00 p.m. meeting time. I was introduced to Natalie and then to Adriane, Gwen, and Brianna, who arrived shortly after us. I was introduced to Camille when she arrived about twenty minutes later. The women, of different heights, weights, skin complexions, ethnicity, cultures, religions, and educational backgrounds greeted me and each other warmly. While feasting on the refreshments that were provided by the host, everyone participated in dialogue about current events, books, authors, the theater, and hobbies. We also participated in a little gossip. The book club meeting was called to order by the host.

"So, ladies, what did you think about Bebe Moore Campbell's book *Brothers and Sisters*?" Natalie asked. After a brief outburst caused by everyone trying to express their opinions at the same time, Natalie took control of the meeting and returned it to an organized state. The exchange of dialogue and comments about the book, the book's characters, and about personal experiences that related to the book were funny, enlightening, and thought provoking. Like a therapist, I did not provide much input; I participated by listening. Two hours later, we had completed our discussion of the book, devoured all the food, selected a book and a host for our next meeting, and said our farewells.

Driving home, Allana asked me what I thought about the book club meeting. My reply to her was, "Cool." In fact, it was better than cool. All of the women were nice, especially Camille. For some reason I was able to relate to a lot of her comments even though Adriane was more vocal. I was certainly looking forward to our next meeting, although I did not tell Allana that. I remember thinking how the women presented themselves so impressively. But first impressions can be deceiving. I'm living proof of that. Most people perceive me as having it all together. What a joke! I am soul searching like the next person, looking for something that is more than a day-to-day existence.

25

DESTINY

It was finally my turn to host the book club meeting. I was looking forward to having the ladies over. My work schedule rarely afforded me the opportunity to entertain. For once everybody was on time, so we started the meeting right at 2:00 p.m. I opened the meeting and Allana jumped right in. I guess you could say the book, *In Search of Satisfaction* by J. California Cooper, inspired her.

"Josephus' decision to bring Yinyang with him was dangerous and selfish. I know my father would not have exposed me to the unknown. My father would have taken his chances and left me where I was. Besides, Yinyang's life could have turned out differently if Josephus had left her in Yoville with Master and her mother, Mistress Krupt."

"Allana, are you saying Josephus should have left his daughter with drunks? Furthermore, are you saying if your father was in the same predicament he would have left you with drunks?" Natalie asked.

"I know Master and Mistress Krupt were drunks, Natalie, and I know the living conditions weren't perfect, but Josephus subjected his daughter to mental and physical cruelty when they took up residence in Virginia."

After flipping through the pages of the book, Gwen exclaimed, "All of this happened around 1890, right? Well, former slaves did not have many choices. The most important thing back then was keeping the family together."

"I know," Allana said. "But if he'd left Yinyang behind maybe—"

"Key word," Camille interrupted, "'maybe.' Maybe Master Krupt would have raped her because she was his wife's bastard, or maybe the mistress would have enslaved her or kicked her out of the house, causing her to be homeless in Yoville."

"Homeless? They didn't have homeless people back then," Allana said. And with that comment the book club members laughed hysterically. Looking back on it now I realize it was easier for me to laugh with the group than to share my personal opinion of Josephus.

I've never known a father-daughter relationship. According to society's standards, I am the product of a fatherless home. However, I'm not a statistic. I was not raised on the welfare system. I have never committed a crime. I did not drop out of school and I don't have a house full of babies. Unfortunately, I have been in several dysfunctional relationships. These may or may not be attributed to a common psychological theory that having a missing or silent father has a negative impact on the ability to maintain loving and sexually fulfilling adult relationships.

I remember filling out my first job application. I was fourteen years old. It was the first time I was asked to identify my father. Name, address, telephone number, age, employer, deceased. I didn't want to leave the lines blank because that would suggest that I was a bastard. And I didn't have the heart to declare a man dead that I so desperately wanted to be a part of my life. So I did the only thing I could have done. I put N/A. Twenty-three years later and I'm still filling out forms. Not only are the forms asking for my father's name but they are also asking for his medical history and the medical history of his parents, my grandparents. Needless to say, my responses to the questions are still N/A. Sometimes I think it would have been simpler to have labeled him dead years ago—as simple as it was for him to give me life and turn his back on me.

From age six to sixteen, I used to wonder if my father knew that his desertion made me feel rejected, ugly, and confused. And I used to wonder if he could sense that I hated and loved him all in the same breath. God I hated him. I hated him for making me fend for myself at such a young age. And I hated him even more for making me want a daddy so badly that I accepted the attention given to me by a great-uncle.

My great-uncle never bought me anything or took me anywhere, but he was always nice and he always had a smile for me. And he always made me feel like I was pretty. We even had our own little secret. My mother used to drop me off at her aunt and uncle's house every morning before she went to work. My great-aunt was usually the one to receive me at the door. Because it was so early in the morning she would put me back to bed and then return to bed herself. My bed was a little pallet on the living room floor. I don't remember whether my pallet was comfortable but I do remember that the apartment was very dark. I wasn't used to the dark because my mother kept a light on in the hallway so I could find my way to the bathroom at night. I also remember a faint ticking sound. I believe it came from the red, green, and black clock that hung on the living room wall over the component set. Maybe the sound of the clock and the darkness of the room prevented my great-aunt from hearing and seeing my great-uncle and me act out our little secret. She probably didn't hear us because my great-uncle whispered. He said no one must ever know our little secret because people would think I was a bad and nasty little girl. I don't recall the incident happening more than a couple of times because my mother quickly changed the babysitting arrangement. I wonder if she knew. My great-uncle died seven years ago but our secret lives within me.

I also hated my father for making me wonder if the people I met day to day or saw on the street were my kinfolk. Especially when I started dating. I used to drill every guy I met about his family. The guys probably thought I was crazy, nosy, or working for the FBI. One guy was so annoyed with all of my questions that he hung up on me right in the middle of the conversation. But that didn't discourage me. I continued the drill. I even added one or two new questions each year. After all, I didn't want to have sex with my brother, uncle, or first cousin, nor did I want to have sex with my father because I had no objections to dating older men.

I hated my father even more for making a wisher out of me. When I was in my late twenties, every Sunday I would sit beside the same elderly gentleman in church. He appeared to have the makings of a good father and grandfather. He was about five-foot-seven and had a head full of white hair. His demeanor seemed very serene and his attire would have been very chic in the early sixties. I believed him to be a man of God because he showed genuine concern for members of the congregation, including me. Therefore, it was easy for me to wish. When holding that man's hand while reciting a prayer, I would pretend he was my dad. A dad that would have picked me up when I fell, comforted me when I was sick, corrected my shortcomings, and embraced me for my accomplishments. A real dad. That is my wish for all children. As the years passed and my experiences and wisdom grew, I stopped wishing and hating. I just lived.

One day two years ago, I was thinking about the yard work that needed to be done and my plans for the long weekend instead of giving my full attention to the prospectus I was editing. I was also listening to the sounds coming from my Sony AM/FM/TV radio. Normally I don't pay any attention to what's on the TV radio because I use the sound as background noise. But on this particular day I found the sounds to be very interesting so I shut the door to my office and turned up the volume. From what I could gather, since I had not tuned in from the beginning, a guest on one of the talk shows had donated his sperm to a sperm bank when he was in college to earn extra money. Now, twenty years later, the offspring from the sperm wanted to meet his biological father. However, the sperm donor believed that the offspring did not have the right to invade his privacy and life. The topic of conversation struck a nerve. I immediately called my mother to ask her if she was watching the talk show.

Of course she was. She'd recently retired and was fast becoming a talk show junkie. My mother and I discussed the show for nearly ten minutes before I announced to her that I had a good mind to contact my father and ask him for my back child support. She laughed and told me where I could probably find him. Even though I didn't know my father I've always known his name and his whereabouts. But neither my mother nor I ever bothered him. My mother used to say some things are best left alone. Mom was right on the money about where to find my father, because I was able to track him down with one phone call. Imagine that, thirty-some years, and he was only a phone call away. I left a message.

A few days later, at 11:37 a.m. to be exact, I answered my business phone with my most professional voice—"Destiny Davis."

The caller asked, "Is this Destiny?"

"Yes it is," I said.

"This is Nathan Long. I'm returning your call," he said.

I don't know what a heart attack feels like but my heart was beating so fast that I thought it was going to jump out of my chest. Sweat began to develop around my nose and underarms and my hands were as clammy as a raw oyster. I was so nervous and shocked that he'd returned my call that I didn't know what to say. So I blurted out that I wasn't sure if I had the right person, but before I could finish my sentence, he said you have the right person. I nearly passed out. I remember thinking—so this is the voice of my father.

We talked for approximately forty-five minutes. Not a lot of time to cover childhood, puberty, young adulthood, and womanhood. But it was enough time to assure him that my mother had provided a wonderful life for me. I also made it clear that the call had no hidden agendas. I was not in need of money, a kidney, or vengeance. The last fifteen minutes of the conversation belonged to my father. He told me that his parents had died years ago, mainly from old age. I was sorry to hear that my grandparents were deceased but it was a blessing to hear that their medical history did not include cancer, high blood pressure, or other genetic disorders. He also told me about his wife of thirty years, their three sons, and grandchildren. And last, but not least, he made a genuine effort to justify why he had not been a part of my life. The tears in my eyes and the emotions running through my head must have distorted my ability to hear all of what he was saying. However, I distinctly heard him say that he never told a living soul about me, nor did he wish to play "To Tell the Truth" at this point in his life. Consequently, there would be no homecoming for me. Father dearest touched my heart when he said that he remembered the date and year I was born. "March 11, 1960," he said. I said, "close but no cigar. I was born on the tenth of March." That long-awaited telephone conversation ended with no maybes or promises. But I thought, hoped, and prayed that he would honor me with a follow-up phone call or a birthday card. I have not heard from Mr. Nathan Long since. At least I know I am my father's daughter, because we both know how to keep a secret.

A few hours had passed and we were just getting around to rating *In Search of Satisfaction*. We had exhausted the discussion of all the characters in the book and the book as a whole, ate all the food I prepared, and discussed several television shows that recently aired.

"The book was very detailed and emotional. I'll give it a 2.0," Camille said.

Natalie asked, "What about you, Allana?"

"Well, I don't think Josephus did the right thing, so you guys know I didn't like him. Nevertheless, J. California Cooper did a fantastic job depicting the characters in the book. I give it a 2.0 also."

"I'll give it a 1.5. It's the best book we've read this year," Natalie said.

"I agree," Gwen said. "The book was one of our better reads. Cooper wrote *In Search of Satisfaction* very passionately. I give it a 1.5."

"One-point-five is my rating too. Even though I cried through most of the book," Brianna said.

Gwen turned to me. "We haven't heard much from our host. What are you doing over there, Destiny, daydreaming?"

"No, I was thinking and formulating my opinion of the book. Cooper painstakingly depicted a family situation in the turn of the century that is very prevalent today. Her recounting of the pain and suffering and loneliness resulting from the dysfunctional family is classic. It's like if you are a member of a dysfunctional family, as were most of the characters in the book, you are doomed before you get started due to preconditions. And the preconditions make it challenging to attain and maintain any level of satisfaction. The book was well written. I'll give it a 1.5 also."

"Well, Adriane, that leaves you. I know you didn't get a chance to finish the book but that never stops you from having a comment." Natalie laughed.

"The little bit I read was depressing as hell. Can we pick up the pace with next month's book?" Adriane whined.

As the ladies prepared to leave, they stood chatting in the open foyer under the spiral wood and black wrought-iron staircase. "Destiny, your home is absolutely beautiful," they said almost in chorus.

"Thank you," I responded as we stepped onto the brick porch.

I take great pride in my home so I was pleased to hear that the ladies liked my efforts. Simply put, I love furniture. While in college, my girlfriends were buying expensive sweaters and designer jeans. I, on the other hand, was purchasing fine furnishings, one piece at a time. My first purchase was a French pine armoire. It took me almost a year to get it out of layaway. Then I bought 1910 French chairs, Chinese plant stands, antique gilded mirrors, a small settee, and the list goes on and on. Decades of shopping set the stage for my formal and informal décor with mixed styles and textures. I like dark and light together so pink, white, and hunter green were chosen for the color scheme throughout the house. All of the upholstered pieces are made up in pink or hunter green toiles, tapestry, cotton damask, and taffeta, except in the family room where I used pink and green suede and leather with some animal print. None of the rooms required much furniture because I had the builder put in architectural designs like built-in bookcases and entertainment units, one-foot ceiling and floor molding, window seats, a fireplace in the kitchen and master bedroom, and arched doorways. I painted the walls salmon-pink and the trimming antique white, installed white plantation shutters, and adorned the walnut hardwood floors with hand-painted sisal and oriental rugs. Then I personalized the rooms with my accent tables and chairs and spotlighted original oil paintings by Bernard Stanley Hoyes and Shona sculpture in serpentine stone by Moses Masaya. My decorating venture is complete except for my bedroom. I'm in the midst of sketching designs for a headboard and nightstands.

Camille and Adriane stayed behind to talk. "Girl, I can't believe you decorated this house yourself. And I definitely can't believe you created the finishes on most of your furniture. You missed your calling, girl. I mean, this stuff is tight. You could probably make millions," Adriane said.

"Yeah, right," I replied, as I led Adriane and Camille to my workshop in the garage to show them one of my latest creations.

"Destiny, you have a little furniture gallery in here. Is this chair for sale?" Adriane asked.

"No, Adriane, that chair is for my bedroom," I replied.

"Well, after you finish yours, make me one," Adriane exclaimed.

"Are these finishes traditional or contemporary?" Camille asked.

"A little of both. The colors are somewhat contemporary, but the antiquing is traditional," I said.

"When do you have time to do all of this?" Adriane piped in.

"Well, if I'm not at work, school, or reading the book club selection, or turning the pages of some interior magazine, or book, or browsing antique and furniture galleries, I'm in the garage. I watch a lot of interior decorating programs on television. Norm is my man."

"Who in the hell is Norm?" Adriane asked.

"Norm Abram, Adriane. Even I know that," Camille said. "Why don't you open up your own business?"

"My own business! Girl, I'm not ready to have my own business. A few years ago I applied for a job at a design center and I sought out positions decorating model homes, but neither one of them materialized because I didn't have work experience or a degree in interior design. Nor did I know anyone in the industry. So I started doing my own thing," I replied.

"Well, your own thing is going on. I want to know when you are going to do my chair?" screamed Adriane from the other side of the garage.

"I'll hook you up for your birthday," I yelled back.

"Destiny, I have a client, a very handsome client I might add, who designs furniture as well as owns a furniture gallery in Georgetown. Maybe I can arrange for you to meet him," Camille commented.

"Do you really think he would be interested in my work, Camille?"

"It's worth a try. I'll mention it to him the next time he comes into the office," Camille said.

"Thanks, Camille," I replied.

"No thanks required, Destiny. When you are rich and famous, just show me the money, girlfriend."

"All I want is my chair and make my cushion black," Adriane demanded.

26

DESTINY

Camille arranged for me to meet with her client, Marshall Wren. The meeting went even better than expected. A partnership was formed immediately. Marshall agreed to invest in my designs and finishes and Camille agreed to handle all of the banking and financing details. After approximately nine months of meetings with Marshall and his assistant Val, buyers, and attorneys and lots of late nights in the garage perfecting my furniture finishes, my dream was going to become a reality. In less than three months Destiny's Designs was going to be featured in fine furniture galleries in Washington, D.C., Manhattan, New York, and Los Angeles. Marshall's brilliant and creative team had orchestrated all the prep work. Photographs of Destiny's Designs were placed in *Architectural Digest*, *Veranda*, and *Metropolitan Home*. Announcements introducing the new line of furniture had been distributed to everybody who's anybody in the furniture and design business, and a private reception had been arranged in New York. Val also arranged for me to interview with an editor of the *Washington Post*'s Home section. I didn't know how I was ever going to repay Marshall for giving me a chance to show my designs to the world. I guessed his percentage of any sales would be sufficient. But what about my girl Camille? Without her, none of this would be happening. To thank her for introducing me to Marshall and encouraging me every step of the way, I named one of the collections *Camille* in her honor.

I recall the day I presented the *Camille* brochure to her. It was at a book club meeting hosted by Brianna. I made the announcement right after we had finished discussing and rating *Native Son* by Richard Wright, and just before my second helping of spring rolls and pancit, a rice noodle dish served with vegetables and meat. Camille was honored beyond words. She must have thanked me a million times. I was happy I'd made her happy. Since her divorce from Eric, she'd been a little preoccupied.

About two years ago, Camille and Eric hosted the best Christmas party I had ever attended. Dressed in a Santa suit, Eric showered the kids and Camille with all kinds of gifts. One gift in particular made every woman in the house squeal with delight—a ten-karat, emerald-cut diamond tennis bracelet. I couldn't help thinking how lucky Camille was. She had everything. A beautiful petite mansion in Potomac, Maryland, overlooking the Potomac River; a booming career that afforded her the opportunity to meet prominent people and wine and dine in restaurants and hotels that I read about in *Gourmet* magazine, two beautiful kids, and a loving husband. Driving home from the party I wondered how Camille got to walk down the aisle twice, first with some jock and then with Eric. Matter of fact, how does any woman get a man, especially a black man, to give up bachelorhood and say "I do"?

Back in the day when my girlfriends and I thought a husband, 2.5 children, a house with a two-car garage, a Mercedes station wagon, and a minivan were required to determine our self worth, we couldn't buy a husband. I mean we tried everything. Well, almost everything. A few of the girls tried shacking up. Some cried pregnant and some actually got pregnant. One or two of us gave the old ultimatum, piss or get off the pot. And all of us were guilty of playing mind games and being manipulative.

When I was twenty-five, Janet, my best friend at the time, finally reeled one in. She was engaged. With my assistance we planned a storybook church wedding. It was the highlight of our year. We went out every weekend for a month until she found the perfect wedding gown. The gown was made out of silk and satin and scattered with sequins. Small pearls outlined the V-shaped neckline and four-inch rear slit. The matching tiara veil was done up in sequins and pearls. As her maid of honor, I purchased a bronze tea-length dress with sequins and small pearls. It was the companion to her gown. The next five months were spent buying accessories for our wedding attire; picking out tuxedoes for Renaldon, the groom, and Sam, the best man; selecting a reception location; choosing a wedding cake; photographer; florist; musicians, for the church; and a band for the reception. Two months before the wedding date all we had left to do was address and mail out the invitations and wait on the big day. Like so many first-time wedding planners, I was so caught up in the moment that I didn't stop to think, or better yet, ask Janet why Renaldon wasn't helping her make the decisions about the wedding. I guess I thought he was allowing the bride to make all of the arrangements, which is typical. "Just tell me the place and the time and I'll be there" is usually the attitude of most men.

The evening of the rehearsal, everything was going according to plan. The catered rehearsal dinner was being set up in the church hall. The florist had placed four flower arrangements that contained white roses and baby's breath with white and bronze sequin ribbons on the altar. And the pastor was arranging white candles in the candelabra while awaiting the rest of the bridal party. I was folding programs and Sam was reading the newspaper. Janet was busy entertaining her parents, grandmother, and Renaldon's parents. The rehearsal time was 6:00 p.m. At 7:30 p.m. we decided to start the rehearsal dinner while waiting for Renaldon.

At 8:30 p.m. the pastor said he had to leave but not to worry; he could conduct the ceremony tomorrow without practice. By 10:00 p.m. everyone had gone except Janet and me. Janet was speechless and Renaldon was a no-show.

The morning of the wedding I called Janet to see if she had heard from Renaldon. She had not. But she said the wedding was still on. Again, everything was going according to plan. Over two hundred guests had arrived, the musicians were playing the love songs we picked out, the pastor and Sam were waiting for Renaldon in his office, and Janet and I waited in the limousine for our signal. After a two-hour delay, we had to admit that Renaldon was not coming to his own wedding. Janet's father apologetically announced that the wedding was cancelled and insisted that everyone join him and his family at the hotel for cocktails and dinner.

Janet had the limousine driver take us back to her apartment. We changed into jeans and T-shirts, put Anita Baker on the CD player, and cursed all men for a couple of hours. When night fell, we turned Anita Baker off and sat in silence. The only sound was Janet's moans. Then sleep. Around noon on Sunday I went home. I called Janet at 5:00 p.m. Sunday evening and did not get an answer. I called her every couple of hours for the next two days and still did not get a response. I called her parents to see if she was there or to find out if they had heard from her. Janet's mother appeared worried but indicated that she probably needed some time. On the third day, I drove over to Janet's apartment. I had been knocking on the door for about ten minutes before the neighbor next door came out of her apartment and said, "Sweetie, I saw Janet leave yesterday morning with two or three suitcases. Looks like she was going on some kind of trip or something." That was twelve years ago.

I had not had a best friend since Janet. During the first few months of her disappearance I must have called her twice a day to tell or ask her something. In the beginning I got a recording telling me the number was disconnected. And later I was apologizing for dialing the wrong number. Not having Janet around was like not breathing because we were as close as our next breath. She was part of me and I was part of her and it had been that way since first grade. We had time, tears, and laughter invested in our friendship. We were nothing less than sisters. That's why it was so difficult to forgive her for the anguish she caused her parents and me when she took off without a word. Not knowing whether she was dead or alive ate at our hearts. Whenever my mind was tranquil—at home, work, in the car, under the hair dryer—I could see and hear Janet so vividly. She was such a character, which made it easy to reminisce. My memories always ended with tears. Sometimes I cried until I ached. I always expected to hear from her. I checked my answering machine all day long while at work and stayed at home as much as possible. Once a month I had Sunday dinner with Janet's parents. It was our way of holding on to our relationship with each other and holding on to Janet. Although we agreed not to discuss her we would talk about what we would say to her when she returned or called. But she never did either. After a year, the detective working on Janet's case filed her folder away and Janet's parents and I halfheartedly moved on with our lives.

I bumped into Renaldon several years ago, ironically, at a coworker's wedding reception and I tried to avoid him like the plague. Eventually he cornered me and I was forced to converse. After the exchange of pleasantries, Renaldon apologized for his disappearing act. He said he never meant to hurt Janet. He also swore on his mother's life that he never asked Janet to marry him. Renaldon insisted that Janet knew he never wanted to get married. Even though I hated him for what he did to Janet, I could see the sincerity in his eyes. I was convinced that he was telling the truth. And he confirmed that when he introduced me to his partner of thirteen years, Paul.

Because of Janet's and Camille's experiences with marriage and men, I am taking Patrick, my significant other, at face value. I met Patrick at an estate sale in Alexandria, Virginia, several years ago. He was neither pleasant nor polite. Actually he was arrogant and rude. Oddly enough, the chemistry was most definitely there for me so I gave him my number when he asked. My first impression of Patrick was that he did not posses the physical attributes that I thought I was attracted to. Supporting two hundred and twenty buffed pounds, and standing at six feet three inches tall, he was too much man for my small frame, I thought. He was also darker than any guy I have ever dated. His skin tone has the richness of mahogany and his almond-shaped eyes are even darker. Contrasting the darkness is a set of beautiful white teeth, a devilish half smile, and a deep dimple. After several months of dating I reached the conclusion that Patrick is all bark and no bite. He is a true gentleman. Patrick has most of the qualities I hold in high regard. He is sensitive, playful, intellectual, well read, and not afraid to communicate and articulate his feelings to me. We make quite a pair. We both enjoy long walks in the park, hot baths together, skiing in Colorado, candlelight dinners for two, and dancing in the nude when drunk. We also like to shop and watch old black-and-white flicks. Sounds too good to be true? He is. I think he is committed to the relationship; he's just not interested in sharing his last name. In other words, he does not want a wife or children, and said so on our fourth date. Since it was the fourth date and I was not certain if there was going to be a fifth, I did not explore his comment. I think it was for the best because I'm having the time of my life with Patrick.

Once, when Patrick and I were sharing intimate fantasies, I told him I used to wonder what it would be like to make out in the back seat of a car. "Like they used to do in the old movies," I told him. Several months later, Patrick invited me over to his place for dinner and to plan our upcoming trip. When I got there he was still in the kitchen mixing up something.

"Do you need some help?" I inquired from the family room.

"No, I'm almost finished," he said. Five minutes later Patrick surfaced from the kitchen saying, "I have a surprise for you."

"Oh yeah, what is it?" I remember asking.

"Follow me." I followed Patrick to his garage. He opened the door and said, "Welcome to Patrick's Drive-In. Tonight we have a double feature." We both stepped into the garage and he led me to the back door of his car. "Get in," he said. I got in the car and immediately saw a bottle of champagne, glasses, and strawberries on the other seat. After my eyes were fully adjusted to the darkness, I also saw an old reel-to-reel movie projector and a large white screen through the front windshield. Patrick turned the movie projector on and slid in the backseat with me, carefully lifting the champagne, glasses and strawberries.

"What is this?" I asked.

"Your fantasy," he said.

Halfway through the 1962 movie *The Music Man*, featuring Robert Preston and Shirley Jones, foreplay got the best of us. My shirt was fully undone exposing my hardened nipples and my pants were tossed somewhere in the front seat. With his pants down near his ankles, Patrick gently guided my body up and down on his hardness in slow circular movements. The tight quarters and the excitement we both felt intensified our lovemaking, and ultimately our explosion.

After a long hot shower together, Patrick and I discussed our upcoming fourteen-day trip to East and South Africa over grilled shell steak with lime, grilled red potatoes, red cabbage coleslaw with jalapeno vinaigrette, and a California merlot. Looking over travel brochures and some Dorling Kindersley travel guides, we decided to tour the city of George, Cape Town, Zimbabwe, and Victoria Falls, then fly to Kenya for game viewing in Amboseli National Park, Samburu National Reserve, and the world famous Masai Mara. I can't wait to take this excursion in the fall. I need a vacation badly. The last time I had some days off, Brianna and I went to St. Croix, Virgin Islands. The accommodations at the Buccaneer were luxurious. We spent our mornings sunbathing and shopping, our afternoons at the spa, and our evenings eating beans and rice, callaloo, and mahi-mahi, and partying at the Parrot Perch and Pier 69.

Camille and I left the book club meeting at Brianna's house to meet Marshall for drinks at Heart and Soul Café on Pennsylvania Avenue. For Camille the evening was undoubtedly about pleasure and an opportunity to show off her *Camille* brochure. But for me the evening was business as usual. Marshall never missed an opportunity to discuss business details. That's probably why he is a millionaire. After a few drinks, I noticed Camille and Marshall talking romantically with their eyes. It was apparent that they enjoyed each other's company. I also noticed that her spirits were high whenever she was in Marshall's company. I knew Camille would not remain out of sorts long because she is a vivacious and resourceful woman. She is also drop-dead gorgeous. Camille is the type of person who will see to it that life treats her fine. Hopefully, life is treating my old friend Janet fine too.

27

DESTINY

I had never been this busy. Juggling work, Destiny's Designs, and life was overwhelming. But I was able to maintain the pace with some serious time management. I worked eight hours a day, five days a week to pay the mortgage. I went to school two nights a week to obtain a degree in interior design so I could apply for membership in the American Society of Interior Designers (ASID). And I worked evenings and all day Saturday on Destiny's Designs to fulfill a dream. I spent Saturday nights and Sundays with Patrick and I read the book club book under the dryer, in the tub, on trains and airplanes, or before bed every night. One of the book club selections was *Tumbling* by Diane McKinney-Whetstone. As Adriane would say, that book was slamming. I think it was one of the best books I'd read since becoming a member of the book club. I couldn't wait to discuss it with the ladies. *Tumbling* was so good, I couldn't put it down. I read it in two days. Thinking back on it now, Allana was probably perturbed with me because I tried to discuss some of the book with her before she had a chance to finish it. I was overzealous. I even called Brianna under the guise of going over final plans for Adriane's baby shower in hopes of discussing some of the book. If I recall correctly she had not purchased the book yet. I was not surprised though, because Brianna, Gwen, and Adriane were always the last to read the book. Adriane did not finish most of the books she started. However, she always finished the books she recommended or those for the meetings she hosted.

At the last book club meeting hosted by Adriane she gave us a tour of the baby's room. She was so proud of her creation. On one wall of the room Adriane painted a Disney Baby mural. The background color was royal blue and Mickey and Minnie Mouse and Pluto were painted in royal blue, green, brown, red, black, and purple. The adjacent walls were painted eggshell white. Adriane installed a royal blue chair rail on those walls to give the room depth and hung sixteen-by-twenty-foot Disney animation portraits on the walls. The maple wood crib was dressed in a Disney character comforter and a royal blue and yellow-striped bed skirt and bumper pad. A maple armoire was placed across from the bed with a matching nightstand beside it. Adriane and I found the pieces at a furniture store that was going out of business. Adriane haggled the prices down to nothing. She made window treatments, a diaper stacker, and other matching accessories out of royal blue and yellow-striped companion sheets.

I didn't see a rocking chair in the room so for her baby shower gift, I designed one using all of the colors in the mural. I told Natalie about my gift so she purchased a white iron floor lamp with a blue shade to place beside the rocking chair. Everybody was so excited about Adriane's pregnancy and the baby shower because it was the book club's first baby. We were already veterans at weddings, divorces, and on-again, off-again relationships.

I remember well the day that Adriane announced her pregnancy. I should have known something was up because she had been glowing for months. Matter of fact, she had been glowing since she proclaimed at one of the book club meetings that her hubby, Tim, was the primary rock of her foundation, her best friend, and the love of her life. I knew in my heart that Adriane and Tim were going to be wonderful parents, like the parents in *Tumbling*. Maybe that's why I liked the book so much. I didn't see Noon and Herbie, two of the main characters in the book; I saw Adriane and Tim.

In one of my many telephone conversations with Adriane she was telling me about her research on Montessori schools in New Columbus. I said, "The baby ain't even here yet and you are already trying to send him to school."

Adriane replied with authority, "Girl, you got to get started early. Most good schools have a waiting list."

"But Adriane, suppose the school loses its reputation for quality over the next couple of years. All your research will be in vain."

"Well, I'll cross that bridge when and if it comes," she shouted. We both laughed. "My actions may be a little premature, but my baby's going to be smart. You hear me, Miss Destiny? I'm going to give him the best that my money, energy, and love can provide," Adriane said with commitment.

"I know that's right, Miss Adriane. Not to change the subject, but did you finish reading *Tumbling*?" I asked.

Adriane responded in her scolding voice, "Destiny Davis, I am not discussing the book with you until Sunday."

"I just want to ask you one thing, Adriane," I said.

"Good-bye," Adriane said and hung up the phone.

I was glad Adriane got me off the phone because I had lost track of time. I had an interview with Ms. Remmington at the *Washington Post* in two hours. I was okay on time because I had my hair and nails done the day before, my clothes were laid out, and I didn't have far to drive to meet her. Neither Ms. Remmington nor Val, who set up the interview, said anything about photographs, but I was prepared nonetheless.

I arrived at The Savoy restaurant thirty minutes before our meeting time. I went in and was told that Ms. Remmington had not yet arrived. So I went straight to the women's restroom to touch up my hair and lips. When I returned to the lobby the young waitress said, "I can show you to your table." I followed her to a "Reserved" table. "Can I get you anything to drink?" she asked as I sat down.

I said, "No, thank you." While waiting for Ms. Remmington, I felt a little twitch in my stomach. I was getting nervous about my first interview. I really didn't know what to expect because she had not sent an advance copy of the questions as was requested by Val. I took a couple of deep breaths and concentrated on the tasks that were on my "To Do" list. After looking over my list, I raised my eyes to scan my dim surroundings. The décor is nice. And the original art strategically placed throughout the restaurant made quite a statement. I was told the food here was to die for, especially the fried chicken livers with spiced garlic and the Cajun pan-fried catfish with roasted cream corn, shaved onion crisps, and mixed greens. I thought I'd order that. Moments after I returned my eyes to my list of things to do, I was interrupted.

"Hi, are you Destiny Davis?" Ms. Remmington asked.

"Yes, I am," I replied.

"I hope you haven't been waiting long; my previous appointment took longer than I expected. Have you ordered yet?" she asked.

"No, I haven't, I thought I would wait for you."

"Well, I'm here and I'm famished, so let's order something to eat." Ms. Remmington, or Kathy, as I was directed to call her, did not look like she sounded over the telephone. Her voice was very deep, but she was short and thin. During lunch Kathy and I spoke as if we were old pals. We talked about the movie *Titanic* with Leonardo DiCaprio and Kate Winslet, careers, and my childhood.

I think I started out by telling Kathy that I am an only child, but I grew up with my older twin cousins Trey and Travis. Their mother, my mother's sister, died in a car accident when they were eight years old, so Mama adopted them. The four of us lived in a brick, ranch-style home in Fort Washington, Maryland. Like the other kids in the neighborhood, the twins and I attended private school, took piano lessons every Saturday morning, went to Sunday school and church on Sunday mornings, and played every sport we were interested in. Oh, and let me not forget about our chores. We had lots of chores because Mama was always busy. As a high school principal she was responsible for the school's budget, curriculum, personnel issues, and the daily operation. Mama assigned me the task of cleaning the interior of the house and Trey and Travis were charged with maintaining the yard, washing the Volvo station wagon, and taking out the trash. I used to rush through my work so that I could get out in the yard with the twins. I wanted to be with them twenty-four-seven. They allowed me to follow them around as if I was their shadow until they turned fourteen. Then they only wanted to be bothered with me when it was convenient for them. Travis teased me constantly while Trey was my knight in shining armor.

Trey was the person who introduced me to wood. He took a wood shop class in the tenth grade. He disliked the instructor and he hated working with wood. I glanced in the basement one day and saw him struggling with his first wood project, a wooden key holder, so I offered my assistance. I completed the project for him. After that Trey completed the readings and examinations for the wood shop class and I made all of his wood projects at home. In addition to the key holder, I made a footstool and a miniature chair. Thanks to me, Trey's final grade was an A.

Once the wood shop class was over, I no longer had a reason

to work with wood nor did I have access to any unfinished wood. A year later, on my thirteenth birthday, my mother presented me with a building kit with paints. Every day I was banging on or painting something. I was punished twice for altering pieces of my mother's furniture, which I ruined. "Leave my furniture alone!" she would yell. I am most proud of a jewelry box I made for Mother's Day some twenty years ago. Of course it's not my best work but my mother treasures it. It still sits on her chiffonier.

I stopped the account of my childhood and personal life there. I didn't tell Kathy that our family structure was a little rocky in the beginning. Trey and Travis were shy and withdrawn when they came to live with us. They hardly ever spoke. Mama thought the sudden death of their mother and the strained relationship with their father, Eugene Ellington, were to blame. One would think Eugene's paternal instincts would have kicked into over-drive after the death of my aunt, but they didn't. It was if Eugene couldn't stand the sight of the twins. They may have been too much of a reminder, I suppose.

After graduating as a Tar Heel, Travis moved to San Francisco, California. He landed a job as a sports agent and is doing quite well. He's always sending us tickets to some kind of sporting event. Trey, Mama, and I have gone to at least five Super Bowls, two summer and winter Olympic Games, and six NBA championship games. I even got to attend the Grammys because Travis needed a date and he couldn't choose one person out of a long list of candidates without getting himself in trouble. Speaking of dates, I have never seen Travis with the same woman twice. He says he's like peanut butter—he likes to spread himself around slowly. Mama's always telling him to slow his lifestyle down. "Or else," she says, "I'll make you move back here with me." Travis laughs.

Trey made North Carolina his home after law school. A few

years ago he became the youngest judge to sit on the bench in North Carolina. He and his partner of four years have a lovely oceanfront home in Hatteras, on the Outer Banks. Because Trey is close in distance and the love of my life, I try to visit him whenever I get a free weekend. Due to his recent terminal illness, I now visit him at least once a month. Other than his partner, the doctors, Travis, and Mama, no one else knows of his condition. And I'm sure it will remain that way because we are a very private family. Mother, strong in her convictions and committed to her God, spent all of our lives teaching us values, educational and work ethics, how to think independently, how to love unconditionally, and how to respect silence.

"So, Destiny, that was yesterday. Tell me about today," Kathy said, breaking my train of thought. "Tell me how Destiny's Designs came to be," she continued. I responded by saying I guessed the whole thing grew out of my desire to communicate my love of solid woods and paints, especially black and gold leaf. Also, I am not totally of the mindset that everything old is better or sturdier. I think technology, materials, and designers have brought about significant changes and improvements in the furniture market. I love antiques. But some things I don't want to buy old. Like dining room chairs. And then there were things that I could not afford to buy old. So I'd purchased new finished and unfinished furnishings with the intent of making a new variation of the aged look. I started out distressing, painting, staining, waxing, and crackle glazing furniture. I also applied gold leaf to some wood-carvings. After working with these mediums for five years, I began changing out tabletops, legs, drawer handles, castors, and seat cushions to create my own furniture style. Most of the furniture techniques you see today aren't new. Designers like Thomas Chippendale Sr. and George Hepplewhite, to name a few, painted furniture as early as the eighteenth century. And they experimented with constructional details, styles, polishes, woods, and veneers to create new products. My experimenting resulted in about a hundred different pencil sketches that I had on drawing paper, napkins, the backs of books, or whatever I could put my hands on at the time the idea popped into my head. However, none of the drawings materialized until I met Anton.

Actually, I stumbled upon Anton. While antique shopping in Kensington, Maryland, I saw Anton working in a garage that he had turned into a workshop, behind one of the storefronts. He was so engulfed in his work that he didn't see me observing him. After twenty minutes or so I walked up to him and introduced myself. I asked him about the project he was working on. Anton, not shy at all, was more than willing to talk to me. After an hour or so I learned how to grain and sand wood properly. I also learned a little about Anton personally and professionally.

He is a cabinetmaker by trade but he enjoys making anything out of wood. He especially likes to work with mahogany.

Anton said, "At home in Honduras, mahogany is a rich mellow brown color with a semi-flat texture. It is so easy to lay the groundwork for veneering, no? Mi fader and me make beautiful things. Wood price not so high. My lady, you should come with me to my home in Honduras and see."

Because he did not speak English well, sometimes it was challenging to communicate with Anton, especially, when he was trying to explain construction details. However, we overcame the language barrier through our drawings. I hired Anton to construct a mahogany nightstand and I painted on a stencil in antique gold and black. It turned out very nice. So I gave him one of my sketches for a full-size headboard. We used the same design as the nightstand. And it too turned out beautifully. Whenever I had extra money, I would take Anton a new sketch. Before I knew it Anton and I had completed ten pieces of furniture.

I told Anton, "I guess that makes you a furniture maker."

"And you, my lady, a furniture designer," he said. "At home a creator signs his masterpiece."

So I signed and dated all of my furniture. I will continue that practice with the new designs that are being showcased.

"When is Destiny's Designs' debut?" Kathy asked.

"February tenth," I answered.

"That's right around the corner. I wish you much success," Kathy responded.

"Thank you. Are we finished?" I asked.

"We sure are. I hope it wasn't too painful," Kathy replied.

"Not at all. I was expecting the typical Q and A," I said.

"I try to stay away from them. They are so boring," Kathy said. I nodded in agreement. Kathy paid the bill and we bid our farewells in front of the restaurant. "Thank you for the interview, Destiny."

"No, thank you," I said.

In the car I pulled out my to-do list and added, "Send Kathy Remmington, *Washington Post*, a thank-you note.

28

DESTINY

T he day had finally arrived. The sign in the window of the furniture gallery read FEATURING DESTINY'S DESIGNS. I pinched myself to make sure I wasn't dreaming. My designs were being showcased in a furniture gallery in the Big Apple. I arrived three hours early for the debut because I wanted to look over the furniture one last time and I didn't want to miss one moment or small detail of this long-awaited event.

Marshall's staff was busy taking care of some last-minute administrative items. The bartender was setting up the bar. Chef Petunza, from the Ritz-Carlton hotel, was arranging the appetizers and the photographer, Jonathan, was working out his lighting dilemmas caused by the room's iridescent painted walls and the low-wattage spotlights. By the looks of things, Marshall and his staff had gone all out. Val even arranged to have a limousine collect Mama, Patrick, Trey, Travis, and Camille from La Guardia Airport. A second limousine picked up Gwen, Adriane, Natalie, Brianna, and Allana from Penn Station. The ladies had agreed to ride the train with Adriane because she didn't like flying.

Guests arrived around 4:00 p.m. Marshall and I greeted them and made introductions. Within an hour I had met so many people that I couldn't remember names or faces. I made a mental note to myself to work on that. The only faces that really mattered were those of my family and friends, who came strutting in around

5:00 p.m. Everybody was so happy for me that we couldn't contain ourselves. We were all laughing and crying at the same time—especially Mama. She must have cried for ten minutes. Trey joked that if it wasn't for his wood shop class we wouldn't be here today. And Patrick whispered in my ear, "I'm so proud of you, baby. By the way, you are wearing that dress! Can I interest you in some wood rubbing after this affair?"

"I'll polish you like you've never been polished before," I whispered back.

At about 5:45 p.m. Val told me I could stop being a greeter. She wanted me to work the crowd by walking around. I liked that arrangement better because it didn't make me feel like I was on display. I met more people and accepted numerous compliments on my designs. The furniture definitely displayed well because the best woods were used. And all of the pieces were handmade, carved and painted. The production costs were narrowing my profits but I told Marshall I was okay with that because I wanted my name on furniture that might one day be collector's items. Just as I was about to converse with another guest, Val signaled for me to join her. I excused myself and made my way across the room. Val introduced me to Jack Schikora, owner of Schikora Interiors, Inc. We both extended our hands for the customary handshake. Val said, "Jack just purchased the hand-painted black and gilded settee with the classical motifs from the *Camille* collection."

"I saw it and fell in love. I just had to have it. It's perfect for one of my clients," Jack added.

"Well, I'm glad you love it. Thank you for your patronage," I responded. Val took his card and jotted down some terms and delivery arrangements on the back. Jack's client had him working under a tight deadline so he purchased the piece on display. Before he left, both Val and I thanked Jack again. Val told him she would call him tomorrow. Once he was out of hearing distance, Val informed me that a partner of a prominent law firm in Chicago wanted to commission me to design some furniture for her estate home, currently being built on a private island in the Bahamas.

"You are scheduled to meet with her in two weeks in Chicago. Everything has been arranged. I'll call you on Monday and give you the details to put in your infamous Franklin Planner." The look on my face must have said, *Pinch me, I must be dreaming.* Because Val did just that and said, "You are doing it, girl."

A little after 6:00 p.m. Marshall officially introduced me. As advised by Val, I kept my comments brief because my biography was printed in the program along with color photographs of some of my designs. I thanked Marshall and his staff for all of their support and hard work and I thanked the guests for attending. Lastly, I took a few minutes to introduce the person whom one of the collections was named after, Camille, and my family and extended family. They were so tickled to be in the spotlight and have their pictures taken. Allana told me later that one of the magazine editors interviewed her. I'm sure she dazzled him because she is a wonderful spokesperson.

The next several hours were spent eating and drinking, meeting more guests, taking photographs, and being entertained by musician and composer Marcus Johnson. Camille sought me out to tell me my family was preparing to leave. I excused myself from some guests I was speaking to and made my way over to my family with Camille in tow. They had already retrieved their coats from the coat check. I hugged my mom and kissed her on the cheek. Close to tearing up again and holding both of my hands in hers, she looked me in my eyes and lovingly expressed how proud she was of me. "You've come a long way professionally and personally, Baby Girl," which was her pet name for me. "It makes me feel good to see you reach your dream and be among girl-friends once again. And your beau, Patrick, is a mighty fine young man. I have been talking to him most of the evening. You have been a good daughter and a good person. You deserve all of this and more."

"It feels good, Ma. Real good," I replied.

I then turned to hug Trey and Travis. Before I could let go of their necks they were already teasing me about the absence of my love handles. I smartly informed them that all of my love is in my heart. Patrick, who was also holding his coat and hat, came over to me and told me he was going to leave with Trey, Travis, and Ma. He said, "This is your big night. Enjoy. I'll meet you in the room." The book club members bid farewell to the four of them as I escorted them to the door. Unlike us they were leaving New York early in the morning so they were ready to call it a night.

When I returned to the room, Camille, Allana, Natalie, Brianna, Adriane, and Gwen were discussing our weekend plans in the Big Apple. We had arranged to shop, see a Broadway production, and dine at Sylvia's in Harlem.

"Oh, don't forget, we have tickets to see the author James Patterson at Barnes & Noble," Allana stated factually.

"His book is our selection for next month. And I am hosting the meeting, right?" I added for confirmation.

Natalie nodded her head in agreement.

At that moment Val signaled me, yet again, to join her on the other side of the room.

Adriane laughed. "Your public is calling."

Smiling proudly, I said, "I will be right back, ladies."

29

DESTINY

More than five weeks after the debut and I was still on cloud nine. Things were going very well. Orders were coming in from furniture stores and the trade. The staff Val assigned to Destiny's Designs was handling all of the details associated with the transactions. However, I too was reviewing all incoming orders, invoices, materials, products, and financial documents. Sunday mornings had become my time for doing this. On this Sunday morning Patrick was lying beside me still fast asleep so I gathered up some folders and went downstairs to my office. Before sifting through the paperwork, I put some coffee on and called Brianna. As I was dialing Brianna's cell phone, which is the best way to reach her because her schedule is so hectic, I took out some red salmon to make salmon cakes for breakfast.

"Hello," Brianna said.

"Hey, girl, what's up?"

"Work. I've been on call all weekend," Brianna responded.

"I didn't know you had to work this weekend. I was calling you to remind you of the book club meeting today at my house," I said.

"Unfortunately, I'm going to miss the meeting. But I did finish the book. It was quite suspenseful. Matter of fact, I purchased another one of James Patterson's books. I can't think of the name right now. My mind is mush," Brianna stated.

"Well, I'm not going to hold you because I'm trying to make

the early service. And maybe you can sneak a nap in before you are paged," I said.

"Yeah, I hope so. Tell everyone at the book club meeting I said hello. I'll call you on Monday," Brianna said emotionlessly.

"Okay," I replied and hung up.

As always, First Baptist's 7:30 a.m. service was rejuvenating. And Reverend Fowler was in rare form. Reverend Fowler's sermon was based on Exodus 12:38 and Numbers 11:45. "Make a radical move in your life," Fowler said. "Don't look backward. Move forward. Don't let your attitude ruin the future God has in store for you. Learn the Word, teach the Word, act on the Word and be strong in your convictions. Press on to a new realm of glory."

Every Sunday I am amazed at the impact the Word has on the church's members and on me. For the last couple of weeks I have been reminiscing about my childhood with Trey and Travis and pondering over some decisions that I made regarding Destiny's Designs. Today's service helped me to realize that the Master's plan is to work in the present, plan for the future, and not dwell on the past.

When I left my lifelong church to join First Baptist, Ma had a fit. She didn't talk to me for a week, which is unheard of because we speak to each other on the phone at least four times a day. I knew she would react that way, which is one of the reasons I stayed at my home church so long. But I had to leave. My inner being had been in a tug of war since I lost my virginity seventeen years ago in some sleazy motel not worthy of a rating. I struggled with the fact that my heart and soul were one with the Lord but my flesh was owned by the devil. Shame and guilt had overcome me. Every Sunday I felt like a hypocrite. I had to do something. So I confided in my pastor. He was neither sympathetic nor tolerant of my plight.

"I have known you all your life, Destiny Davis. I even baptized you into this church. You are a respectful woman from a respect-ful family. You know the Bible. Keep your dress down until you are married," he said. He was right and I knew it. But I didn't "keep my dress down." After my discussion with Pastor I felt guiltier. I couldn't even look him in the eye. Whenever I was in his presence, I was paranoid. I thought sermons about virtues and morals were being directed at me. Slowly my attendance started to drop and then I stopped going to church altogether until I found First Baptist. The rule on fornication didn't change at First Baptist and my shame and guilt did not subside. The only saving grace was my sin was not in the open. Just in my heart. I often wonder how other Christian men and women slay this dragon. Or do they?

When I opened the garage door that leads into the mud room, I could smell fried potatoes with onions, salmon, and King's Caribbean coffee that I'd purchased in St. Croix. Entering the kitchen, I said, "Good morning, sleepy head."

"Good morning to you, early riser. I finished the breakfast you started," Patrick responded.

"Wonderful." Patrick was already sitting at the kitchen island so I joined him. Over breakfast we discussed the dinner engage-ment we'd attended last night. Patrick had to entertain an out-of-town client who'd brought his wife and children with him. We took them to—no, let me rephrase that—the company's chauffeur took us to Dave & Buster's. It was a good choice, because every-body had a good time, especially the kids. Patrick and I also discussed some minor details of our trip to Africa.

After finishing up his third cup of coffee, Patrick said, "I better get going. You have a big day. You're playing host, right?"

"Yeah, and I need to prepare a few more refreshments."

"What are you doing after the book club meeting?" Patrick asked.

"I don't know, why?"

"Just asking, I'll give you a call around six."

"We should be finished by then," I responded. After Patrick gathered up all of his belongings, I walked him to the door. We kissed gently on the lips.

"See you later, baby."

"See ya."

I made up the bed, changed my clothes, and started preparing for the meeting. The day was so beautiful I decided to open the shutters to let the sunlight in. I also changed the menu to include some lighter refreshments.

30

DESTINY

Awakened by a sudden movement on the sofa, I jumped up, startled. *Where am I?* I thought. It took me a minute to get my bearings. I was still at the hospital.

"Are you alright?" Camille asked, somewhat dazed herself.

"Yeah, I'm okay. I must have been dreaming," I answered.

Stretching, Camille said, "I'm going to take a walk. Do you want something from the vending machines?"

I glanced at the clock. I had been asleep for well over an hour. Still drowsy, I managed to lift my can of Pepsi—empty.

"Any word yet?" I asked.

"Not since Natalie came in to tell us that Adriane had started dilating," Camille responded.

"That was more than three hours ago," I said.

Allana opened her eyes and adjusted her torso on the sofa to sit at attention. "Did I hear you say you were going to the vending machines? I could use another cup of coffee. Black. Can you bring me some, Camille?" Allana yawned.

"Sure. And I'll also check in at the nurse's desk to see if there's any word on Adriane. Be back shortly," responded Camille.

While rubbing the back of her neck, Allana asked how I was holding up.

"Pretty good," I answered as I popped a mint in my mouth to remove the stale taste. "I wonder how things are going with Adriane,

Natalie, Brianna, and Gwen back there in Labor and Delivery. They must be exhausted."

"I know. But babies come in their own sweet time," Allana said. Shifting the focus, I asked Allana how she was doing, especially since I knew she had been experiencing some physical and emotional discomforts of late. Although I was unable to relieve her of her condition, I had listened to her woes and accompanied her to several holistic seminars and nutritional workshops.

"I'm hanging, girlfriend, I'm hanging," was her reply.

Speaking of hanging, I forgot all about Patrick. We were supposed to have gotten together after the book club meeting. I got up to call him, thinking, *He's probably wondering what happened to me*.

31

GWEN

Walking down the hall of Labor and Delivery, I heard laughter coming out of Adriane's room.

"Hey girls, what's so funny?" I asked as I entered the room.

"Oh, we're just talking about this whole delivery thing," Adriane said. "I don't understand how this baby is going to fit through there." She pointed to her genital area. "I guess it's too late to worry about that. At this point, the baby is going to come out."

"Oh, Adriane, don't even focus on that. Where is Tim now?" Natalie said.

"He called me from the plane just before you came in. He's nervous as hell. I can hear it in his voice. You know how he sounds when he's excited. Don't get me wrong. You know I love Tim to death, but I'm kinda glad he's not here. He'd be all over the place, asking questions and in somebody's way."

"Don't be so hard on Tim. I think it's the husband's responsibility to get in the way when his wife is in labor!" With this comment, both women let out a loud laugh.

I smiled. I thought they were being too hard on Tim, but I have to admit that this is how first-time fathers usually are.

I had been looking at the fetal heart tracing on the monitor in the doctor's lounge and I didn't like what I saw. Sometimes the tracing looks worse on the monitor in the lounge, so I decided to come take a look for myself. I glanced at the fetal heart tracing and frowned. "I'm going to check your cervix now. Do you want Natalie to step out while we do the exam?" I asked.

"Girl, you know I don't care about that now. Natalie's going to be here for the delivery and she's definitely going to see everything then," Adriane replied.

"Guess what, you are completely dilated. It's time to have a baby," I said.

Adriane yelled, "Not yet, we have to wait for Tim!"

I squeezed Adriane's hand and said, "Sorry, girlfriend, it's time. I don't like the fetal heart tracing. The baby needs to come out now."

Adriane responded with her eyes. "I trust you. Do what you got to do. Tim will understand." The nursing staff was called in to get the labor bed ready for delivery and the warmer for the much-anticipated newborn. The delivery table was uncovered, and I got gowned and gloved for the task.

"Adriane, we're ready to start pushing now. With the next contraction, I want you to push as if you're constipated and really want to have a bowel movement, okay? Natalie, I'm going to need you to hold one of Adriane's legs so that we get more room in the pelvis to allow the baby's head to get through the birth canal," I said.

"Oh, wait, I feel like I need to throw up," Adriane stated as she reached for the emesis basin. A steady stream of dark green emesis erupted from Adriane's mouth. "I feel better. Now, I'm ready to push!" exclaimed Adriane. With the next contraction, Natalie and the nurse held Adriane's legs back toward her chest as Adriane pushed with all her might. By the next contraction everyone in the room except Adriane could see the baby's hair. We all cheered her on, telling her that soon she would be holding her baby. Our cheering must have ignited a fuse within Adriane because with the next contraction, Baby Buttler was out.

"Adriane, slow down. No more pushing. I need to suction the baby's mouth and nose," I said. After clearing the mouth and nose of mucous, the rest of the baby was delivered and then placed on Adriane's chest. The umbilical cord was clamped and then I turned to Natalie and asked, "Do you want to cut the cord?"

Natalie gave me a look that screamed, *"I think I'm going to be sick."*

"Oh, Natalie, go ahead and cut the cord. You'll be fine. If I just pushed this baby out, you certainly can muster up the guts to cut the umbilical cord." Adriane laughed. I handed the scissors to Natalie and she cut the baby's lifeline that it no longer needed. Baby Buttler was finally here. Ten fingers and ten toes. Already bright eyes and a big smile.

Just as I pulled off my surgical gown and shoe covers, I saw a figure moving a million miles per minute. I stuck my head out the doorway to see where this person was going in such a rush. To my surprise, it was Tim.

"Hey, Tim, we're in here. Congratulations! Come see your son," I said as I gave Tim a big hug.

Tim had a look of total amazement as he walked in the room to greet his new son. With tears in his eyes, he hugged and kissed Adriane vigorously. He touched his son's small legs so gently that one would have thought he was stroking Waterford crystal.

"I'm sorry we couldn't wait for you to get here, but we had to get the baby out. Adriane wanted me to wait. With Natalie's help, your wife was a true pro. She pushed this baby out in three pushes," I said.

After giving Adriane hugs and kisses, holding Baby Buttler, and taking pictures of the new family, I turned to Adriane and said, "Adriane, I didn't like the vomiting you had right before your delivery, so I'm going to check some lab work to make sure there are no problems with your liver and gall bladder. I'm also going to order an ultrasound of your liver and gall bladder. I'll be right back."

Natalie and I left the family to spend some time together. Natalie made her way to the waiting room to inform the ladies and Adriane's mother of the good news and I stayed at the nurse's station to finish my delivery note and postpartum orders. I couldn't shake this feeling that something was going on with Adriane. But instead of jumping the gun I decided to wait for the lab results.

As the doors of Labor and Delivery opened to let me out, I saw five eager faces begging for answers. I remembered then that I had started the day going to the book club meeting. Natalie had already joined Camille, Destiny, Allana, and Brianna, who was on a break, in the family waiting area. For a moment, I stood still in the doorway to reflect on this group. Gosh, we had grown. Not only collectively as a book club, but also individually as women. The group was full of energy. Poor Natalie was fielding questions from all of them at the same time. She was used to this deluge of questioning, though, since she was always the first person on the scene when her senator put his foot in his mouth on some issue.

Look at Destiny. I don't think she said a single word at the first book club meeting. Now, she was our keeper of order, our parliamentarian. She was busy scribbling something in her Franklin Planner. It was probably key information such as time of birth, gender, weight, and length so that she could email all the other book club members with the good news. In her personal life, she was embarking on an adventure that would surely change her forever. With Camille's help, and all of our encouragement, she had launched her own collection of furniture designs.

My eyes shifted to Allana. Some people seem uncomfortable

being in a hospital even if it's for a joyous occasion. They are restless and always seem to be looking over their shoulder as if someone is going to wisk them away on a stretcher to the operating room. That's how I would have pegged Allana initially. But I would have been wrong. She was a pillar of strength. When she was having problems with her hormones and her doctor suspected that she may have had a large ovarian cyst, she'd called me for my opinion and she'd accepted all of the information I'd given her with a stiff upper lip.

Brianna looked tired. I was probably the only one who could spot that fatigue since I have known Brianna since medical school. Brianna and I could always sense when something was wrong in each other's lives. And I believe that Camille had these same senses. Maybe it's because she's the proverbial mom who knows everything. Tonight I hoped that I could disguise my concerns, although perhaps premature, about what was going on with Adriane. I figured Brianna and Camille would be the hardest to fool. Ideally, Natalie would be included in that group too, but I think she was too emotionally drained after the delivery to notice anything. I plotted my approach to the group. I would walk up and put my long arms around Brianna and Camille, forming a semi-circle. That way, they would never see the concern in my eyes that I was trying so desperately to blink away. I would face Natalie, Allana, and Destiny and discuss the details about Adriane and her new family. I counted to three and I made my way toward the group.

"Hey, you guys, I'm sure Natalie has filled you in," I began.

In unison, they all responded, "Yes."

We all came together and hugged. You could feel how much joy everyone felt for Adriane. My plan was working perfectly. I had Brianna and Camille on either side of me and I held them with my arms extended. I was concentrating very hard on keeping a light tone.

"Everything went really well. I wished that we could have waited for Tim to get here before delivering Baby Buttler, but it was time to get that boy out. Adriane was a great pusher and Natalie was the best pinch hitter a girl could ask for," I continued.

"Yeah, we saw Tim bust through the doors like a thoroughbred at the start of the Kentucky Derby," Camille said.

"Well, the whole family is together now and doing well. The little guy is so adorable."

Just at that moment, Tim and Adriane's mother appeared with Baby Buttler in his bassinet, followed by the nurse. They were headed over to the nursery for the baby's first bath. The book club members were introduced to Baby Buttler for the first time. The nurse didn't give us much time with the newborn because she was afraid that he would get too cold. "Newborns sometimes have difficulties with temperature regulation," the nurse said. Once Tim and Baby Buttler made their exit, we all went into the labor suite to visit with Adriane.

Congratulations and hugs were abundant. Adriane replayed the whole labor and delivery, blow by blow. She had us laughing the hardest when she described Natalie not wanting to hold her leg during the pushing stage. Camille made us laugh ever harder when she described how her first husband, Everett, dropped her leg when she was delivering her first child.

"My leg was so numb from the epidural that I couldn't feel a thing. Here I am pushing with all my strength because I wanted to get the whole thing over with and I look down and see my leg hanging off the side of the bed. I look at Everett and he's turning gray with crusty lips as if he is going to pass out at any moment. You know, I should have left him then."

By this time Tim had returned from the nursery. We all said our good-byes. Once outside the room, we rescheduled the book club meeting for Wednesday night at my house. Brianna waved good-bye and headed to her locker. I stopped at the computer terminal on Labor and Delivery to see if the lab results had come back yet but the phlebotomist was just getting to the floor to draw blood. I reminded the nurse to page me once the results were back and then joined Natalie, Camille, Destiny, and Allana on the elevator. There was still a lot of excitement within the group. No one seemed to have noticed my concern. I preferred to keep it that way until I had something substantial to be concerned about.

32

ALLANA

Early the next morning Rodney and I stopped by the hospital to see Adriane before going to work. We hoped to catch Tim at the hospital also. I held Rodney's hand as we made our way through the maze of hospital corridors. When we entered Adriane's room, Tim beamed at us. He was happy to see Rodney with me today.

"Hey, man. How's it going?" asked Rodney.

"It's all good man," Tim answered.

I hugged Tim and kissed him on the cheek. Rodney gave Tim that handshake-hug where men grab right hands and lean into each other, touching right shoulders and wrapping the left arms around each other's backs. They stayed connected that way for about a minute. It was as if Rodney, the "big brother," was infusing the "little brother" with some of his strength, physically holding him up to let him know he had a strong shoulder to lean on.

Swinging his arms, Tim asked, "Did your handicap fall below intermediate level? If not, you will be buying the Heineken this spring."

"Man, you must be kidding. The links are going to be mine. Pretty soon I'll be playing with the pros."

"The pros!" Tim replied. They both laughed.

"New fathers don't get to play a lot of golf. You will be playing house, my man."

Rodney was speaking from experience.

"I know. Adriane has been reminding me every chance she gets." Tim laughed and winked at us.

"Where is Adriane?" I asked.

"They are running some tests."

"Where is the baby?"

"In the nursery."

"I'll be back," I said.

I left the fellows and headed straight to the nursery. Looking in on Baby Buttler I began thinking about my family, especially my sister. In so many ways, Adriane reminded me of my little sister. So I treated her like she was. I was always protective of her and gave her the benefit of my years of wisdom. Not that she listened. Most of the time she was trying to tell me what to do. Sometimes her advice was good, so I used it. If my real sister lived in this area, I'm sure we would have double-dated. Since she does not, Rodney and I double-date with Adriane and Tim. We like the same activities, except Adriane doesn't like to eat out at restaurants much so we usually have dinner at her house since she loves to cook and play host. Many times she would invite other people to dine with us because Adriane loves to be in the company of people. I always wondered when she and Tim found time to be alone because they always had a house full of people or overnight guests. Some guests stayed a few days, others for weeks.

Baby Buttler was smiling in his sleep. His beauty and innocence brought tears to my eyes. I blew him a kiss and returned to Rodney and Tim. The guys were still discussing sports. I heard Jordan's name so I assumed they were discussing basketball.

I interrupted. "Are they still running tests?"

"I guess."

"Well, we'd better get going if we want to get in the office before 10:00 a.m. Tell Adriane we came to visit. And tell her I will call her later."

"Okay," Tim responded.

While reaching to embrace Tim, I said, "Tell her we love her."

"You got it," he said.

"Later, man," Rodney chimed in.

33

DESTINY

Monday mornings are catastrophic for me when Sunday night does not afford me the luxury of eight hours of sleep. I left the hospital around nine-thirty for the forty-five-minute drive home. By the time I got home, tidied up the kitchen and the family room from the earlier book club meeting, took a shower, and packed an overnight bag for the firm's monthly business trip to New York in the morning, I was dog tired. But I couldn't fall asleep and when I finally did it was time to get up.

It took me an hour to get from La Guardia Airport to 2 World Trade Center. My meeting was at 9:30 a.m. so I was doing okay on time. I was the first to arrive so I selected my favorite seat, facing the window with a view of the Hudson River. These meetings usually dragged on for eight to ten hours so I needed as much distraction as possible so as not to fall asleep. I placed my black Samsonite overnight bag and Coach briefcase on the chair behind me and arranged my Franklin Planner and the conference room telephone in front of me. Before checking my voice mail, I called Brianna to check on Adriane and the new little one. I knew I would get her answering machine, so I was prepared to leave a number for the Marriott hotel at the World Trade Center. My visits were so frequent I knew the number by heart. I thought about calling Allana, but figured she would not have any additional information since we'd left the hospital at the same time last night. I changed the greeting on my voice mail to say I would be out of the office until Wednesday and sat the telephone back on the glass and chrome credenza.

The last time I was in New York, Camille, Allana, Adriane, Natalie, Brianna, and Gwen were here with me. What a time we had at Sylvia's. We ate so much fried catfish, grits, collard greens, macaroni and cheese, and corn bread and clowned around so bad, I thought Adriane was going to burst. Now that I think about it, she almost did burst when the waiter tripped over his own feet and dropped the dinner salad with ranch dressing in Brianna's lap. Brianna maintained her composure, but we all knew she was hotter than a firecracker. "That's okay," she kept saying while the waiter raked the salad out of her lap with his white linen cloth. "I'm fine," she said. As soon as the waiter left we all roared with laughter and teased Brianna mercilessly. Adriane laughed until her face turned the color of a maraschino cherry and tears rolled down her puffy cheeks. We fell silent when the waiter returned with a lady who turned out to be the manager.

"Your waiter explained to me what happened. I'm so sorry," she said. "Did the salad dressing ruin your blouse and pants? Please, please allow me to pay for the dry cleaning."

"No, that won't be necessary. I think they're fine. It's washable silk," Brianna responded.

"Well, allow me to pay for your dinner and provide a complimentary bottle of cabernet sauvignon from our 1992 Sonoma Valley Artist Series for you and your friends. And when you are ready for dessert, peach cobbler and vanilla French roast coffee will be on the house too."

Brianna was fixing her lips to say thank you, but we said it for her. "Thank you, thank you very much." We ate and drank everything that was put before us, paid our bill, and tipped the waiter handsomely because barring the spill he was very attentive. Before we rolled our stuffed selves out of the booth seats, the waiter, still aiming to please, arranged to have two yellow taxis pick us up and deliver us to Reade Street in Tribeca.

Back at the colossal four-bedroom, four-bathroom loft we'd borrowed for the weekend from one of Camille's clients who was out of town, we sprawled all over the living room. The owner had a nice collection of John Coltrane as well as other antiques and collectibles. We put some music on and turned on the gas fireplace to accompany our mellow mood. Snapping our fingers and swaying our heads, we fell into a conversation about our good ol' days. Hot pants, wet look boots, bush balls, blue lights in the basement, smoking Kools, Larry Graham concerts, slow jams by the Ohio Players, and the annual family reunion. Brianna stood up and said she was going to soak her clothes in cold water.

"Check to see if there is some white vinegar in the kitchen cabinets. I read somewhere that vinegar removes stains from silk," Allana said.

"I'll look," Brianna responded, walking into the kitchen. Adriane also got up and followed Brianna into the kitchen. She brought back some popcorn and soft drinks, set them on the coffee table, and reenacted the tripping incident at the restaurant. She began laughing uncontrollably again and so did we. Brianna, who witnessed the scene from the kitchen, said, "That's right, have fun at my expense. I'm going upstairs to soak my clothes."

When Gwen was certain that Brianna could not hear her, she whispered to the rest of us, "I have something that I want to discuss with you."

"You and Sloan are off again," guessed Camille.

"No, it's not about me this time; it's Brianna," Gwen said, looking concerned.

"Brianna, what's wrong with Brianna?" Natalie asked.

"I have reason to believe that Brianna's friend Sarah had or is having an affair with one of the partners at my old job," Gwen said.

Adriane nearly choked on the soda she was drinking. "Weren't the partners all women?" She gasped. After clearing her throat to make sure her soda went down the right pipe, she went on, "Well then, how in the hell can Sarah be having an affair with one of the partners?"

"What do you mean, how? Sarah could be a lesbian or at least bisexual, I guess," Gwen replied with a puzzled expression on her face.

"Maybe Brianna doesn't know Sarah likes girls," Adriane said.

"Gwen, how do you know Sarah was having an affair with one of the partners? Are you sure?" Allana asked.

"Yeah, pretty much. Although I did not see Sarah with my ex-boss, I overhead them having a sexual conversation at the office one night. During the conversation, I overheard my ex-boss call her companion 'Sarah.'"

"What were you doing, spying?" Adriane asked with excitement.

"No way. I was working late and I accidentally stumbled upon them. But I didn't let my presence be known. And when I met Sarah at the baby shower, I thought to myself, her voice and name sound familiar. And then it clicked. Brianna's Sarah is the same Sarah who was with my ex-boss," Gwen explained.

"So how do you plan to tell Brianna that you suspect Sarah likes women?" Natalie asked.

"First of all, do you tell her?" I asked.

"I was hoping the group could help me answer all of these questions," Gwen said thoughtfully.

"Does this mean Brianna likes girls too?" Adriane asked.

We all looked at Gwen.

"Don't look at me. I don't know." Gwen laughed to lighten up the conversation.

"Well, I think we tell her your suspicions. Because we are her friends we owe her that. She and Sarah are both adults so they can work out the rest," Allana said.

Camille, Natalie, and I agreed. Adriane was still digesting the situation.

Brianna came downstairs, now smelling like distilled vinegar. "Anybody want anything from the kitchen?" she asked.

We answered no.

Brianna plopped on the sofa and adjusted a pillow behind her back. With one of Coltrane's up-tempo beats in the background and us looking on like clients in a group therapy session, Gwen said, "Brianna, how much do you know about your friend Sarah?"

"What do you mean, how much do I know? I know where she lives, I know what kind of food she likes, I know she's crazy about basketball, I know her favorite wines, I know what kind of car she drives, I know where she likes to vacation, I know she likes to live life to its fullest and I know we have a great time when we are together," Brianna responded with a perplexed look on her face.

Gwen, who is not long on words, asked, "What do you know about her sexual preferences?"

"I haven't asked Sarah about her sexual preferences because it is not an issue to me. Why do you ask?" Brianna shot back.

"I asked, because I believe she is or was having an affair with one of the partners at my old job. A female partner."

"Uhmmm, I'll ask her," was Brianna's only response.

All of us interpreted that response to mean "I know Sarah's sexual preference and I have no interest in discussing it with you—end of conversation."

"Good morning, Destiny. Always the first to arrive," Charlie said.

"Good morning, how was your flight?" I asked.

"The trip from Atlanta to New York wasn't bad," he replied.

As Charlie and I continued to talk shop, a woman walked in with coffee, hot water, pastries, bagels, muffins, and condiments. A few of the other meeting attendees came in as well. I was glad we were getting the show on the road, because I didn't want to be here all night. I had hoped that I would have enough time to do some shopping in SoHo.

Two-thirds of the agenda was completed by early afternoon. While waiting for lunch to be set up by the same lady who served the continental breakfast, I, along with the rest of the team, checked voice mail messages. Hmmm, no messages from the ladies; only business calls. I responded to a few and saved the rest. I checked my voice mail at home and all that awaited me was that familiar recording, "There are no new messages." I fixed myself a sandwich, added some pasta salad to my plate, picked up a Pepsi, and took my seat.

"The next item on the agenda is the JustCo project. James, do you have copies of the Work Breakdown Structure to hand out? And are you ready to discuss the business plan, Destiny?"

My man Frank, president of international marketing, was on a roll. James and I captivated our team members with our knowledge and preparedness. Once we'd answered questions, we were able to strike that item off the agenda in record time. I like teaming up with James because he is thorough, unlike some of my other team members. Two more items to discuss. Maybe I'd have enough time to check into the hotel and drop my bag and laptop off before I went to SoHo. That is, if someone on the team didn't suggest dining together. What's up with that? We were together all day and then they wanted to spend half of the night looking at each other, drinking and smoking and discussing the same old stuff.

I only had a couple of hours to shop in SoHo. But it seemed like less than two hours because my overnight bag and laptop were weighing me down, hindering my progress. I was able to browse a couple of jewelry stores, a few new boutiques, and a French antique store. I wanted to do more shopping and get something to eat in SoHo but it was getting late. So I thought it best to hail a taxi and go to the hotel.

The hotel accommodations were wonderful as usual. Once situated in the room, I ordered a jumbo shrimp cocktail and a Caesar salad from room service, unpacked my overnight bag, and set up my laptop to respond to the voice mail messages that I'd saved earlier. When the food arrived, I was at a good point to wrap things up, so I turned off the computer, turned the television on, and ate. After several yawns I looked at the Rolex on my wrist, which was a Christmas present from Trey and Travis several years ago. Ten-thirty, no wonder I'm so tired. I took a shower and went to bed.

34

CAMILLE

Natalie called me around lunchtime to tell me about Adriane. She had been moved to the ICU because of some complications that had arisen since the birth of her son. I said a silent prayer, and then I said, "Natalie, this must be a horrible ordeal for Adriane and her family."

Natalie responded, "Yes, it has been very hard. They have not left the hospital since the birth of the baby."

"Please let me know if there is anything I can do," I said.

"I'll keep you posted. Oh, can you call Allana and Destiny for me?"

"I will." After we hung up, I called both Allana and Destiny and got their answering machines. I didn't want to leave this kind of news on the machine so I hung up. I also called Gwen to check on her, but of course, I got no answer.

35

DESTINY

I woke up to the sounds of elevators moving between floors and the hotel staff moving around in the hallway. Damn, I forgot to set the alarm. It was 6:09 a.m. I had to rush to make the 7:30 a.m. staff meeting. Quickly, I jumped in the shower, then into my clothes. I packed up my stuff, checked out of the hotel, and hailed a cab, which was my only means of transportation in New York besides walking. I definitely was not the first to arrive for the meeting this morning. I just made it by the skin of my teeth. Again the continental breakfast was set up. Thank goodness, I was starved and I needed a cup, if not two, of caffeine. The bagels looked good. Too many choices though. I selected a cinnamon raisin, fixed a cup of coffee, and took my favorite seat, across from the window. I think the team purposely did not sit in it, knowing that it was my favorite. Apparently Frank wanted to conclude the meeting at noon because he began day two's half-day agenda at 8:00 a.m., which is rare. Normally we spend forty-five minutes to an hour talking about politics, stocks, golf, and whatever else the good ol' boys want to talk about.

The early start was fine with me. I had several things I wanted to do in the city before I flew home. First, I wanted to go across town to see how Destiny's Designs were being displayed in The Home Design Gallery. Secondly, I wanted to shop for shoes.

The bullet points on the agenda consisted of administrative

and human resource issues. Not much input required on my part. I found myself scribbling a to-do list.

—design gallery
—shoes
—purchase sketch paper
—pick up theater schedule
—call insurance company

That's when it hit me. Brianna didn't return my call yesterday. Or did I sleep through the ring? I usually have a difficult time falling asleep when on travel. Not last night, though. It was like I was drugged. I wonder if Patrick called. I rushed out of the room so fast this morning I didn't have time to check the message light on the telephone. We should be taking a ten-minute break soon; I'll call Patrick and Brianna then. With my to-do list complete I focused my attention back on the meeting. Frank was describing the backgrounds of the final two candidates for the vacant vice president of international marketing position. It was clear that one of them was a woman. No matter what he said about her, she already had my vote. Women are under-represented in our division.

"Before you give me your comments, let's take ten minutes," he said.

After a much-needed stretch, I picked up one of the telephones to check my voice mail messages. I had two messages from Patrick and one from Brianna. Brianna's message simply said, "Hey, girl, give me a call. If not, I'll see you Wednesday night." I erased all three of the messages and called Patrick at work. His secretary answered.

"Hi, this is Destiny. Is he available?"

"Hi, Destiny, he's in a meeting with a client. He's probably going to be tied up for the next couple of hours. Then he has another meeting at one o'clock. Do you want to leave a message?"

"No, just tell him I called. Thanks."

"Will do. 'Bye."

The remainder of the morning flew by. Around 11:30 a.m. the group departed to catch trains and planes. I, on the other hand, caught a taxi to Park Avenue.

It was a bright but chilly early afternoon in New York. Everything was hustle bustle like always, and I needed to join the frenzy if I was going to do all of the things I wanted to do and catch my scheduled 5:30 p.m. flight. As soon as I walked into the poshly decorated Design Gallery that obviously specialized in eclectic styles, I saw Destiny's Designs. I liked the positioning immediately. And after forty minutes with the owner, Jean, and his staff, I liked the people, too. Jean invited me to lunch, but I graciously declined, telling him about my other errands. I promised to take him to lunch the next time I was in the city. He accepted.

I spent the next couple of hours in and out of stores—Céline, Saks, Ferragamo, Gucci, Bloomingdale's, Fendi, and Bergdorf Goodman. I found seven pairs of shoes that I could have killed for. But I couldn't afford any of them. Instead I settled for a pair of tan and black skins by Gucci and a Ferragamo multi-color sling. I also found the cutest little top in Bergdorf Goodman that I bought as well. Walking in the direction of Lee's Art Shop to pick up my sketch paper, I passed Tiffany & Company. I always wanted to give a baby a silver spoon as a gift but no one close to me had a baby, not until now. I turned around and went into Tiffany & Company. Once inside, I got carried away. Not only did I purchase the Elsa Peretti Padova feeding spoon in sterling silver, but I also bought the matching baby cup. I had the salesperson wrap them separately. "What about engraving?" she asked.

"I'll have that done later," I responded. I paid the sales representative and walked out with a medium-size blue bag.

As usual, the airport was crowded and my flight was delayed. But I didn't care. I was going home to see both of my babies, Patrick and Baby Buttler.

36

DESTINY

It felt weird having a book club meeting on a Wednesday night. Due to Adriane's unexpected labor and delivery last Sunday, we didn't get a chance to discuss the book and the plans for our first coed book club meeting this summer. I sure hope everybody shows up on time because I don't know how long I can hang with this night-owl group. When I spoke to Allana this morning, she said Gwen had been spending a lot of time at the hospital because Adriane had developed some kind of complication shortly after we left the hospital on Sunday. I asked Allana a lot of questions but she was unable to answer them. So I figured I would wait and ask Gwen about it at the meeting.

I could tell Allana was preoccupied, so I asked her what was up.

"Rodney has been in New Orleans on business since Tuesday. He's returning home about six this evening, and of course he's not thrilled with the fact that I won't be home to greet him," she had said.

"Well, why don't you skip the book club meeting tonight and go home and be with your man?"

"I don't know, girl; I guess he'll be okay with this. I fixed him his favorite meal, meatloaf, before I left home this morning and I laid out his silk pajamas and my red teddy. He knows what that means." Allana had chuckled.

"Sounds like you got it all worked out. So I'll see you tonight then."

"I'll be there," Allana had said.

Gwen, not her usual cheerful self, greeted us one by one as we arrived at her house. Although she was involved in the group's idle discussion, you could tell her mind was a million miles away. Several of us attempted to ask her questions about Adriane's condition, but she refused to answer any questions about Adriane until we were all there. Gwen's silence and the look in her restless eyes were unsettling.

Once everyone had gathered around the table, all eyes were on Gwen. She started off by telling us that Adriane was critically ill but holding her own. "Adriane is young and was very healthy until this illness. Therefore, her chances for recovery are good. Adriane has something called Thrombotic Thrombocytopenic Purpura. It is a disorder where a person's blood platelets don't work. Your platelets are the cells that cause blood to clot. When the platelets don't work, you can get internal bleeding which can cause the blood volume to be depleted, therefore there is less blood getting to the vital organs such as the kidneys, liver, heart, and brain. With less perfusion of the vital organs, they begin to shut down in an effort to spare the heart and the brain. Right now, Adriane's liver and kidneys are shutting down."

Camille interrupted Gwen's medical dissertation for clarification. Gwen continued, saying, "Your liver is responsible for producing various proteins and your clotting factors. If the proteins are depleted, then the body has a hard time holding the fluid in the intravascular space so all the fluid leaks out into the extra-vascular space. The extravascular space is the area under your skin. People with low protein become swollen because extra fluid accumulates under the skin. Some of this fluid can also accumulate in the area around the heart, lungs, and in the abdominal cavity. Extra fluid in these spaces makes it harder for these organs to function. In addition, without clotting factors, a person is even more prone to bleeding.

"The terrible thing about Thrombotic Thrombocytopenic Purpura is that the body goes haywire and causes clots or thrombosis to occur where they shouldn't. Adriane could develop clots in her blood vessels supplying her heart to cause a heart attack, or in the vessels supplying the brain to cause a stroke, or in vessels supplying any of the organs, which would cause them to not only fail but to necrose or die."

"So Adriane doesn't have platelets to allow her to clot correctly but her body is doing its own thing, making arbitrary clots?" I asked.

"That's absolutely correct, Destiny," Gwen answered.

Brianna added, "It's like when your cell phone battery is dying and you can't make a phone call but all sorts of messages or numbers will flash on the screen like it's in overdrive, and then the screen will go blank and you know the battery is dead."

The blank expressions on our faces prompted Gwen to ask us if this made any sense to us. We all hesitantly nodded our heads up and down. But I was clueless.

"The most important thing that I want you guys to understand is that as one organ system starts to fail, the others will follow. Everything in the body has an action and reaction to something else. This is not to say that once the cascade of failure begins, we can't stop it. Sometimes we can, although it's difficult. The doctors are doing everything they can at this time," Gwen further explained.

Natalie didn't have any questions or comments because she had been at the hospital every day since Adriane arrived. She sat at the table staring at nothing in particular.

I think Gwen realized she was giving us more details than we could handle so she ended the conversation and tried to reassure us that everything was going to be okay. But despite Gwen's best efforts, the reassurance was futile. At that moment, the pain and fear in our hearts were strong enough to support one of the Egyptian pyramids.

Allana attempted to bring the book club meeting back to order by suggesting that we outline the agenda for the co-ed meeting first. But all of us were preoccupied with Adriane's health. However, we did manage to agree on a book, *The Genocide Files* by N. Xavier Arnold, and select a date, place, and time. While eating pizza and taking a break from the meeting, we redirected our attention to Adriane and the baby. Natalie said the baby was doing fine. Brianna asked Gwen if we could visit Adriane and Gwen said, "Only immediate family members are allowed to visit right now. But I will call you as soon as that changes."

Allana, being her efficient self, asked if we could discuss the menu for the co-ed meeting. And with that a new discussion started. But most of us had no interest in this discussion. We were still focused on what was going on with Adriane.

"Let's see, we need paper products, condiments, side dishes, meats, and beverages," Allana said.

"What about desserts?" Brianna yelled from the kitchen.

"We should probably discuss how many people we are going to invite before we discuss the menu so we know how many people we have to prepare for," Camille said with very little enthusiasm.

"Yeah, that's a good idea," Allana said.

I could tell people were not interested in talking about anything but Adriane, so I said, "Hey, ladies, it's after eight. Can we table the discussion of the co-ed book club meeting for right now?"

"Yeah, I think we have enough to get started on the co-ed thing," replied Gwen.

Allana changed the subject, trying to lift our solemn mood. "We need to finish our discussion from Sunday on *Jack & Jill* and rate the book. Did you notice that Patterson did not elaborate on the facial and physical appearances of his characters? I found his writing style very different from that of Terry McMillan, Octavia Butler, Amy Tan, Anita Richmond Bunkley, E. Lynn Harris, Gabriel Garcia Marquez, and Walter Mosley, to name a few. These authors usually described every inch of a character in their books," she commented.

"Yeah, I noticed that too. Initially, I didn't know the race of Alex Cross, the main character," Brianna responded.

"This is not Patterson's first book. He probably assumed the readers were familiar with Alex Cross," responded Camille.

"Well, whatever the reason, I found Patterson's lack of detail refreshing," replied Natalie dryly, "because I don't think characteristics like lip size and dress size are necessary unless they have some impact on the story. However, I did think a few of the scenes in the book were unrealistic."

"Which ones?" I asked.

"Well," Natalie said, "Patterson described a scene in which Alex visits with Christine at her home, late at night, while her husband is asleep upstairs. Now tell me, how many men would have slept through that?"

"I know Rodney wouldn't. And he would have come downstairs to see what a strange man was doing in his house, at night, while he's asleep," Allana said.

"I know that's right," Camille said. For the first time that night, we all laughed and gave each other five. Even Gwen mustered up a brief smile. I could see that all of this was really taking a toll on Gwen and Natalie.

One word led to another about Alex seeing a psychiatrist and somehow or another the discussion of *Jack & Jill* led to a discussion on how black and white men and black and white women view stress, financial security, parenting, relationships, and careers.

After forty-five minutes or so, I commented on the time again. "Can we rate the book, ladies?" I asked. Everybody enjoyed the thriller mystery and the ratings supported that. *Jack & Jill* received a 1.5.

It was 10:30 p.m. and I was exhausted. I told the ladies that I was going to retire. "Allana, if you guys sign up for food for the co-ed club meeting tonight, put me down for anything."

"Okay," she responded.

I said good night to Allana, Gwen, Brianna, Natalie, and Camille and hugged them as if it was the last time I was ever going to see them again. I told Gwen and Natalie that I would call them tomorrow to check on Adriane.

Driving home I felt numb, helpless and blessed for my current good health all at the same time. What had Gwen laid on us and what did it really mean? I had heard of conditions like gestational diabetes and preeclampsia, also called toxemia, but I never heard of Thrombotic Thrombocytopenic Purpura. Maybe it's not as bad as it sounds. The explanations from Gwen and Brianna simplified things for me a little. And Gwen did say that Adriane's vital signs were improving and that she no longer needed assistance breathing. But she also said we should pray. As I pulled up to the traffic light that turned yellow, then red, I closed my eyes.

"Lord, you are my light and salvation. I do not fear. You are my rock. I do not bend. You protect and watch over me. I am not concerned. I pray and you listen. I ask and you deliver when it is your will. Tonight, Lord, I ask that you keep my sister, your child Adriane, safe."

As I opened my eyes and proceeded through the intersection,

I thought, *Adriane will be up and about in no time. All she needs is some rest.* Her schedule has been so hectic. She was organizing a cotillion with her sorority sisters, preparing for the baby, working on a political campaign, working on a major account at work, and doing what she does best—being a friend to everybody, a sister, a daughter, and a wife to Tim.

37

Morning. But it feels like night. I shake my head to clear the fog that seems to be engulfing me. But the fog doesn't clear; it intensifies instead. I see Tim. His eyes are bloodshot and his face is gaunt. He's not eating. He is holding Adriane's hand and telling her how much he and Baby Buttler love her. Adriane is silent. There are tubes and machines everywhere and the doctors have given her drugs to make her rest. They say she must conserve her energy. I don't quite know what that means. I don't want to think about it. On the wall beside her bed are two pictures. One picture is of Adriane and the baby taken right after his birth. In it, Adriane is smiling. The other picture is of Adriane and Tim on their wedding day. The nurses told us it is good to have things in the room that will inspire Adriane to fight, so Tim and I put them up yesterday. I wonder if she can hear Tim. I hope so.

Sometimes I can't look. I am afraid. It makes me ashamed. I don't want her to see me cry. I want to help, but don't know how. What can or should a friend do? Everything is inadequate. I guess you just have to be there. Adriane has always been there for me. She always had a bright idea, always a solution. More often than not, the solution involved food, friends, fun, and sometimes a new business venture. She was forever coming up with new business ideas. She was a true entrepreneur, always bringing disparate people together in all sorts of amazing combinations. She was the creative one, the one who finally got me to put up pictures on my blank walls after I had been in my house for over two years. Of course she had to buy a picture or two to help me along with this task. She was also so proud and encouraging when I learned how to do something totally mundane, like making lasagna.

Adriane was truly an unselfish person, which is so rare. She was so generous with her time and her money even if she didn't have any. She was always inclusive and wanted all of her friends to be friends. None of that proprietary bullshit and jealousy you sometimes encounter. She was the one with whom I shared all my secrets and juicy gossip, and she with me; except most of the secrets weren't ours to share, but we shared them religiously anyway. Adriane was not perfect. Her bark could be so biting that in less than a minute she could tear you to shreds, but if you did the same to her, even less eloquently, her little face would scrunch up and turn red with tears. Even so, she was always there to back me up when I stumbled. Now she needed help and I was powerless to help her.

One of the things I admired most about Adriane was that she was a content person. She liked her life. She had her family and friends close by, just like she wanted it. She was happy. Most of us are always searching for more. Always in a hurry to get to the next phase in life, better job, more money, new relationship. We don't take the time to enjoy the journey, and sometimes the journey is all it will ever be. *What am I doing with my life?* I think to myself. I work all the time. I don't have real time to spend with my friends and family. I don't have a husband or children. I realize I am still searching. Maybe, in light of the recent events with Thorton and Adriane, I need to rethink my life. Maybe I should stop and smell the roses and embark on a real life—my life.

I shake my head to clear my mind. Is this a nightmare? If it is, I must wake from it because it is too painful. I blink my eyes and stare at the pictures on the wall. I hear a commotion in the hallway and turn to look. I see a gurney racing down the hall. An old man with an oxygen mask is lying on the gurney while two physicians in blue scrubs run on either side of him. I see the old man, whose hair is all white and thinning, raise his frail arm weakly. His arm is shaking and covered with age spots. I wonder what is wrong and whether he is scared. As I lose sight of the gurney the doors to the ICU open, then close. I look down at my hands, and then cover my face with them to hide my eyes as they well up with tears. Fully aware of my heart breaking, I realize this is no dream. It is reality. A reality I never knew existed.

Life is not guaranteed. I vowed to no longer take it for granted.

38

GWEN

In our modern culture, the term "God complex" has been synonymous with "arrogance, domineering, omniscient, and omnipotent." The best illustration of this concept that I have ever seen was a scene in the movie *Malice* where a charismatic surgeon removes the diseased as well as the healthy ovary of a young woman. When the surgeon is asked why he removed both ovaries even though one was totally healthy, his response is that he thought it was in the patient's best interest. The patient then accuses the doctor of playing God. The surgeon smugly answers, "I am God. I can make all patients better and give them life."

If ever there was a time that I wished that life imitated art, it was now. I just got paged from the doctor in the ICU who is taking care of Adriane. He asked me to come up to the unit because she isn't doing well. Of all the doctors taking care of Adriane, couldn't one of them have the power of God thrust upon him? Or, better yet, I'd settle for witnessing a miracle. I didn't think that was far-fetched because doctors witness miracles every day. Like the patient I had in residency whose uterus ruptured, yet she and the baby both lived.

I climbed the stairs to the ICU since I never took the elevators in the hospital unless I was really, really tired. Surprisingly, I didn't feel that tired even though it was 2:30 a.m. Friday morning. And I really hadn't slept since Sunday, the day Adriane had her baby.

The waiting area to the ICU was adjacent to the unit. As I approached, I could see Tim's and Adriane's parents asleep on the sofas. They had not left the hospital since the day Adriane had arrived. My heart went out to them. How could one have expected this to happen to Adriane? I thought, *We never know what the future holds for us. Some things we can control and others we can't.* My thoughts turned back to Adriane.

When I walked into the unit, I felt like I was in Times Square. There was a large nursing area in the center with central monitors, computer terminals, multiple phone lines, and ample counter space with books and charts or clipboards sitting in orderly piles. In the front of the counter there was a place for the unit secretary to perch him or herself to oversee anyone coming in or out of the unit and everything that was happening within the unit. The patients' rooms were arranged around the outside. These were not the typical hospital rooms. They were small cubicles filled with all kinds of instruments to monitor and sustain life. The rooms didn't have typical doors. The whole front wall of the room was a sliding glass door. The reason why the doors have to be so wide is that most patients don't walk into the intensive care unit. Most are brought in on stretchers after surgery or from the emergency room. This setup reminds me of Times Square because as you approach the square from the north, you see the island-like land mass that houses the big Times Square billboard and clock in the center, like the nursing station in the center of the unit. Then on the outside of the square where Broadway and Avenue of the Americas intersect, you have all the stores with their lights on and doors open, no matter what time of day, like the ICU. Even though it was pitch-black outside, this place was as bright as Times Square. All kinds of alarms were buzzing and beeping and everyone was scurrying around. The movement wasn't chaotic but it was constant. I guess it has to be this way in the unit when all the patients have complex medical/surgical problems such that if one system fails, it has a domino effect on all the other body systems.

"Hey, Mark. What's going on?" I asked as I approached Adriane's bed. Mark was the doctor taking care of Adriane now that she was in the ICU.

"Oh, hi, Gwen. Thanks for coming up here. I thought you would want to know that we're having a hard time ventilating Adriane. Her oxygen saturations were dropping and her pulse was creeping up. We increased her FiO2 and increased her PEEP. Look, here's her last ABG."

I looked at the piece of paper with five numbers. To someone not in the medical field, this slip might look like a receipt you would get after using your ATM card at the gas station. But for Adriane, this piece of paper was telling us how well her body was holding up.

I felt a sense of relief. "These numbers don't look so bad. I'm a little concerned about her CO2."

"Yeah, I saw that starting to increase with the last blood gas. Adriane's electrolytes and CBC look fine and her urine output has been okay. The renal team will be here later this morning."

We both glanced at the clock when he said that. It was 2:45 a.m. He must have been reading my mind because then he said, "Well, if I see a trend of the CO2 increasing, I'll call the renal team in early."

I felt better with this answer. This increase in the CO2 in Adriane's blood could be the first sign that Adriane's kidneys were shutting down. I didn't want to be too hasty in my thoughts because the level could also be an indication that Adriane's ventilator settings needed to be changed, and they had been.

I looked up from all of the many flow sheets that had been tracking every blood pressure and heart rate reading, laboratory result, and X-ray test from the last several days. Despite everything that was happening to her, she still had that look on her face that said, "I may be small and petite, but I'm tough." I moved in closer to Adriane and quietly told her to hold on while the doctors tried to stabilize her various body systems. I told her about the book club meeting held Wednesday night; how everyone—Brianna, Destiny, Alan, and Camille—sent their love. I reminded her that her son was waiting for her. And I reassured her that he was doing fine in the nursery and that all the nurses were spoiling him. At that moment, the monitor started beeping, indicating that Adriane's pulse had increased and I thought I saw a quick smile on her face. I think she heard me talking to her and probably was wondering why I was rousing her out of a sound sleep at 3:00 in the morning.

ONE YEAR LATER...

39

DESTINY

I can't believe I had to wake up by means of an alarm clock this morning. Normally my body awakens every morning at 5:00 a.m. Apparently my nine-to-five and Destiny's Designs, coupled with my relationship with Patrick, my family, and my book club family are taking a wonderful but fatiguing toll on me. Everything is moving so fast and I with it. Destiny's debut has come and gone. As a result, I have four interviews with magazine editors, eight invitations to furniture trade shows and another trip to Exuma, Bahamas, to look at a new home under construction. My intimate friendship with Patrick seems to be blossoming. Mama, Travis, and I have been spending more quality time with Trey because his stamina has returned due to the new clinical regimen prescribed by his doctor and the alternative medicine therapy. And the lives of my friends are ever-changing.

It was a few hours before I had to leave. I wasn't hungry, so I got a glass of orange juice. I threw a load of clothes in the wash while reading *The Between* by Tananarive Due, this month's book club selection. The phone rang and startled me because this supernatural horror novel had me spooked. "Hello," I said.

"Good morning, baby. How are you?" Patrick asked.

"Pretty good," I responded.

"Sorry I couldn't be with you today. I thought I was going to be able to get an earlier flight home."

"That's okay. I'm probably going to spend all day with the ladies."

"I'll see you tonight, then."

"I can't wait," I said with a little more emotion. We said our good-byes and hung up.

After showering and applying my makeup, I stepped into the new dress that I'd purchased for today. Looking in the mirror, I couldn't help but laugh aloud. I've never owned anything this color. The color on the garment label read "Raspberry." I didn't even know what color shoes to wear. Did I wear black leather, black patent leather, white, or bone? I tried on one of each and decided on the black patent leather pumps. Now all I needed was my black patent leather handbag and I'd be ready to go.

I looked in the full-length mirror for a final inspection. Damn, I look good. What a difference a couple of years can make. I'm exercising routinely. I visit the spa monthly for manicures, pedicures, facials, and massages. My short hairstyle is maintained once a week. My health is good. My financial portfolio is starting to burst at the seams thanks to Destiny's Designs. And my spirituality has been heightened since Patrick and I have been going to church together every Sunday. Patrick is even thinking about signing up for the Men's Mentoring Program sponsored by Brother Malik.

As I set the house alarm, the phone rang. I didn't answer it for fear of being delayed. I shut the door to the house, hit the garage door opener, and got into the car. Once started, I gave the engine a little gas and pulled out of the garage. Waiting for the garage door to close, I put on my sunglasses, turned on the radio, and adjusted the rearview mirror. "Dreamer," I said, "take me to my destiny."

40

CAMILLE

I have mixed feelings as I lie in bed waiting for the second alarm to go off. I know that Marshall is already up and has probably already made his green tea in his tea maker and picked up the paper even though it's only 7:00 a.m. on a Sunday morning. I think about the events ahead of me for this day. I need to wake my kids up, which is no easy task since they inherited their late-night/late-morning habits from me. Ever since our wedding, I knew it would be one of many adjustments Marshall and I would encounter as we endeavor to combine our lives into one blissful union. Marshall gives me plenty of reason to believe that this time we will overcome the obstacles I faced in my other relationships because he is so understanding, confident, and flexible yet firm. He was the one man whom I could believe in and depend on to be consistent, supportive, and loving. Although I had serious concerns, the kids have made a remarkably smooth transition despite changing schools, athletic teams, friends, and homes. They have little to complain about on that last point— both Jade and Tyler have rooms that are double the size of the rooms they had at my old house, and Jade was thrilled to have a new bedroom set complete with her own TV, telephone, and computer. I'll be amazed if we ever see her at any time other than mealtime. Tyler has discovered a gang of new kids in the neighborhood and has already been rollerblading, bicycling, and skateboarding with the locals.

I planned to be at the church by 10:00 a.m. I felt an overwhelming desire to take the opportunity while in church to thank God for the blessings he has bestowed on me, and to give thanks for finally finding my soul mate in a man who loves my children enough to make them a large part of his life. I had to overcome my fear of commitment because of my prior baggage. But Marshall convinced me that I should not judge him by the "idiots" of my past but that I should look at this relationship for what it is, something pretty wonderful.

41

ALLANA

Chirp, chirp, chirp. Chirp, chirp, chirp. The sounds of the birds in the woods woke me from my peaceful sleep. I rushed to the bedroom window, hoping to get a glimpse of the returning robins that nest nearby. As I slowly raised the shade, I laid eyes on three huge ravens striding across the green manicured lawn toward a bed of azaleas.

"They're raptors! Little dinosaurs," Rod would say. Somehow on this spring morning, Mother Nature had a divine order for everything.

"Come back to bed, baby," said the husky voice behind me. Rodney had stirred.

"I didn't mean to wake you," I said.

"Come here. You didn't." I slid into his embrace. He smothered me in his strong arms so tightly, I could barely breathe.

"Good morning, my queen."

"Good morning, my king." We kissed and made love sweetly, then passionately, holding on to each other for dear life.

"Honey, I really need to get ready to go," I said.

"I know. Last one downstairs is a rotten egg!" he teased. We jumped out of bed and raced to separate showers to expedite matters. As I shampooed my new short haircut, I smiled. The length was so easy, and I loved the convenience. A neighbor did say I looked ten years younger.

Taking dong quai root capsules and increasing my intake of vitamins B and E has made me feel better. I finally made the decision to retire and it has also made a difference in my health. I decided to use my experience in corporate America to start my own company. After serious soul searching and discussion with Rod about our finances, we agreed that I would follow my professional passion in organization development and business consulting. The mild depression lifted—I believe my mood swings and irritability were directly related to feeling stuck in a dead-end job. I have accepted the symptoms of perimenopause and started managing them by reading, sharing experiences with other women, and learning all I can about this "middle passage."

As I stepped from the shower, I noticed the results from doing crunches. I'm glad I started counting fat grams. I have also limited my intake of sugar and increased my intake of fresh fruits and vegetables. *I'm becoming comfortable with my proportions again,* I thought, as I slipped on my pantyhose. Back in the bedroom, I quickly got into my new spring suit. Out of the corner of my eye, I saw Rod's muscular six-foot-four frame as he put on his shirt. His forty-six-inch shoulders tapered down to his thirty-eight-inch waist. I told him, "I feel lucky to have found you. I'm thankful we have our health and each other for the rest of our lives." Then I said a silent prayer of thanks and ran downstairs to the garage.

42

BRIANNA

Getting up in the morning is always hard for me. Despite the fact that I've been getting up at 6:00 a.m. every day for the past ten years, I still like to hit the snooze button at least three times. This Sunday morning, however, I decided not to set the alarm. To my surprise, my body woke up at 8:00 a.m. instead of 6:00 a.m. as I'd expected. I guess my body knew that I really needed the extra rest.

The first thing I had to do was make coffee. I have become addicted to Jamaican Blue Mountain coffee grown and roasted by King's Caribbean Coffee. I discovered this gem of coffees on my trip to St. Croix with Destiny. Thank goodness for mail order. Once I was jump started, I proceeded to make a Filipino breakfast of chicken tocino with ensamada and sliced mango. The marinated chicken doesn't look good because it's red in color like Chinese pork, but it is extremely tasty. I save this meal to have as a treat to myself because of the high fat content. I allow myself to splurge every once in a while.

Just as I was about to slice the mangos, the phone rang. I answered, "Hello?"

"Hey, Bre, it's Bro."

"Hi, Brandon, what's up?"

"The sky."

"You're so corny. Some things will never change. What's up?"

"I'm calling to check on you."

"I appreciate you acting like a big brother but remember you're Little Bro to me. Don't forget that."

"Yeah, yeah, yeah, whatever. Look, please speak on my behalf today. I wish I could be there in person. Are you sure you'll be okay?"

"Yes, Brandon. Thanks for thinking of me, especially today. I appreciate your support. Good luck, by the way, on the verdict tomorrow. Call me and let me know what the outcome is."

"Alrighty, Sis. Check you later."

I signed off. "Ciao." Short and sweet. That's the way our conversations usually went. We both knew that if more needed to be said, we would say it.

I looked up for a moment to appreciate the beautiful day that was before me. I loved my new home. The kitchen nook was one of my favorite spots in the house. Windows surrounded the entire area and allowed the bright, early morning sun to gleam in. I finished setting the table and noticed the fine detail on the hand-painted Mexican plates that Camille gave to me for Christmas. While noting the pattern of dots, swirls, and curls that made each plate unique, I realized that it really is the small things in life that one should appreciate. So much can change in so little time. I act upon that fact daily at work, but not so much in my personal life. That has now changed. I want to live each day to its fullest, as if it's my last. I want to be happy and enjoy life despite what anyone else thinks. I feel like I'm finally living my life for me and not anyone else. Everyone has good intentions when giving advice or sharing information. Like when Gwen advised me that she thought Sarah was having an affair with her former boss. Not that it mattered much to me, but I asked Sarah about it, and she told me it was a brief relationship in her past, during which she'd acted irresponsible and immature. She said she regretted that it ever happened. I could definitely relate to that sentiment, so Sarah and I agreed to leave our pasts in the past.

I suddenly heard the shower water running. I was glad that she was up, getting ready. I cannot be late today of all days. I shouted upstairs, "Sarah, breakfast is ready!"

43

NATALIE

Today is going to be a good day, a beautiful day, I say to myself, as I adjust my eyes to avoid the sun streaming through my window. I love the sun. Usually it's all I need to get me started every morning. The past year has been unbearably hard though; even the sun hasn't been enough to get me up in the morning. I think of all of the nights in the hospital. I never knew one could feel so helpless. Work has been just as bad. The fallout from the *Meet the Press* debacle was worse than even I'd imagined. Nick Charles, the chairman of the state chapter of the NAACP, called for Thorton's resignation and staged protests at Thorton's state and Washington, D.C. offices. The media attention was unrelenting, and Thorton was compared to the likes of David Duke.

I was torn. Thorton was my boss and a man I had come to admire in many respects. He was a mentor to me and rewarded me professionally. He was a good and dedicated legislator. He also was the only senator, or House member for that matter, to hire an African-American chief of staff. He had several other blacks in key positions on the committee and in his personal office and always had. He was also a very powerful member who was not only on the right side of the issues, but in a position to affect change. On the other hand, he lived in a mansion, practically a plantation, with all black servants, and this was not the first time he had made statements that demonstrated little regard for persons of African descent.

This situation was hard for me because I generally saw things in black and white. I had always believed that actions had consequences. People who made statements such as those uttered by Thorton, should have to pay the price. An example had to be made so that others did not perceive the same latitude. You seldom heard anyone disparage Jews or the Holocaust. That's because if and when they did, they paid a price. It was not tolerated. I believed the same should be true of persons who disparaged black people. Of course, it is very easy to be judgmental about others' actions when they are far removed from you. It is much harder to assign the same blame and punishments to people you care about. Even though the aversion I felt for Thorton's statement was strong, it hurt me to see him struggle for his job. I knew of course that no matter what happened he would be okay. White men of his stature always were. But his name and legacy would be irreparably sullied. The questions I struggled with most were, "What should my role be? Should I publicly denounce him and quit my job or rally around him and show my loyalty?" In the end, I chose neither of these options. Instead I chose a political solution. I went to Nick Charles and asked him what he wanted. I told him he could bring down Thorton, a major ally in the Senate, or he could help me develop a plan that extracted a public price from Thorton immediately, and kept Thorton beholden to the black community for a long while to come. Charles, who has political aspirations of his own and is thus quite pragmatic, chose the latter. Nick and I worked together to craft yet another, much more strongly worded apology, and arranged for Thorton and Charles to do a series of public forums on race in the state. Additionally, Thorton arranged for a coalition of black leaders to meet with key committee members to discuss their legislative priorities. I couldn't guarantee legislation, but I could promise access. When I presented the plan to Thorton, he accepted it because, as a skilled politician, he was a master at the game of compromise.

I decided to put this situation out of my mind. *Today is going to be a good day*, I say to myself, *a day to rejoice*. I see that it's only 7:18 a.m. I don't have to get up until 7:30 a.m. and I'm glad to have a few minutes to wake up. I turn on my side and look at Chris. His head is almost completely covered by his pillow. He doesn't have the same appreciation for morning sun as I do. Having his support and confidence over the last year helped keep me sane. It took all the courage I could muster to make the call. We had kept in touch only sporadically over the years since we broke up, but he knew Adriane well and would have wanted to know she was in the hospital. So I called and he came to the hospital with me that night and the one after that and has been by my side ever since. I had missed him so much but would never admit it. My emotions were a roller coaster, but Chris just rolled with the flow. He held my hand when I needed it and held me close when I cried. Spending time with him again was hard at first but given all that had happened, and maybe a little maturing on my part, I found I could be much more open with him. I told him why I had been so afraid and how worried I was that we couldn't overcome our differences. His response was to squeeze my hand and say, "Chill out, Nat, don't make it harder than it is." Of course he was right, I chilled out and it wasn't hard at all. We are different, but given all that has happened, the differences I used to worry about have lost their meaning. What I know is that he is there for me and he makes me happy. I am still searching but in love I am content. I look at Chris and smile fully awake. I wrap my arm around his chest and snuggle closer. Chris gives me a peck on the forehead and murmurs a sleepy, "I love you." He adjusts his pillow to eliminate any remaining sunlight and then drifts back to sleep.

Chris has brought a calm to my personal life, but I still had some decisions to make about work. I think it's time for Thorton and me to part ways. I stuck around to make sure the public forums on racism happened and that he made good on his promises to bring minority organizations to the table on critical legislation. But now I think I have done all I can or am willing to do. I'm ready for change. I'm mulling over a couple of job offers and even considering a career change. I guess I don't have to make all of these decisions right away. I think I'll take each day as it comes. It's time to enjoy the journey.

44

GWEN

I glanced over at Sloan as he was shaving. I watched him methodically move the razor from right to left, then up to down and then finish with down to up movements. I was paying such close attention because the night before I'd had a hard time getting to sleep, anticipating the events of today. When I finally dozed off, I was awakened by the sound of a bug whizzing by my ear. I never made it back to sleep. So I turned on the TV and found myself channel surfing with the remote control. I settled on *The Newlywed Game*. I did not even know this show was still on TV. The twenty-five-point bonus question that was being posed to the wives was—"In what direction does your husband shave—top to bottom or bottom to top?" Since Sloan and I would soon be newlyweds, I thought that I should know the answer to that question. I was relieved to know that I would have gotten the twenty-five-point bonus if Sloan and I had been on the show. At 4:00 a.m., sitting alone on the sofa, I had answered the television, "Top to bottom."

Over the last two years, I had changed jobs, salvaged my relationship with Sloan, and dealt with some highs and some lows. I now know what Brianna means by her mantra, "That which does not kill you, makes you stronger."

When I first met Sloan, I was a naïve college coed. I think I fell in love with him at first sight. The love was based on nothing and

I never thought it would amount to anything. It was a schoolgirl crush, something to talk to your girlfriends about. Then in medical school when we were first reunited in the middle of the frozen food section of Krueger's out in Los Angeles, I thought I had died and gone to heaven. At this point I was a mature young woman, poised with charm as well as confidence; at least I thought so. I was ready for a fun and easy-going relationship with no pressures of marriage or major compromises.

When I left the West Coast and headed for Washington, D.C., for residency, I did not spend nights crying myself to sleep because I would be leaving Sloan. I had two wonderful years with Sloan. Our relationship had been a full one. We had parted on good terms and I thought that we would remain friends. Although I often found myself thinking about what my life would have been like if Sloan and I had married then.

It was not until our third reunion that I clearly understood all the dynamics and complexities of an adult relationship. Some people would call these things baggage. I now recognized the value that I brought to the relationship; I knew my wealth. I understood my expectations of Sloan and he understood his of me. We were both looking in the same direction at the same time. This reunion was not initiated by a chance meeting but by a purposeful telephone call. It was not characterized by a "girl meets boy and falls madly in love and lives happily ever after" theme. This was a relationship that had been molded and remolded and then molded again. I was happy with the end result. I guess the third time is the charm.

I nudged Sloan with my hip to move over so I could share the sink to brush my teeth. As I picked up my toothbrush, I glanced at the clock that shared the shelf with the toothbrush holder. It was 8:30 a.m. already. Sloan and I had to be ready to leave the house within thirty minutes. I had promised myself that I was not going to be the last one to arrive today. I felt myself go into overdrive. You know the feeling. Your heart starts to race. Your face gets a little flushed, and you feel like you are going to trip over your feet because they can't move as fast as you think they can. At 9:15 a.m., I was sitting on the front porch of the house that Sloan and I shared, enjoying the clean, crisp air of the morning.

"Hey, there you are," Sloan said as he opened the screen door. "I thought you were still upstairs."

"No, I've been out here waiting for you. You're late," I said as I winked at Sloan.

We both chuckled because I hardly ever had to wait for Sloan. Sloan reached for my hand and we walked off, hand-in-hand, headed in the same direction, at last.

45

FOURTH SUNDAY

The closest things to heaven that are yet rooted to earth are mountains. Rising from a mountainous area in Great Falls, Maryland, sits an oval-shaped, gothic church; not like a fortress, but like a vision of glory. Assorted wildflowers and ivy formed a living kaleidoscope around the century-old house of worship. Judging from the preserved discolored bricks, the mahogany door, the brilliantly colored stained-glass windows, and the worn wooden pews, it was obvious that the church had witnessed many sacred events. And today's event would be no exception.

At 11:00 a.m. the church bells chimed while family and friends congregated in the church for the second time, almost one year to the date. The first time had been to say good-bye to a loved one, and this time it was to rejoice and celebrate the beginning of a life of faith. Even the gates of heaven opened up and all the angels flocked to the church to witness the blessed event.

At half past eleven, Reverend Hawthorne Jones, clothed in a long white robe with gold embroidery, followed the choir down the center aisle to start the service. After two musical selections and an opening prayer, Reverend Jones announced the addition of a new member to the Family. Anthony Buttler, dressed in a white satin tuxedo jacket with matching shorts, a white cotton shirt, a white satin tie, and white socks with white shoes, was carried to the altar by his father, Tim. Tim was dressed in a black suit, white shirt, black and white tie, and black shoes.

Adriane pushed her way through the angels so nothing was obstructing her view when Anthony appeared on the altar with Tim.

"Look at my son—my beautiful gift to the world—my husband, my family, and my friends! Baby Anthony has dimples. And he's going to have curly hair like his father.

"Everybody is here except me. It was so hard for me to leave. Everything happened so fast. One minute I was asleep and the next minute every memorable event in my life paraded before my eyes. Each event played out to the same song. I can't recall the name of the song nor the music. But I do remember that I was so tired when the music ended. My mind and spirit put up one hell of a fight, but my body—it got so weak. It was a good weakness, though, because I was not in pain. And I was not afraid. The light welcomed me and I welcomed it. I had accomplished my worldly goals. I was a daughter, a sister, a wife, a mother, and a friend. That's all I ever really wanted.

"Looking around the church, I see my family and friends smiling. I know they are smiling because Anthony is so handsome. And look at the ladies from the book club. They look so chic. So strong. So dynamic. They are certainly divas with a capital D. I remember all the times we shared together and the times I shared with each one of them individually. The good times outweighed the bad so I remember laughing a lot. I recall our many telephone conversations, my need to debate any issue that had more than one point of view, get-togethers at my house, which always included lots of good food and loud music and voices, shopping for bargains to turn into treasures, all the books that we read that I didn't finish, and our conversations about the teachings that I had planned for my son.

Smiling, I continue my gaze around the church. It's packed. Some people are standing because there aren't enough seats. Man, everybody I know must be here. What a true testament to our relationship. I'm gone but they are carrying on as if I'm here and a part of their lives. They are still loving and supporting me. Now my eyes are filled with tears. Happy tears though. Because I realize how blessed I was to have had wonderful family and friends.

Reverend Jones summoned Gwen, Natalie, Brianna, Camille, Allana, and Destiny to take their places at the altar. Outfitted in some of Adriane's favorite colors and sporting fuschia scarves in her memory, they took their positions one by one alongside Tim and Anthony.

"Are we all here?" Reverend Jones asked, after taking a quick count.

Tim said, "I think so."

"That's mighty fine," Reverend Jones muttered. "I can't say that I've ever performed a ceremony with this many people before, but that's okay. Thank you, Jesus."

The church replied with a little laughter and then, even louder, "Thank you, Jesus!"

While Anthony was being presented to Reverend Jones, Reverend Jones explained the duties. "You are spiritual guardians," he said. "It is your duty to love, protect, nurture, discipline, and honor Anthony. As godmothers, you are also responsible for assisting Brother Tim in his efforts to raise Anthony to be a child of God. Like a parent, your responsibilities and commitment are never-ending. Because love is forever."

Reverend Jones placed Anthony in all of our arms. Administering prayers and anointing Anthony with oil, Reverend Jones said, "I baptize Anthony Buttler in the name of the Father, the Son, and the Holy Spirit. May God watch over all of you and guide your footsteps in a righteous path. Amen."

In unison Gwen, Natalie, Brianna, Camille, Allana, and Destiny said, "Amen!"

A CONVERSATION WITH
THE AUTHORS OF "FOURTH SUNDAY"

Q: What does B. W. Read stand for? How did you come up with that pen name?

A: B.W. Read stands for "Because We Read." The name was derived during a brainstorming session.

Q: What prompted you to write the book?

A: In the summer of 1996, our book club read a well-reviewed book by a respected author. However, our consensus was that we could not identify with the author's characters and style. Unfortunately, it was not the first time we had such an opinion. We have found that the number of books that speak to our lives and portray our experiences is too few. This occurrence inspired several of the book club members to write a book. Our book is a fictionalized account of the lives of seven women. Each woman has a personal story but the characters remain linked through friendship and the book club.

Q: You are a diverse group of women. How were you able to partner to write this book?

We are first-time authors who are diverse in careers, educational backgrounds, and personal status. The book is the culmination of over a decade of starts and stops, conference calls, weekend retreats, Sunday afternoon meetings, and overcoming the challenges associated with balancing the schedules, moods, and talents of six strong-minded women.

We see ourselves as "Synergistas." The term *Synergista* describes the positive energy that fuses our lives together. Collectively we achieved our goals using the "Synergista Principles."

Synergista Principles
1. So let it be written; so let it be done
2. Whatever your heart desires, listen to it.
3. Whatever your mind conceives can be achieved.
4. Don't limit yourself; the possibilities are endless.

Q:Was the book club in the novel real or imagined?
A: The authors are members of the same book club. However, the book club in the novel, *Fourth Sunday*, is fictional.

Q:What is the major theme of the novel?
A: This story chronicles the lives of seven women. The reader learns about each woman, as well as how all the women relate to one another during paramount events in their lives.

Q:What message do you hope to convey to readers?
A: *Fourth Sunday* is not just a book—it's about embracing your goals and making them happen. We hope our book is not only a fun read, but that it can serve as an example to empower and inspire women of every age and hue to work together to accomplish what can't be done solo. Often women are so focused on being caretakers that they forget to take care of themselves. The "Fourth Sunday" movement encourages women to make themselves their top priority, if only for a day. So embrace your "Fourth Sunday" and make it count. The possibilities are endless!

READING GROUP
DISCUSSION QUESTIONS

1. Each character had a personal challenge. What do you think they were for Gwen, Camille, Natalie, Adriane, Allana, Destiny and Brianna?

2. Which character(s) are you drawn to and why?

3. Which character(s) are most like you and why?

4. Human beings often want what they don't have. What did Gwen want that she did not have?

5. Why do you think Camille fell in love so easily?

6. Did Natalie sacrifice her love life for her career?

7. As Adriane prepared to give birth, how did it change her?

8. Newly married Allana finds her body betraying her. Have you experienced peri-menopause? Or menopause?

9. Destiny has a "Type A" personality. How does she find time for her passion, design?

10. Brianna, who is at the top of her profession, seems confused about her sexuality. What would you do if you were in her shoes?

11. This story is about women in a book club that takes place in 1997. Where were you? And what were were you doing in 1997? How have things changed for women since 1997?

12. If you were going to cast *Fourth Sunday*, the movie, which actresses would you choose to play Gwen, Camille, Natalie, Adriane, Allana, Destiny and Brianna? Which actors/actress would you choose to play the significant others in their lives?

ABOUT THE AUTHORS

FRANCESCA COOK received a B.A. in biology from Mount Holyoke College and a M.P.H. from Yale University. Ms. Cook is an executive at a biotechnology company. Previously, Ms. Cook spent several years working in both the United States Senate and in consulting. Ms. Cook lives in Maryland with her daughter.

CHYLA EVANS was born in Chicago, Illinois and attended prep school in Massachusetts before heading south to Nashville to attend Vanderbilt University, where she received a B.A. in economics. After graduation, she returned to the Chicago area to work in the 1st Scholar program of First Chicago while attending Northwestern's Kellogg School of Management. After receiving an M.B.A., Ms. Evans began a career in business. Ms. Evans lived in Denver, Colorado and Los Angeles, California before moving to her present home in Washington, D.C. She is a divorced mother of two and works in Sustainable Energy Lighting & Signage.

CLARITA FRAZIER was born in Washington, D.C. She received a B.S. degree in Zoology from Howard University and a M.D. from the University of Maryland. She completed a residency in Anesthesiology at Tufts–New England Medical Center and fellowship in Obstetric Anesthesiology at Harvard–Brigham and Women's Hospital. She is in private practice and resides in Glenelg, Maryland. She lives with her husband and beautiful daughter.

ALLITA IRBY holds a M.A.S. degree in Business from The Johns Hopkins University, and is retired from a major telecommunications company. Trained at Georgetown University in organization development, Ms. Irby is also a business consultant in the public and non-profit sectors. In addition, she is a visual artist who works in mixed media and is active in the arts community in the Washington, D. C. metropolitan area and surrounding counties. She is married and lives in Mitchellville, Maryland with her husband and two small schnauzers. To learn more about her artistic endeavors you may go to these sites: http://princegeorges artistsassociation.org/ or www.allitairby.webs.com

DONNA NEALE holds a degree in Human Biology from Brown University and received a M.D. from Boston University School of Medicine. She completed her residency in Obstetrics and Gynecology at the Georgetown University School of Medicine and fellowship in Maternal Fetal Medicine at the Yale University School of Medicine. She is now an Assistant Professor in Gynecology and Obstetrics at The Johns Hopkins University School of Medicine and specializes in Maternal-Fetal Medicine. Dr. Neale is married with two children and a chocolate lab. In addition to cherishing time with her family, she also enjoys skiing, running, traveling and participating in community service.

YOLANDA YATES is a Manager at a telecommunications company. She holds a B.A. degree in Public Communications from The American University and an M.G.A. in Marketing from the University of Maryland. Ms. Yates was born in Washington, D.C. She currently resides in Maryland with her husband.

B.W. READ Contact Information:
Email us at bw.read@yahoo.com, or visit us on the web at www.bwread.com or http://www.simonandschuster.com.